NECESSARY
FICTIONS

Especially for
Peter & Jean —
and quality writing
and quality friendships —
Yrs,
Dirt-bag Stan

NECESSARY FICTIONS

Selected Stories from
The Georgia Review

Edited by
STANLEY W. LINDBERG
and
STEPHEN COREY

THE UNIVERSITY OF GEORGIA PRESS
ATHENS AND LONDON

© 1986 by the University of Georgia
Published by the University of Georgia Press
All rights reserved
Text designed by Ronald F. Arnholm
Set in Janson typeface with Caslon display headings and printed
by letterpress on 50 pound Warren's Olde Style at Heritage Printers,
Inc., Charlotte, North Carolina

The paper in this book meets the guidelines for permanence and
durability of the Committee on Production Guidelines for Book
Longevity of the Council on Library Resources.

Printed in the United States of America

90 89 88 87 86   5 4 3 2 1

Library of Congress Cataloging in Publication Data

Necessary fictions.

1. Short stories, American.   2. American fiction—
20th century.   I. Lindberg, Stanley W.   II. Corey,
Stephen, 1948–   .   III. Georgia review.
PS648.S5N33   1986   813'.01'08   86-16079
ISBN 0–8203–0882–X
ISBN 0–8203–0883–8 (pbk.)

This book is dedicated by the current editors of
The Georgia Review

to the memory of

JOHN DONALD WADE (1892–1963)
Founder & Editor, 1947–50
JOHN OLIN EIDSON (1908–1983)
Editor, 1950–57
WILLIAM WALLACE DAVIDSON (1901–1978)
Editor, 1957–68

and to the honor of

RALPH STEPHENS
Business Manager, 1947–49
MARION MONTGOMERY
Business Manager, 1950–52
BETTY L. SARGENT
Business Manager, 1965–77
Assistant Editor, 1977–82
JAMES B. COLVERT
Editor, 1968–72
WARREN LEAMON
Assistant Editor, 1968–71
EDWARD KRICKEL
Assistant Editor, 1971–72
Editor, 1972–74
STEPHEN MALONEY
Assistant Editor, 1972–74
JOHN T. IRWIN
Editor, 1974–77
SARAH S. EAST
Managing Editor, 1982–83

Contents

339   CONTRIBUTORS

NECESSARY
FICTIONS

Stanley W. Lindberg
and Stephen Corey

Introduction

THE stories collected in this book first appeared in various quarterly issues of *The Georgia Review* and are being reprinted here as part of our retrospective celebration of *The Review*'s fortieth year of continuous publication. Of all the fiction that has been featured in *The Review* during those years, these are the stories we have found to be most compelling. Their subjects and styles engaged our attention on first readings, then offered up even more each time we went back to them. In the words of Wallace Stevens—certainly one of the greatest avatars of faith in the imagination—a literary artist is one who "creates the world to which we turn incessantly and without knowing it and . . . gives to life the supreme fictions without which we are unable to conceive of it." Furthermore, as Elizabeth Bowen reminds us, "The first necessity for the short story, at the set out, is *necessariness*. The story, that is to say, must spring from an impression or perception passing through, acute enough to have made the writer write. Execution must be voluntary and careful, but conception should have been involuntary, a vital fortuity." In the dual spirit of these writers' words, we are presenting here our selection of what we believe to be some of America's most telling and necessary fictions.

In 1947 John Donald Wade, a native Georgian and one of the Nashville Agrarians, founded *The Georgia Review* with the avowed intent of trying "to confine it, at least for the time being, to topics that bear somewhat closely upon the history, literature, art, and social activities of Georgia." While he acknowledged from the start that *The Review*'s program would not always be "explicitly Georgian," his second editorial made it clear that he felt no obligation "to publish here anything devised pointedly for the approval of the current smart-set in Omaha. Or anywhere else like Omaha. . . ." Provocative ideas and the best writers, however, are seldom confined by geographical boundaries, and subsequent editors steadily enlarged the reach of the magazine. Over the years *The Review* acquired contributors from, and readers in, all regions of the United States (as well as many foreign countries), and its expanded role in American letters has subsequently become well recognized. That approximately half of the stories in this present collection come from Southern-born writers no longer signals an editorial mission; instead, it acknowledges the continuing and undeniable vitality of fiction in a region that, since 1920, has produced a disproportionate number of America's finest authors.

With this gathering we salute all the fiction writers who have appeared in the pages of *The Georgia Review*, together with the editors and staff members who preceded us in shaping the contents of the magazine. We believe that the range of voices and the variety of styles collected here serve both as a testimony to the richness of American writing during the past four decades and as a reflection of the eclectic vision of *The Review*'s different editors.

Many of the nearly four hundred stories published by *The Georgia Review* since 1947 still speak with such vital force that choosing from the already-once-chosen turned out to be far more difficult than we had anticipated. We share the regrets of those authors, former editors, and readers whose favorites were not ultimately selected, and we realize that probably none of our predecessors would have picked exactly the same stories we have. But even as the original selections were made by the individuals in charge of *The Review* during their various tenures, so our choices had to be based, finally, on our own tastes and judgments.

We knew from the start that space limitations would not permit us to reprint all the stories that merited inclusion. Among the first decisions we were forced to make was to offer no more than a single story by any author, despite the multiple contenders offered by several contributors who have appeared in *The Review* more than once, often under different editors. Other, more arbitrary determinations we made reluctantly were to include no work by any author who had subsequently served on *The Review* staff and to exclude several fine novellas that, despite their unquestioned merits, would have drastically reduced the total number of stories we could present. Finally, we chose not to reprint any stories from the issues of the last two years, even though there were some splendid candidates from that period. It would be fairer to readers and authors alike, we decided, to present less readily available work.

Behind and beyond the admittedly arbitrary ground rules came our own editorial perceptions and predilections. Although many readers will doubtless draw their own conclusions about what kinds of stories we apparently prefer, it may be useful if we outline broadly what *we* see as our editorial tastes—tastes that we hope are eclectic enough to keep us open to the new and the unexpected, yet palpable enough to let us be aware of them, at least in retrospect.

Most of these stories, in our opinion, put more overt importance on telling us about the world than on calling attention to themselves as literary artifacts; and even those stories that do exhibit certain meta-fictional techniques—such as Gary Gildner's "Sleepy Time Gal" and A. B. Paulson's "College Life"—do so at the same time that they maintain for-ward-moving narratives of human situations. These narratives are often accompanied by sharply defined settings: Barry Hannah's Alabama, Siv Cedering's Sweden, David Wagoner's Pacific Northwest, Jesse Stuart's Kentucky. A sense of history (long a vital factor in Southern fiction) also operates in many of these stories—more often, perhaps, than might be found in other anthologies of short fiction. And each of the authors represented here, in his or her own way, pays especially loving attention to language, refusing to settle for the dull flatness of presentation that is all too often promoted as honest and "real."

It would be unfortunate, however, if such remarks imply more uni-formity to this collection than it possesses, for in fact the widely divergent styles of these thirty-three different voices give us great pleasure. Al-though we made no special editorial effort to balance equally such factors as gender, the degrees of authorial renown, the themes employed, or the phases of *The Review*'s history, we are delighted with the final blend of writers and stories. We are not offering here a literary history of forty years, nor is it a perfect representative sampling of *The Review*'s fiction during that period. But we hope we have captured one magazine's con-tinuing practice of featuring excellent fiction, whether by Nobel lau-reates like William Faulkner or by never-before-published authors like Judith Hoover, whether by Georgia natives like Harry Crews and Mary Hood or by Louisiana's Ernest J. Gaines, Montana's Mary Clearman Blew, and Ohio's Jack Matthews.

Most of the stories published in *The Georgia Review* (including nearly all of those gathered here) arrived initially as unsolicited manuscripts, having been sent to us directly by the authors rather than by literary agents or other representatives. Special mention is in order, however, for the unusual circumstances involving two of the stories featured in this collection: "A Portrait of Elmer" by William Faulkner and "Fra Lippi and Me" by Harriette Simpson Arnow. Both of these works were written in the 1930's but—for very different reasons—did not see publication until their 1979 appearances in *The Review*.

Beginning in 1925, Faulkner worked off and on for ten years on various manuscripts (both novels and short stories) focusing on a vaguely autobiographical character named Elmer. When a short-story version that satisfied him finally went out to Bennett Cerf at Random House in 1935, plans were drawn up to present it in a special limited edition the following year. Cerf, however, had some reservations about the work, and publication was postponed. At that point, Faulkner apparently set the manuscript aside, never considering further attempts to see it into print; "A Portrait of Elmer" remained unknown to the public until it was uncovered in the 1970's by the critic Joseph Blotner, who was working with the Faulkner papers at the University of Mississippi. Thanks to the cooperation of Professor Blotner (and Random House), *The Review* was able to feature the first printing of the story in the Fall 1979 issue.

While Faulkner was at the height of his writing powers in the 1930's, Harriette Simpson Arnow was a virtually unknown beginner, trying to survive in Cincinnati by waitressing and typing to support her writing career. Not until some twenty years later, with the publication of her best-selling novel *The Dollmaker*, did her talent achieve significant recognition. Although she published a few stories in the thirties, most of her energy went into working on novels; she continued to write stories occasionally, but seldom took the time and effort to try to market them. Only by the efforts of scholar Glenda Hobbs did "Fra Lippi and Me" come to light, and it was through her good services that we obtained permission from Mrs. Arnow to feature the story in our Winter 1979 issue. (We mark with deep regret the death of Harriette Simpson Arnow in late March 1986, shortly after we had received her permission to include her story in this collection.)

In the cases of Faulkner and Simpson, then, the writers' appearances in *The Georgia Review* obviously came well after their importance in American letters had been recognized. For many other well-known authors in this collection, however, their initial appearance in *The Review* came early in their careers and aided them in finding a receptive audience for their works. Harry Crews's "A Long Wail" is a notable case in point. Although he is now widely known as a storyteller *par excellence*, combining a vivid (and often violent) realism with a satirist's sense of the fantastic and the grotesque, he was an unpublished writer—fresh from the Marines and college—when he began submitting short fiction to *The Review* in the early 1960's. Even though his first submission was declined, he received an encouraging letter from editor William Wallace Davidson, and his next story—"A Long Wail"—was accepted for publication early in 1963. It was his first acceptance.

An editor's eyes must always be on the work before him on the desk, but he must also be able to envision those as-yet-unwritten works likely to emerge from the potential exhibited by the manuscript under examination. William Wallace Davidson accepted a single manuscript from an unknown writer, and perhaps only time and circumstance have made Davidson look like a prophet of things to come from Harry Crews. Perhaps, however, *something* in the editor felt what was coming, sensed it more clearly and confidently than the writer himself. In any case, Davidson and those who have followed him in editing *The Review* have frequently presented early work by authors who have subsequently achieved substantial reputations. Among such writers are several others included in this collection: Max Apple, Mary Hood, Judith Hoover, Patrick Worth Gray, and Leigh Allison Wilson.

Many commercial magazines publishing fiction today select their stories by solicitation—extending invitations to well-known authors and essentially closing out all others—or by giving primary attention only to work represented by literary agents. Other magazines control their contributors in a less direct way, ostensibly reading submissions from anyone but in fact giving serious consideration only to a preselected few. At *The Georgia Review*, however, all fiction manuscripts are read with care, regardless of whether or not we recognize the authors' names. Only by remaining open to new voices, we believe, can a literary quarterly serve one of its primary missions, that of finding and fostering the upcoming generation of writers. Such a practice is, we believe, good not only for the writers, but for our readers, for the magazine itself, and for the vitality of contemporary American literature.

Several years ago *The Christian Science Monitor*, in a survey of America's literary magazines, cited *The Georgia Review* as "the best of them all" and singled out our "marvelous fiction" for special praise. Since that time others have joined in—including the London *Times Literary Supplement*, which recently saluted the "spirit of adventure" that reigns in *The Review*'s stories—even as the annual prize anthologies (*Best American Short Stories*, *The O. Henry Awards*, *Editors' Choice*, and *The Pushcart Prize Anthology*) continue to honor many of our fiction selections. And in April of this year *The Georgia Review* received the prestigious fiction prize in the 1986 National Magazine Awards, in competition with such eminent finalists as *The Atlantic*, *Esquire*, *The North American Review*, and *Vanity Fair*. Honors of this kind are, of course, deeply gratifying to those working on *The Review*, but we would be much more pleased if such accolades could be converted directly into a wider audience for the fine authors featured in our pages. It is our sincere hope that this collection, these necessary fictions, will help to serve that larger purpose.

Athens, Georgia
May 1986

Lee K. Abbott

The Final Proof of Fate and Circumstance

HE liked to begin his story with death, saying it was an uncommonly dark night near El Paso with an uncommon fog, thick and all the more frightful because it was unexpected, like ice or a parade of gray elephants tramping across the desert from horizon to horizon, each moody and terribly violent. He was driving on the War Road, two lanes that came up on the south side of what was then the Proving Grounds, narrow and without shoulders, barbed-wire fences alongside, an Emergency Call Box every two miles, on one side the Franklin Mountains, on the other an endless spectacle of waste; his car, as I now imagine it, must have been a DeSoto or a Chrysler, heavy with chrome and a grill like a ten-thousand-pound smile, a car carefully polished to a high shine, free of road dirt and bug filth, its inside a statement about what a person can do with cheese-cloth and patience and affection. "A kind of palace in there," he'd always say. "Hell, I could live out of the back seat." He was twenty-eight then, he said, and he came around that corner, taking that long, stomach-settling dip with authority, driving the next several yards like a man free of fret or second thought, gripping that large black steering wheel like a man with purpose and the means to achieve it, like a man intimate with his several selves, scared of little and tolerant of much. I imagine him sitting high, chin upturned, eyes squinty with attentiveness, face alight with a dozen gleams from the dashboard, humming a measure of, say, "Tonight We Love" by Bobby Worth, singing a word of romance now and then, the merry parts of the music as familiar to him as a certain road sign or oncoming dry arroyo. "I'd just come from Fort Bliss," he said. "I'd played in a golf tournament that day. Whipped Mr. Tommy Bolt, Jr.; Old Automatic, that's me. Show up, take home the big one." He was full of a

[9]

thousand human satisfactions, he said—namely, worth and comforts and renewals. He could hear his clubs rattling in the trunk; he could hear the wind rushing past, warm and dry, and the tires hissing; and he was thinking to himself that it was a fine world to be from, a world of many rewards and light pleasures; a world (from the vantage point of a victory on the golf course) with heft and sense to it, a world in which a person such as himself—an Army lieutenant such as himself, lean and leaderly— could look forward to the lofty and the utmost, the hindmost for those without muscle or brain enough to spot the gladsome among the smuts; yes, it was a fine world, sure and large enough for a man with finer features than most, a grown-up man with old but now lost Fort Worth money behind him, and a daddy with political knowledge, and a momma of substance and high habit, and a youth that had in it such things as regular vacations to Miami Beach, plus a six-week course in the correct carving of fowl and fish, plus a boarding school, and even enough tragedy, like a sister drowning and never being recovered, to give a glimpse of, say, woe— which is surely the kind of shape you'd like your own daddy's character to have when he's about to round a no-account corner in the desert, a Ray Austin lyric on his lips, and kill a man.

It was an accident, of course, the state police saying it was a combination of bad luck—what with the victim standing so that his taillight was obscured—and the elements (meaning, mostly, the fog, but including as well, my daddy said, time and crossed paths and human error and bad judgment and a certain fundamental untidiness). But then, shaken and offended and partly remorseful, my daddy was angry, his ears still ringing with crash noises and the body's private alarms. "God damn," he said, wrestling open a door of his automobile, its interior dusty and strewn with stuffings from the glove box, a Texaco road map still floating in the air like a kite, a rear floormat folded like a tea towel over the front seat, a thump-thump-thump coming from here and there and there and there. It was light enough for him to see the other vehicle, the quarter moon a dim milky spot, the fog itself swirling and seemingly lit from a thousand directions—half dreamland, half spook-house. "There was a smell, too," he told me, his hands fluttering near his face. A smell like scorched rubber and industrial oils, plus grease and disturbed soils. His trunk had flown open, his clubs—"Spaldings, Taylor, the finest!"—flung about like pick-up sticks. His thoughts, airy and affirming an instant before, were full of soreness and ache; for a moment before he climbed back to the road he watched one of his wheels spinning, on his face the twitches and lines real sorrow makes, that wheel, though useless, still going round and round, its hubcap scratched and dented. He was aware, he'd say every time he came to this part, of everything—splintered glass and ordinary night sounds and a stiffness deep in his back and a trouser leg torn at the knee and a fruit-like tenderness to his own cheek pulp. "I felt myself good," he said, show-ing me again how he'd probed and prodded and squeezed, muttering to himself, "Ribs and necks and hips," that old thighbone-hipbone song the foremost thing on his mind. He said his brain was mostly in his ears and his heart beat like someone was banging at it with a claw hammer, and there was a weakness in the belly, he remembered, which in another less stal-wart sort might have been called nausea but which in this man, he told himself as he struggled to the roadway, was nothing less than the true discomfort that comes when Good Feeling is so swiftly overcome by Bad.

At first he couldn't find the body. He said he walked up and down the road, both sides, yelling and peering into the fog, all the time growing angrier with himself, remembering the sudden appearance of that other automobile stopped more on the road than off, the panic that mashed him in the chest, the thud, the heart-flop. "I found the car about fifty yards away," he said, his voice full of miracle and distance as if every time he told the story—and, in particular, the parts that go from bad to worse—it was not he who approached the smashed Chevrolet coupe, but another, an alien, a thing of curiosity and alert eyeballs, somebody inno-cent of the heartbreak human kind could make for itself. The rear of that Chevy, my daddy said, was well and thoroughly crunched, trunk lid twisted, fenders crumpled, its glowing brake light dangling, both doors sprung open as if whatever had been inside had left in a flurry of arm and legwork. My daddy paced around that automobile many times, look-ing inside and underneath and on top and nearabout, impatient and anxious, then cold and sweaty both. "I was a mess," he said. "I was think-ing about Mr. Tommy Bolt and the duty officer at the BOQ and my mother and just every little thing." He was crying, too, he said, not sniveling and whimpering, but important adult tears that he kept wiping away as he widened his circle around the Chevy, snot dribbling down his chin, because he was wholly afraid that, scurrying through the scrub-growth and mesquite and prickly cactus and tanglesome weeds, he was going to find that body, itself crumpled, hurled into some unlikely and unwelcome position—sitting, say, or doing a handstand against a bush— or that he was going to step on it, find himself frozen with dread, his new GI shoes smack in the middle of an ooze that used to be chest or happy man's brain. "I kept telling myself Army things," he said one time. "Buck up. Don't be afraid. Do your duty. I told myself to be calm, methodical. Hope for the best, I said." And so, of course, when he was hoping so hard his teeth hurt and his neck throbbed and his lungs felt like fire, he found it, bounced against a concrete culvert, legs crossed at the ankles, arms folded at the belt, with neither scratch nor bump nor knot nor runny wound, its face a long and quiet discourse on peace or sleep.

"At first, I didn't think he was dead," my daddy told me. He scrambled over to the body, said *get up*, said *are you hurt*, said *can you talk*, *wake up, mister*. His name was Valentine ("Can you believe that name, Taylor?" Daddy would say. "Morris E. Valentine!") and my daddy put his mouth next to the man's earhole and hollered and grabbed a hand— "It wasn't at all cold"—and shook it and listened against the man's nose for breaths or a gurgle and felt the neck for a pulse. Then, he said, there wasn't anything to do next but look at Mr. Valentine's eyes, which were open in something like surprise or marvel and which were as inert and blank and glassy, my daddy said, as two lumps of coal that had lain for ten million years in darkness. It was then, my daddy said, that he felt the peacefulness come over him like a shadow on a sunny day—a tranquility, huge and fitting, like (he said) the sort you feel at the end of fine drama when, with all the deeds done and the ruin dealt out fairly, you go off to eat and drink some; yup, he said one night, like the end of the War Road itself, a place of dust and fog and uprooted flora and fuzzy lights where you discover, as the state police did, a live man and a dead one, the first laughing in a frenzy of horror, the second still and as removed from life as you are from your ancestral fishes, his last thought —evidently a serious one—still plain on his dumb, awful face.

He told me this story again today, the two of us sitting in his backyard, partly in the shade of an upright willow, him in a racy Florida shirt and baggy Bermudas, me in a Slammin' Sammy Snead golf hat and swim trunks. It was hooch, he said, that brought out the raconteur in him, Oso Negro being the fittest of liquors for picking over the past. Lord, he must've gone through a hundred stories this afternoon, all the edge out of his voice, his eyes fixed on the country club's fourteenth fairway which runs behind the house. He told one about my mother meeting Fidel Castro. It was a story, he said, that featured comedy in large doses and not a little wistfulness. It had oompphh and running hither and hoopla when none was expected. "Far as I could tell," he said, "he was just a hairy man with a gun. Plus rabble-rousers." He told another about Panama and the officers' club and the Geists, Maizie and Al, and a Memphis industrialist named T. Moncure Youtees. It was a story that started bad, went some distance in the company of foolishness and youthful hugger-mugger and ended, not with sadness but with mirth. He told about Korea and moosey-maids and sloth and whole families of yellow folk living in squalor and supply problems and peril and cold and, a time later, of having Mr. Sam Jones of the Boston Celtics in his platoon. "You haven't known beauty," he said, smiling, "till you see that man dribble. Jesus, it was superior, Taylor." He told one about some reservists in Montana or Idaho—one of those barren, ascetic places—and a training exercise called Operation Hot Foot which involved, as I recall, scrambling this way and that, eyes peeled for the Red Team, a thousand accountants and farmboys and family men in nighttime camouflage, and a nearsighted colonel named Krebs who took my daddy bird watching. My daddy said that from his position on a bluff he could see people in green scampering and diving and waving in something approaching terror, but that he and Krebs were looking through binoculars for nest or telltale feather, listening intently for warble or tweet or chirp, the colonel doing his best, with nose and lipwork, to imitate that sort of fear or hunger or passion a rare flying thing might find appealing. "It was lovely," my daddy said, the two of them putting over two hundred miles on the jeep in search of Gray's Wing-Notch Swallow or something that had been absent from the planet, Daddy suspected, for an eon. There were trees and buttes and colors from Mr. Disney and a kind of austerity, extreme and eternal, that naturally put you in mind of the Higher Plane.

For another hour he went on, his stories addressing what he called the fine—events in which the hero, using luck and ignorance, managed to avoid the base and its slick companion, the wanton. I heard about a cousin, A. T. LeDuc, who had it, let it slip away, and got it back when least deserved. I learned the two things any dog knows: Can I eat it, or will it eat me? I learned something about people called the Duke and the Earl and the Count and how Mr. Tommy Dorsey looked close up. I was touched—not weepy, like my wife Nadine gets when I tell her a little about my Kappa Alpha days at TCU or how I came out looking like a dope when I had gone in imagining myself a prince. To be true, I was in that warm place few get to these days, that place where your own daddy—that figure who whomped you and scolded you and who had nothing civil to say about the New York Yankees or General Eisen-hower, and who expressed himself at length on the subjects of hair and fit reading matter and how a gentleman shines his shoes—yes, that place where your own daddy admits to being a whole hell of a lot like you, which is sometimes confused and often weak; that place, made habitable by age and self-absorption and fatigue, that says much about those here-tofore pantywaist emotions like pity and fear.

Then, about four o'clock, while the two of us stood against his cinder-block fence, watching a fivesome of country-club ladies drag their carts up the fairway, the sun hot enough to satisfy even Mr. Words-worth, my daddy said he had a new story, one which he'd fussed over in his brain a million times but one which, on account of this or that or another thing, he'd never told anyone. Not my momma Elaine. Not my Uncle Lyman. Not his sisters, Faith and Caroline. His hand was on my forearm, squeezing hard, and I could see by his eyes, which were watery and inflamed by something I now know as purpose, and by his wrinkled, dark forehead and by his knotted neck muscles—by all these things, I knew this story would not feature the fanciful or foreign—not bird, nor military mess-up, nor escapade, nor enterprise in melanchody; it would be, I suspected while he stared at me as though I were no more related to him than that brick or that rabbit-shaped cloud, about mystery, about the odd union of innocence and loss which sometimes passes for wisdom, and about the downward trend of human desires. There was to be a moral, too; and it was to be, like most morals, modern and brave and tragic.

This was to be, I should know, another death story, this one related to Valentine's the way one flower—a jonquil, say—is related to another, like a morning glory, the differences between them obvious, certain, and important; and it was to feature a man named X, my daddy said; a man, I realized instantly, who was my father himself, slipped free of the story now by time and memory and fortunate circumstance. X was married now, my daddy said, to a fine woman and he had equally fine children, among them a youth about my own age, but X had been married before and it would serve no purpose, I was to know, for the current to know about the former, the past being a thing of regret and error. I understood, I said, understanding further that this woman—my daddy's first wife!—was going to die again as she had died before.

She was a French woman, my daddy said, name of Annette D'Kop-

man, and X met her in September 1952 at the 4th Army Golf Tournament in San Antonio, their meeting being the product of happenstance
and X's first-round victory over the professional you now know as Mr.
Orville Moody. "X was thirty-one then," my daddy said, filling his glass
with more rum, "the kind of guy who took his celebrating seriously." I
listened closely, trying to pick out those notes in his voice you might
call mournful or misty. There were none, I'm pleased to say, just a voice
heavy with curiosity and puzzlement. "This Annette person was a guest
of some mucky-muck," my daddy was saying, and when X saw her, he
suspected it was love. I knew that emotion, I thought, it having been produced in me the first time I saw Nadine. I recalled it as a steady knocking
in the heart-spot and a brain alive with a dozen thoughts. This Annette,
my daddy said, was not particularly gorgeous, but she had, according to
X, knuckles that he described as wondrous, plus delicate arches and close
pores and deep sockets and a method of getting from hither to yon with
style enough to make you choke or ache in several body parts. So, X
and Annette were married the next week, the attraction being mutual, a
Mexican JP saying plenty, for twenty dollars, about protection and trust
and parting after a long life of satisfactions, among the latter being health
and offspring and daily enjoyments.

As he talked, my daddy's face had hope in it, and some pride, as
though he were with her again, thirty years from the present moil, squab-
bling again (as he said) about food with unlikely and foreign vegetables
in it, or ways of tending to the lower needs of the flesh. X and Annette
lived at Fort Sam Houston, him the supply officer for the second detachment, she a reward to come home to. "It wasn't all happy times," Daddy
was saying, there being shares of blue spirits and hurt feelings and mis-
understandings as nasty as any X had since had with his present wife.
"There was drinking," he said, "and once X smacked her. Plus, there was
hugging and driving to Corpus Christi and evenings with folks at the
officers' club and swimming." I imagined them together and—watching
him now slumped in his chair, the sun a burning disc over his shoulder—
I saw them as an earlier version of Nadine and me: ordinary and doing
very well to keep a healthful distance from things mean and hurtful. The
lust part, he said, wore off, of course, the thing left behind being close
enough to please even the picky and stupid. Then she died.

I remember thinking that this was the hard part, the part wherein
X was entitled to go crazy and do a hundred destructive acts, maybe
grow moody and sullen, utter an insulting phrase or two, certainly drink

immoderately. I was wrong, my daddy said. For it was a death so unexpected, like one in a fairy tale, that there was only time for an "Aaaarrr-
ggghhh!" and seventy hours of sweaty, dreamless sleep. "X didn't feel
rack or nothing," my daddy said. "Not empty, not needful, nor abused
by any dark forces." X was a blank—shock, a physician called it—more
rock than mortal beset with any of the familiar hardships. "X did his
job," Daddy said, "gave his orders, went and came, went and came." X
watched TV, his favorite being Mr. Garry Moore's "I've Got a Secret,"
read a little in the lives of others, ate at normal hours, looked as steadfast
as your ordinary citizen, one in whom there was now a scorched and
tender spot commonly associated with sentiment and hope. Colonel Buck
Wade made the funeral arrangements—civilian, of course—talking patiently with X, offering a shoulder and experience and such. "X kept
wondering when he'd grieve," Daddy said. Everyone looked for the
signs: outburst of the shameful sort, tactless remark, weariness in the
eyes and carriage, etc. But there was only numbness, as if X were no more
sentient than a clock or Annette herself.

"Now comes the sad part," my daddy said, which was not the ceremony, X having been an Episcopalian, or the burial because X never got
that far. Oh, there was a service, X in his pressed blues, brass catching
the light like sparkles, the minister, a Dr. Hammond Ellis, trying through
the sweep and purl of learnedness itself to put the finest face on a vulgar
event, reading one phrase about deeds and forgiveness and another about
the afterworld and its light comforts, each statement swollen with a
succor or a joy, yet words so foreign with knowledge and acceptance
that X sat rigid, his back braced against a pew, his pals unable to see anything in his eyes except emptiness. No, the sadness didn't come then—
not with prayer, not with the sniffling of someone to X's left, not at the
sight of the casket itself being toted outside. The sadness came, my daddy
said, in the company of the driver of the family car in which X rode alone.
"The driver was a kid," my daddy said, "twenty, maybe younger, name
of Monroe." Whose face, Daddy said, reflected a thousand conflicting
thoughts—of delight and of money and of nookie and of swelter like
today's. Monroe, I was to know, was the squatty sort, the kind who's
always touchy about his height, with eyeballs that didn't say anything
about his inner life, and chewed nails and a thin tie and the wrong brown
shoes for a business otherwise associated with black, and an inflamed
spot on his neck that could have been a pimple or ingrown hair. "Stop,"
X said, and Monroe stared at him in the mirror. "What—?" Monroe was

startled. "I said stop." They were about halfway to the gravesite, funeral coach in front, a line of cars with their lights on in back. "Stop here. Do it now." X was pointing to a row of storefronts in Picacho Street—laundry, a barber's, a Zale's jewelry.

My daddy said he didn't know why Monroe so quickly obeyed X, but I know now that Monroe was just responding to that note in my daddy's voice that tells you to leave off what you're doing—be it playing Canasta, eating Oreos with your mouth open, or mumbling in the favorite parts of "Gunsmoke"—and take up politeness and order and respectfulness. It's a note that encourages you toward the best and most responsible in yourself, and it had in it a hint of the awful things that await if you do not. So the Cadillac pulled over, Monroe babbling "Uh-uh-uh," and X jumped out, saying, "Thank you, Monroe, you may go on now." It was here that I got stuck trying to explain it to Nadine, trying to show that funeral coach already well up the street, Monroe having a difficult time getting his car in gear while behind him, stopped, a line of headlamps stretching well back, a few doors opening, the folks nearest startled and wild-eyed and looking to each other for help, and X, his hat set aright, already beginning a march down the sidewalk, heels clicking, shoulders squared, a figure of precision and care and true strength. I told Nadine, as my daddy told me, about the cars creeping past, someone calling out, Colonel Buck Wade stopping and ordering, then shouting for X to get in. X didn't hear, my daddy said. Wade was laughable, his mouth working in panic, an arm waving, his wife tugging at his sleeve, himself almost as improbable as that odd bird my daddy and another colonel had spent a day hunting years ago.

"X didn't know where he was going," my daddy said. To be true, he was feeling the sunlight and the heavy air and hearing, as if with another's ears, honks and shouts, but X said he felt moved and, yes, driven, being drawn away from something, not forward to another. The sadness was on him then, my daddy said, and this afternoon I saw it again in his face, a thing as permanent as the shape of your lips or your natural tendency to be silly. X went into an ice-cream parlor, and here I see him facing a glass-fronted counter of tutti-frutti and chocolate chip and daiquiri ice, and behind it a teen-age girl with no more on her mind than how to serve this one then another and another until she could go home. X ordered vanilla, my daddy said, eating by the spoonful, deliberately and slowly, as if the rest of his life—a long thing he felt he deserved—depended on this moment. It was the best ice cream X ever ate, my daddy

said, and for three cones he thought of nothing, not bleakness, not happiness, not shape, nor beauty, nor thwarts, nor common distress—not anything the brain turns toward out of tribulation. It was then, my daddy
said, that X realized something—about the counter girl, the ice cream itself,
Colonel Buck Wade, even the children and the new wife he would have
one day, and the hundreds of years still to pass—and this insight came to
X with such force and speed that he felt lightheaded and partially blind,
the walls tipping and closing on him, the floor rising and spinning, that
mountain of sundae crashing over his shoulders and neck; he was going
to pass out, X knew, and he wondered what others might say, knowing
that his last thought—like Mr. Valentine's in one story—was long and
complex and featured, among its parts, a scene of hope followed by
misfortune and doom.

When Nadine asked me an hour ago what the moral was, I said, "Everything is fragile." We were in the kitchen, drinking Buckhorn, she in her
pj's; and I tried, though somewhat afflicted by drink and a little breathless, to explain, setting the scene and rambling, mentioning ancient times
and sorrows and pride in another. It was bad. I put everything in—the
way of sitting, how the air smelled when my daddy went inside, gestures
that had significance, what my own flesh was doing. But I was wrong.
Completely wrong. For I left out the part where I, sunburned but shiv-
ering, wandered through X's house, one time feeling weepy, another
feeling foolish and much aged.

The part I left out shows me going into his kitchen, reading the note
my momma wrote when she went to Dallas to visit my Aunt Dolly; and it
shows me standing in every room, as alien in that place as a sneak thief,
touching their bric-a-brac and my daddy's tarnished golf trophies, sitting
on the edge of the sofa or the green, shiny lounger, opening the medicine
cabinet in the guest bathroom, curiosity in me as strong as the lesser
states of mind. It's the part that has all the truth in it—and what I'll tell
Nadine in the morning. I'll describe how I finally entered my daddy's
room and stood over his bed, listening to him snore, the covers clenched
at his chest, saying to myself, as he did long ago, headbone and chinbone
and legbone and armbone. Yes, when I tell it I'll put in the part wherein
a fellow such as me invites a fellow such as him out to do a thing—I'm
not sure what—that involves effort and sacrifice and leads, in an hour or
a day, to that throb and swell fellows such as you call triumph.

Max Apple

My Real Estate

I

I have always believed in property. Though a tenant now, I have prospects. In fact, Joanne Kefir, my realtor, thinks I have the greatest prospects in the world. She has always dropped in on me now and then, but these days she comes up almost every time she leaves her seat for popcorn or a coke. She brings her refreshments with her and she refreshes me. She has done so right from the start, ever since I first realized that I really wanted to own my own home.

She picked me up outside my apartment house. She gave me her card. We shook hands. She looked me over.

"You want a bungalow," she said, "two bedrooms, one and a half baths, central air, hardwood floors. You don't need the headache of a lawn."

In her big Oldsmobile we cruised the expressways. Short skirts were the style then. Joanne drove in bursts of speed. She was learning conversational Spanish from a Berlitz eight-track recording that played as we headed toward the fringes of the inner city where she said there were "buys."

"*Haga me usted el favor de . . .*" said the tape.

"There are a lot of Spanish speakers entering the market," said Joanne. A small card on her dashboard, the type that usually says "Clergy," proclaimed "*Se Habla Español*." "Once you show someone a house," she said, "it's a moral obligation. You take them in your car, buy them lunch, introduce them to some homes in their price range. It's as if you've been naked together." She had long thin legs, all shin until they disappeared only a few inches below where her panty hose turned darker. When the tape ended, she asked if I was a wounded veteran and then if I had ever been in the army at all. She was sorry.

"With a VA loan you could float into a house. Conventional will be tougher. Still, you've got thirty years to cushion one or two percent." She shrugged her small shoulders, asked me about how much I earned.

I declined to say. Her skirt edged higher. I never knew what a VA loan meant. When I saw the VA signs around the housing developments, I thought that the whole thing was exclusively for veterans, that there were lots of crutches and wheelchair ramps and VFW halls in there. She laughed when I told her this.

"There is a lot to know in real estate." She was twenty-eight, she said, and divorced from a man who had liked furnished apartments. My efficiency in the beams is also furnished, but with great luxury. Simmons hideabed, chrome and glass coffee table, Baker easy chair, Drexel maple bed and dresser. There is a hunting tapestry on my living-room wall. My bathroom fixtures are gold leaf and the tub has a tiny whirlpool. When she wants nothing else, Joanne sometimes comes up just to soak her toes in the hot bubbles.

When she was the salesperson and I the client, she told me I was her first bachelor. "I know your type," she said. "When I went to singles bars you were all I ever met. You think apartments are where you'll meet people, you believe the managers who show you game rooms and swimming pools. Listen to how people talk. In apartments they don't have 'neighbors'; they say, 'he lives in my complex.' If you want to meet people, you buy a house."

Joanne refused to believe that I wanted a house for reasons other than neighbors and schools. "So what if you have no wife and children," she said. "Why not be near kids that are well educated, less likely to soap your windows on Halloween and put sugar in your gas tank."

I told her the simple truth. "I want a house because my people have owned land and houses in Texas for four generations. We lived here with the Mexicans and the Indians. I'm the first Spenser who hasn't owned a tiny piece of Texas."

"You still can live with Mexicans," she told me, "in the Fifth Ward. But if you go there, you'll go without me."

She drove extravagantly and used no seat belts. I slid toward her on all the turns. She used the horn but not while listening to the tape. "In the suburbs," Joanne said, "I can put you into a two-bedroom plus den and patio for eighteen five. I can get you all-electric kitchens and even sprinkler systems for a lot less than you'll pay for an old frame bungalow close in." But no matter what she said, she couldn't convince me to look at Sharpstown and Green Acres and Cascade Shores. They sounded like Hong Kong and Katmandu. I grew up in Houston and never knew about these faraway places until I started noticing some of the addresses printed on the checks we took in at the store. Sometimes it was a long-distance call to trace down a local bad check.

"My great-grandfather fought at the Alamo," I told her. "He was one of those who left when Santa Anna gave them a last chance. My granddad owned a farm near where the Astrodome is now." This was the first time the Dome entered our conversation. Joanne was unimpressed and it didn't seem very important to me either. The Dome was just another big building, the Colonel who owned it just another big business-man, and my granddad just another old memory, dead fifteen years.

In my case she was wrong about the suburbs, but Joanne did have an instinct for a client's needs. She was flexible. The one thing she could not do was pretend to like a house. If she didn't like the place, she got out fast, sometimes without leaving her card. She held her nose all the way to the car and refused to answer questions about the place. "Go back without me," she said. "Go alone or take a lawyer or an interior decora-tor." Even when she liked a house, she made the home owners open their drapes. "I want to see everything in the bright light," she said. She came into a house like an actress to center stage. Buyers and sellers moved close to the walls. She sized places up as she walked through in long strides. She noticed inaccuracies in thermostats and recommended plasterers and electricians as she passed needed repairs. Whenever there was a child, she chased him down to pat his head. On our first day, we spent three hours together. At four-thirty, she told me there was a Mexican couple, thus the tape. At seven there was an Open House in Sharpstown. I should call her in the morning.

The next day, Sunday, she was at my door at eight A.M. She had a tennis dress so white that it literally blinded me as the sun reflected from it into my dark apartment.

"Sorry to wake you," she said, "but I was in the neighborhood and I need to use a phone, please." While I showered she made what seemed like dozens of calls. She had played tennis from six A.M. to eight. "Sunday is my big day. I have three listings in Montrose and one in Bellaire. With good weather we'll close something today." She joined me for what was her second breakfast. I knew that as she ate she was itemizing my establishment and judging my taste. She was doing even more than I thought. We finished breakfast at eight-forty-five. "I don't have to be in Bellaire until ten-fifteen," she said, and took off her tennis dress.

Joanne's style was flawless, efficient. She was done in time to have a quick shower herself and give me a brief rundown on mortgage rates.

Later in the week, as she led me from house to house, I learned more personal information, facts from the life of Joanne Kefir. She rattled them off as briskly as the square footage of a room. Born in Chicago, moved to Houston at fourteen, married high school sweetheart; at twenty-five, childless, living in a furnished apartment, where Chuck still resided, only a few complexes east of me; left Chuck and job as legal secretary; became cocktail waitress. There amid "tips that would make your head swim," she met Vince, her sales manager. "What the hell," Vince asked her, "is a girl with your personality doing as a waitress? You should be out on the street." He opened his Multiple Listings Book and started to show her some pictures. "There's a five-bedroom rancher that can bring you a $4,000 commission." Vince told her to think of herself as an obstetrician. A house on the market was like a pregnant woman. She had to go, she would burst if nobody helped. You wanted to make it fast, painless, smooth.

She worked days for Vince, nights as a waitress. "At the end of the month I sold that five-bedroom rancher that Vince had randomly picked out of the book." "It was no accident," he said, "it was your career. I showed you the picture of it." She sold close to a million dollars in each of her first two years. This year she wanted to go over.

"The kind of house you want is chicken feed," she told me, "but I've got the time for it. And who knows, you might one day have a rich friend who'll use me to buy a mansion in Green Meadows."

Because I was in the eighteen to twenty-two thousand range with conventional mortgage, mediocre credit, and less than ten percent down, Joanne could not give me her best hours. I drew dinner times and late nights usually, but this made it convenient for us to eat and occasionally sleep together. She did not have to mix business and pleasure, any more than she had to hurry. Speed and pleasure and business all combined in her like the price and sales tax. The only noise she made was a small grinding of the teeth like a nervous signature on a deed. We rarely kissed and used only the most explicit embraces.

And Joanne did not pressure me to buy a house. As I wavered and mused upon closing costs and repair bills and termites and cockroaches, she just paid less and less attention to me. Finally, in spite of mutual fondness, we never saw each other at all. I kept up with her though by her signs around the city. She married Vince, but because his Italian name was so long, they both used hers. Kefir and Kefir signs, bright orange with a green border, sprang up throughout various better neighborhoods. Whenever I saw the sign, I knew that there Joanne had once opened drapes and frightened owners. She and Vince made a good team. He ran the office and took care of all the paperwork. This left her free to sell. Judging by the frequency of her signs, I guessed she now sold many millions in a year and had forgotten me as a truly bad investment of her time.

I underestimated her loyalty and her memory. Months after our last encounter, I met her in the express lane at Kroger's. It was around supper time and she was buying three Hershey bars.

"With all the money you must earn now," I asked, "can't you take time out for a regular dinner?"

"Sweetheart," Joanne told me, "you never did understand real estate." She bought me a Hershey bar too. I left my less than eight purchases in the cart and followed her to a long white Cadillac. "Deductible," she said, "might as well." She made a U-turn and parked across the street among a group of vans belonging to plumbers who had gone home for the evening. She checked the clock on the panel. "I should be in River Oaks in thirty minutes to show five bedrooms, but they'll wait a few minutes if they have to."

They didn't have to. In the back seat of the Cadillac Joanne was her old self. I looked up and saw wrenches and plungers hanging from the ceilings of the plumbers' vans. "I haven't forgotten you, Jack," she said. "Everytime I see a two bedroom one bath in the medical center area I mean to give you a call."

"Congratulations," I said, "on your marriage"—I had read about it in the financial pages; they took out a quarter-page ad—"and your own business."

"Yes," she said, "it's wonderful. If interest stays down we might even go into our own development."

II

When I next saw her, it was at my own apartment complex. I was on the balcony looking out at the tennis courts below me. Joanne saw me, halted her doubles match and invited me to bring them all some Cokes after the set.

Vince was as tall as Joanne but so thick-set that she seemed to tower above him. He played the net and she took the long ones that he couldn't reach. She wore a tennis dress exactly like the one I remembered. Joanne introduced me to my landlords, Ben and Vera Bloom.

"I'm glad to have a tenant like you," Ben Bloom said. "You know the kind of people that usually rent these: twenty-two-year olds that like to drink beer and screw and write on the walls. They never dump their garbage, but every time they see a roach they run to call the manager. You can't satisfy people like them. No matter what you do they move out. They break leases. Who's going to take a traveling salesman to court?"

Vince treated me like an old friend, claimed that he recognized my name as a former client of their old company. When he and Joanne went into business for themselves, most of the old company came along with them. "We closed the deal for the land you're standing on," Vince said, "so you might say we did a little bit to help you find a place." He seemed to feel guilty that their company had not matched me with a house. "It's his own fault," Joanne said. "He had chances. By the time he decides someone else has put in a bid."

"Oh, one of those," Vince said. Still, he invited me to join them that night at the ball game. The Astros were playing the Cubs. "I've never been to the Dome," I admitted.

"It's a separate world," Ben Bloom said. He wiped the perspiration from his eyes and took off his tennis glove. "People like me put up these developments and tract houses and zoned subdivisions, but not the Colonel. The Colonel left us to screw around with the small stuff. He went for the pie in the sky."

"And he made it," Vera said, "he put us on the map more than the moon did. Nobody even remembers the moon anymore, but just mention Houston at a convention and they all ask about the Dome."

They were going to a party celebrating the fifth anniversary of the stadium. Joanne asked me to meet them at the Colonel's penthouse.

That night, watched by ushers and security guards, I entered the penthouse in the beams. I felt underdressed in my corduroy trousers and sports shirt. Joanne, I noticed, was wearing a black dress with a cut-out back, but Vince was as casually dressed as I. They made me feel very comfortable in the Colonel's living room. The Blooms were there and many other couples. The tuxedoed ushers carried trays full of martinis and Tom Collinses.

"It's nickel beer night in the grandstand," Vince said. "No matter how much you drink you won't be able to keep up with the slobs down there. You couldn't get me to nickel beer night. They piss down all the corridors leading to the men's rooms."

Joanne took me by the elbow and introduced me to some guests. She was relaxed and elegant. I had never seen her in company before, only in business and in bed. She was not even wearing a watch.

"What can I do," she told me when I asked. "I'm here for the evening just like the baseball players. When there's nothing to do, I play ball. That's something else you don't know about real estate."

If I could have looked out from this Dome toward the east, I would have seen my grandfather's former seventy-five acres only a city block away. There are gas stations and motels on the property now, and the roller coaster of an amusement park. My grandfather died broke in the Christian Brothers Home for the Aged. He sold his land right before World War II to buy a liquor store. My dad ran the store.

While I was thinking what might have been if Granddad had held onto the land instead of going into the liquor business, the Colonel rolled in, a big gray-bearded man in an expensive-looking wheelchair. An Astros blanket lay across his knees. A nurse in white and an usher in her gown stood on either side of the chair. Ben Bloom proposed a toast, "To the head of the Dome," he said. "To the man who made it all possible." We clinked our glasses. The Colonel could neither drink nor hold the glass.

"A bad stroke," Joanne whispered to me, "during the first football season. He's never even felt the Astroturf, poor man." She smiled and went over to pat the Colonel on the shoulder. He seemed to understand everything but could barely speak.

As the nurse wheeled him through the guests, it came my turn to meet the great man. The room seemed more crowded; Joanne was nowhere in sight.

"Jack Spenser, sir," I said, not really knowing how to explain my presence. "My grandfather once owned seventy-five acres on Old Spanish Trail. I'd like to buy myself a house in this area."

I could not be sure if he had even heard me. The nurse pushed with some effort his polished chair over the thick carpeting. The room was quite full now, of people with drinks and loud voices. Nobody was watching the TV or cared about the game itself hundreds of feet below.

"Lyndon Johnson used to stay in this suite," I heard someone say, "and get drunk on his ass for the whole weekend. He'd send the Secret Service out to the ranch so everyone would think he was there worrying about Vietnam. It would have taken a pretty shrewd assassin to look for him way up at the top of the Dome."

The splendor of the Astrodome was not the baseball I knew. My dad and I used to go to Texas League games at Buff Stadium for Saturday night doubleheaders. We packed a lunch and a lot of mosquito repellant and sat out in the bleachers for twenty-five cents each. My hero was a black first baseman named Eleazer Brown who never made it to the big leagues. He was six-foot-eight and for awhile did play with the Globetrotters. When my dad closed the liquor store after the eighth robbery and his second bullet wound, the police brought him to a line-up to identify one of the holdup men. It was a cinch. Even slouched over and in dark glasses, Dad knew the big torso of Eleazer Brown. "It was a sad day for me," Dad said, "fingering that coon who could hit the ball five hundred feet. That's him, I told the cops—and you know, in spite of everything, I almost went up and asked that black bastard for his autograph." At least Brown hadn't shot at Dad; the gunman was Brown's friend, an average-sized numbers runner from Dallas.

The roof of the Dome was so high, I had read, that you could put the Shamrock Hotel into it. I tried to imagine the biggest thing I could, the Goodyear Blimp, dwarfed against the ceiling. As a store manager, I was entitled to one ride a year in the Blimp. When I first met Joanne, I had taken her as my guest. She pointed out landmarks to the children of other managers. When we landed, she ran toward her car. "It made me nervous," she said. "It reminded me of a mobile home."

"I've been looking for you," Joanne said. "The Colonel wants to see you. He never asks for anybody."

"Why does he want me?"

"Who knows," Joanne said, "but it's a great honor. Vince and Ben thought you went down to the game. Go ahead—he's in the other room with his nurse." I knocked at the door.

The Colonel and his nurse awaited me in a smaller sitting room. I was surprised that he smoked a pipe. The nurse held it for him between puffs. As I waited for the Colonel to begin, the nurse played with the pipe stem. With a small knife, she shaved the dark tobacco and repacked the bowl. She caressed the stem. It took the Colonel a long time to say anything. He had to get his mouth in the right position. I could see how difficult it was for him. When he did begin, the words came out loud and uneven, like a child writing on a blackboard.

"Your grandpa," he got out, "was a dumb-ass son of a bitch." He puffed on the pipe and then the nurse repacked it. I waited for the second sentence.

"He could have had a piece of the world . . . wanted a liquor store instead." As the Colonel, between puffs and silences, got out his story, I learned that he had bought most of the Dome land from Granddad and had offered my ancestor a part of what, at that time, was going to be a housing development. Just as I hesitated with Joanne over my would-be bungalow, so Gramps had hemmed and hawed with the Colonel and finally taken his money instead for the liquor-store enterprise.

"We grew up together on Buffalo Bayou," the Colonel said. "He sold booze during Prohibition and never forgot that he made easy money then. Before he kicked off, I told him about the Dome and he laughed in my face. Now," the Colonel went on even more slowly, "now the laugh is on me. I put the top on baseball. I made my own horizon. I shut out the sky. But I've got no arms and legs and no sons and daughters." He took a long, long pause and rejected the pipe. The noise from the party in the outer rooms surrounded our silence. It made the Colonel's slowness even more dramatic.

"I never liked Old Jack Spenser" (I was named for Granddad) "and I jewed him out of his land. Fifty bucks an acre was a steal even in those days. He had liquor on his mind all the time."

While the Colonel kept pausing, I tried to remember what I actually had heard about the land on the Old Spanish Trail. I knew it had been Gramps's land, but when he went senile, I was just a boy. All I remember is his crazy laugh in the Christian Brothers Home. We used to have to bring him dolls when we came as if he were a baby. He died in '56 and Dad only made it two years beyond that. The liquor store was busted. Mom moved to Colorado with my sister.

"For a liquor store, he gave up this." With difficulty the Colonel made a neck gesture that suggested arms wide open. "I can't stand all these outsiders that keep coming down here. I'd like the dome to be just for us Texans. That real-estate girl told me you wanted your own house.

You're smarter than your granddad." Then the Colonel made me an offer.
I thought about it overnight, asked Joanne's advice the next day. "I only
think of single dwellings," she said. "The family is the unit I work with.
Ask someone who knows big spaces." But without further advice, I did it
on my own. What was there to lose?

III

That was almost three years ago. Now I don't work for Goodyear anymore. I don't have to. The Colonel pays me two hundred a week plus
room. He only leaves the Dome to go to the doctor's office in Plaza Del
Oro across the street. I have my own apartment next to his and my only
real job is getting up to turn the Colonel at three each morning so he
won't get bedsores. The night watchman lets me in. The Colonel is
asleep on his right side. He snores quietly into his beard. Since I'm pretty
tired too, it's all a blur. I pull the special pad from beneath his hips and
put it on the other side of him. I grab his arms as if they're ropes and
give a good hard pull, then I go back to the other side of the bed and roll
his hips over. He never wakes up.

Lately Joanne has been saying that I'll inherit the Dome someday
because he's got no heirs. "He picked you because you're a Texan, because he knew your grandpa. He doesn't need other reasons. What else
is he going to do with it?" When she tells me how rich I'm going to be she
snuggles up close and spends an extra few minutes. The high interest
rates since '73 have really hurt her business and her marriage. She doesn't
talk about it too much, but things are not working out between her and
Vince. "He wants to go commercial," she says, "I can't work beyond the
family. He wants to use leverage. He talks about a real-estate trust. I look
at houses as walls and roofs. Vince calls them instruments and units."
They have filed for divorce.

This year, for the first time, Joanne bought an Astros season ticket.
Sometimes I go down to watch an inning or two and when I come back
there she is in my whirlpool. She is as fast and smooth as ever. Interest
rates and marriage have not changed her. She doesn't look around for
Jack Spenser's perfect house any longer. "You'll own the Dome soon,"
she says. "You'll call all the shots."

I don't think the Colonel is likely to make me his heir, but there is
no doubt that it's possible. He calls for me every few weeks just to talk.
He's getting weaker but he still likes to tell me what a dumb ass Grandpa

was. I agree and have taken over the nurse's job with the pipe. So far it's been no problem. If the Colonel wants to call Granddad a dumb ass all the time, that's his privilege.

In most ways my life is pretty much the same, but living in the Dome has killed my interest in baseball. When I do watch an inning or two it's only to look at the scoreboard or the mix of colors in the crowd or to listen to the sound of the bat meeting the ball. What I like to do most is walk behind the grandstand and watch the people buying refreshments. There are one hundred and twenty-six places in the Dome where you can buy beer. People line up at each one of them. There are eight restaurants and six of them have liquor licenses. While Astros and Dodgers and Cubs and Giants are running the bases and hitting the balls, the Colonel is making a fortune on beer and liquor. My grandpa, I think, wasn't such a dumb ass. He just had the wrong location.

Joanne has lots of plans for later. She wants to marry me. She says that we could keep the name of her business and use all the signs she has left over from her years with Vince.

"We won't need the money," I tell her. "We'll take a vacation around the world."

"No," she says, "first we'll evict the baseball team and the conventions. We can make a big profit on these auditorium seats. Then we'll put up modern bungalows, just the kind you wanted. They'll be close to downtown and have every convenience. There's room here for dozens. Even the outdoors will be air conditioned. We'll put good private schools in the clubhouses and lease all the corridor space for shops and supermarkets. A few condominiums down the foul lines," she says, "and a hospital in center field. The scoreboard will be the world's biggest drive-in movie."

I go along with her. She gets more passionate when she talks this way, more involved with me. She's been saying these things for quite a while now and keeping track of the Colonel's health. He is so slow these days that he falls asleep between words. I don't think he can last much longer. Joanne gets very excited when she sees his pale face being wheeled past my door. "We'll move into his place," she says, "and use this as my office." I'm sad when I think of the Colonel becoming something like my grandpa playing with dolls, but I didn't take Joanne too seriously until a few days ago when after some drinks and a whirlpool bath she put on a long hostess gown and went back to her box behind third base. I followed because I was suspicious of the gown. She walked right over the railing onto the field. She took the third-base umpire by the arm and led him to the mound. "Let's get some sunlight in here," she yelled to the top of the Dome, "let's see what it would be like with new tenants. It's a good neighborhood. There's lots of shade and well-kept lawns, and the neighbors," she looked at Walt Alston in the visitors' dugout, "the neighbors seem friendly and sincere." She left the umpire at the pitcher's mound and started taking her long strides toward the outfield.

"Rates can't go much higher," she told the Dodger infield, "but if they do you'll be extra glad you bought now. A house isn't like other investments. Stocks and bonds don't give you the direct benefits of housing. There is nothing like it on God's earth. Yearly deductions, shelter, comfort, and all of it at capital gains rates."

"Do you have children?" she asked the second baseman who looked on in bewilderment. "If you do you'll appreciate the lack of traffic. You can send three-year-olds to the store without any worries." By center field her stride was almost a gallop. "Don't worry," she called to the Dodgers' black left fielder, "you'll be able to live here too. It will take a few years but the whole world is changing."

A squadron of park policemen caught up with her on the way to the bullpen. They led her back to the third-base box where I waited alongside the manager who knew me and told the police to let her go in my custody. The policemen were gentle with her, and the crowd cheered as she put those long smooth legs easily over the high railing. She threw kisses in all directions. The scoreboard spelled out "Charge" and the organist played "Funny Girl." I led her up the ramp toward the escalator. "The place will sell, Jack. Everybody loves it. That Astroturf will save a bundle on gardening too. We can do it, Jack, I know we can. When the Colonel leaves it to you, can we go ahead with it?"

She was all motion in my apartment. I could hardly restrain her from going into the Colonel's penthouse and smothering him with a pillow. "I'm only kidding about that," she said. "We're at the top now; we can wait."

As she ran the water for another whirlpool bath to relax her, I thought of my great-grandfather saying goodbye to Davy Crockett and walking out of history, his son selling out to the Colonel, and my own dad bankrupt by liquor. Far below us, someone was stealing a base. Next door, the Colonel was struggling for a word. Cartoons blinked from the scoreboard. I took off my clothes. "It must run in the family," I said, thinking of Gramps laughing in the empty hallway of the Christian Brothers Home. I laughed out loud too. "If I get the Dome, do anything you want with it," I said. "Just save me room for the world's largest liquor store." In the midst of bubbles, I joined her. We sparkled like champagne.

Harriette Simpson Arnow

Fra Lippi and Me

I didn't know she was mad. A minute before she looked at the man and smiled. That was when I heard it first. That name, Fra Lippi, I mean. She was saying something about it when I brought her tea. She looked at the cup. She looked at me. "But I wanted cream," she said. She didn't look at me the way she looked at the man.

I smiled my all mouth and no eyes smile. "I'm sorry," I said. "I didn't know you wanted cream instead of lemon."

"You could have asked," she said. Another woman called across the aisle, "You brought me rolls when I wanted corn muffins."

I smiled again. I turned and said, "I'm sorry. I didn't know." I picked up the plate of rolls and the cup and saucer with the lemon. I hurried. But I wasn't quick enough. The blue-chinned man by the post glared at me. I knew he would. He had ordered a steak well done. He was in a hurry. "My wife could have skinned and cooked a whole cow while I've been waiting here," he said.

I smiled. "I'm sorry, but—"

I couldn't say any more. He slapped the table. "Sorry. You waitresses are always sorry. Sorry." His last loud, "Sorry," brought Ridgeways on the run. She was the hostess. She followed me into the kitchen. "That man's been waiting half an hour," she said, and made her voice loud. I heard it above the dish washers and the order caller and the long curses of the black meat cooks and the sizzling sound of broiling meat. I started to tell her the man had lied. I changed my mind. I knew it was no good. She would believe him. That was her job—believing them. "Don't come back without that steak," she yelled, and rushed into the dining room.

It didn't matter. Nothing much would matter if I. . . . I would have to get a manicure. But I wouldn't. I knew I wouldn't. It made me sick to think about it. I told myself I thought I might because I was tired. The people seemed so hard that day, all in a hurry. My feet hurt and my back ached and something inside me ached from just knowing—that tomorrow was today. I was tired of people's chewing mouths and their hands, reaching and beckoning and fumbling with gloves and purses and napkins—and sometimes silver. But I knew I wouldn't do it. I knew I wouldn't.

I pried hot corn muffins from a greasy sticky iron, and then I pulled the order caller's sleeve. "What about a small sirloin well for number twelve?"

I waited while he called, "Lamb chops on two, T-bone well, sirloin rare, chicken on three, roast beef, dry, medium, filet two, tenderloin . . ."

I pulled his sleeve again. "What about—"

He did not look at me. "Get the hell outa my way. Get back on the floor. Tenderloin . . ."

"But," I began, and felt Ridgeways' hand shaking my shoulder. "Patsy, do you know, do you realize—" she gulped her words so fast they choked her—"that you walked off and left Mrs. George Henry Wakefield without so much as a cup for her tea. Not even a cup—and here you stand arguing with Shadoan."

"I couldn't pick up the lemon in my fingers. It's against the rules. And you said for me not to—"

"None of your back talk."

I grabbed a cup and saucer and a creamer. I hurried. Ridgeways kept right behind me. She talked—loud so I could hear. "Do you know who that woman is? She said you were impertinent. Same as told her that it was her place to tell you she wanted cream. And then you must run off. You ought to lose your job for this. You ought to know better. Remember you've been reported twice for not smiling." I was glad when we got into the dining room. There we both had to smile. She followed me to this Mrs. George Henry Wakefield. "I found her," she said.

I set down the cup and saucer. The woman talked to Ridgeways. She did not look at me. "You'd think that with all this fuss about unemployment that those who are fortunate enough to have jobs would try to do their work properly. I would not tolerate dining-room service such as this for one moment, not for a single moment." I can't remember all she said. She didn't talk loud and fast like Ridgeways. I guess she was well bred. She took her time.

I had to stand and listen. I saw the woman who wanted muffins instead of rolls. She was getting mad. I had her muffins but I couldn't go. I couldn't move while this Mrs. George Henry Wakefield complained. That would have been impertinence. The four women at the corner table were ready for dessert. A fat woman by the wall was waving her cup for more coffee. I knew the man's steak was done. It would be cold. I would get bawled out. But I couldn't move. I had to listen to the woman. She said that while she waited for the cup her lunch had grown cold. She talked about courtesy. She said she liked to be served by a pleasant waitress. People must learn to smile, she said.

I stood by her elbow, but I didn't look at her. I looked at the man with her. He wasn't half as old as the woman. But he wasn't a boy. Some men are always boys. This one looked as if he had been a boy just a little while—maybe never at all. He drew pictures on the tablecloth with the handle of a spoon. I couldn't see the pictures. The way he looked at the tablecloth was how I knew. Sometimes he would look at the woman. Once he looked at me. I smiled the way I've learned. He did not look at me again. I hated him. Not because the woman seemed to like him so. I hated him for his shoulders. They were not so big, but they looked strong. I've wished for shoulders like that. Strong shoulders and big shoulders like the ones some of the women I waited on had. Their strong shoulders and long arms and big hands seemed mostly wasted. With me they wouldn't have been. I always thought that maybe big shoulders wouldn't ache so, get so tired. But I don't know. The man looked as if he might have thought about things like that. Not about shoulders, I mean, but things like rent money. They are all the same.

The woman finished. She listened then while Ridgeways explained and apologized. "I know your food is cold by now," Ridgeways said. "The waitress will take it away, and I will see to it that she brings back everything fresh and hot from the kitchen. You won't have to wait a moment."

The woman smiled. "If it doesn't take too long. We can't sit here all day, you know."

"My lunch is quite all right," the man said.

The woman wanted him to have me take it away. They argued about it. I had to stand and listen. Then the woman had me get her another pot of tea, and more hot cheese rolls for her chicken salad, and put more ice in their drinking water, and bring her a slice of lemon for the salad, and bring the man another pat of butter. He didn't have enough, she said. He didn't say anything.

I hurried. But after that I knew it was no use. I wouldn't make any money. I was behind from spending so much time with her. I never got caught up until the rush was over. Ridgeways followed me around. That didn't help. The man with the steak raised a row. He waited a long while. When his meat came it was cold. That was my fault.

The rush was over. I had thirty cents. This Mrs. George Henry Wakefield and the man were still there. It was after two o'clock. I couldn't leave while I had customers. They had been talking a long while. Mostly she talked. He listened. I listened, too. I had nothing else to do while I stood against the wall and waited. I tried to stand up straight and not fidget. "An appearance of haste or restlessness creates an unpleasant atmosphere for guests." That was what our rule book said. My feet hurt and my shoulders had that two o'clock feeling. I guess I must have fidgeted. The man looked at me—more than once.

I could see he wasn't used to servants. Good servants, I mean. The kind that are like pieces of furniture. I could see he didn't want me to stand and listen. I was glad she talked. I wanted to listen to something. I kept thinking about how easy it would be—in a way. It wasn't like I had never been married. It wasn't like I was young and not knowing. I was almost twenty years old. It would be so easy. But I wouldn't do it. I knew I wouldn't. I didn't want to think about it, so I listened to this woman. She was talking about this Fra Lippi, and another man Browning. The man Browning had said things about Fra Lippi. A painter I made him out. "I read that," she said, "when I was only sixteen, and terribly, terribly impressionable. The effect of Fra Lippi on me was tremendous, just tremendous." She lit another cigarette and looked sad like she wanted to cry. I took her a clean ashtray. I hoped she would notice she was keeping me and go. She didn't though. She talked some more. "I vowed then," she moved the ashtray a little and looked at it, "that if it ever lay within my power to save a struggling young artist from the fate that strangled that genius I would do it."

She looked at the man. He didn't say anything. She went on. "That was so cruel, to smother him so, to stifle him. They made him paint as they wished, and shut out all beauty, all realism, all life one might say." She raised her head and looked full in his face. She leaned towards him. Her big breasts seemed ready to fall on the table. "Can't you see? . . . Your little petty job . . . this—this horrible commercial work will deaden you, blunt you. . . . I will not expect that—"

"Want me to stand a minute, Patsy? If you don't grab a bite now you'll get nothin'. Them cooks are shuttin' down the steam table."

I didn't look around. I knew it was Thelma. She worked the station next to mine. I looked straight ahead. I talked low and hardly moved my lips. That way a hostess wouldn't notice. "I'm not hungry," I said.

"Don't let Ridgeways get you down. She'll ride me tomorrow and leave you alone."

"Ridgeways don't worry me."

"Thinkin' on your boyfriend?"

"Not so much. Since he got that job in Detroit he hardly ever gets a chance to write."

"You know I don't mean the one you're married to. That oldish guy that eats on your station ever' night."

"I feed a lot a oldish guys."

"The one gettin' thick in the belly and thin in the hair that likes you so."

"He's lonesome as ever," I said.

"There's a heap a ways a man has a bein' lonesome."

"He's just plain lonesome."

"Lonesome like Adam and a boar hog in December?"

"Yes," I said. I wished she would hush. I didn't want to think about that old man. He had so much money. I wanted to listen to the woman. "Don't be silly." I heard that. "I am the one who will be grateful." I heard that, too.

"Still a tryin' to get you to lighten his lonesomeness?" Thelma asked.

"Yes."

"You aimin' to?"

"I'll have to get a manicure and maybe get my eyebrows fixed first."

"Your hair'll do as it is, though."

"Yes. Lucky, it curls in dampish weather like this."

"And when are you aimin' to begin this lonesome work."

"And if you are so squeamish about . . . a loan . . . there are always portraits. I could get some of my friends—"

"I was thinking maybe tonight," I said.

"Does he know it?"

"No, he said call him any afternoon at the hotel where he stays, or let him know at dinner."

"They'd love it. I always find my sittings disappointingly short. You are so . . . so—"

"Don't tell the old fool at dinner. Excite him so he'd maybe choke to death."

"I'll telephone."

"I would ask nothing, expect nothing . . . only now and then perhaps . . . a view of your work . . . and of you. I am so interested."

"You'll come in here to eat, and throw me a quarter tip, pretty as you please, I bet."

"I'd make it fifty cents. He tips that much. Sometimes more."

"I wish I had a few customers like that. He's not hard to wait on either, is he?"

"No. Most generally takes the same thing. Says once he likes a thing he always likes it."

"I would save you from that. When I first saw your work—and you—I came home and read that poem again."

"If he's by his women like he is by his grub you're settin' pretty."

"I saw that child Fra Lippi, hungry . . . watching people's faces to see who would fling a crust of bread. I thought of you . . . and wondered . . ."

"I figure I will be . . . easy with the world."

"Forgive me. I'm only a sentimental old fool. No, not old. . . . Henry is good . . . and kind; he just doesn't understand, doesn't realize that I need . . . that I am not old, too old to be interested in . . . art. That child, hungry, watching, haunted me when—"

"Well, Patsy, I'll be lookin' for you any day now. I'll see you come strollin' in—in a mink coat."

"I think I'll take beaver," I said. I knew Thelma was joking. I wondered if I was. I was glad when she went away. I wanted to get the hang of this man Fra Lippi. I wondered what it was he did to keep from starving. I never did find out—exactly. The man never did talk loud enough for me to hear.

The woman began to get ready to go. She was smiling now. Glad about something. I couldn't tell about the man. I didn't watch him so much. I kept looking at the woman. She was going to pay the check herself. Still, I hoped a little. Maybe she'd leave me anyhow a quarter. She was in a good humor—now. I watched her. The man watched me. I didn't care. I made three dollars a week in wages. I had to make tips.

She fumbled in her purse. She took out a five-dollar bill. She shut the purse. She picked up her lorgnette, twirled it a moment on its silver chain. She unsnapped it, set it on her nose, and squinted at the check. She frowned. She opened the purse again. Fumbled awhile, and brought out a penny. "This tax is such a nuisance," she said. "Eleven cents on this. I hate pennies, don't you." She looked at him, smiled a moment, and then she got up.

The man rushed around and helped her with her coat. She looked down the dining room. "Why if there isn't Florence Sangster. She's one of the kind you must meet. She's an old friend of mine."

The man looked like he wanted to frown. But he didn't. He did look at his wristwatch, a cheap one. "I really ought to hurry on to that—"

She cut him off. "Don't be silly," she laughed. She shook her finger at him. "Remember now I'm saving you from dashing away to see people you don't want to see. Florence might like you to do her portrait when I tell her you're doing mine."

She took his arm. They walked away. I went over to the table. I looked under her finger bowl and under his finger bowl. Nothing was there. I knew there wouldn't be. I didn't care. It wouldn't matter. With yesterday and today I had enough for what I needed. I picked up the crumpled napkin the man had used. Under it was his cigarette lighter. I saw him then, coming back alone.

"You forgot your cigarette lighter," I said.

He smiled. He looked nice when he smiled. "On purpose," he said, and laid two quarters on the table. "I'm sorry my companion was so—"

I didn't want his quarters. I wouldn't let him finish. "Keep 'em, Fra Lippi," I said.

All the smile went out of his eyes. His face looked hard and red. "Don't call me that," he said.

I felt giddy and not caring. That name had popped first into my head. "You oughtn't to mind," I said. "The man with that name must have been pretty smart to have people writing and talking about him."

His face didn't change.

"He must have done something bad then," I said.

"He didn't want to starve, so he worked to please. When he was sorry he couldn't change."

"Didn't he please himself?"

"No."

"He didn't starve and had a easy time."

"Yes."

I looked him in the eye. "Is that a sin?"

"It is—for some."

I picked up a finger bowl. I didn't look at him. "I see," I said. "I guess I owe you an apology for calling you that name."

"No, no apology—for me. Fra Lippi would be the one . . . he was a child, and I'm not, but it's all . . . you wouldn't understand."

I picked up the other finger bowl. "I do understand," I said.

He looked me over. "You are studying to be an artist, too—perhaps. I thought your face was—"

"I'm not an artist—exactly," I cut in, "but, well . . . if you're Fra Lippi, I guess I'd be Sister Lippi."

"I'm afraid I don't understand."

I put both finger bowls in one hand and picked up the water glasses. "I'm not an artist, but it's all the same—in some ways," I said.

By the swinging door I turned and looked at him. He was walking away toward the woman. He didn't hurry. I thought about him again that day when I went to the telephone. I walked slow, too.

Mary Clearman Blew

Forby and the Mayan Maidens

IT is your belief, I take it, that undertaking this narrative will, in shedding light upon my *alleged* role in Richard's death, allow me to sleep nights. I have no faith at all in the efficacy of this project. The events leading up to Richard's choice, insofar as they had to do with me at all, were a part of my adult and conscious life. I have no reason to feel guilty. It is the irrevocability of his turning from me that I simply cannot . . . allow myself to dwell upon.

But lest I be charged with unwillingness to cooperate in my own cure, I have begun this account, to use your words, of the authoritarian figures of my childhood. What a phrase! Its illogic is manifest, for all children stand in the shadows of giants. My particular giants, my parents, were ordinary farm people. I am the younger of two brothers. My brother, Miles, still farms the old ground. He and I remain on good, if remote, terms. My father is dead, my mother senile.

It is not at all unusual for a man like me to come from such a background. Few of my graduate-school acquaintances (as I recall them) or of my present colleagues enjoyed the advantages of a cultured or even sympathetic background. My personal history is depressingly commonplace: the bookish and sensitive child, rebuffed and belittled by puzzled or contemptuous parents and playmates, turns more and more to the rewards of scholastic achievement that eventually lead to escape through a scholarship at the state university and thence to the teaching assistantship and the painfully acquired advanced degree which in its turn, if one is fortunate, returns one to the teaching position at the undistinguished four-year college. The infrequent rewards, the Richards whose sensitivity and promise provide one with the opportunity to perform the rescue that was once provided for oneself, must suffice. Hundreds, possibly thousands, can tell my story. Reason enough for my reluctance to re-examine it. In my case I was fortunate to have a brother like Miles who, in fulfilling perfectly the expectations of our little community, lessened the need to press me into the same deadening mold.

As I think upon it now, however, I admit that few among those thousands can boast of overcoming an initial encounter with public education as stultifying as was mine. For even in my boyhood, rural schools were beginning to disappear from farming communities just as remote as ours. Hardly a one of those schools can exist today. In his Christmas letter Miles mentioned that our very school had recently been purchased by a neighbor and hauled away to serve as a grain bin. A far more useful function than it had served in many years!

It was their inability to hire a teacher, wrote Miles, that convinced the local school board to bow to the inevitable. High time, indeed. Even in my boyhood it was difficult to find a teacher who would accept a position isolated by miles of muddy or snowbound roads beyond even the reach of telephone lines, without plumbing and without electricity and with the very drinking water carried from the spring—do I bore you? Those teachers were hardly the authoritarian figures you imagined. Only the halt, the blind, the dregs of the profession would accept positions in the rural schools.

It was my brother Miles's teacher's dropping dead in his shoes before the astonished eyes of the school's ten or eleven pupils that delayed my own enrollment in school for two fatal years. I do not exaggerate. It was during those two years that I grew into myself—or are you curious about poor old Professor Wentworth who dropped dead? Do you want to know the details? I really know very little, having been only six years old and kept in the dark at the time it happened. I do know that Professor Wentworth was ninety years old when they hired him. He had had a respectable teaching career but at his age no town school would have taken a chance on him. He was spry and alert but he, too, bowed to the inevitable shortly before Thanksgiving. Miles had to be driven ten miles to a school in the next district for the rest of the year, and I, who should have started the first grade in the fall, was kept at home by my mother for two more years. She was worried, I suppose, about the effect the sudden death might have upon me. Its effect upon Miles? You may well ask. I've never known. Did he, I wonder, lie awake at night as I do and watch the electric streetlight outside my window bleach the unresisting

elm leaves and slowly fade as they resume their daylight greens one
more time?

Why, why in the name of God must I bother with all this? Can you
tell me what point it has? Do you think I can possibly care about elm
leaves or Miles or country schools? I was begotten, born, and will—should
I be fortunate enough to follow Professor Wentworth's example—drop
dead before the momentarily startled eyes of thirty freshman-composition
students. Meanwhile I cannot sleep. You have implied that you can grant
oblivion in return for these details, and God knows it is an exchange
I would make joyously if only I believed in its terms; what else could I
ask at three in the morning when, brain aching from the unrelenting roller
coaster of associations it can no longer contain, I prowl from window to
window in the dark and note how still the leaves hang in the artificial
light? If only I could ask him, talk with him, have ten minutes back out
of all time to plead my cause—as I say, it is the irrevocability of a suicide
that leaves the living without an alternative.

In any event, I was at last enrolled in school, the wife of a neighboring farmer having agreed to open ours. Large for my age, self-taught
to read from my brother's schoolbooks, longing for school with a mis-
placement of expectations that is pathetic in retrospect, I was set up for
disillusionment in a way no one recognized.

"I think he'll be all right," I remember my mother saying. I remember that she sounded doubtful, but memory is a notorious liar. Certainly
it seems as though I recall perfectly her sharp voice and the line gouged
between her eyes as she turned in the long September twilight to carry
the supper dishes to the drainboard—but do I? Of course it was September, time for school to start. Of course she frowned; her frown was
permanent. But if, by one of the technological feats that have reduced
our young to illiterate victims of a box of flickering shadows, I could
witness a (so to speak) metaphysical videotape of my mother's kitchen
on that September evening, what would I see? Or hear (assuming a sound
track)? Was she doubtful? Angry? Relieved to get me off her hands?

I think I remember her turning as my father pushed back from the
wooden table and lifted his cup of coffee in a hand horny and permanently grimed from his fields: "Why wouldn't he be all right? Only
place for him. Goddamn kid would get himself killed if I let him around
the machinery. Even if you could get his nose pried out of his book he'd
forget his head if it wasn't for Miles keeping track of him. Miles, now—"
Some of this diatribe he may have repeated to my mother on that September evening, some of it at other times. How I feared him, and feared

the certainty of his voice and the wallop of his hand! His assessment of me was the assessment which my first schoolmates made immediately and which has been made of me repeatedly since then: in a world split between the real and the unreal, my only province lies in the latter.

Miles, for example, knew what to expect. He drove grain trucks up to the day school started. Then he submitted reluctantly to a bath and clean clothes—"If I could skip the first week, Dad, and help you finish harvest?"—but at last dug out his baseball bat and glove and cheered a little at the sight of them.

But I couldn't wait to get to school. I tried to get out of the car before it came to a full stop in the schoolyard that morning, earning me a shout from my mother, but my feet were on the sod by then and nothing could stop me. I stood in the dry September grass that was still knee-high on the playground, squinting against the glare of the sun on white siding and smelling the fields of stubble and the dust that converged from the horizon from all directions upon one point.

The school was cool in the anteroom. Underfoot the old pine flooring was hollowed from the feet of hundreds of children. Under the row of coat hooks sat the earthenware water cooler with its tap at the bottom and its row of drinking cups on the shelf behind it. In the classroom itself, light flooded through a dozen long north windows and fell in blotches across the waxed floor and the rows of desks in graduating sizes that were connected with the back of each seat supporting the desk of the next. The blackboard was clean. At the front of the school was the teacher's desk and a large flag. At the rear was the oil heater. A door behind the heater led to the teacherage, as everyone but me knew. Perhaps even in that first excitement, something about the teacherage warned me off. I do remember its smell, yeasty and cramped from the generations of women who had lived and cooked for themselves behind the schoolroom.

"And this is Wayne," said my mother, catching me by the neck and pushing me forward with a smile so unlike her that I struggled to escape her fingers. "Oh yes?" smiled the teacher and I got my first good look.

You understand, don't you, what a crime it was? From Miles's social studies and science readers I had not only taught myself to read but had also caught a glimpse, or so I thought, of a heaven on earth made concrete in a third- or fourth-grade classroom presided over by a smiling Miss White or Miss Bell who guided twenty or so small companions all united in their desires to examine the sources of weather changes or common modes of transportation or the lives of children around the world. Do you understand what I imagined lay ahead?

Mrs. Skaarda had taught for several years previously at our school, its proximity to her home being, I suppose, its one attraction. She was considered to be a fine teacher with a proper regard for phonics, those tiresome objects whose unpredictable fallings in and out of pedagogical fashion so worry the parents of young children—Mrs. Skaarda, as I have said, was strong on phonics, and her willingness to teach at our little school was considered a stroke of fortune for the neighborhood until her unexpected illness forced her to a long stay in a distant hospital and brought about the hiring, after a frantic schoolboard meeting, of poor old Professor Wentworth. Miles, my senior by four years—and six grades ahead of me because of my late start—had already gone to school under Mrs. Skaarda and liked her. This fall, after nearly three years of an illness I never heard named, Mrs. Skaarda felt well enough to return to the school, and my mother thought it safe at last to enroll me.

I do not remember ever seeing Mrs. Skaarda before that morning. Unlike my mother and the other farm women, who were heavy-handed and heavy-hammed from work and fatigue and over-feeding, Mrs. Skaarda was a small slim woman with bones as insubstantial as a bird's. While considerably older than the Miss Whites and the Miss Bells of Miles's old readers, she radiated something of their storied warmth. Her hair was dark and her eyes, too, were dark and apprehensive in their setting of fine wrinkles. Her smile for me was tremulous: "And this is Miles's little brother? Wayne? Oh-h-h-h-h! We'll be fine!"

After all the parents drove away, Mrs. Skaarda rang a little bell and called the small children off the swings and Miles and the big Snapp girls and Charlie Connard away from the baseball diamond to crowd through the cloakroom into the fresh sun-dappled schoolroom to try out desks for size. Mine, I remember, had hardly room for my legs under it; as the year wore on I was continually being cursed by Shelley Snapp for tripping her on her way to the pencil sharpener, which I could not help—my desk having been assigned me because of my primary status and not my size. Yes, from that first day I was paired with Forby Weston.

But back to Mrs. Skaarda. As I recall her small, anxious face, the way she cupped her chin in her hands while her eyes searched our twelve faces for reassurance, I must ask myself again: how well do I really remember her? And I answer firmly: oh surely I remember her as she was! For on that first day, whether she knew it or not, I recognized a kindred spirit in her, a fellow sensitive in the land of the unfeeling. From the time when, instead of beginning an arithmetic lesson, Mrs. Skaarda leaned across her desk and began to tell us how glad she was to be well again and how she looked forward to learning with us, I knew her for what she was.

For Mrs. Skaarda, too, stood in the shadows of giants. Her sister-in-law, her father-in-law, her professors at college, a man who taught her niece in a city school, the director of a theater group to which she had once belonged—"I begged her to understand the man was dying!" Mrs. Skaarda's tremulous whisper reduced us to silence as we sat in our rows between the north windows and the blackboard. "But it didn't matter to her! It didn't matter!"

The accounts of her conflicts, begun in lieu of opening exercises, swelled through the mornings and sometimes continued after we had eaten our sandwiches at noon. We were a willing audience, for none of us had heard such tales; and, as though by agreement, we never discussed what we heard with our parents or even among ourselves. More and more those long mornings and lengthening afternoons became a matter of awe among us.

Mrs. Skaarda's brother was dying of cancer. Every morning she brought us reports, not only of the callousness of her sister-in-law, but of each step her brother took as he yielded his body to decay. "Cancer has its own terrible smell," she whispered. "I gag when I sit at my own brother's bedside. Anybody would. And to think that he must lie there, never able to walk away from the putrid smell of his own body! And we'll all come to the same thing in the end. Every body in the room will someday be putrid!"

"I'd shoot myself before I died like that," said daring Shelley Snapp.

"It's all the same in the end," Mrs. Skaarda told her sadly.

A few days later she told us that her brother could eat nothing. For three days he had eaten nothing. Then it was a week.

"He can't eat nothing! He'd die!" said my brother Miles stoutly.

"They give him liquids through a tube," she explained. "But it isn't enough nourishment to live on. He would starve to death if he weren't dying first of cancer." Then she told us the dreadful family secret: it didn't matter to her sister-in-law whether her brother died or not.

One morning she came to school red-eyed. "He's dead," she told us and burst into tears. The youngest Snapp girl cried, too, and the rest of us tried not to cry. Only Forby Weston showed no emotion, and, not for the first time, I focused my anger on Forby, my companion in the first grade, for his lack of sensitivity. He sat coloring in his workbook and paid no attention. I had always disliked him for his appearance and his inability to read; now I whetted my dislike by staring at him. He was as large-framed as I, with pale skin and fishy eyes and a large mouth like a fish.

"I sat up with him all night," Mrs. Skaarda recovered enough to tell us as we waited, rapt, for more. "I held his hand. No one else would stay with him. It happened about three o'clock this morning."

The schoolroom was so quiet that I could hear the soft rub of Forby's crayon across the paper. "Did you know that dead bodies fart?" Mrs. Skaarda confided. "His did."

After her brother died, Mrs. Skaarda became fearful. For a few days fitfully spent on ordinary lessons, her eyes searched the schoolroom, lingering on the three shelves of old library books I had already read from cover to cover, the wainscoted cabinet that held chalk and paper, the twelve of us in our three rows—and coming to rest more and more often on our old oil heater.

"If it exploded, it would kill us, of course," her voice broke the silence. We looked up hopefully from our science readers, blinking against the sunlight now strained thin through frost-covered windows. "They might be able to identify my body. My desk is on the far side of the room. But most of you would be mutilated beyond recognition."

We all turned to look at the glowing heater, once our ally against the freezing December weather that kept us cooped in the schoolhouse during recess, but now transformed into a squat smug force capable of blotting us all out of existence.

"If it started to explode, I'd jump up and run," said Shelley loudly.

"You wouldn't have time to run," said Mrs. Skaarda.

For the rest of the week before school mercifully was dismissed for Christmas, we all watched the oil heater and breathed as tentatively as we could. For as Richard once took pains to point out to me, it is the threat from the familiar, from the recognized companion, that is the true rack of anxiety. Not, of course, that those were his words—no. You do not need to hear his words. I will never rid myself of them, and that they are drawn from the impoverished vocabulary of his generation does not make them the less poignant. Let it suffice that not only did he hold me responsible for his growing estrangement with his background but he found insubstantial what I could offer in return. But this you have heard before. I have, as I have said, no reason to feel guilty.

I must say! (For you see, I am determined not to stray long from the assigned subject.) Although I earlier described my first educational experience as stultifying in the extreme, it strikes me now that in some respects, at least, Mrs. Skaarda's brand of education far exceeded the trite doses fed most farm children stuck in a snowbound country school. If I remember anything exactly as it was, it is the way we sat through those winter mornings, hands folded on our desks and mouths slightly ajar as we listened to the unfolding installment of the slow death of one of Mrs. Skaarda's relatives or of the details of Mayan sacrifice. And oh, yes! Her teaching went much farther.

I had long thought of myself as one of Mrs. Skaarda's own, a member of a small loyal flock that stood firm against the insensitives of the world. Gradually I became aware that all of us, however, were not of the flock. Mrs. Skaarda's eyes lingered more and more—no, not upon me, but upon Forby Weston.

Because of our common grade assignment, Forby and I were often enforced companions. We took the pail for water together when it was our turn. We were supposed, ridiculously, to be doing lessons together. And oftener than not we were paired in the recess games like Last Couple Out or Prisoner's Base that the older children taught us. Forby, although large for his age, was in fact rather better coordinated than I; my clumsiness had rapidly won for me the dishonor of always being the last chosen for sides (out of doors, mind you! In schoolroom games I was always first in spite of my age). "You may be the smartest one in school, but you're the dumbest one outside it!" Shelley Snapp once taunted me. Such designations come early, as you see.

Forby was content to sit quietly at his desk and color while Mrs. Skaarda talked to the rest of us, and for a long time he gave no indication of being aware of her increased scrutiny. Perhaps he, too, assumed that as one of the chosen he was safe.

"There is something the matter with Forby," Mrs. Skaarda confided to Shelley over the water cooler. I, eavesdropping as usual, turned with Shelley to look at Forby where he sat coloring peaceably in his spelling workbook. "Why does he always color with the black crayon?" whispered Mrs. Skaarda. "Or the brown?"

"Why don't you use the red crayon?" she asked Forby. I winced, for her voice held the forced good will my mother turned on her neighbors. "Okay," said Forby, picking up another crayon at random and going on with what he was doing. Mrs. Skaarda turned and shrugged significantly at Shelley.

Even in retrospect I can offer little insight into the mystery of Forby. I once tried to explain the incident to Richard—"He probably just didn't know his colors," said Richard. I was disappointed. I had looked forward to sharing the story with him; Richard, I had felt sure, would understand, if not the causal relationship that sent Forby crashing out of his small world, at least the effect his crash has had upon me ever since. But it was not to be. I misjudged Richard, as I have misjudged so many others. But to return.

At the time I only knew that Forby had unaccountably taken the place of the Mayan civilization in Mrs. Skaarda's interests. We had considered the Mayans with her for—days? weeks? I don't remember. Sometimes it seems as though we were occupied with the Mayans for most of the winter, and yet surely at one time or another we did ordinary lessons? Wouldn't my mother, or some other mother, have become suspicious sooner than she did and visited the school? And yet I recall only the Mayans.

Mrs. Skaarda had lent to Miles, her favorite, a book about the Mayan civilization to read over Christmas vacation. He shared generous portions of it with me. One episode haunted me for nights. It had to do with the sacrifice of Mayan maidens into a pool thought to be bottomless until recently fathomed by curious archaeologists who fetched up skeleton after delicate skeleton of hapless children cast down to appease their ancestor the sun. I daresay neither I nor the now-forgotten author of the book understood the mythology, but no matter. It was important, he said, that the maiden be cast into the pool at the precise moment dawn cracked over the horizon. He himself was so fascinated with the maidens that one night he waited by the pool until sunrise and, with its first rays, cast himself into the pool (but survived the fall and swam out). He said the pool smelled bad.

Mrs. Skaarda was, as I said, fascinated with the Mayans and their sacrifices until Forby claimed her attention. Loyally we shifted our attention with hers.

"There is something the matter with Forby," Mrs. Skaarda whispered to Miles. "I'm so thankful you're here." Such was her intensity that even my unimaginative brother looked at Forby, while I trembled in my impotent rage that it was to Miles her clouded eyes turned for reassurance. Who was Forby to cause us such distress? Fish-eyed Forby!

"If he were ever to—you know—lose control, it would be more than any one of us could do to subdue him. The insane have strength beyond all normal measures," she explained to Miles in her troubled whisper. "That's what I'm afraid of. That he'll slip over the divide and overpower us all."

By this time every pair of eyes in school was glued on Forby. Could we have possibly believed the child was insane? was Richard's question. I don't know. Perhaps more accurate to say that, stimulated by the vicarious threat of death and destruction and awakened to the promise of sacrifice, we suspended our disbelief for the course of the action. For who could say what Forby might do? Was it impossible that his was the pale mien of homicidal mania? And Forby gradually looked up from his crayons and his paste and his other simple pursuits to find a wall around him.

Within doors and out—for by this time winter had yielded to early spring mud—we all watched Forby. No longer chosen on anyone's side in games, he took to hovering at a distance of a few yards and pawing with his overshoes at the greening sod, while I, once the clumsy outcast, shone in a new role. For I, who had been Forby's peer against my will, was now privileged to be his licensed tormentor.

"Get away!" Shelley might bellow across the few yards of unthawing prairie grass at dumb, uncomprehending Forby in his thick winter coat and cap. "Keep away from us! We don't want you hanging around us, so quit being so stupid!"

But Shelley could do no more than shout; anything further would be "picking on the little kids" and outside the pale of country-school convention. But—"You chase him off, Wayne!" Shelley could urge. "Kick him. That's right. See? He's even scared of Wayne." And I, riding on a crescendo of encouraging yelps from the other children, ran at Forby and made him withdraw another ten or fifteen feet. "That's right!" "Kick him, he's got it coming!" they shrilled, and I raised an overshoed foot and planted its mud on Forby's undefended leg. For the first time in my life, I was flooded with joy. How thankful I was for Forby! How I fed my dislike upon his thick pale features! How I doted on his otherness that made me complete! Oh, the pure joy of my new mindlessness! How I capered in the April sun, freed by Forby from my old self as surely as though, snakelike, I had shed a skin!

As for what follows—the particular occasion when two mothers converged—that incident, as you will understand, I never confessed nor wished to confess to Richard. For it is one thing, is it not, to confess to the pleasure I took in another child's torment, but quite another to admit to its reverse? Why, indeed, continue now? Only because it is almost dawn and a few more paragraphs will suffice.

I even had some small part in bringing to an end my time in the sun, for I took to bragging of my exploits to my parents—little enough I had had to brag of in the past—at about the same time that Forby's mother somehow divined through her son's phlegmatic exterior that all was not well with him, bringing the two women separately and coincidentally to school the day Forby was at last driven out of his skin.

Driven out of the circle and pelted with mud balls by the older children and teased and kicked and even bitten by me, Forby had made no attempt to defend himself. His eyes withdrew into the stolid white plane of his face as though no taunt, no pummel, could penetrate. But that day, I bolted my sandwiches and raced out of doors, quite beside myself in the mellow young sunlight—"Get away!" I shrilled at Forby. "Get away!" Screwing my face into ferocious indignation, I hurtled myself at the unmoving figure in the plaid cap and coat and decently buckled overshoes just like mine, only to stop in astonishment when he broke and ran.

After my first surprise, I ran after him, of course. We all ran, ten of us pelting across the mushy, wet grass back of the school. (Miles, whose presence might have made a difference, had taken to staying in the schoolhouse and talking to Mrs. Skaarda during recess), down the coulee that sliced the schoolyard and panting up the other side, gulping the sharp spring air that stung our young lungs, ecstatic because we saw we were going to corner Forby against the barbed-wire fence that separated the schoolyard from the neighboring grain fields—but the others had unaccountably fallen back and I was alone at Forby's heels when, instead of turning to accept his punishment from my hands, he crashed into the barbed wire and set it vibrating for yards in both directions.

Forby hung on the wires. Gradually they ceased their humming. Shelley and the others stood in a silent group. They had seen, as I had not, Forby's mother coming across the back lot. As I turned, she broke into a run with her coat flapping around her legs. She ran past me without looking at me and plucked Forby off the fence. Carrying him, she turned back toward the school. In his mother's arms Forby looked astonishingly long and limp.

The others turned and trailed in her wake back toward the school. I tried to catch up. "Did you see how dumb old Forby ran?" I tried.

Nobody would look at me. "You're the dumb one," Shelley muttered.

My mother and Mrs. Skaarda were waiting on the steps as we came around the corner. Forby's mother had put him in her car and had just slammed the door on him, but I caught a glimpse of his white face lolling against the seat.

I hardly dared to breathe, for Mrs. Skaarda's chin was trembling and her eyes were wells of fear. Even in that moment so indelibly etched that I can still remember the warm rotten smell of the spring thaw and the whistle of a meadowlark from the gatepost and the force of all eyes fixed on me, it was her fear I pitied.

Her hands were clenched in two small white fists at her waist. "I have been so worried," she said to my mother. Her voice shook. "I didn't know what to do. He's been worse and worse since the weather turned warm—hasn't he?" Her appeal was to my schoolmates. Solemnly they all nodded.

My mother's face was bright red. "You go in the teacherage," she said to me, "and stay there until we're ready for you."

I remember I took two steps toward the cloakroom door and stopped, still too dazed to cry or protest, to squint against the glare of eyes that pinned me there against the peeling white siding of the school. The realization, if not the comprehension, was dawning on me that it was *I* who was to be offered up to whatever gods she feared.

As I walked through the cloakroom and past the cold and harmless oil heater, I heard the burst of voices eager to tell what I had done. I walked into the teacherage and shut the door on all but an unintelligible buzz.

No one had lived in the teacherage since the days of old Professor Wentworth. The shades were pulled over the windows and a single beam of sunlight glared through a torn place. On the bed was a mattress. Mrs. Skaarda's coat hung on the back of the door.

I sat down on the bed to wait, where, in a sense, I have been waiting ever since. After a while, I got up and stood by the door and put my face against her coat. The moment on the steps, when I knew it was I who had been fixed outside the circle, had been as painful as a rotten tooth under a probe; but it has been the aftermath that has returned in the wake of Richard's choice to overwhelm me with its dim associations of dust and yeast. As you see, I can go no further. No, I am not responsible for Richard's death. It is the awful suspicion that once again the tables have been turned that keeps me here, blear-eyed but unable to sleep, as a raucous sunrise breaks into my window.

T. Coraghessan Boyle

I Dated Jane Austen

HER hands were cold. She held them out for me as I stepped into the parlor. "Mr. Boyle," announced the maid, and Jane was rising to greet me, her cold white hands like an offering. I took them, said my good evenings, and nodded at each of the pairs of eyes ranged round the room. There were brothers, smallish and large of head, whose names I didn't quite catch; there was her father, the Reverend, and her sister, the spinster. They stared at me like sharks on the verge of a feeding frenzy. I was wearing my pink boots, "Great Disasters" T-shirt, and my Tiki medallion. My shoulders slumped under the scrutiny. My wit evaporated.

"Have a seat, son," said the Reverend, and I backed onto a settee between two brothers. Jane retreated to an armchair on the far side of the room. Cassandra, the spinster, plucked up her knitting. One of the brothers sighed. I could see it coming, with the certainty and illogic of an aboriginal courtship rite: a round of polite chitchat.

The Reverend cleared his throat. "So what do you think of Mrs. Radcliffe's new book?"

I balanced a glass of sherry on my knee. The Reverend, Cassandra, and the brothers revolved tiny spoons around the rims of teacups. Jane nibbled at a croissant and focused her huge unblinking eyes on the side of my face. One of the brothers had just made a devastating witticism at the expense of the *Lyrical Ballads* and was still tittering over it. Somewhere cats were purring and clocks ticking. I glanced at my watch: only seventeen minutes since I'd stepped in the door.

I stood. "Well, Reverend," I said, "I think it's time Jane and I hit the road."

He looked up at the doomed Hindenburg blazing across my chest and smacked his lips. "But you've only just arrived."

There really wasn't much room for Cassandra in the Alfa Romeo, but the Reverend and his troop of sons insisted that she come along. She hefted her skirts, wedged herself into the rear compartment, and flared her parasol, while Jane pulled a white cap down over her curls and attempted a joke about Phaetons and the winds of Aeolus. The Reverend stood at the curb and watched my fingers as I helped Jane fasten her seat belt, and then we were off with a crunch of gravel and a billow of exhaust.

The film was Italian, in black and white, full of social acuity and steamy sex. I sat between the two sisters with a bucket of buttered popcorn. Jane's lips were parted and her eyes glowed. I offered her some popcorn. "I do not think that I care for any just now, thank you," she said. Cassandra sat stiff and erect, tireless and silent, like a mileage marker beside a country lane. She was not interested in popcorn either.

The story concerned the seduction of a long-legged village girl by a mustachioed adventurer who afterward refuses to marry her on the grounds that she is impure. The girl, swollen with child, bursts in upon the nuptials of her seducer and the daughter of a wealthy merchant, and demands her due. She is turned out into the street. But late that night, as the newlyweds thrash about in the bridal bed—

It was at this point that Jane took hold of my arm and whispered that she wanted to leave. What could I do? I fumbled for her wrap, people hissed at us, great nude thighs slashed across the screen, and we headed for the glowing EXIT sign.

I proposed a club. "Oh, do let's walk!" Jane said. "The air is so frightfully delicious after that close, odious theatre—don't you think?" Pigeons flapped and cooed. A panhandler leaned against the fender of a car and drooled into the gutter. I took Jane's arm. Cassandra took mine.

At *The Mooncalf* we had our wrists stamped with luminescent ink and then found a table near the dance floor. The waitress' fingernails were green daggers. She wore a butch haircut and three-inch heels. Jane wanted punch, Cassandra tea. I ordered three margaritas.

The band was re-creating the fall of the Third Reich amid clouds

of green smoke and flashing lights. We gazed out at the dancers in their
jumpsuits and platform shoes as they bumped bums, heads, and genitals
in time to the music. I thought of Catherine Morland at Bath and decided
to ask Jane for a dance. I leaned across the table. "Want to dance?" I
shouted.

"Beg your pardon?" Jane said, leaning over her margarita.

"Dance," I shouted, miming the action of holding her in my arms.

"No, I'm very sorry," she said. "I'm afraid not."

Cassandra tapped my arm. "I'd love to," she giggled.

Jane removed her cap and fingered out her curls as Cassandra and I
got up from the table. She grinned and waved as we receded into the
crowd. Over the heads of the dancers I watched her sniff suspiciously at
her drink and then sit back to ogle the crowd with her black satiric eyes.

Then I turned to Cassandra. She curtsied, grabbed me in a fox-trot
sort of way, and began to promenade round the floor. For so small a
woman (her nose kept poking at the moribund Titanic listing across my
lower rib cage), I was amazed at her energy. We pranced through the
hustlers and bumpers like kiddies round a Maypole. I was even beginning to enjoy myself when I glanced over at our table and saw that a
man in fierce black sideburns and mustache had joined Jane. He was
dressed in a ruffled shirt, antique tie, and coattails that hung to the floor
as he sat. At that moment a fellow terpsichorean flung his partner into
the air, caught her by wrist and ankle, and twirled her like a toreador's
cape. When I looked up again Jane was sitting alone, her eyes fixed on
mine through the welter of heads.

The band concluded with a crunching metallic shriek, and Cassandra and I made our way back to the table. "Who was that?" I asked Jane.

"Who was who?"

"That mustachioed murderer's apprentice you were sitting with."

"Oh," she said. "Him."

I realized that Cassandra was still clutching my hand.

"Just an acquaintance."

As we pulled into the drive at Steventon, I observed a horse tethered to
one of the palings. The horse lifted its tail, then dropped it. Jane seemed
suddenly animated. She made a clucking sound and called to the horse
by name. The horse flicked its ears. I asked her if she liked horses. "Hm?"
she said, already looking off toward the silhouettes that played across the
parlor curtains. "Oh yes, yes. Very much so," she said, and then she

released the seat belt, flung back the door, and tripped up the stairs into the house. I killed the engine and stepped out into the dark drive. Crickets sawed their legs together in the bushes. Cassandra held out her hand.

Cassandra led me into the parlor where I was startled to see the mustachioed ne'er-do-well from *The Mooncalf*. He held a teacup in his hand. His boots shone as if they'd been razor-stropped. He was talking with Jane.

"Well, well," said the Reverend, stepping out of the shadows. "Enjoy yourselves?"

"Oh, immensely, father," said Cassandra.

Jane was grinning at me again. "Mr. Boyle," she said. "Have you met Mr. Crawford?" The brothers, with their fine bones and disproportionate heads, gathered round. Crawford's sideburns reached nearly to the line of his jaw. His mustache was smooth and black. I held out my hand. He shifted the teacup and gave me a firm handshake. "Delighted," he said.

We found seats (Crawford shoved in next to Jane on the love seat; I wound up on the settee between Cassandra and a brother in naval uniform), and the maid served tea and cakes. Something was wrong—of that I was sure. The brothers were not their usual witty selves, the Reverend floundered in the midst of a critique of Coleridge's cult of artifice, Cassandra dropped a stitch. In the corner, Crawford was holding a whispered colloquy with Jane. Her cheeks, which tended toward the flaccid, were now positively bloated, and flushed with color. It was then that it came to me. "Crawford," I said, getting to my feet. "*Henry* Crawford?"

He sprang up like a gunfighter summoned to the OK Corral. "That's right," he leered. His eyes were deep and cold as crevasses. He looked pretty formidable—until I realized that he couldn't have been more than five three or four, give or take an inch for his heels.

Suddenly I had hold of his elbow. The Tiki medallion trembled at my throat. "I'd like a word with you outside," I said. "In the garden."

The brothers were on their feet. The Reverend spilled his tea. Crawford jerked his arm out of my grasp and stalked through the door that gave onto the garden. Nightsounds grated in my ears, the brothers murmured at my back, and Jane, as I pulled the door closed, grinned at me as if I'd just told the joke of the century.

Crawford was waiting for me in the ragged shadows of the trees, turned to face me like a bayed animal. I felt a surge of power. I wanted to call him a son of a bitch, but, in keeping with the times, I settled for cad. "You cad," I said, shoving him back a step, "how dare you come sniffing around her after what you did to Maria Bertram in *Mansfield Park*? It's people like you—corrupt, arbitrary, egocentric—that foment all the lust and heartbreak of the world and challenge the very possibility of happy endings."

"Hah!" he said. Then he stepped forward and the moon fell across his face. His eyes were like the birth of evil. In his hand, a riding glove. He slapped my face with it. "Tomorrow morning, at dawn," he hissed. "Beneath the bridge."

"Okay, wise guy," I said, "okay," but I could feel the Titanic sinking into my belt.

A moment later the night was filled with the clatter of hoofs.

I was greeted by silence in the parlor. They stared at me, sated, as I stepped through the door. Except for Cassandra, who mooned at me from behind her knitting, and Jane, who was bent over a notebook, scribbling away like a court recorder. The Reverend cleared his throat and Jane looked up. She scratched off another line or two and then rose to show me out. She led me through the parlor and down the hall to the front entrance. We paused at the door.

"I've had a memorable evening," she said, and then glanced back to where Cassandra had appeared at the parlor door. "Do come again." And then she held out her hands.

Her hands were cold.

Siv Cedering

Family Album

THIS is their wedding picture. Pappa wears a tuxedo, and Mamma is wearing a white satin dress. She is smiling at the white lilies. This is the house Pappa built for Mamma, when they were engaged. Then this house, then that; they were always making blueprints together.

Mamma came from Lapland. She was quite poor and dreamed of pretty dresses. Her mother died when Mamma was small. Pappa met her when he came to Lapland as a conscientious objector. He preached in her church. There he is with his banjo.

Pappa was quite poor too; everyone was in those days. He told me he didn't have any shoes that fit him, one spring, and he had to wear his father's big shoes. Pappa said he was so ashamed that he walked in the ditch, all the way to school.

Pappa was one of eleven children, but only five of them grew up. The others died of tuberculosis or diphtheria. Three died in a six-week period, and Pappa says death was accepted then, just like changes in the weather and a bad crop of potatoes. His parents were religious. I remember Grandfather Anton rocking in the rocker and riding on the reaper, and I remember Grandmother Maria, though I was just two when she died. The funeral was like a party: birch saplings decorated the yard, relatives came from all around, and my sister and I wore new white dresses. Listen to the names of her eleven children:

Anna Viktoria, Karl Sigurd, Johan Martin, Hulda Maria, Signe Sofia, Bror Hilding, Judit Friedeborg, Brynhild Elisabet, John Rudolf, Tore Adils, and Clary Torborg.

We called the eldest Tora. She was fat and never got married. Tore was the youngest son. I remember sitting next to him, outside by the

[57]

flagpole, eating blood pancakes after a slaughter, and also calf-dance—
a dish made from the first milk a cow gives after it has calved. Tore
recently left his wife and took a new one. He once told me that when
he was a boy, he used to ski out in the dark afternoons of the North and
stand still, watching the sky and feeling himself get smaller and smaller.
This is Uncle Rudolf in his uniform, and this is Torborg, Pappa's youngest sister. Her fiancé had tried to make love to her once before they were
married, and—Mamma told me—Torborg tore the engagement ring off
her finger, threw it on the floor of the large farmhouse kitchen, and
hollered, loud enough for everyone to hear: "What does that whore-
monger think I am?" He was the son of a big-city mayor and well educated, but you can bet he married a virgin. Don't they look good in this
picture? Three of their five children are doctors. They say that Torborg
got her temper from Great-grandfather. When he got drunk he cussed
and brought the horse into the kitchen. This is the Kell people from the
Kell farm. I am told I have the Kell eyes. Everyone on this side of the
family hears ghosts and dreams prophecies. To us it isn't supernatural;
it is natural.

Mamma's oldest brother Karl went to America when he was eighteen. There he is chopping down a redwood tree, and there he is working in a gold mine. He married a woman named Viviann, and they visited
us in Sweden. Let me tell you, the village had never seen anyone like her.
Not only had she been married and divorced, but she had bobbed hair,
wore makeup, and had dresses with padded shoulders, matching shoes,
and purses. Vanity of all vanities was quoted from the Bible. So of course
everyone knew the marriage wouldn't last—besides, they didn't have any
children. Uncle Karl is now old and fat, the darling and benefactor of
a Swedish Old Folks Home in Canada. Silver mines help him. This is
Mamma's second brother. He had to have a leg amputated. I used to think
about that leg, all alone in heaven. This is Aunt Edith. She once gave
me a silver spoon that had my name written on it. And this is Aunt
Elsa who has a large birthmark on her face. I used to wonder what mark
I had to prove that I was born. Mamma's father was a Communist and
he came to Lapland to build the large power plant that supplies most of
Sweden's electricity. He told me, once, that he ate snake when he was
young and worked on the railroad. His wife Emma was a beauty and a
lady, and when the household money permitted, she washed her face
with heavy cream and her hair with beer or egg whites. My hair? Both
grandmothers had hair long enough to sit on.

I am talking about my inheritance—the family jewelry that I wear in my hair, so to speak, the birthmark that stays on my face forever. I am motherless in Lapland, brought down to size by the vastness of the sky. I rock in the rocker of old age and ride the reaper, while some part of me has already preceded me to heaven. I change one husband for another, and toss my ring, furiously moral at any indignation. I am a pacifist, I am a Communist, I am a preacher coddling my father's language and abandoning my mother tongue forever. I eat blood pancakes, calf-dance, snake, and I bring the horse into the kitchen. I build new houses, dream of new dresses, bury my parents and my children. I hear ghosts, see the future and know what will happen. If I step on a crack and break my mother's back, I can say the shoes were too large for my feet, for I know, I know: these are the fairy tales that grieve us. And save us.

Fred Chappell

The Snow That Is Nothing in the Triangle

"IF a man construct an equilateral triangle on a sheet of paper, what is in the triangle?"

Silence, consternated head-wagging. . . . Nothing is in the triangle. What did Herr Professor Feuerbach want his students to answer? They were not yet so disturbed as they would later become at his bizarre behavior, as when he would enter the classroom with an unsheathed sword and seriously threaten to behead any student who could not solve the problem that he would propose. But they were beginning to know that things were not straight, not clear.

"You will say, Nothing," Feuerbach went on, "but that is wrong. The correct answer is *Snow*. It is snow inside the triangle."

Snow.

They looked at his unclean sparse hair, dressed, or rather not dressed, in the old long fashion, falling in raddled strings on his shoulders. He was not much older than his students, the youngest man ever appointed to such a position at the Gymnasium in Erlangen, yet his thin and greasy hair was white and his long fingernails tough and horny like the talons of a man in his seventies.

"Ha, but wait—you will not be quite wrong either. For snow is nothing, yet it is a Substantive Nothing. If a man plunge into a snow-bank up to his neck, or even over his head, has he fallen into Nothing?" He nodded, heavily grave. "He has, yes he has fallen into Nothing, and who can tell what consequences will ensue?"

They no longer called him *the Pope of the Theorems*, referring to his magisterial brilliance as a geometrician and to his physique. His body, like that of the famous English poet of seventy-five years before, was crushed into the shape of a question mark, and he got himself about with obvious pain. But his manners had become so odd that the students no longer called him anything but *Feuerbach*, as if his true name were descriptive beyond the power of other words. For a brief time he had been called *old Feuerbach*, but then they had discovered that he really was only thirty-two years old. In any case, he seemed no age at all, but rather outside time, like a topological proposition that could not be proved.

"That it is snow in our constructed triangle is true, indubitable, but you gentlemen are not to noise this fact abroad. It is to be our secret." As soon as he had said this, he began to look about the classroom apprehensively. Then, with a sudden expression of alarm, he crossed to the door and flung it open. The hallway was empty, but he looked up and down it with the greatest intensity, as if suspecting that something escaped his gaze.

The students stirred uneasily. It had been hard to believe that their Herr Professor F. was the same man who had produced the most beautiful theorem in plane geometry since the time—perhaps—of Euclid. It bore his name, the Feuerbach theorem: "For any triangle, the nine-point circle is tangent to the incircle and to each of the three excircles of the triangle." And there was a further lovely corollary, because the nine-point circle also passes through the three feet of the altitudes of the triangle and the three points bisecting the joins of the orthocenter to the three vertices. This was a theorem so elegant that some of the students had decorated the flyleaves of their textbooks with drawings of it.

Now Feuerbach trotted back and perched his crooked little shape on the edge of his desk. "Secret secret secret," he cooed, and leaned forward in earnest confidentiality. "*Secret* is another word that, gentlemen, you must never utter. Do you know why?"

He waited; they waited.

"Because it is destructive to your health. Do you not observe the shape of my body, gentlemen, which is twisted like a curve in space? That is because there is a logically unbreakable linkage between the word *secret* and the prison cell and the triangle full of snow which is Nothing. Oh you may try"—and now he leaned forward even more, and they feared that he might tumble—"you may try, gentlemen, gentlemen, to cut the veins in your feet, but they will not let you die. No, you cannot bleed to death that way—there is a guard who coughs and shuffles and then they take you to the infirmary and bind up the veins again and you are alive after all. Of twenty of you, only one may die, that much is clear. Look, I will demonstrate."

He tipped to the floor and scurried back to the blackboard. He seized a piece of chalk, but he had already covered the board with partial constructions, numbers, mottoes, Greek and Latin abbreviations, scraps of poetry. He stood looking at this wilderness of scrawl in bafflement.

Peremptorily, he turned back to the class and indicated the whole of the board with a languid hand. "Klaus Hörnli will now solve this problem," he said.

The eleven students turned involuntarily to survey the back of the classroom. There was no Klaus Hörnli among them, and no unknown person in the room. Finally one of them dared to say, "There is no Klaus Hörnli here, Herr Professor."

He put the chalk down and rubbed his hands together briskly. "So. You see. By now it is evident, it is evident as daylight, is it not? There is no Klaus Hörnli among us." His voice quavered and his cheek trembled with irrepressible sorrow. "And he was the best of us, gentlemen, the very best." He brightened triumphantly. "But that is our proof. Klaus is absent from us, while I am here. The snow that is Nothing in the triangle has rejected me, but it has accepted Klaus. *Quod erat*, gentlemen. This is clear, this is clear as daylight."

Again the feckless student ventured to demur. "Herr Professor, I am afraid that we do not completely understand."

"Why can you not understand? It is clear, it is evident, a fool, even an idiot, can understand." Anger stopped his voice in his throat for a moment. His face reddened; he coughed, gagged. Then his whole body shuddered convulsively as if it might tear apart. But then settled. Suddenly now he seemed to be possessed by a peaceful gravity. His expression softened, his eyes were wise and glistening.

"Let us begin again from the beginning. Here is the basic proposition. Two young men are walking along the street. A quite ordinary day, and these two young men are merely walking along, chatting as any of you gentlemen might be chatting with one of your friends." He stopped and looked at them anxiously. "Do you understand where we are? Do you comprehend our premise?" Klaus Hörnli was the other young man with Feuerbach. Blond Klaus, high-spirited, sardonically witty, that is the way of young and brilliant students, when suddenly two policemen—two agents, that is—in dark unseasonable overcoats, you would not have known them for policemen, you could not decipher, decipher—"Gentlemen, how could a geometrician be an anarchist? Is not anarchy disorder? But do not the propositions of Euclid—including even the famously troublesome fifth proposition—follow one another with the inevitability of the leaves falling in autumn? Let us begin again from the beginning. Two young men walking, and let us say that the town is Hof, a wealthy and respected town with a reputable Gymnasium," *anarkhos*, without a ruler, no constructions without a ruler, he Klaus Hörnli was no anarchist, he Karl Feuerbach was no anarchist, "Gentlemen, you have mistaken the loose and spirited talk of students in the beer gardens for plots and conspiracies; that is a false conclusion as I will now demonstrate," he went back to the blackboard but could not find the chalk anywhere, meanwhile they were questioned endlessly, taken from their cells and asked to elucidate faulty conclusions to problems without being given the necessary premises, there was a guard or there were many guards who paced the corridor outside the blind doors of the cells, all these guards in delicate health, coughing and snuffling and sputtering, racking their poor lungs for bits of phlegm to swallow down again, shuffling always, not lifting their feet, with a dull sound that kept erasing the thoughts of him *Hörnli* Feuerbach in the cell, the feet wiping out the clear mathematical propositions, a hexagon would appear shining white on black paper and then the feet would come shuffling and the hexagon would disappear, that was in early fall, the first fall in the prison cell, and when the snows began the sound of falling snow was quite loud, much louder than you would expect, it sounded like the shuffling of the feet of many guards in the corridor there, the snow that fell into the interiors of any closed construction and filled it up with the sound of shuffling, the lines no longer discernible on the black paper covered over with snow, Feuerbach flapped his arms helplessly at the blackboard then turned around and came back to his desk, in the cells bitter cold and dank, many of us fell ill, twenty of us all told, "Do you understand, from a group of twenty, one by one, or as it might be in some cases, by twos and threes, abstracted subtracted distracted distracted from the numerical order of their lives?" and put into cells by featureless heavy men and loutish foul guards and asked to fabricate in a pitiless given time and without any proper tool a geometry of anarchism, "The mind, gentlemen, the mind is not anarchical, geometry for instance as it occurs in nature, the snowflake let us say with its infinitely varying but unvarying hexagon, is a clear proof the mind is not anarchical, for the mind has in it all the shapes of geometry and does not require that nature supply it with example, but here let us say in the snowflake nature reaches out to touch us reassuringly, gentlemen, to suggest that the mind is not mistaken in apprehending intimations of a high and eternal order, an order though we can but guess at it as certain and clear as the Pythagorean theorem," but then all the little hexagons of the snow filled up the greater hexagon in the mind with the sounds of coughing and shuffling until gradually gradually by minute gradations, you understand, the Greater Proposition began to show clear, in burning letters it appeared in his mind on the blank paper, melting away the detritus of snow on top, letters of yellow fire, IF ONE MAN DIE THE OTHERS SHALL BE FREED, there was no doubting this intuition written in pure fire, the way such intuitions must have come in antique time to Plato, to Euclid, to Aristotle, and no doubting the further certain corollary, that he Karl Wilhelm Feuerbach must be the man to die, the cough and shuffle of snowy hexagons fell upon these burning letters but could not obscure them, disappearing in the space above the black page in his mind with the letters of yellow flame, and Feuerbach began to weep and turned suddenly on his heel away from the students to wipe his eyes on his sleeve, he was becoming a bad example, to give them to think that geometry is a cause for weeping, "You must understand, gentlemen, you must forgive, we must all learn to understand and to forgive," and so he cut the veins in his feet, slowly, painfully with a bit of dull metal he had got, and then it began to disturb him that he could not remember where he had got that little bit of metal and he began to weep afresh and turned again away from his students, he could not bear for high-spirited Klaus Hörnli cheerfully smiling in the back of the classroom to see him weeping when he Feuerbach had so much less reason for tears than Klaus who was after all dead, Feuerbach must keep it in mind that Klaus had died, accepted into the Nothing triangle while he Feuerbach had been rejected, it was the medal with the portrait of Euclid he had won as a school prize and kept on a little chain round his neck, the mathematics prize he had won in fifth form, a medal whose edges he had kept honing honing against the stone wall of his cell until he had achieved a sort of keenness not very satisfactory, and so had managed to cut or to saw through the veins in his feet and lay back to die, now they would free the others, Feuerbach's death a surety for their innocence their youthful harmlessness, now he remembered and his feet began to hurt and he hopped up on the desk and held his left foot in both hands, cooing to it as a mother to her child, gentlemen gentlemen gentlemen, but as the snow of sleep began to settle on the letters in his mind and now at last not melting away but covering over the letters he closed his eyes, he tried not to sleep but the heavy inevitable snow kept falling on the yellow-flame letters, gray snow like greasy ash, snow as warm and sleepy as it was cold, and finally the burning letters could be seen no longer though they must be burning somewhere still, and then he awoke, awoke oh God, in the infirmary and a white pure snow was falling outside the window on the sharp angles of the roofs, on the triangles of the gables, on the curves in space of bare oak limbs, a pure white cold snow and in a little while he knew he was alive, he had not died, and when he knew that fact the sound of shuffling feet returned into the falling snow and no clean geometric constructions would appear on black paper in his mind any more, and his friends and colleagues were still miserable in their cells, and now the greasy ash of snow began to melt off the black paper and the letters appeared burning once again IF ONE MAN DIE THE OTHERS SHALL BE FREED the characters of yellow fire hotter and brighter than before, and he turned in the narrow infirmary bed to face the wall though the turning made his feet hurt as if scalded and begin to bleed again, and he wept copiously and bitterly because he had not managed to die, he had failed, "Gentlemen gentlemen gentlemen, did Plato and Euclid and Aristotle fail the intuitions that were so clearly delivered unto them, appearing in their minds as sharp as flame? Gentlemen, they did not, ours is an age of pygmy cowards with tedious little secrets and we are called upon to solve problems that are not problems, anarchical geometry, that is no problem, it is a whim of unlettered tyrants who cannot know the proper use of words, do not be taken in, gentlemen, by the spurious fancies of our own puny century," and he let go his foot as if it were a burning thing and let it swing like a pendulum back and forth under the open desk, the directive still imperative in his mind, *if one man die*, and he Feuerbach still determined to carry it out but stricken breathless on the paradox that in order to die he must a little at least regain his health, and turned again in his infirmary bed to stare out the window at the shuffling snow which had begun to cough quietly, falling on roof-ridge and gable-angle, if he could not produce clear geometric constructions in his mind there were yet these angles in nature to be looked at through the window, and the coughing snow could not obliterate them, that much was clear, could soften but not obliterate, and so he began to grow cunning, oh he was very crafty he was, not speaking unless spoken to, and obeying all the instructions of the doctor and the guards, though they persisted of course in asking those moronic questions that were not questions, he had no answers to the questions not questions but began to smile at them, gently wisely forgivingly smiling whenever they started with those propositions of anarchical geometry, and little by little the season turned into deep winter, the snow kept falling and its shuffling-coughing sound always grew louder, "Gentlemen, it is hard to think with so much noise in this classroom, can you not keep your feet quiet, must you always?" and he had formed a plan while smiling to win their confidence so that one day he might casually stroll to the window and open it as if without thinking and leap out and be killed, IF ONE MAN, and kept smilingly to his plan and did just that, opened the window just so, gracefully, while humming a tune, and hopped up on the ledge and plunged three stories to his death   no   for as it happened, in his descent through the icy air, his bed robe flapping about him like broken wings, he saw the triangle of infirmary wall as base and the two courtyard walls as sides, the triangle rising to meet him, a triangle without architectural reason here, cramped out of the way behind the infirmary, "Gentlemen it is important, it is imperative gentlemen that we teach our workmen and the designers of our buildings proper appreciation and knowledge of geometry so that we may prevent such pervasive ugly and expensive public construction," and the cruel useless triangle that rose to meet Feuerbach had filled up completely with snow during this strange long winter and he plummeted into it, plummeted into a burning pain that was not death and which collapsed his youthful scholarly body like a field telescope, now finally the letters of yellow fire on the black paper in his mind were obliterated not by the snow which was Nothing but by the towering hotter white fire of pain, he died but did not die in that triangle, the snow that was a Substantive Nothing had held him back from death and held him back from giving his comrades freedom, for when he came to himself again they told him it was many weeks later but he was not certain of that there in the same infirmary room in the same bed, disbelieving them because outside the window the same snow was still falling, and told him that Klaus Hörnli had died while he Feuerbach was unconscious, drifting back to the world of men again out of the triangle of Substantive Nothing, he Klaus Hörnli had died, his health broken in the cold and horrible cell, and of course they were to be freed, the death had brought the anarchical geometers and even King Maximilian Joseph to good sense, IF ONE MAN, Feuerbach thought, but he could not remember the rest, the fire of pain had burned off the letters of fire, he must attempt to, it was imperative that, what was the

He snapped his fingers repeatedly. "You must forgive me, gentlemen. I fear that I have been digressing. You must help me to recall the topic under discussion."

He looked at them imploringly. But how could they help him? They were strangers to him, and senile, these eleven old men who sat in the students' desks, their stringy white hair unclean on their shoulders and their unclean fingernails long and horny.

"Gentlemen, please!" Feuerbach said, but they would not answer. They began to shuffle their feet, a whispery sound at first but growing louder; and this noise caused an ashy gray snow to begin falling inside the classroom. It fell furiously and covered the floor and the desks and Feuerbach's hands.

Harry Crews

A Long Wail

THE old man looked out the window at the darkened fields slipping
past in the rain and said, "Tonight, you ring the bell before supper.
I want to eat with him one more time."

Sarah Nell sat stiff on the seat, both hands holding firmly to the
steering wheel, and did not answer. Out of the corner of her eye she
could see her father's twisted profile. No matter how hard she concentrated on the road, his face was always there like a piece of gravel under
the lid.

The old man turned on the seat toward her, half of his face melting
away into shadow.

"You ain't fer it, are you?" he asked.

"You're Pa, so I ain't against it," she said. "It's you that's got to care
it around, that's going to bed with it and gittin up with it, so I cain't be
against it."

"You always was a sensible girl," he said.

"I just don't know about tollin Gaff in and shutting the door on
him like you'd pen a hog. He ain't gone understand that."

"He don't have to understand," said the old man. "I'm the only one
who has to understand. I'm sick to death of doctors."

"Don't put it on him," she said. "Dr. Threadly's a good man."

"He's a fool and I'm worse. When it gits that time, you go. That's
all there is to it. All there ever was to it." His voice was soft, the words
slightly blurred, as though coming from a great distance. "Remember
your Ma, an how he wagged his wonderful tongue over her an how we
follered her right on down to the grave with him still talking."

Sarah Nell caught at the word "Ma" and held it to her as though it were a talisman. She moved her lips over the sound of it, breathing it into the darkness and sucking it back again until finally the sound and the word became an odor and an image; and the image burned cleanly before her: hot blue eyes, dry and faded with pain, set above high cheek-bones over which the thin flesh stretched like parchment.

"But Ma never rung a bell for Gaff," she said, the words bursting from her lips before she knew she would say them. "Never a bell for Gaff to take me to Big Creek Church."

"That was your Ma, and she had me," he said. "Besides, women can walk up face to face with things that men can only back up to."

"I'll pray," she said softly, almost inaudibly.

"For me?" he asked.

"No," she said. "For Gaff and me."

She turned the car into the lane leading down from the big road, through old, winter-naked pecan trees, past the lot where the hesitant bray of a mule joined the sound of the wind. A great, brindle-colored mastiff waited at the yard fence. He had not barked when they drove up, and sat now with his huge head hanging forward. The old man spoke to him softly as he passed through the gate and the dog raised himself, long and lean, his belly curving sharply upward from his chest. The old man lifted his arm in the direction of the mule barn and the mastiff turned and walked away in the rain.

In the kitchen her father sat silently with his elbows on the faded oilcloth of the table, his chin propped in his hands, while Sarah Nell set out cold meat and bread.

"Is they clabber?" he asked through the web of his fingers.

"Yessir," answered Sarah Nell.

"Set it," he said.

She set the clabber out and put an earthen bowl beside his plate. In the yellow light of the kerosene lamp, the surface of the clabber took on a bluish tinge. He turned his eyes on the bowl and gently his fingers drummed the bandages partially covering his mouth where cancer had broken through in an open sore. Slivers of cheek and segments of gum had been removed leaving the right side of his face concave as though his jawbone had been half split away. As it always did when he was about to eat, his odor grew stronger, the heavy, half-sweet odor of decay that swarmed about him like flies.

"Git that syrup, too," he said, the words far away, muffled by the bandage.

She took the syrup bucket down from the screen-wire safe, pried up the lid with a case knife, and set it beside him. Before she could sit down at her place, he said without looking up from the bucket, "Ring the bell for Gaff."

She stepped out onto the porch, and the night air met her cold and clean. She stood a moment breathing deeply against the scent in her nostrils, but it was no good. On her tongue was the taste of decay and it drew her mouth like alum. The rain had stopped, but a mist still hung in the air as fine as fog. There were no stars now, no moon. The lamp from the kitchen window gave enough light to see the triangular rod of iron hanging from a piece of hay wire at the end of the porch. She struck it three times with an iron cylinder. The sound came back again and again, bouncing out of the black forest of pine that bordered the field at the back of the house.

"I ain't there, I'm here."

Sarah Nell shrank into herself, the breath catching at the base of her throat, her hand still poised to strike. The voice had come out of the darkness at the edge of the porch.

"Gaff?"

"Yeah. I've already come. I was just waiting out there for the bell." The voice was at the steps now; then the sound of his booted feet was on the porch and she saw him, tall, his felt hat pushed back, his brow very smooth and damp.

"How . . . ?" she began.

"Seen the lights of the automobile when it come up," he said.

"He's waiting," she said.

Gaff went into the kitchen ahead of her, stooping slightly in the door, the black hat still on his head.

"That was quick," her father said without looking up from the clabber he had dipped and was now stirring.

"I was out there waiting," said Gaff.

Sarah Nell sat at the table opposite her father. Gaff remained standing just inside the door.

"You had your supper?" asked her father.

Gaff shifted his weight and reached up and pulled his hat farther down on his forehead.

"No sir, I ain't," he said, "But I don't . . ."

"Git him a plate Sarah Nell."

Gaff was rock-still now, his back pressed into the wall by the door.

"I ain't hongry," he said evenly.

"You said you didn't eat," said her father, still without looking at him. "Set and be welcome."

Sarah Nell set a plate, a bowl, and a spoon at the end of the table, and then the three of them sat very still, their plates empty, while the old man loosened the bandage at the right side of his face so he could eat. Both Gaff and Sarah Nell looked directly at him, at his fingers working slowly and delicately as though unwrapping a fine and treasured secret.

He was the first to eat and the clabber had to be kept in the left side of his mouth because the right cheek had been partially cut away to expose the grinding teeth.

"You want some of this clabber?" asked the old man, gesturing toward the bowl at his elbow.

"No sir, I don't," said Gaff. He had put a biscuit in the middle of his plate and was making an effort to keep his eyes on it, but the naked, working spot in the old man's face was too fascinating, and his eyes would invariably come off his plate and slowly move up the denim work shirt to the dry, seamed neck to the teeth.

"It's mighty good with a little syrup."

"Yessir," Gaff said, his eyes trying to make it back to the biscuit, "But I really ain't too hongry."

"You ain't, huh?"

"No sir, I ain't and if it's the same to you, I'll just step to the door and smoke till you ready to talk."

"No, no," said the old man quickly. "Smoke there if you like. And's for talking, now's as good as any."

Gaff took out a book of cigarette leaves and a can of tobacco.

"Did you start breaking the back field yet?"

"Yessir, I did."

"And did you get the cloth on the beds all right?"

"Yessir."

"Any sign of blue mold?"

"No sir."

The old man had cleared his mouth of food and his words were more distinct now.

"Good, good. You're a worker Gaff. Always have been. What you need is a wife."

The cigarette broke in Gaff's fingers, and the tobacco dribbled off onto his lap. He looked at Sarah Nell. She sat stiff in her chair, her cheeks ashen, looking directly across the table at her father.

"Sir?" said Gaff.

"You a young man and you able," he said. "You cain't expect to go on working another man's land in a cabin without a woman for the rest of your life." He had begun spooning clabber into his mouth again. There was a brittle silence over the table for a long minute. Then he looked up over his poised spoon and asked, "Can you?"

Sarah Nell and the old man watched Gaff across the table, and he, still holding the torn cigarette paper between his fingers, stared at the biscuit in his plate. Finally he pushed his chair back slowly and took off his hat. The band across his forehead where the hat had been was red and damp with sweat.

"They is some that has," said Gaff.

"Do you want to be one that has?" asked the old man, pushing the clabber bowl across to Gaff.

Gaff reached for the spoon and without lowering his eyes began to dip clabber.

"No," said Gaff.

"When you take Sarah Nell to Big Creek Church tonight, you oughto start looking," he said. "They's lots of girls just waiting."

Gaff stopped dipping.

"When I take her where?"

"I want you to drive her over there to the revival. The roads is bad with the rain."

"Tonight?" asked Gaff.

"She wants to go," said the old man.

Sarah Nell, her face set like a gray mask, leaned forward and with a steady hand ladled two spoons of syrup into Gaff's bowl.

"Clabber and syrup makes right good eatin," she said. "It's a wonder anything could look so bad and be so good."

A loud silence hung in the room. Gaff picked up his spoon, stirred the clabber, looked at Sarah Nell, then stirred again, his face as gray as hers. A drop of sweat broke from his forehead and trembled at the end of his nose. Only the old man had the color of life in his face.

"It *is* a wonder," said Gaff.

The old man moved his chair closer to the table, leaned on his elbows, and said, "Sarah Nell and me was talking on the way from town."

"You was, huh," said Gaff.

"Would you like another one of these biscuits, boy?" asked the old man.

"No sir, I ain't finished this un yet."

"We was talking about you and the doctor. Tell Gaff what the doctor said, Sarah Nell."

"About the doctor and *me?*" asked Gaff.

"Tell him, Sarah Nell."

"Doctor Threadly says Pa has to have his tongue taken off."

Gaff's mouth opened, worked over a word, then closed. His pink under-lip caught the light and trembled.

"His tongue?" he finally managed to say.

"That's the next thing," said Sarah Nell woodenly.

"The doctor says," said the old man, his mouth doing the best it could with a smile, "That if I don't have it taken off I'll die."

Gaff opened his mouth as though he would speak, but instead put a spoon of clabber into it.

"That's mighty good eatin once you get started," Sarah Nell said. Gaff raised his eyes to hers and she saw his throat work over the clabber.

"It's mighty good, thank you," said Gaff. "You going to have it taken off?"

"No, I ain't," said the old man.

"I'll have another one of them biscuits," said Gaff.

The old man looked past Gaff to the door, and his vision was distant, stretching past the porch, past the field and even the night, down to the forest of pines. "Since the first frost of November in this country, living on land I growed out of as a boy, I been a stranger. Not eating with any-body, not talking with anybody, and follered by a scent that'ed sicken a hog." His eyes suddenly snapped back, and Gaff met them steadily, suck-ing at a front tooth, and wiping his mouth with the back of his hand. "Now I'm supposed to fix it so I cain't even holler when I hurt."

"And Pa and me was just talking on the way this evening," said Sarah Nell, her face still ashen, but her eyes bright and moist.

"And I just wanted to set again . . ." said the old man, his voice trailing off, his eyes wandering to the door again. ". . . to set to the table again. . . ."

"It was mighty good," said Gaff. "That syrup's got a good taste."

"That syrup's a tad too sharp, son," said the old man. "You biled it too long."

"You think so, huh," said Gaff, dabbing his finger on the rim of the syrup can and touching it to his tongue.

"Next year you cook it slower and not so long. It'll lose that tart."

"I'll do that," Gaff said. "I will."

"I smell myself," said the old man. "You'd think I couldn't smell it wouldn't you? To be able to smell it after all this time." He shook his head slowly, and pulled the clabber to his bowl again.

"We'd best be going, Miss Sarah Nell," said Gaff.

She went around the table to her father and kissed him on the scarred side of his face.

"Goodbye, Pa."

"Bye, Sarah Nell." He did not look at her.

When Gaff opened the door, the huge dog was sitting on the other side of the screen, his yellow eyes dull and unblinking. Gaff pushed back the screen and the dog walked through to the old man and lay at his feet. As they were going through the door the old man spoke again.

"Take the dog too," he said.

"Sir?" asked Gaff, already standing on the porch, but still holding the door open behind him.

"Take him out of here," said the old man.

Joe Gaff looked from the dog to Sarah Nell, who refused to meet his eyes, and then back to the dog.

"It ain't me that can make him leave you, sir," Gaff said.

The old man looked at the dog for a long, still moment and then raised his arm and pointed toward the door and the night.

"Go out of here. Git," said the old man.

The dog raised himself slowly and passed through the door between Gaff and Sarah. Outside, the wind was up again and it was raining. They left the dog standing by the car shed, tail and ears drooping, his body slicked black with rain. The car was already past the mule lot, halfway down the lane between the rows of pecan trees, before they heard the dog howl the first time, a long, moon-reaching wail breaking over the night.

Gaff turned to Sarah Nell as though he would speak, but did not. Instead, he pulled his hat lower over his eyes and guided the old car carefully through the mud out of the lane onto the big road.

"Pa always was a fool about clabber," Sarah Nell said, her wooden voice breaking over the last word.

Pam Durban

This Heat

IN August, Beau Clinton died. He was playing basketball in the high-school gym when his bad heart finally set him free, and he staggered and fell and blew one bloody bubble that lingered, rising and shimmering, then burst, leaving a shower of blood like rust spots on his pale skin. The school phoned Ruby Clinton but they wouldn't say what the trouble was, just that Beau was sick, in trouble, something—it was all the same trouble—and could Ruby or Mr. Clinton come right down. "Isn't any Mr. Clinton," Ruby snapped, but the woman had already hung up the phone. So she figured she'd best go down to see what he'd done this time, her son with his long slanted eyes exactly like his father's.

Ruby walked down the hall working herself up for the next show-down with Beau or the principal or whoever crossed her. No one made her angrier than Beau. She could get so angry that bright points of light danced in front of her eyes. Of course it didn't matter, not at all; she might as well rave at the kudzu, tell it to stop suffocating everything under its deadly green. A woman with a worried face directed Ruby toward the clinic room and Ruby quickened her step. But when she got there, a man blocked the doorway. "You can't go in there," he said. Ruby didn't answer and she didn't stop. She was used to plowing past men such as he, and she knew her strength in these matters. There were things that wouldn't give but you put your shoulder against them and you shoved.

"The hell you say," Ruby said. "If he's having one of his spells I know what to do."

"He's not having one of his spells," the man said. "I'm afraid he's dead."

She squinted and watched while the man collapsed into a tiny man

[75]

and grew up life-size again. She had a steady mannish face, and when something stunned her that face turned smooth and still, as if everything had been hoarded in and boarded up back of her eyes somewhere. Younger, she'd had a bold way of memorizing people, but that look had narrowed until she looked as if she were squinting to find something off in the distance. At the time of Beau's death Ruby was thirty-two, but she looked worn and strong as if she'd been out in the weather all her life. Her face had settled like the straight dense grain of wood. She'd been what they called *hot-blooded*, a fighter, all her people were fierce and strong, good people to have on your side. There was once something of the gypsy in her: a lancing eye and tongue and the gypsy darkness shot with a ruby light. But that seemed like a long time ago.

She'd gone there ready to scream at Beau, to smack him good for whatever he'd done, to drag him back one more time from hurting somebody—he'd heard what the judge had said—or from playing ball—he'd heard the doctor say that he was not to move faster than a walk if he wanted to live through the summer. She'd gone there ready to smack him, breathing harshly through her nose. She still had faith in the habit of hitting him—he came back then for a second from where he lived most of the time—a numb sort of habit that began as pressure behind her eyes and ended with the blunt impact and the sound of the flat of her hand brought hard against his skull.

The words she would have said and the force of the blow she'd gone ready to deliver echoed and died in her head. Words rushed up and died in her throat—panicked words, words to soothe, to tame, to call him back —they rushed on her, but she forgot them halfway to her mouth, and he lay so still. And that's how she learned that Beau Clinton, her only son and the son of Charles Clinton, was dead.

From then on it was just one surprise after another. She was surprised to find herself standing outside on the same day she'd left when she'd gone inside the school building. Everything should have been as new and strange as what had just happened. But the dusty trees stood pinned and silent against the tin sky, and below in the distance Atlanta's mirrored buildings still captured the sun and burned. Then the word *dead* took her by surprise, the way it came out of her mouth as though she said it every day of her life. "Well, that's that," she said to Mae Ruth as her sister sat there, hands gripping the steering wheel, exactly the way she'd been caught when Ruby had dropped the word onto her upturned face.

Then she was surprised by her sister's voice, how it boiled on and on shaped like questions, while Ruby breathed easily, lightheaded as a little seed carried on the wind. It was the most natural thing in the world that Beau should be dead; it had never been any other way. She patted her sister's hand: "That sneaky little thing just slipped right out on me," she said, chuckling to herself and wiping her eyes with the backs of both hands. And her heart gave a surge and pushed the next wave of words at him, as though he were standing right in front of her again: "That sneaky little bastard," she said, "goddamn him."

Mae Ruth drove like a crazy woman—running red lights, laying on the horn, heading back towards Cotton Bottom at sixty miles per hour, gripping Ruby's wrist with one hand. "We got to get you home," she said.

"You do that," Ruby said. It would be nice to be back there among the skinny houses that bunched so close together you could hear your neighbor drop a spoon. She could slip in there like somebody's ghost and nobody'd find her again. That was the comfort of the village—the closeness made people invisible. She could hide there and never come out again, the way old lady Steel did after her kid got run over by a drunk: rocking on her porch day and night and cringing anytime tires squealed and crying out at the sight of children in the street. That was a good use for a life, she thought. She just might take it up like so many of the rest of her neighbors. They saw something once, something horrible, and it stuck to their eyes and the look of it never left them.

When they turned onto Rhineheart Street, Ruby sat up. "This ain't right, Mae Ruth, you took a wrong turn somewhere," she said anxiously. Her eyes never left the road which ran into a lake of white sun, a mirage. In the glare, her street looked like a place she'd seen once, and forgotten. Then there was her house and the neighbors three deep on the narrow porch because somehow the news had gotten loose and run home before them. And she saw that the emptiness was a trick of the light on the windshield and she sat back and said, "Oh, now I get it. Fools you, don't it?" And she chuckled to herself. Someone had played a fine joke, and now it was revealed.

The village where Ruby lives is called Cotton Bottom because of the cotton mill and because of the fact that the main street is down in a slump in the earth. All the streets above and below the main street run straight between the mill on one end of the village and the vacated company store on the other. In February when the weather settles in and the rain falls straight down, the air turns gray and thin and there's silence as though the air had all been sucked into the big whistle on top of the mill and scattered again to the four corners of the earth. But in the summer, this place comes alive: the kids all go around beating on garbage-can lids, the air is so full of the noise you couldn't lose them if you tried, and the heat is heavy so you drag it with you from place to place.

The other border of this place is an old city cemetery with a pauper's field of unmarked graves down in a low meadow. Ruby used to go there between shifts or after work if it was still light and sit and listen to the wind roughing up the tops of the trees. Sometimes she thought of the roots of the trees, and it gave her a funny cold knot in the pit of her stomach to think of the way the roots were all tangled up with the bodies and of how people's bones fertilized the trees. She sat very quietly then, listening, as if she might catch that long faithful story as it's told from the ground up, as it ends in the wind, in the tossing crowns of the oaks, in the way they bend and sigh and rise and lash the air again.

By eight o'clock the morning after Beau's death the sun looked brassy, as though it had burned all day. You had to breathe shallow for fear you'd suck in the heavy heat and choke on it. Ruby didn't question how the night had passed; she watched while the sweating men struggled and pushed Beau's coffin up the narrow steps. And as she watched them coming closer she had one of her thoughts that seemed to come out of nowhere: Who is that stranger coming here? And she must have mumbled it to herself because Dan Malvern and Mae Ruth both leaned over at the same time to catch what she'd said. "You'd think that'd be the easy part," she said, nodding towards the men with the coffin. Her arms hung at her sides; her face was slack, red, and chafed looking; her feet were planted wide to keep her upright. When they passed with Beau's coffin, her mouth went dry and her knees gave a little and Dan squeezed her arm and whispered: "Ruby you hold on now." His warm breath on her ear annoyed her.

She tried not to listen to the rustling of the undertakers, the whispers as they arranged the casket. They opened the casket and draped an organdy net from the lid to the floor and arranged it in a pool around the legs of the coffin stand and it all seemed to be happening beyond glass somewhere in front of her face. The open lid was lined with shirred satin gathered into a sunburst and below it her son floated on his cushions with the stubborn look stuck to his face as though he were about to say *no* the way he did: jutting out his chin and freezing his eyes and defying the world to say him *yes.* "I never believed it," she said, and the words were cold drops in her ears, "not for a minute, and now look." And with that, a heaviness in her chest dragged on her, and she turned on them and said: "What was the way he should've come, tell me that. What other road could he have gone, why don't you tell me?" She grabbed Mae Ruth's arm.

It seemed that she'd been strong forever and in everything. Just after Beau was born sick she'd been strong in her faith. Her religion had leapt on her one day like something that had been lying in wait, preparing itself. Afterwards, she'd gone about preaching the word to anyone who'd stand still long enough to hear. That's when Charles Clinton had left for the first time. She'd worked herself into raptures: down on her knees, voice about to break with the joy of it, the joy dilating, pressing against the walls of her chest, the walls of her skull, till the spirit was so restless it threatened to tear her open. She swooped down on her neighbors' houses then, praying, singing, weeping for all who lived inside sunk in the sin and error of their ways, all their sin a pressure inside her as though she lived inside their lives too. She sang the hymns with the force and flatness of a hammer hitting a rock, and she beat the tambourine so loudly that no one could stand close to her, and her face looked angry as if she were defying something.

Then she'd been strong at work in the mill. First, she wielded the sharp razor, slashed open the bales so the cotton tumbled out. She roughed up the cotton and set it going toward the other room to be wooed and combed straight into fiber. They took note of how she worked and she was promoted to spooler. She stood beside the machines until she thought the veins in her legs might burst. She worked there yanking levers, guiding the threads as they sped along from one spool to the next. You had to yank the levers because the machines were old and balky, but the habit of it became the same as its action, and the habit felt like anger after a while. The threads flew by never slowing, drawing tighter, flying from one spool to the next, the separate strands twisting, making miles of continuous threads for the big looms in the room beyond. The noise could deafen a person. The machines reared up and fell forward in unison and grabbed the fiber with witchfingers and twisted the strands and rose and grabbed and fell again in rhythm all day and all night. The machines crashed like sacks full of silver being dropped again and again until she couldn't think, she could only watch the threads as they came flying out of the dark door and caught and flashed around the spools and flew out the other door.

At night she used to go to prayer meetings or to church singings. And once when they'd prayed, and something ugly had come into their presence, something with the smell of burning hair, she'd known what to do. She'd been strong for them all and had led them in raising their voices louder in praise till the smell had ebbed. She felt so strong then, every fiber set against the thing that had entered and filled the room so completely, the thing that had swamped them in the middle of prayer. She'd known right away that whatever it might be, it was between this thing and Beau that she needed to stand. She already knew that much. "Don't be afraid," she said, "that's what it wants." She made *quiet down* motions with her hands and she said: "You know ladies, it comes to me to say there isn't nothing strange under the sun. There is this thing—we don't want to call it the devil, because once you give it a name it's got half of what it wants—and it turns things inside out and upside down just that quick, and what you've got there staring you in the face is an empty lining, ain't that right?" That is where the work begins, she told them.

But it didn't stop there, oh no. The work went on working and people began to mistake the lining for the whole cloth, and it made them bitter and sad, and it made them call themselves shameful and monstrous before God. You could see it all the time, she told them, in the sad empty eyes around you. And the worst of the work, the end of the work came when people's lives were x'd out—not by death, but by life. When people turned into living tombstones over their own lives, when people hid their faces from each other, when human life turned foreign, then the work was finished, she told them. "Now you've all seen it happen," she said. "Every single one of us in this room's seen it happen. But the way I figure it, we got to go one better than that. We got to stand up and say 'All right then, I got something for you better than what you got for me.' That's what we're all put here to do on this earth, and we can't ever let each other forget."

But that all seemed to have happened in another lifetime, in another country, a long time ago. Now there was this: the undertakers finished their business and left the house. Ruby dragged the reclining chair right next to the steel-gray coffin and eased herself down, feeling like a bag of flesh with a cold stone at the center. The coffin looked cold and shiny as coins and her mind wandered there, counting the coins.

The green vinyl of the chair arms sucked to the back of her arms and she saw the looks go around the room from Mae Ruth to her aunts, to Granny Brassler and the rest of them. Looks and sighs that flew around the room, passed from one to the other, but she didn't care. She knew what they were thinking; she'd thought the same herself many a time about someone else: they were worrying that all the fight had gone out of her and wondering what they would do with another one to feed and wipe clean. In the village, that's the worst that can happen. "I'm here to stay," she said, "don't want no bath, don't want no supper, so don't start on me about it, just tend to your business and let me tend to mine."

She thought of that business and how she'd learned it well. To work, to live, you had to be angry, you had to fight—that much she remembered. Her father had fought for his life, for all their lives, the time half the mill walked out and the mill police came muscling into their house on fat horses. She could still see the door frame give, see her father's arm raised, all the veins standing up before he brought the stick of stove wood down hard across the horse's nose. That was what life was for—fighting to keep it. That's how she'd been raised. All the good sweet passion and flavor of life soured if you just let it sit. Like milk left out, it could spoil. You had to be strong.

She smelled her own exhausted smell, like old iron, leaving her. Someone had drawn the curtains across the front window. Someone wiped her face with a cloth. They bent over her one after the other. "Ruby, trust in the Lord," someone said. The thought rolled over her.

"I do," she said automatically, because the Lord was still a fact, more or less, "but that's all there is to it and it's got nothing to do with him." She nodded toward her son. There. She was afraid to say it, but that was the truth. She snapped up straight, defying any of them to say differently. And just then she was taken by grief that pushed up in waves from the dead center of her. Each wave lifted her out of the chair and wrenched her voice from her throat, and that voice warned them: "I can't bear it." She couldn't open her eyes and inside the darkness there was a darker darkness, a weight like a ball, rolling against the back of her eyes. "I can't support it," she said, and everything obliged inside her and fell in, and there was a quick glimpse of Beau the way he'd come home one time after a fight: the tatters of blood in the sink, too much blood to be coming out of his nose and no way to stop it, and she was falling, tumbling over and over. Someone shouted her name; hands held her face, her hands. They bobbed all around her, corks on a dark water.

And when finally she could open her eyes, she glared at them as if they'd waked her from a deep sleep. She looked at Beau's face: it was rosier than in life, and dusted with a chilly-looking powder. The blue-gray lips were likewise frosted. The hair looked washed straight back by a wave, so silky and fine. He'd taken to dyeing his hair—the roots were dark and a soapy cloying smell rose through the organdy—and she said on the last receding wave of grief: "Lord, don't I wonder what's keeping him company right now."

"Now don't you go wandering off there all by yourself," Mae Ruth said. Her eyes were inches from Ruby's own. She looked at her sister and almost laughed in spite of herself at that funny veiny nose, more like a beak than a nose, the eyes like her own, two flat dark buttons. Now Mae Ruth's life was hard too, but there seemed to be more room for it. She made more room. She could tell funny stories, then turn around and tell somebody off just as neat and they'd stay told off. Once they'd both gone to a palm reader out by Doraville and the woman had scared Ruby, and Mae Ruth had said, "Lady, far's I'm concerned you get your jollies out of scaring people half to death." That was Mae Ruth for you. Just then, her face looked like she was about to imitate the way the woman had looked. Mae Ruth could pull her face down long as a hound's and say "Doom" in this deep funny voice and you'd have to laugh.

"You know Mae Ruth, you're right," Ruby said. They had a way of picking up pieces of conversation and weaving them together again. "I can't remember a time when anything was much different than it is now, but I know it must have been. Because sometimes I get a thought and it seems like it's not a new thought at all, it's something I can almost remember, like I've thought the same thought before, you know? The way you turn a corner and think you've been there before or hear a noise or catch something off the corner of your eye?"

Someone new had come into the room. She felt it in the stirring among the crowd around her chair, the way they coughed and got quiet. "Dan?" she said. He'd left after the coffin was carried inside and had gone to stand with the men on the porch. She looked up, expecting to find Dan's narrow brown face, and there stood Charles Clinton and his new wife, looking cool and pastel in spite of the heat. She said: "Well, look who's here, everybody, look who's showing his face around here again." The welcome in her voice would have chilled you to the bone. "Look who's come back to the well," she said. "Well's all dried up, Charles Clinton," she said. Her breathing turned down like a low gas flame. His new wife tried to get in her line of vision, but Ruby kept ducking around her in order to keep an eye fixed on Charles. And doesn't it always happen this way? When she was most in need of the blessing of forgetfulness—just then, she remembered everything.

She was sixteen, up from Atlanta to Gainesville for the Chicopee Mill picnic. He stood apart from everybody, working a stick of gum. The lights inside the mill had come winging out through the hundreds of small windows. Like stars, they'd winked on the water of the mill-pond. And the roaring of the mill barely reached them across the mild night, and it was no longer noise that could make you deaf. The air was clean of cotton lint and clear, and the mill glittered. Everything glittered that way. Oh yes, she remembered that glittering very well. He had eyes like dry ice. She should have known; she should have turned and run with what she knew instead of thinking she could sass and sharp-tongue her way out of everything. He said: "You're Ruby Nelson from Atlanta, aren't you?"

"How'd you know?" she said.

"I have my ways," he said. And thinking about those ways had thrilled her down to the soles of her feet.

She should have bolted for sure. She was supposed to have married Hudger Collins, and she had no business forgetting that. But Hudger was dull next to this one who had hair like corn silk, a sloped and angled face, and tilted eyes that watched and watched.

"I take you for a soldier," she said. And he smiled that smile that rippled out across his face and was gone so fast you couldn't catch it.

"Now you're a right smart girl," he said, wrapping one hand around the top of her arm. "I was in the Navy. You're real smart. I bet you could teach me a lot."

Later that night he said the word *love* over and over, as if he would drive it into her. Now when she saw him again a pit opened and all the fiends let fly. She looked at Beau jealously, as if he might rise up and join his father and together they'd waltz away into the night. "Why doesn't he come closer?" she said. "I'm not a rattlesnake." She hated her voice when it got quavery like that. She said: "Charles Clinton, who's going to hurt you now? Why don't you come here and look at your boy? He's dead, he isn't going to get up and bother you anymore. You don't even have to be ashamed anymore." And she heard a dry crackling sob burst out of his throat and nose, and she leaned her head back and smiled at the ceiling.

"Ruby," Mae Ruth rasped in her ear, "everyone's suffering, let him be."

Ruby hooted and smacked the arm of the chair. "Who's suffering?" she said. "How can you tell he's suffering?"

"Oh Lord," someone said from the corner of the room, "there's just no end to it."

He stepped closer then, and for the first time she looked directly into his eyes. She was afraid to do it because she believed in what she saw in people's eyes. When she saw his eyes she bit her lip halfway into another bitter word. His eyes were washed out, drained, the color broken. And his mouth turned down, and something elastic was gone from under his skin. He'd lost a tooth and in spite of the powder-blue leisure suit, the backs of his knuckles looked permanently grimy. And those were the very eyes I searched and searched, she thought, the ones where I tried to see myself for so long. And those eyes stared at her, void of anything but a steady pain that threatened to break from him. And it scared her so much she couldn't speak, and she leaned over and fussed with the net over Beau's coffin.

She didn't love Charles, never had; she'd known that from the start, and that was the crime. But it acted like love; it kicked like a horse colt inside. And it was time: Ruby saw that in the eyes of the men on the streets of the village when she passed them by, and she saw it in her mother's eyes. And love was something that grew: that's what she'd been taught. That's what she'd believed.

She wore a tight dress of lilac-colored imitation linen all the way to Jacksonville on the bus. It was their honeymoon trip, but all the while she had the sense that she was riding along beside herself. Away over there was the girl who was wild crazy in love, but she, Ruby, couldn't get to her. All the while she waited for that special feeling to come up in her throat, the way a spring starts up out of the ground. She wanted that feeling, but it didn't come. She didn't love him, but she shut that feeling away. That was her secret. She always believed it would be different, and that was her secret. And her faith, and her shame.

So, love or no love and faithful to another law, Beau was born barely moving, hardly breathing through his blue lips. And both times—after the birth when the doctor had come in peeling off his rubber gloves, and now—Charles had stood there looking like something broken, his face taking on no more expression than the dead boy's. Only his eyes still spoke, and his hand that trembled like an old man's hand as he lifted it to wipe his mouth. Why I'm better off than he is, she thought. For all this, I'm better off. It was cold, proud comfort. The sweet vengeful cry she'd hoped for, the hot bass wire she'd hoped to hear sing at the sight of him broken by the death of his only son, wouldn't sound. She grabbed for Mae Ruth's hand because the falling sensation was creeping in behind her eyes again.

The fact of the boy had stuck in Charles like a bone in his throat. She spent her days sitting in clinics with Beau's heavy head lolling over one arm, because there had to be an answer. You'd have thought the boy was contaminated the way Charles' hands had stiffened when he picked up the baby. You'd have thought the boy was permanently crippled or contagious the way Charles had held him away from his body. "Lots and lots of people's born with something just a little off," she said. "Lord, some of them never even know it," she told Charles pointedly. Of course, as things had gone on, the depth of the damage had been revealed as it always is. By the time Beau had surgery on his heart at the age of five, Charles wouldn't even come up to sit with him. He said it was too humiliating to sit in the charity ward, where people treated you like you were something to be mopped off the floor.

And after Beau had managed to grow up and after he started coming home with pockets full of dollar bills, Charles could only say "What's going on?" She could almost see the words forming on his lips as he looked at his son in the coffin. Charles never understood a thing; that was his sorrow. She didn't want him near her.

She remembered her own sorrow, how it had struck so deep it had seemed to disappear inside her the first time Beau got caught in Grant Park in a car with a rich man from the north side of town. He was nothing but a baby, twelve years old. The police cruiser brought him home— because the other man was not only rich, he was also important, and he didn't want trouble on account of Beau. Her son smelled like baby powder and dirty clothes. He was growing a face to hide behind. His lips were swollen as though someone had been kissing them too hard, and she stared and wondered whether that brand was put on his mouth by love or hate or by some other force too strange to be named. She had to drag

Charles into the room. "It's not the money," Charles had shrieked at his son. "I know it isn't the money." That's as much of the discovery as he could force out of his mouth; the rest was too terrifying.

"Why?" she asked her son. Her voice was a tool, boring into him. She held onto his skinny arm and watched the skin blanch under her fingers.

"They talk nice to me," Beau said.

"Honey, those men don't care about you," she said, watching Charles turn away; watching Beau watch him turn away.

When Charles left, he said their life wasn't fit for human beings and he moved to Marietta. He'd never lifted a hand against her. By village standards, he was a good man. But she felt that violence had been done to her; there was a hardness and a deadness inside that made her swerve away from people as though she might catch something from them.

During that time, she went to Dan Malvern. It was right: he was her pastor as well as her friend, and together they'd puzzled over that deadness and prayed endlessly for forgiveness for her. She was never quite sure for what sin she needed to be forgiven, but she'd kept quiet and prayed anyway.

Now, sitting beside Beau's coffin, she'd come a whole revolution: she felt like asking for forgiveness about as much as she felt like getting up and walking to New York City. Forgiveness belonged to another lifetime, to people like Dan who had a vision left to guide them. Once Dan had seen armies of souls pouring toward heaven or hell while he stood at the crossroads, and he was still standing there, frantically directing traffic. Dan stood just outside the door with his big black shoes sticking out of his too-short pants. You had to be gentle with Dan; he always had to be invited so she said: "Dan'l, you're always welcome here." He crossed the room with one long country stride and grabbed her hand and rubbed it and said: "Are you holding up all right in the care of the Lord?"

"Getting by," she said. His eyes looked old and sad. She took his hand more warmly and said: "Dan, bless you." But when she took her hand away, it hung in front of her, bare and powerless. And there was Beau, dead, his life full of violence in spite of that hand, and she said "Oh," and bit her knuckle, and Dan hauled her up and pulled her into the kitchen and shut the door behind him. He rested a hand on her shoulder and threw back his head, and the tears squeezed out through the lashes like beads. She moved to embrace him but he stopped her. He was maneuvering into the current, she saw that, setting his back to the wind. He shifted and hunched his shoulders: "Kneel down with me, sister," he said.

"Oh, all right, Dan," she said, sighing. She knew this part of the ritual, when they had to forget each other's names in order that God might hear their prayers. She knelt down facing him. She had to endure this, because when Dan wasn't busy acting like God's own special riding mule, he was one who shed a steady light onto her life, a light in which she could stand holding all her shame and be known without shame. Mae Ruth was another, only her light was barer and warmer. Dan remembered her and could remind her sometimes of ways she'd been that she could barely recall. He knew her practically all the way back. She could go to him feeling small and cold, the way lights look in winter, and come away after talking about nothing for a few hours, with her feet set squarely on this earth again.

But something happened when he talked about God, when he started to pray. They didn't have much in common then. He became hard then, he saw things in black and white and spoke of them harshly through his teeth. His jawbone tried to pop through the skin, and his black hair began to tremble with indignation, and he jerked at the words as if he were chewing stringy meat. He strained after the words as though he could pull them from the air: "Lord, help her to see that sin is there," he began, "that sin has taken away her son. Help her to see the sin, to look on the *wages* of sin and to ask forgiveness, and help this woman, your servant, to know in her HEART the sin and to call OUT to the Lord in her hour of need."

She would have laughed had she not felt so lonely. Dan could let himself down into it any time and drink of the stern comfort there. She envied him that plunge. She imagined the relief must taste hard and clean. She closed her eyes and tried to pray, to sink into that place. It would be so good to believe again in the laws, she thought, because those laws named the exile and the means of coming home in such clear ringing tones. First there was sin, a person drifting in some foreign land, then confessing the sin, then redemption, then hallelujah sister and welcome home. She felt for her heart, for its secret shame, and found only a sort of homesickness, a notion that there was someplace else that she'd forgotten, a place where there were no such people as foreigners, a place big enough to hold sin, grief, ugliness, all of it.

But forgetfulness, that was the sickness, the worm in the heart. Words like good and evil and death simplified things and rocked you and lulled you and split things apart. There was something else moving back there; she could barely feel it but it was there.

She watched his face move through the prayer, laboring against a current. "The grave," Dan said with a shiver, and when he came back to himself with a great bass "Amen" she said Amen too, and a sob broke from her at the sound of that blank word. Her shoulders shook and her head wagged from side to side and she said: "Dan, where'd you learn all that? It must tire out the Lord himself to listen to all that talk about sin all the time. There must be some wages due to you for that, wouldn't you say?"

"Ruby," he said, "don't blaspheme now, don't go piling sin on sin."

And at that she labored to her feet and shook herself. "The way I understand it," she said, "we're all born fools, ain't that right? Nothing we can do about that. What's the sin in that? Seems like everything we do has got wages." The man of God with thunder and sword faded, his face was restored to him, and the Daniel she knew came back, looking sheepish, pulling on his bottom lip. "So where are you going to look for better wages is what I want to know?"

"I know you're under a terrible strain," he said, "but I don't know where you get such talk." But by then she was halfway into the other room. And seeing her son in his coffin again, she felt she was coming on him fresh, and she saw how much Beau's face looked like her own—much more like her own than like Charles' face—and it scared her. The hard life he'd led showed in the set defiance of the chin, in the squint marks around the eyes that the mortician's powder puff couldn't erase. That look was stuck there for all eternity, and he was only sixteen years old.

It was the same look he'd given her any time she'd asked him about those men and why he went with them. She'd fought for him for so long, and the fatigue of that fight caught up with her again and she was tossed up on a fresh wave of grief. She began to sob and twist, turning this way and that, trying to escape from the people who pressed in from all sides, suffocating her. Strong hands gripped her and shook her, and she recognized Dan and Mae Ruth though neither of them spoke and her eyes were squeezed tight. "Get it out," Mae Ruth said. "You go on and get it all out, then you come on back here with us."

"I think I want to sleep for a while now," she said, opening her eyes.

"You want a nerve pill?" Mae Ruth asked. She shook her head no. She stopped beside the coffin.

"Well now," she said softly, "don't he look sweeter without that harsh light on him?" During the minute that she'd had her spell of grief, the light had shifted and softened and turned gray and round as a belly pressing back against the dark outside. As the light softened in the room, her son's face softened too; he looked younger and not so angry at the air. He hadn't looked that way since he was a baby, and she loved him with a sweetness so sharp she felt she might be opened by it.

And what became of that sweetness, she thought, as she pushed through the curtains into her bedroom. By what devilish sly paths did it run away, leaving the harsh light that never ceased burning on him? It took too much effort to remember that he was not just that strange being who'd thrashed his way through her life and out, leaving wreckage in his path. He was also another thing, but it made her head hurt to think of it. She pulled off her slippers and unhooked her slacks at the waist. It was easier to think that the march he'd made straight to his grave was the sin. To call that life ugly and be done with it. But the changing of the sweet to the ugly was the most obvious trick in the book. Anyone with eyes could see through that one. There was a better trick. She thought how much she wished she could still believe that the devil dreamed up the tricks. That would explain the ashes around her heart.

But never mind: the better trick was that the soft curtains of forgetfulness dropped so quietly you did not hear them fall. It was forgetfulness that made things and people seem strange: that was sin if ever there was sin. Still, remembering things made you so tired. Better to live blind, she thought.

Once she'd begged Beau to remember who he was. She'd meant *her* people, the Nelson side, dignity and decency deep enough to last through two or three lifetimes. But they were as strange to him as the whole rest of the wide world. "Sure," he'd said, "I know who I am. I'm a Nelson from the cotton patch and a Clinton straight from hell." Seeing her shocked, hand pressed to her throat the way she did, he'd laughed and said: "Well ain't I? You're always saying 'goddamn your daddy to hell.'" The way he'd imitated her, his mouth drawn back like a wild animal's, had terrified her. "That means I come from hell, don't it, mama?"

She shook her head in frustration and eased herself down onto her bed. She wished that he were there, given back to her for just one minute, so that she could collect, finally, all that she'd needed to tell him, so that she could tell him in words he'd have to understand: that if one person loved you, you were not a chunk of dead rock spinning in space. That was what she'd tried to tell him all during the long winter just past.

That was the winter when the mill had stepped up production again and had taken on everyone they'd laid off. She'd gotten a job in the sewing room. All day she sat there sewing, while her mind worked to find an end to the business with Beau. Last winter he was gone more than he was home, and his face was pale and sunken around the cheekbones. Every so often she'd start way back at the beginning and come forward with him step by step, puzzling out the way and ending always in the same spot: the place she'd seen him staring into. She turned it over and over like the piecework in front of her, looking for the bunched thread, the too-long stitch that would give, the place where her mind had wandered and the machine had wandered off the seam.

Once she'd taken half a sick-day and had gone home to find him staring at nothing. She'd barely been able to rouse him, and when she'd bent over him she'd been repelled by his sweet sick odor. But it was the way he'd looked that stuck in her mind: tight blue jeans, a black shirt, a red bandanna wound tightly around his neck. And his face, when he'd finally turned it up to her and smiled dreamily into her screaming, had looked serene and sly as the face of a wrecked angel. It was the smile that made her blood shut off. When he smiled that way, there was a shudder in the room like the sound that lingered in the air if the looms shut down, and she knew that he was bound to die, that he was already looking into that place. She saw it in his eyes all winter.

The cotton came in baled through enormous doors and was pulped, twisted, spun, woven, mixed with polyester and squeezed and pressed and dyed, printed with tulips, irises, gardens of blowing green, and made into sheets and blouses.

It wasn't right that she should worry herself the way she did all winter. She was up all hours of the night waiting for him, but half the time he never came home. And then one day she went to his room and nailed the window shut and when he went into his room that night, she locked him in and sat in the living room with arms folded and cried as he bumped and crashed around and screamed awful names at her. It was for his own good and because she loved him. And if you loved somebody, she told herself, you had to make a stand and this was her stand, and in the morning she'd explain to him that she did it out of love in words he'd have to understand.

Afterwards she was ashamed, and she never told anyone—not even Mae Ruth. She felt that she'd been in a dream, a fever dream, where crazy things made perfect sense and everything hung suspended way up high in clear air. But it didn't matter anyway, because when she unlocked the door to set him free in the morning, he was gone. There was glass all over the floor and the window was kicked out.

She woke up after dark, groping around with one hand, looking for something on the bedspread. She'd been dreaming of black rocks looming over her, while at the base of the rocks hundreds of people scrambled around picking up busted-off pieces of the largest rock and holding them up in the moonlight. She groped her way out into the living room, and people patted her and helped ease her down into her chair again.

All night she slept and woke, and whenever she woke, one pair of hands or another reached for her, and once she tried to say: "I want to thank you all for being so good." But her voice broke when she said "good," and someone said: "Hush, you'd do the same."

The voices went around and around her, a soothing drone that filled the room. And then the sun was up, the day was up bright and blazing, and she looked at her son beside her in his coffin and the thought of his going was borne fully onto her. And as the day rushed back at her, so did her memory of Beau, which was as sharp as if he were still alive. In fact, they were hardly memories at all, they were more like the smaller sightings we keep of someone's day-to-day life.

This is how he came in: her body had threshed with him for two days and a night. Then his sickness: she walked him day and night, while over on Tye Street, Granny Brassler and the others went down almost to their knees, taken by the spirit, shouting: "Devil, take your hands off that baby."

He was never full of milk and quiet; he was long and gangly and he never fleshed out. And all the while he was growing a man's mind. By the time he was twelve, right after Charles left, he'd stay gone for days without even a change of clothes. Until the June just past, when he and his friends had started sticking closer to home and robbing the men in the park nearby. Then she'd set herself against him in earnest. The last time she'd smacked him good was for calling somebody a nigger motherfucker. She'd grabbed his face and squeezed and said: "Don't you never let me hear you talking like trash again. You are not and never will be trash, and don't you forget it."

"Everybody calls me trash," he said. "What makes you any different?"

"Cause I'm your people," she said. "Cause you're mine."

"Ain't that funny?" he said. "That's what they say too."

Every time, somebody else was holding the gun, but the next time or the time after that she knew it would be Beau, and then he would be tried as an adult and sent away to the real prison and that would be that. But last June they'd only taken him as far as the jumping-off place—the juvenile evaluation center, they called it. But it was a prison as surely as the other place where he'd end up someday.

She wasn't like the other mothers, the ones who wept or pleaded or shouted. That time was long gone and she knew it. She was there for another reason but it had no name, only a glare, like the harsh sunlight on the white white walls of his room. She listened. He beat time on his thigh with the heel of one hand and talked, and sometimes he looked up and said: "Ain't that right?" And with knees spread, elbows resting on her knees, hands loosely knotted and fallen between her knees, she looked back at him and said: "Yes, it is," in the strongest voice she could muster.

But staying, listening and staying, was a habit she'd had to learn. The first visit had ended with her reeling out of the room, driven back by his words that were so ugly they seemed to coil like tar snakes out of his mouth. But she went back, *she did go back*, and she knew she must never let herself forget that. She went back and she listened to every word, and she had never felt so empty, so silent. The city and the room turned strange around her, and the only familiar face was the one just in front of her—the one with the mouth that opened and said: "You ought to see their faces when Roy shows them the gun."

She looked up quickly, hearing that voice again just as clear as if it were still ringing off the walls of the jail. She looked at his dead face, and her head began to tug with it, and she stood and bore down on him while all around her the dark closed in as it does when a person's about to faint. Only she was far from fainting. The dark narrowed around her until she stood inside a dark egg looking down at her son, the stranger made up for his grave, who rested in a wash of light that lingered at the core of the outer dark shell. And as she watched and listened—watching and listening with every cell—the stranger's face dropped away and below it there was another, older face, and the whole harsh chorus of his life tangled in her and sang again, and she remembered what she'd seen in the jail, what she'd seen a long time before the jail and had forgotten and carried with her the whole stubborn way and had never wanted to believe, and had believed: he was lost, and she loved him.

She sat down in her chair with a moan and began to rock herself and to pat the edge of the coffin in time with her rocking. She saw the panic start up on every face, and she pressed a hand to her chest to quiet herself. "Things should slow down," she said, "so that a person can have time to study them."

As though they'd been held back, people crowded into the room again. The air got sticky and close, and the smell of flowers and sweat and not quite clean clothes and the soapy smell over Beau's coffin began to make her dizzy. So she focused on Charles and a prickly rash began to spread over her neck and arms and her vision began to clear. Finally she said, in a lazy kind of voice—lazy like a cottonmouth moccasin stirring the water—"Charles, you and your wife's taking up more than your share of the air in here. Why don't you just step out onto the porch?" They ignored her. But Mae Ruth clucked her tongue.

"Ruby, shame, he's still the boy's father; you can't deny him that," she said.

"I know that," Ruby snapped. "Don't I wish I didn't."

She closed her eyes and wished for the old way, the old law that said *such as gives, gets back in kind*. She wished that the weight of that law might lie in her hand like a rock. She wished for some revenge sweet enough to fit his crimes, the kind of revenge that came from a time before people were condemned to stand linked to one another. She could make him order the tombstone and have Beau's name drilled there, yes, and be gone before the funeral started. She tried it out on herself but the little cold thrill the thought gave her wasn't enough to satisfy. Oh me, she said to herself, there isn't no country far enough away where I could send him. She opened her eyes and searched the room for a single unfamiliar face on which to rest her eyes, and found not a one. And she felt the whole dense web of love and grief descending, settling over her shoulders as it had before, in the prison. "This don't ever stop," she said out loud. And she thought of how she had never loved Charles, not in the way that a woman loves a man, and how, still, he was part of the law that turned and turned and bound them all together, on each turn, more deeply than before.

And then there was the vault out under the strong sun without a tent to cover it, and the flowers were wilting under the sun, and Mae Ruth's strong voice led off a song. Then Daniel spoke of heaven and hell for a long time. They were in a new cemetery and the lots were parceled out of a flat field. Through the thin soles of her shoes, Ruby could feel the rucks and ripples of once-plowed ground. She wore a dress of hard black cloth that trapped the heat inside and made the sweat trickle down her sides. Charles stood on the edge of the crowd, his chin sunk onto his chest, and he looked faded under the light that seemed to gather into a center that was made of even whiter and hotter light.

Ruby barely listened to the resurrection or the life. She saw her son's face: that fierce look into the darkness which now rolled around him. Those words Dan said, they weren't the prayers, she thought, not the real prayers. The prayer rested in the squat coffin, in the dark there. Her eyes followed its deaf, dumb lines. The prayer was his life that she couldn't save, and the prayer was her own life and how it continued. And the prayer never stopped; lives began and ended, but the prayer never stopped. She looked at the ground and had the sensation that she'd been standing there for a very long time, trying to memorize each one of the scrappy weeds that had begun to grow again out of the plowed-over land. Those weeds were like the threads, she thought; she watched them in the same way. The threads flew towards her like slender rays of light and twisted spool to spool and disappeared through another door toward the looms beyond. The sound of their coming and going made one continuous roar.

Because she wanted it that way, they all stayed as the coffin was lowered into the hole. She stepped up to the side of the grave and saw her own shadow, thrown huge, on the lid of the vault. It startled her so much she stepped forward instead of back and the edges crumbled under her shoes. Then there were hands on her arms, and she looked down again and saw Mae Ruth's shadow and Dan's beside her. It was as though they were in a boat together, looking over the side. And the sun beat down on them all: on the living, and into the grave, and on those who had lived and died.

William Faulkner

A Portrait of Elmer

I

ELMER drinks beer upon the terrace of the Dome, with Angelo beside him. Beside him too, close against his leg, is a portfolio. It is quite new and quite flat. Sitting so among the artists he gazes across the boulevard Montparnasse and seems to gaze through the opposite gray building violetroofed and potted smugly with tile against the darkling sky, and across Paris itself and France and across the cold restless monotony of the Atlantic itself, so that for the twilit and nostalgic moment he looks about in lonely retrospect upon that Texas scene into which his mother's unselfish trying ambition had haled at implacable long last his resigned and static father and himself, young then still and blond awkward, alone remaining of all the children, thinking of Circumstance as a tireless detachment like the Post Office Department, getting people here and there, using them or not at all obscurely, returning them with delayed impersonal efficiency or not at all.

He remarks on this. Angelo awaits his pleasure with unfailing attentive courtesy as always, with that spirit of laissez-faire which rules their relationship, claims the same privilege himself and replies in Italian. To Elmer it sounds as though Angelo is making love to him, and while autumn and twilight mount Montparnasse gravely Elmer sits in a warm bath of words that mean nothing whatever to him, caressing his warming beer and watching girls in a standardised exciting uniformity of dress and accompanied by men with and without beards, and he reaches down his hand quietly and lightly and touches the portfolio briefly, wondering which among the men are the painters and which again the good painters,

[95]

thinking *Hodge, the artist. Hodge, the artist.* Autumn and twilight mount Montparnasse gravely.

Angelo, with his extreme vest V-ing the soiled kaleidoscopic bulge of his cravat, with a thin purplish drink before him, continues to form his periods with a fine high obliviousness of the fact that Elmer has learned no Italian whatever. Meaningless, his words seem to possess an aesthetic significance, passionate and impersonal, so that at last Elmer stops thinking *Hodge, the artist* and looks at Angelo again with the old helpless dismay, thinking How to interrupt with his American crudeness the other's inexhaustible flow of courteous protective friendship? For Angelo, with an affable tact which Elmer believed no American could ever attain, had established a relationship between them which had got far beyond and above any gross question of money; he had established himself in Elmer's life with the silken affability of a prince in a city of barbarians. And now what is he to do, Elmer wonders. He cannot have Angelo hanging around him much longer. Here, in Paris, he will soon be meeting people; soon he will join an atelier (again his hand touches lightly and briefly the briefcase against his leg) when he has had a little more time to get acclimated, and has learned a little more French, thinking quickly *Yes. Yes. That's it. When I have learned a little more French, so that I can choose the best one to show it to, since it must be the best. Yes yes. That is it.* Besides, he might run into Myrtle on the street any day. And to have her learn that he and Angelo were inseparable and that he must depend on Angelo for the very food he eats. Now that they are well away from Venice and the dungeon of the Palazzo Ducale, he no longer regrets his incarceration, for it is of such things—life in the raw—that artists are made. But he does regret having been in the same jail with Angelo, and at times he finds himself regretting with an ingratitude which he knows Angelo would never be capable of, that Angelo had got out at all. Then he thinks suddenly, hopefully, again with secret shame, Maybe that would be the best thing, after all. Myrtle will know how to get rid of Angelo; certainly Mrs Monson will.

Angelo's voice completes a smooth period. But now Elmer is not even wondering what Angelo is talking about; again he gazes across the clotting of flimsy tables and the serried ranks of heads and shoulders drinking in two sexes and five languages, at the seemingly endless passing throng, watching the young girls white and soft and canny and stupid, with troubling bodies which he must believe were virginal, wondering why certain girls chose you and others do not. At one time he believed that you can seduce them; now he is not so sure. He believes now that they just elect you when they happen to be in the right mood and you happen to be handy. But surely you are expected to learn from experience (meaning a proved unhappiness you did get as compared with a possible one that missed you) if not how to get what you want, at least the reason why you did not get it. But who wants experience, when he can get any kind of substitute? To hell with experience, Elmer thinks, since all reality is unbearable. I want what I think I want when I think I want it, as all men do. Not a formula for stoicism, an antidote for thwarted desire. Autumn and twilight mount Montparnasse gravely.

Angelo, oblivious, verbose, and without self-consciousness, continues to speak, nursing his thin dark drink in one hand. His hair is oiled sleekly backward; his face is shaven and blue as a pirate's. On either side of his brief snubbed nose his brown eyes are spaced and melting and sad as a highly bred dog's. His suit, after six weeks, is reasonably fresh and new, as are his cloth topped shoes, and he still has his stick. It is one of those slender jointed bamboo sticks which remain palpably and assertively new up to the moment of loss or death, but the suit, save for the fact that he has not yet slept in it, is exactly like the one which Elmer prevailed on him to throw away in Venice. It is a mosaic of tan-and-gray checks which seems to be in a state of constant mild explosion all over Angelo, robbing him of any shape whatever, and there are enough amber buttons on it to render him bulletproof save at point-blank range.

He continues to form his periods with a fine high obliviousness, nursing his purplish drink in his hand. He has not cleaned his fingernails since they quitted Venice.

II

He met Myrtle in Houston, Texas, where he already had a bastard son. That other had been a sweet brief cloudy fire, but to him Myrtle, arrogant with youth and wealth, was like a star: unattainable for all her curved pink richness. He did not wish to know that after a while those soft distracting hips would become thicker, heavy, almost awkward; that straight nose was a little too short; the blue ineffable eyes a trifle too candid; the brow low, pure, and broad—a trifle too low and broad beneath the burnished molassescolored hair.

He met her at a dance, a semipublic occasion in honor of departing soldiers in 1917; from his position against the wall, which he had not altered all evening, he watched her pass in a glitter of new boots and spurs and untarnished proud shoulder bars not yet worn thin with salutes; with his lame back and his rented tailcoat he dreamed. He was a war veteran already, yet he was lame and penniless, while Myrtle's father was known even in Texas for the oil wells which he owned. He met her before the evening was over; she looked full at him with those wide heavencolored eyes innocent of any thought at all; she said, "Are you from Houston?" and "Really," with her soft mouth open a little to indicate interest, then a banded cuff swept her away. He met Mrs Monson also and got along quite well with her—a brusque woman with cold eyes who seemed to look at him and at the dancers and at the world too even beyond Texas with a brief sardonic perspicuity.

He met her once; then in 1921, five years after Elmer had returned from his futile and abortive attempt at the war, Mr Monson blundered into three or four more oil wells and Mrs Monson and Myrtle went to Europe to put Myrtle in school, to finish her, since two years in Virginia and a year in the Texas State University had not been enough to do this.

So she sailed away, leaving Elmer to remember her lemoncolored dress, her wet red mouth open a little to indicate interest, her wide ineffable eyes beneath the pure molasses of her hair when he was at last presented; for suddenly, with a kind of horror, he had heard someone saying with his mouth, "Will you marry me?" watching still with that shocked horror her eyes widen into his, since he did not wish to believe that no woman is ever offended by a request for her body. "I mean it," he said; then the barred sleeve took her. I do mean it, he cried silently to himself, watching her lemoncolored shortlegged body disseminating its aura of imminent fat retreating among the glittering boots and belts, to the music become already martial which he could not follow because of his back. *I still mean it, he cries soundlessly, clutching his beer among the piled saucers of Montparnasse, having already seen in the* Herald *that Mrs Monson and Myrtle are now living in Paris, not wondering where Mr Monson is since these years, not thinking to know that Mr Monson is still in America, engaged with yet more oil wells and with a certain Gloria who sings and dances in a New Orleans nightclub in a single darkish silk garment that, drawn tightly between her kind thighs and across her unsubtle behind, lends to her heavy white legs an unbelievably harmless look, like drawn beef; Perhaps, he thinks with a surge of almost unbearable triumph and exultation, They have seen me too in*

the papers, maybe even in the French one: Le millionnaire americain
Odge, qui arrive d'être peinteur, parce-qu'il croit que seulement en France
faut-il l'âme d'artiste rêver et travailler tranquille; en Amérique tout gagne
seulement

III

When he was five years old, in Johnson City, Tennessee, the house
they were temporarily living in had burned. "Before you had time to
move us again," his father said to his mother with sardonic humor. And
Elmer, who had always hated being seen naked, whose modesty was
somehow affronted even in the presence of his brothers, had been snatched
bodily out of sleep and rushed naked through acrid roaring and into a
mad crimson world where the paradoxical temperature was near zero,
where he stood alternately jerking his bare feet from the iron icy ground
while one side of him curled bitterly, his ears filled with roaring and
meaningless shouting, his nostrils with the smell of heat and strange
people, clutching one of his mother's thin legs. Even now he remembers his mother's face above him, against a rushing plume of sparks like
a wild veil; remembers how he thought then, Is this my mother, this
stark bitter face? Where [is] that loving querulous creature whom he
knew? and his father, leanshanked, hopping on one leg while he tried to
put on his trousers; he remembers how even his father's hairy leg beneath the nightshirt seemed to have taken fire. His two brothers stood
side by side nearby, bawling, while tears from tight eyesockets streaked
their dirty faces and blistered away and that yelping scarlet filled their
gaping mouths; only Jo was not crying, Jo, with whom he slept, with
whom he didn't mind being naked. She alone stood fiercely erect, watching the fire in dark scrawny defiance, ridiculing her wailing brothers by
that very sharp and arrogant ugliness of hers.

But as he remembers she was not ugly that night: the wild crimson
had given her a bitter beauty like that of a Salamander. And he would
have gone to her, but his mother held him tight against her leg, binding
him to her with a fold of her night gown, covering his nakedness. So
he burrowed against the thin leg and watched quietly the shouting vol-
unteers within the house hurling out the meagre objects which they had
dragged for so many years over the face of the North American continent: the low chair in which his mother rocked fiercely while he knelt
with his head in her lap; the metal box inscribed Bread in chipped curl-

ing gold leaf and in which he had kept for as long as he could remember a dried and now wellnigh anonymous bird's wing, a basket carved from a peachstone, a dogeared picture of Joan of Arc to which he had added with tedious and tonguesucking care an indigo moustache and imperial (the English made her a martyr, the French a saint, but it remained for Hodge, the artist, to make her a man), and a collection of cigar stubs in various stages of intactness, out of an upstairs window onto the brick walk.

She was not ugly that night. And always after that, after she had disappeared between two of their long since uncounted movings and there was none of the children left save himself, the baby—after he saw her one more time and then never again, when he remembered her it was to see her again starkly poised as a young thin ugly tree, sniffing the very sound of that chaos and mad dream into her flared nostrils as mobile as those of a haughty mare.

It was in Jonesboro, Arkansas, that Jo left them. The two boys had before this refused the gambit of their father's bland inactivity and their mother's fretful energy. The second one, a dull lout with a pimpled face, deserted them in Paris, Tennessee, for a job in a liverystable owned by a man with a cruel heavy face and an alcoholcured nose and a twenty-two-ounce watch chain; and in Memphis the eldest, a slight quiet youth with his mother's face but without her unconquerable frustration, departed for Saint Louis. Jo left them in Jonesboro, and presently Elmer and his mother and father moved again.

But before they moved, there came anonymously through the mail ("It's from Jo," his mother said. "I know it," Elmer said) a box of paints: cheap watercolors and an impossible brush bristling smartly from a celluloid tube in which the wood stem would never remain fixed. The colors themselves were not only impossible too, they were of a durability apparently impervious to any element, except the blue. It compensated for the others, seeming to possess a dynamic energy which the mere presence of water liberated as the presence of spring in the earth liberates the hidden seed. Sultry, prodigious, it was as virulent as smallpox, staining everything it touched with the passionate ubiquity of an unbottled plague.

He learned to curb it in time, however, and with his already ungainly body sprawled on the floor, on wrapping paper when he could get it or on newspapers when not he painted blue people and houses and locomotives. After they had moved twice more however the blue was exhausted; its empty wooden dish stared up at him from among the other glazed discs, all of which had by now assumed a similar dun color, like a dead mackerel's eye in fixed bluish reproach.

But soon school was out, and Elmer, fourteen and in the fourth grade, had failed again to make the rise. Unlike his brothers and sister, he liked going to school. Not for wisdom, not even for information: just going to school. He was always dull in his books and he inevitably developed a fine sexless passion for the teacher. But this year he was ravished away from that constancy by a boy, a young beast as beautiful to him as a god, and as cruel. Throughout the whole session he worshipped the boy from a distance: a blind and timeless adoration which the boy himself wrote finis to by coming suddenly upon Elmer on the playground one day and tripping him violently to earth, for no reason that either of them could have named. Whereupon Elmer rose without rancor, bathed his abraded elbow, and emotionally free again, fled that freedom as though it were a curse, transferring his sheeplike devotion once more to the teacher.

The teacher had a thick gray face like heavy dough; she moved in that unmistakable odor of middle-aged virgin female flesh. She lived in a small frame house which smelled as she smelled, with behind it a small garden in which no flowers ever did well, not even hardy Octoberdusty zinnias. Elmer would wait for her after school on the afternoons when she remained with pupils who had failed in the day's tasks, to walk home with her. For she saved all her wrapping paper for him to paint on. And soon the two of them, the dowdy irongray spinster and the hulking blond boy with almost the body of a man, were a matter for comment and speculation in the town. Elmer did not know this. Perhaps she did not either, yet one day she suddenly ceased walking home through the main streets, but instead took the nearest way home, with Elmer lumbering along beside her. She did this for two afternoons. Then she told him not to wait for her anymore. He was astonished: that was all. He went home and painted, sprawled on his stomach on the floor. Within the week he ran out of wrapping paper. The next morning he went by the teacher's house, as he had used to do. The door was closed. He went and knocked, but got no answer. He waited before it until he heard the school bell ringing four or five blocks away; he had to run. He did not see the teacher emerge from the house when he was out of sight and hurry also toward the still ringing bell along a parallel street, with her thick doughlike face and her blurred eyes behind her nose glasses. Then it became spring. That day, as the pupils filed from the room at noon, she stopped him and told him to come to her house after supper and she would give him some more paper. He had long since forgot how at one time his blond slow openwork inner life had been marked and fixed in simple pleasure between walking home with her by afternoon and coming by her house in the mornings to walk with her to school until she stopped him; forgetting, he had forgiven her, doglike: always with that ability to forgive and then forget as easily; looking, he did not see her eyes, he could not see her heart. "Yessum," he said. "I will."

It was dark when he reached her door and knocked; high above the reddening bitten maples stars flickered; somewhere in that high darkness was a lonely sound of geese going north. She opened the door almost before his knock had died away. "Come in," she said, leading the way toward a lighted room, where he stood clutching his cap, his overgrown body shifting from leg to leg; on the wall behind him his shadow, hulking, loomed. She took the cap from him and put it on a table on which was a fringed paper doily and a tray bearing a teapot and some broken food. "I eat my supper here," she said. "Sit down, Elmer."

"Yessum," he said. She still wore the white shirtwaist and the dark skirt in which he always saw her, in which he perhaps thought of her in slumber even. He sat gingerly on the edge of a chair.

"Spring outside tonight," she said. "Did you smell it?" He watched her push the tray aside and pick up a crust which had lain hidden in the shallow shadow of the tray.

"Yessum," he said. "I heard some geese going over." He began to perspire a little; the room was warm, close, odorous.

"Yes, spring will soon be here," she said. Still he did not see her eyes, since she now seemed to watch the hand which held the crust. Within the savage arena of light from the shaded lamp it contracted and expanded like a disembodied lung; presently Elmer began to watch crumbs appear between the fingers of it. "And another year will be gone. Will you be glad?"

"Ma'am?" he said. He was quite warm, uncomfortable; he thought of the clear high shrill darkness outside the house. She rose suddenly; she almost flung the now shapeless wad of dough onto the tray.

"But you want your paper, dont you?" she said.

"Yessum," Elmer said. *Now I will be outside soon* he said. He rose too and they looked at one another; he saw her eyes then; the walls seemed to be rushing slowly down upon him, crowding the hot odorous air upon him. He was sweating now. He drew his hand across his forehead. But he could not move yet. She took a step toward him; he saw her eyes now.

"Elmer," she said. She took another step toward him. She was grinning now, as if her thick face had been wrung and fixed in that painful and tragic grimace, and Elmer, still unable to move, seemed to drag his eyes heavily up the black shapeless skirt, up the white shirtwaist pinned at the throat with a bar pin of imitation lapis lazuli, meeting her eyes at last. He grinned too and they stood facing one another, cropping the room with teeth. Then she put her hand on him. Then he fled. Outside the house he still ran, with the noise in his ears still of the crashing table. He ran, filling his body with air in deep gulps, feeling his sweat evaporating.

O and thy little girlwhite all: musical with motion Montparnasse and Raspail: subtle ceaseless fugues of thighs under the waxing moon of death:

Elmer, fifteen, with a handleless teacup, descends steps, traverses sparse lawn, a gate; crosses a street, traverses lawn not sparse, ascends steps between flowering shrubs, knocks at screen door, politely but without diffidence.

Velma her name, at home alone, pinksoftcurved, plump sixteen. Elmer enters with his teacup and traverses dim quietness among gleams on nearmahogany, conscious of tingling remoteness and pinksoftcurves and soft intimation of sheathed hips in progression, and so on to the pantry. Helps to reach down sugar jar from where it sits in a pan of water against ants, but sees only in white cascade of sugar little white teeth over which full soft mouth and red never quite completely closed and her plump body bulging her soiled expensive clothing richly the aromatic cubbyhole in the halfdark. Touched sugar hands in the halfdark hishing cling by eluding, elude but not gone; bulging rabbitlike things under soiled silk taut softly, hishing ceaseless cascade of tilted sugar now on the floor hishing: a game.

It whispers its blanched cascade down the glazed precipice of the overflowed cup, and she flees squealing, Elmer in lumbering pursuit, tasting something warm and thick and salt in his throat. Reaches kitchen door: she has disappeared; but staring in vacuous astonishment toward the barnyard he sees a vanishing flash of skirts and runs after across the lot and into the high odorous cavern of the barn.

She is not in sight. Elmer stands baffled, bloodcooling, in the center of the trodden dungimpregnated earth; stands in baffled incertitude, bloodcooling in helpless and slowmounting despair for irretrievable loss of that which he had never gained, thinking *So she never meant it. I reckon she is laughing at me. I reckon I better try to scrape up that spilled sugar before Mrs Merridew gets home.* He turns toward the door, moving. As he does so a faint sound from overhead stops him. He feels a surge of triumph and fright that stops his heart for the moment. Then he can move toward the vertical ladder which leads to the loft.

Acrid scent of sweated leather, of ammonia and beasts and dry dust richly pungent; of quiet and solitude, of triumph fear change. Mounts the crude ladder, tasting again thick warm salt, hearing his heart heavy and fast, feels his bodyweight swing from shoulder to shoulder upward, then sees yellow slants of cavernous sunlight latticed and spinning with golden motes. Mounts final rung and finds her, breathless and a little frightened, in the hay.

In the throes of puberty, that dark soft trouble like a heard forgotten music or a scent or thing remembered though never smelt nor seen, that blending of dread and longing, he began consciously to draw people: not any longer lines at full liberty to assume any significance they chose, but men and women; trying to draw them and make them conform to a vague shape now somewhere back in his mind, trying to imbue them with what he believed he meant by splendor and speed. Later still, the shape in his mind became unvague concrete and alive: a girl with impregnable virginity to time or circumstance; darkhaired small and proud, casting him bones fiercely as though he were a dog, coppers as though he were a beggar leprous beside a dusty gate.

IV

He left his mother and father in Houston when he went to the war. But when he returned, someone else had the house, as usual. He went to the agent. A bright busy bald youngish man, the agent stared at Elmer's yellow hospital stick in a fretful hiatus, visibly revolving the word Hodge in his mind. Presently he rang a bell and a brisk pretty Jewess smelling of toilet water not soap, came and found the letter

[they] had left for him. The agent offered Elmer a cigarette, explaining how the war kept him too busy to smoke cigars. Our War, he called it. He talked briefly about Europe, asking Elmer a few questions such as a clothes dealer might ask of a returned African missionary, answering them himself and telling Elmer a few facts in return: that war was bad and that he was part owner of some land near Fort Worth where the British government had established a training field for aviators. But at last Elmer read the letter and went to see his people.

His father had liked Houston. But his mother would want to move though, and sitting in the daycoach among the smells of peanuts and wet babies, nursing his yellow stick from whose crook the varnish was long since handworn, he remembered and thought of that Joblike man with pity tempered by secret and disloyal relief that he himself would no more be haled over the face of the earth at what undirected compulsion drove his mother. From the vantage point of absence, of what might almost be called weaning, he wondered when she would give up: this too (compensating for the recent secret disloyalty) tempered by an abrupt fierce wave of tenderness for her bitter indomitable optimism. For he would return to Houston to live, now that his parents did not need him and hence there was none to expect him any longer to do anything. He would live in Houston and paint pictures.

He saw his father first, sitting on the small front porch; already he had known exactly what the house would look like. His father was unchanged, static, affable, resigned; age did not show on him at all, as it never had, on his cunning cherubic face, his vigorous untidy thatch. Yet Elmer discerned something else, something his father had acquired during his absence: a kind of smug unemphatic cheeriness. And then (sitting also on the porch where his father had not risen, also in a yellow varnished chair such as may be bought almost anywhere for a dollar or two) without any feeling at all, he listened to his father's cheery voice telling him that his mother, that passionate indomitable woman, was dead. While his father recited details with almost gustatory eulogism he looked about at the frame house, painted brown, set in a small dusty grassless treeless yard, recalling that long series of houses exactly like it, stretching behind him like an endless street into that time when he would wake in the dark beside Jo, with her hand sharp and fierce in his hair and her voice in the dark fierce too: "Elly, when you want to do anything, you do it, do you hear? Dont let nobody stop you," and on into the cloudy time when he had existed but could not remember it. He sat in his yellow varnished chair, nursing his yellow varnished stick, while his father talked on and on and dusk came for two hundred unhindered miles and filled the house where his mother's fretful presence seemed to linger yet like an odor, as though it had not even time for sleep, let alone for death.

He would not stay for supper, and his father told him how to find the cemetery with what Elmer believed was actual relief. "I'll get along all right," Elmer said.

"Yes," his father agreed heartily, "you'll get along all right. Folks are always glad to help soldiers. This aint no place for a young man, no-how. If I was young now, like you are—" The intimation of a world fecund, waiting to be conquered with a full rich patience, died away, and Elmer rose, thinking if his mother had been present now, who re-fused always to believe that any flesh and blood of hers could get along at all beyond the radius of her fretful kindness. Oh, I'll get along, he repeated, now to that thin spirit of her which yet lingered about the house which had at last conquered her, and he could almost hear her rejoin quickly, with a kind of triumph, That's what your sister thought—forgetting that they had never heard from Jo and that for all they knew she might be Gloria Swanson or J. P. Morgan's wife.

He didn't tell his father about Myrtle. His father would have said nothing at all, and that brisk spirit of his mother's energy would have said that Myrtle wasn't a bit too good for him. Perhaps she knows, he thought quietly, leaning on his stick beside the grave which even too seemed to partake of her wiry restless impermanence, as clothes assume the characteristics of the wearer. At the head was a small compact pal-pably marble headstone surmounted by a plump stone dove, natural size. And above it, above the untreed hill, stretched an immeasurable twilight in which huge stars hung with the impersonality of the mad and through which Adam and Eve, dead untimed out of Genesis, might still be seeking that heaven of which they had heard.

Elmer closed his eyes, savoring sorrow, bereavement, the senti-mental loneliness of conscious time. But not for long: already he was seeing against his eyelids Myrtle's longwaisted body in the lemoncolored dress, her wet red halfopen mouth, her eyes widening ineffably beneath the burnished molasses of her hair, thinking Money money money. *Any-way, I can paint now* he thought, striking his stick into the soft quiet earth *A name. Fame perhaps. Hodge, the painter*

V

Angelo is one of those young men, one of that great submerged mass, that vigorous yet heretofore suppressed and dominated class which we are told has been sickened by war. But Angelo has not been sickened by war. He had been able to perform in wartime actions which in peacetime the police, government, all those who by the accident of birth or station were able to override him, would have made impossible. Naturally war is bad, but so is traffic, and the fact that wine must be paid for and the fact that if all the women a man can imagine himself in bed with were to consent, there would not be time in the allotted three score and ten. As for getting hurt, no Austrian nor Turk nor even a carabinier is going to shoot him with a gun, and over a matter of territory he has never seen and does not wish to see. Over a woman, now—He watches the seemingly endless stream of women and young girls in hushed childish delight, expressing pleasure and approbation by sucking his breath sharply between his pursed lips. Across the narrow table his companion and patron sits: the incomprehensible American with his predilection for a liquid which to Angelo is something like that which is pumped from the bowels of ships, whom he has watched for two months now living moving breathing in some static childlike furious brooding world beyond all fact and flesh; for a moment, unseen, Angelo looks at him with a speculation which is almost contempt. But soon he is immersed again in his own constant sound of approbation and pleasure while autumn, mounting Montparnasse, permeates the traffic of Montparnasse and Raspail, teasing the breasts and thighs of young girls moving musical in the lavender glittering dusk between old walls beneath a sky like a patient etherised and dying after an operation.

Elmer has a bastard son in Houston. It happened quickly. He was eighteen, big blond awkward, with curling hair. They would go to the movies, say twice a week, since (her name is Ethel) she was popular, with several men friends of whom she would talk to him. So he accepted his secondary part before it was offered him, as if that was the position he desired, holding her hands in the warm purring twilight while she told him how the present actor on the screen was like or unlike men she knew. "You are not like other men," she told him. "With you, it's different: I dont need to be always. . . ." In the sleazy black satin which she liked,

staring at him with something fixed and speculative and completely dissimulate about her eyes. "Because you are so much younger than I am,
you see; almost two years. Like a brother. Do you see what I mean?"

"Yes," Elmer said, statically awash in the secret intimacy of their
clasped faintly sweating hands. He liked it. He liked sitting in the discreet darkness, watching the inevitable exigencies of human conduct
as established and decreed by expatriate Brooklyn button- and pants-
manufacturers, transposing her into each celluloid kiss and embrace, yet
not aware that she was doing the same thing even though he could feel
her hand lax and bloom barometrically in his own. He liked kissing her
too, in what he believed to be snatched intervals between mounting the
veranda and opening the door and again when noises upstairs had ceased
and the tablelamp would begin to make her nervous.

Then they went to four movies in succession, and then on the fifth
evening they did not go out at all. Her family was going out and she
did not like to leave the house completely untenanted. He was for starting the kissing then, but she made him take a chair across the table while
she took one opposite and told him what type of man she would someday marry; of how she would marry only because her parents expected
it of her and that she would never give herself to a man save as a matter
of duty to the husband which they would choose for her, who would
doubtless be old and wealthy: that therefore she would never lose love
because she would never have had it. That Elmer was the sort of man
she, having no brothers, had always wanted to know because she could
tell him things she couldn't even bring herself to discuss with her mother.

And so for the following weeks Elmer existed in a cloying jungle
of young female flesh damply eager and apparently unappeasable (bal-
looning earnestly at him, Elmer with that visual detachment of man suffering temporary or permanent annihilation thought of an inferiorly
inflated toy balloon with a finger thrust into it) though at first nothing
happened. But later too much happened. "Too much," she told him from
the extent of her arms, her hands locked behind his head, watching his
face with dark dissimulate intentness.

"Let's get married then," Elmer said, out of his mesmerism of en-
veloping surreptitious breasts and thighs.

"Yes," she said. Her voice was detached, untroubled, a little resigned; Elmer thought *She's not even looking at me* "I'm going to marry
Grover." This was the first he had heard of Grover.

I'm not running away, Elmer told himself, sitting in the inkblack boxcar while the springless trucks clucked and banged beneath him; it's because I just didn't think I could feel this bad. The car was going north, because there was more north to go in than south. And there was also in his mind something beyond even the surprise and the hurt and which he refused to even think was relief; what he told himself was, Maybe in the north where things are different, I can get started painting. Maybe in painting I can forget I didn't think that I could feel this bad. And again maybe he had but belatedly reached that point at which his sister and brothers had one by one broken the spell of progression which their mother had wound about them like the string around a top.

Oklahoma knew him; he worked in Missouri wheatfields; he begged bread for two days in Kansas City. At Christmas he was in Chicago, spending day after day erect and sound asleep before pictures in galleries where there was no entrance fee; night after night sitting in railroad stations until the officials waked them all and the ones who had no tickets would walk the bitter galeridden streets to another station and so repeat. Now and then he ate.

In January he was in a Michigan lumbercamp. For all his big body, he worked in the roaring steamopaque cookshack which smelled always soporific of food and damp wool, scrubbing the bellies of aluminum pots which in the monotonous drowse of the long mornings reminded him of the empty wood dish of blue in the paint box of his childhood.

At night there was plenty of rough paper. He used charcoal until he found a box of blue washing powder. With that and with coffeedregs and with a bottle of red ink belonging to the cook, he began to work in color. Soon the teamsters, axmen, and sawyers discovered that he could put faces on paper. One by one he drew them, by commission, each describing the kind of clothing, dress suit, racecourse check, or mackinaw in which he wished to be portrayed, sitting patiently until the work was finished, then holding with his mates gravely profane aesthetic debate.

When February broke, he had grown two inches and filled out; his body was now the racehorse body of nineteen; sitting about the steaming bunkhouse the men discussed him with the impersonality of surgeons or horseracers. Soon now the rigid muscles of snow would laxen, though reluctant yet. Gluts of snow would slip heavily soundless from the boughs of spruce and hemlock and the boughs would spring darkly free against the slipping snow; from the high blue soon now the cries of geese would drift like falling leaves, wild, fantastical, and sad. In the talk of sex nightly growing more and more frequent about the bunkhouse stove,

Elmer's body in relation to women was discussed; one night, through some vague desire to establish himself and formally end his apprenticeship to manhood, he told them about Ethel in Houston. They listened, spitting gravely on the hissing orange stove. When he had finished they looked at one another with weary tolerance. Then one said kindly: "Dont you worry, bub. It's harder to get one than you think."

Then it was March. The log drive was in the river, and over the last meal in the bunkhouse they looked quietly about at one another, who perhaps would never see the other faces again, while between stove and table Elmer and the cook moved. The cook was Elmer's immediate superior and czar of the camp. He reminded Elmer of someone; he coddled him and harried him and cursed him with savage kindness: Elmer came at last to dread him with a kind of static hypnosis, letting the cook direct his actions, not joyously but with resignation. He was wiry and hightempered; when men came in late to meals he flew into an almost homicidal rage. They treated him with bluff caution, shouting him down by sheer volume while he cursed them, but not offering to touch him. But he kept the kitchen clean and fed them well and mended their clothes for them; when a man was injured he tended the invalid in a frenzy of skillful gentleness, cursing him and his forebears and posterity for generations.

When the meal was over, he asked Elmer what he intended to do now. Elmer had not thought of that; suddenly he seemed to see his destiny thrust back into his arms like a strange baby in a railroad waitingroom. The cook kicked the stove door to savagely. "Let's go to that goddam war. What do you say?"

He certainly reminded Elmer of someone, especially when he came to see Elmer the night before Elmer's battalion entrained for Halifax. He sat on Elmer's bunk and cursed the war, the Canadian government, the C.E.F. corps brigade battalion and platoon, himself and Elmer past present and to come, for they had made him a corporal and a cook. "So I aint going," he said. "I guess I wont never get over. So you'll just have to do the best you can by yourself. You can do it. By God, dont you take nothing off of them, these Canucks or them Limey bastards neither. You're good as any of them, even if you dont have no stripes on your sleeve or no goddam brass acorns on your shoulders. You're good as any of them and a dam sight better than most, and dont you forget it. Here. Take this. And dont lose it." It was a tobacco tin. It contained needles of all sizes, thread, a pair of short scissors, a pack of adhesive tape, and a dozen of those objects which the English wittily call French letters and the French call wittily English letters. He departed, still cursing. Elmer never saw him again.

Soldiering on land had been a mere matter of marching here and there in company and keeping his capbadge and tunic buttons and rifle clean and remembering whom to salute. But aboard ship, where space was restricted, they were learning about combat. It was with hand grenades and Elmer was afraid of them. He had become reconciled to the rifle, with which a man aimed and pulled the trigger with immediate results, but not this object, to which a man did something infinitesimal and then held it in his hand, counting three in the waiting silence before throwing it. He told himself that when he had to, he would pull the pin and throw it at once, until the stocky sergeant-major with eyes like glass marbles and a ribbon on his breast told them how the Hun had a habit of catching the bomb and tossing it back like a baseball.

"Nah," the sergeant-major said, roving his dead eyes about their grave faces, "count three, like this." He did something infinitesimal to the bomb while they watched him in quiet horrified fascination. Then he pushed the pin back and tossed the bomb lightly in his hand. "Like that, see?"

Then someone nudged Elmer. He quit swallowing his hot salt and took the bomb and examined it in a quiet horror of curiosity. It was oval, its smug surface broken like a pineapple, dull and solid: a comfortable feel, a compact solidity almost sensuous to the palm. The sergeant-major's voice said sharply from a distance: "Come on. Like I showed you."

"Yes, sir," Elmer's voice said while he watched his hands, those familiar hands which he could no longer control, toying with the bomb, nursing it. Then his apish hands did something infinitesimal and became immobile in bland satisfaction and Elmer stared in an utterly blank and utterly timeless interval at the object in his palm.

"Throw it, you bloody bastard!" the man beside him shouted before he died. Elmer stared at his hand, waiting; then the hand decided to obey him and swung backward. But the hand struck a stanchion before it reached the top of the arc and he saw the face of the man next to him like a suspended mask at his shoulder, utterly expressionless, and the dull oval object in the air between them growing to monstrous size like an obscene coconut. Then his body told him to turn his back and lie down.

How green it looks, he thought sickly. Later, while he lay for months on his face while his back healed and young women and old looked upon his naked body with a surprising lack of interest, he remembered the amazing greenness of the Mersey shores. That was about all he had to think of. These people didn't even know where Texas was, taking it to be a town in British Columbia apparently as they talked to him kindly in their clipped jerky way. On a neighboring cot and usually delirious was a youth of his own age, an aviator with a broken back and both feet burned off. It's as hard to kill folks as it is to get them, Elmer thought, thinking *So this is war*: white rows of beds in a white tunnel of a room, grayclad nurses kind but uninterested, then a wheelchair among other wheelchairs and now and then lady lieutenants in blue cloaks with brass insignia; thinking *But how green it looked* since it was quiet now, since the aviator was gone. Whether he died or not Elmer neither knew nor cared.

It seemed greener than ever when he saw it again from shipdeck as they dropped down with the tide. And with England at last behind, in retrospect it seemed greener still, with an immaculate peace which no war could ever disturb. While they felt through the Zone and into the gray Atlantic again he slept and waked, touching at times his head where endless pillows had worn his hair away, wondering if it would grow out again.

It was March again. For eleven months he had not thought of painting. Before they reached midocean it was April; one day off Newfoundland they learned by wireless that America had entered the war. His back did not hurt so much as it itched.

He spent some of his backpay in New York. He not only visited public and semipublic galleries, but through the kindness of a preserved fat woman he spent afternoons in private galleries and homes. His sponsor, a canteen worker, had once been soft pink and curved, but now she was long since the wife of a dollarayear man in Washington, with an income of fifty thousand. She had met Elmer in the station canteen and was quite kind to him, commiserating the mothy remnant of his once curling hair. Then he went south. With his limp and his yellow stick he remained in New Orleans in an aimless hiatus. Nowhere he had to go, nowhere he wanted to go, he existed not lived in a voluptuous inertia mocking all briskness and haste: grave vitiating twilights soft and oppressive as smoke upon the city, hanging above the hushed eternal river and the docks where he walked smelling rich earth in overquick fecundity—sugar and fruit, resin and dusk and heat, like the sigh of a dark and passionate woman no longer young.

He was halted one day on Canal Street by a clotting of people. A hoarse man stood on a chair in the center of the throng, a fattish sweating prosperous man making a Liberty Loan speech, pleading on the streets for money like a beggar. And suddenly, across the clotting heads, he saw a slight taut figure as fiercely erect as ever, watching the orator and the audience with a fierce disgust. "Jo!" Elmer cried. "*Jo!*"

money we earn, work and sweat for, so that our children   not have to face what we are now   able to earn this money? By the protection which this country, this American nation showing the old dying civilizations   freedom   she calls on you what will you say

The crowd stirred in a slow hysteria and Elmer lunged his maimed body, trying to thrust through toward where he still saw the fierce poise of her small hat. "For Christ's sake," someone said: a youth in the new campaign hat and the still creased khaki of recent enlistment; "whatcher in such a rush about?"

boys over there   finish it before others must die   duty of civilization to stamp forever

"Maybe he wants he should enlist," another, a plump Jewish man clutching a new thousand dollar bill in his hand, shrieked. "This var— In Lithuania I have seen yet O God," he shrieked in Elmer's face.

"Pardon me. Pardon me." Elmer chanted, trying to thrust through, trying to keep in sight the unmistakable poise of that head.

"Well, he's going in the wrong direction," the soldier said, barring the way. "Recruiting office is over yonder, buddy." Across his shoulder Elmer caught another glimpse of the hat, lost it again.

price we must pay for having become the greatest nation   Word of God in the Book itself

The crowd surged again, elbowing the filaments of fire which lived along his spine. "This var!" the Jew shrieked at him again. "Them boys getting killed already O God. It vill make business: In Lithuania I have seen—"

"Look out," a third voice said quickly; "he's lame; dont you see his stick?"

"Yes, sure," the soldier said. "They all get on crutches when assembly blows."

"Pardon me. Pardon me." Elmer chanted amid the laughter. The black hat was not in sight now. He was sweating too, striving to get through, his spine alive now with fiery ants. The orator remarked the commotion. He saw the soldier and Elmer's sick straining face; he paused, mopping his neck.

"What's that?" he said. "Wants to enlist? Come here, brother. Make room, people; let him come up here." Elmer tried to hold back as the hands touched began to push and draw him forward as the crowd opened.

"I just want to pass," he said. But the hands thrust him on. He looked over his shoulder, thinking, I am afraid I am going to puke, thinking, I'll go. I'll go. Only for God's sake dont touch my back again. The black hat was gone. He began to struggle; at last his back had passed the stage where he could feel at all. "Let me go, goddam you!" he said whitely. "I have already been—"

But already the orator, leaning down, caught his hand; other hands lifted and pushed him up onto the platform while once more the sweating man turned to the crowd and spoke. "Folks, look at this young man here. Some of us, most of us, are young and well and strong: we can go. But look at this young man here, a cripple, yet he wants to defy the beast of intolerance and blood. See him: his stick, limping. Shall it be said of us who are sound in body and limb, that we have less of courage and less of love of country than this boy? And those of us who are unfit or old; those of us who cannot go—"

"No, no," Elmer said, jerking at the hand which the other held. "I just want to pass: I have already been—"

"—men, women, let everyone of us do what this boy, lame in the very splendor of young manhood, would do. If we cannot go ourselves, let everyone of us say, I have sent one man to the front; that though we ourselves are old and unfit, let everyone of us say, I have sent one soldier to preserve this American heritage which our fathers created for us out of their own suffering and preserved to us with their own blood; that I have done what I could that this heritage may be handed down unblemished to my children, to my children's children yet unborn—" The hoarse inspired voice went on, sweeping speaker and hearers upward into an immolation of words, a holocaust without heat, a conflagration with neither light nor sound and which would leave no ashes.

Elmer sought for another glimpse of that small hat, that fierce disdainful face, but in vain. It was gone, and the crowd, swept up once more in the speaker's eloquence, as suddenly forgot him. But she was gone, as utterly as a flame blown out. He wondered in sick despair if she had seen, not recognising him and not understanding. The crowd let him through now.

Dont let the German Beast think that we, you and I, refused, failed, dared not, while our boys our sons are fighting the good fight bleeding and suffering and dying to wipe forever from the world

He shifted his stick to the palm which had become callous to it. He saw the Jew again, still trying to give away his thousand dollar bill; heard diminishing behind him the voice hoarse and endless, passionate, fatuous, and sincere. His back began to hurt again.

VI

Musical with motion Montparnasse and Raspail: evening dissolves swooning: a thin odor of heliotrope become visible: with lights spangling yellow green and red. Angelo gains Elmer's attention at last and with his thumb indicates at a table nearby heavy eyes in sober passive allure, and a golden smile above a new shoddy fur neckpiece. He continues to nudge Elmer, making his rich pursed mouthsound: the grave one stares at Elmer in stoic invitation, the other one crops her gold-rimmed teeth at him before he looks quickly away. Yet still Angelo grimaces at him and nods rapidly, but Elmer is obdurate, and Angelo sits back in his chair with an indescribable genuflexion of weary disgust.

"Six weeks ago," he says in Italian, "they fetched you into the political dungeon of Venice, where I already was, and took from you your belt and shoelaces. You did not know why. Two days later I removed myself, went to your consul, who in turn removed you. Again you did not know how or why. And now since twenty-three days we are in Paris. In Paris, mind you. And now what do we do? We sit in caffees, we eat, we sit in caffees; we go and sleep. This we have done save for the seven days of one week which we spent in the forest of Meudon while you made a picture of three trees and an inferior piece of an inferior river— this too apparently for what reason you do not know, since you have done nothing with it, since for thirteen days now you have shown it to no one but have carried it in that affair beside your leg, from one caffee to another, sitting over it as though it were an egg and you a hen. Do you perhaps hope to hatch others from it, eh? or perhaps you are waiting until age will make of it an old master? And this in Paris. In Paris, mind. We might as well be in heaven. In America even, where there is nothing save money and work."

Musical with motion and lights and sound, with taxis flatulent pale-vaporous in the glittering dusk. Elmer looks again: the two women have risen and they now move away between the close tables with never a backward glance; again Angelo makes his sound of exasperation explosive but resigned. But musical with girlmotion Montparnasse and Raspail and soon Angelo, his friend and patron forgotten in the proffered flesh, expresses his pleasure and approbation between his pursed lips, leaving his patron to gaze lonely and musing through the gray opposite building and upon that Texas hill where he stood beside his mother's grave and thought of Myrtle Monson and money and of Hodge, the painter.

Someone died and left the elder Hodge two thousand dollars. He bought a house with it, almost in revenge, it might be said. It was in a small town innocent of trees where, Hodge said in humorous paraphrase, there were more cows and less milk and more rivers and less water and you could see further and see less than anywhere under the sun. Mrs Hodge, pausing in her endless bitter activity, gazed at her husband sedentary, effacing, as inevitable and inescapable as disease, in amazement, frankly shocked at last. "I thought you was looking for a house that suited you," Hodge said.

She looked about at those identical rooms, at the woodwork (door-frames and windows painted a thin new white which only brought into higher relief the prints of hands long moved away to print other identical houses about the earth), at walls papered with a serviceable tan which showed the minimum of stains and drank light like a sponge. "You did it just for meanness," she said bitterly, going immediately about the business of unpacking, for the last time.

"Why, aint you always wanted a home of your own to raise your children in?" Hodge said. Mrs Hodge suspended a folded quilt and looked about at the room which the two older boys would probably never see, which Jo would have fled on sight; and now Elmer, the baby, gone to a foreign war.

It could not have been nature nor time nor space, who was impervious to flood and fire and time and distance, indomitable in the face of lease contracts which required them to rent for a whole year to get the house at all. It must have been the fact of possession, rooting, that broke her spirit as a caged bird's breaks. Whatever it was, she tried to make morningglories grow upon the sawfretted porch, then she gave up. Hodge buried her on the treeless intimation of a hill, where unhampered winds could remind her of distance when she inevitably sickened to move again, though dead, and where time and space could mock at her inability to quicken and rise and stir; and he wrote Elmer, who was lying then on his face in a plaster cast in a British hospital while his spine hurt and the flesh inside the cast became warmly fluid like a film of spittle and he could smell it too, that his mother was dead and that he (Hodge) was as usual. He added that he had bought a house, forgetting to say where. Later, and with a kind of macabre thoughtfulness, he forwarded the re-turned letter to Elmer three months after Elmer had visited home for that brief afternoon and returned to Houston.

After his wife's death Hodge, cooking (he was a good cook, better than his wife had ever been) and doing his own sloven housework, would sit after supper on the porch, whittling a plug of tobacco against tomorrow's pipe, and sigh. Immediately that sigh would smack of something akin to relief, and he would reprimand himself in quick respect for the dead. And then he would not be so sure what that sigh signified. He contemplated the diminishing future, those years in which he would never again have to go anywhere unless he pleased, and he knew a mild discomfort. Had he too got from that tireless optimist an instinct for motion, a gadfly of physical progression? Had she, dying, robbed him of any gift for ease? As he never went to church he was intensely re-ligious, and he contemplated with troubled static alarm that day when he too should pass beyond the veil and there find his wife waiting for him, all packed up and ready to move.

And then, when that had worn off and he had decided since he could not help that, to let Heaven's will be done since not only was that best but he couldn't do anything about it anyway, three men in boots came and, to his alarmed and pained astonishment, dug an oilwell in his chickenyard so near that he could stand in the kitchen door and spit into it. So he had to move again, or be washed bodily out of the county. But this time he merely moved the house itself, turning it around so he could sit on the veranda and watch the moiling activity in his erstwhile henyard with static astonishment and, if truth be told, consternation. He had given Elmer's Houston address to one of the booted men, asking him if he would mind looking Elmer up next time he was in Houston and telling him about it. So all he had to do then was to sit on his front porch and wait and muse upon the unpredictableness of circumstance. For instance, it had permitted him to run out of matches tonight, so instead of shredding his whole plug for smoking, he reserved enough to chew until someone came tomorrow who had matches; and sitting on the veranda of the first thing larger than a foldingbed which he had ever owned, with his most recent tribulation skeletoned and ladderlatticed high again the defunctive sky, he chewed his tobacco and spat outward into the immaculate dusk. He had not chewed in years and so he was a trifle awkward at first. But soon he was able to arc tobacco juice in a thin brown hissing, across the veranda and onto a parallelogram of troubled earth where someone had once tried to make something grow.

The New Orleans doctor sent Elmer to New York. There he spent two years while they fixed his spine, and another year recovering from it, lying again on his face with behind his mind's eye the image of a retreating shortlegged body in a lemoncolored dress, but not retreating fast now, since already, though lying on his face beneath weights, he was moving faster. Before departing however he made a brief visit to Texas. His father had not changed, not aged: Elmer found him resigned and smugly philosophical as ever beneath this new blow which Fate had dealt him. The only change in the establishment was the presence of a cook, a lean yellow woman no longer young, who regarded Elmer's presence with a mixture of assurance and alarm; inadvertently he entered his father's bedroom and saw that the bed, still unmade at noon, had obviously been occupied by two people. But he had no intention of interfering, nor any wish to; already he had turned his face eastward; already thinking and hope and desire had traversed the cold restless gray Atlantic, thinking *Now I have the money. And now fame. And then Myrtle*

And so he has been in Paris three weeks. He has not yet joined a class; neither has he visited the Louvre since he does not know where the Louvre is, though he and Angelo have crossed the Place de la Concorde several times in cabs. Angelo, with his instinct for glitter and noise, promptly discovered the Exposition; he took his patron there. But Elmer does not consider these to be painting. Yet he lingered, went through it all, though telling himself with quick loyalty, It wont be Myrtle who would come here; it will be Mrs Monson who will bring her, make her come. He has no doubt but that they are in Paris. He has been in Europe long enough to know that the place to look for an American in Europe is Paris; that when they are anywhere else, it is merely for the weekend.

When he reached Paris, he knew two words of French: he had learned them from the book which he bought at the shop where he bought his paints. (It was in New York. "I want the best paints you have," he told the young woman, who wore an artist's smock. "This set has twenty tubes and four brushes, and this one has thirty tubes and six brushes. We have one with sixty tubes, if you would like that," she said. "I want the best," Elmer said. "You mean you want the one with the most tubes and brushes?" she said. "I want the best," Elmer said. So they stood looking at one another at this impasse and then the proprietor himself came, also in an artist's smock. He reached down the set with the sixty tubes—which, incidentally, the French at Ventimiglia made Elmer pay a merchant's import duty on. "Of course he vants the best," the proprietor said. "Cant you look at him and tell that? Listen, I vill tell you. This is the vun you vant; I vill tell you. How many pictures can you paint vith ten tubes? Eh?" "I dont know," Elmer said. "I just want the best." "Sure you do," the proprietor said; "the vun that vill paint the most pictures. Come; you tell me how many pictures you can paint vith ten tubes; I tell you how many you can paint vith sixty." "I'll take it," Elmer said.)

The two words were *rive gauche*. He told them to the taxi driver at the Gare de Lyon, who said, "That is true, monsieur," watching Elmer with brisk attentiveness, until Angelo spoke to him in a bastard language of which Elmer heard *millionnaire americain* without then recognising it. "Ah," the driver said. He hurled Elmer's baggage and then Angelo into the cab, where Elmer already was, and drove them to the Hotel Leutetia. So this is Paris, Elmer thought, to the mad and indistinguishable careening of houses and streets, to canopied cafes and placarded comfort stalls and other vehicles pedaled or driven by other madmen, while Elmer sat a little forward, gripping the seat, with on his face an expression of static concern. The concern was still there when the cab halted before the hotel. It had increased appreciably when he entered the hotel and looked about; now he was downright qualmed. This is not right, he thought. But already it was too late; Angelo had made once his pursed sound of pleasure and approbation, speaking to a man in the dress uniform of a field marshall in his bastard tongue, who in turn bellowed sternly, *"Encore un millionnaire americain."* It was too late; already five men in uni-

form and not were forcing him firmly but gently to sign his name to an
affidavit as to his existence, and he thinking *What I wanted was a garret*
thinking with a kind of humorous despair *It seems that what I really
want is poverty*

He escaped soon though, to Angelo's surprise, astonishment, and
then shrugged fatalistic resignation. He took to prowling about the
neighborhood, with in his hand the book from which he had learned
rive gauche, looking up at garret windows beneath leads and then at the
book again with helpless dismay which he knew would soon become
despair and then resignation to the gold braid, the funereal frock coats,
the piled carpets, and the discreet lights among which fate and Angelo
had cast him, as though his irrevocable horoscope had been set and closed
behind him with the clash of that barred door in the Palazzo Ducale in
Venice. He had not even opened the box of paints. Already he had paid
a merchant's duty on them; he could well have continued to be the merchant which the French had made him and sold them. Then one day
he strayed into the Rue Servandoni. He was merely passing through it,
hopeful still with fading hope, when he looked through open doors, into
a court. Even in the fatal moment he was telling himself *It's just another
hotel. The only difference will be that living here will be a little more
tediously exigent and pettily annoying* But again it was too late; already
he had seen her. She stood, hands on hips in a clean harsh dress, scolding
at an obese man engaged statically with a mop—a thin woman of forty
or better, wiry, with a harried indefatigable face; for an instant he was
his own father eight thousand miles away in Texas, not even knowing
that he was thinking *I might have known she would not stay dead* not
even thinking with omniscient perspicuity *I wont even need the book*

He didn't need the book. She wrote on a piece of paper the rate for
the rooms; she could have made it anything she wished. He told himself
that, housed again, static, dismayed, and relieved, while she nagged at
him about his soiled clothes, examining and mending them, prowling
furiously among his things and cleaning his room furiously (Angelo lived
on the floor above him) while she jabbed French words and phrases into
his mouth and made him repeat them. *Maybe I can get away some night,*
he told himself. *Maybe I can escape after she is asleep and find an attic
on the other side of town;* knowing that he would not, knowing that
already he had given up, surrendered to her; that, like being tried for a
crime, no man ever escapes the same fate twice.

And so soon (the next day he went to the American Express Co. and left his new address) his mind was saying only Paris. Paris. The Louvre, Cluny, the Salon, besides the city itself: the same skyline and cobbles, the same kindlooking marbles thighed as though for breeding— all that merry sophisticated coldblooded dying city to which Cézanne was dragged now and then like a reluctant cow, where Manet and Monet fought points of color and line; where Matisse and Picasso still painted: tomorrow he would join a class. That night he opened the box of paints for the first time. Yet, looking at them, he paused again. The tubes lay in serried immaculate rows, blunt, solid, torpedolike, latent. There is so much in them, he thought. There is everything in them. They can do anything; thinking of Hals and Rembrandt; all the tall deathless giants of old time, so that he turned his head suddenly, as though they were in the room, filling it, making it seem smaller than a hencoop, watching him, so that he closed the box again with quiet and aghast dismay. Not yet, he told himself. I am not worthy yet. But I can serve. I will serve. I want to serve, suffer too, if necessary.

The next day he bought watercolors and paper (for the first time since reaching Europe he showed no timorousness nor helplessness in dealing with foreign shopkeepers) and he and Angelo went to Meudon. He did not know where he was going; he merely saw a blue hill and pointed it out to the taxi driver. They spent seven days there while he painted his landscape. He destroyed three of them before he was satisfied, telling himself while his muscles cramped and his eyes blurred with weariness, I want it to be hard. I want it to be cruel, taking something out of me each time. I want never to be completely satisfied with any of them, so that I shall always paint again. So when he returned to the Rue Servandoni, with the finished picture in the new portfolio, on that first night when he looked at the tall waiting spectres, he was humble still but no longer aghast.

So now I have something to show him, he thinks, nursing his now lukewarm beer, while beside him Angelo's pursed sound has become continuous. Now, when I have found who is the best master in Paris, when I go to him and say Teach me to paint, I shall not go emptyhanded; thinking *And then fame. And then Myrtle* while twilight mounts Montparnasse gravely beneath the year turning reluctant as a young bride to the old lean body of death. It is then that he feels the first lazy, implacable waking of his entrails.

VII

Angelo's pursed sound has become continuous: an open and bland ur-
banity, until he sees that his patron has risen, the portfolio under his
arm. "We eat-a, eh?" he says, who in three weeks has learned both of
French and English, while Elmer has not yet learned how to ask where
the Louvre and the Salon are. Then he indicates Elmer's beer. "No
feeneesh?"

"I've got to go," Elmer says; there is upon his face that rapt, in-
turned expression of a dyspeptic, as though he is listening to his insides,
which is exactly what Elmer is doing; already he moves away. At once
a waiter appears; Elmer still with that rapt, not exactly concerned expression but without any lost motion, gives the waiter a banknote and
goes on; it is Angelo who stays the waiter and gets change and leaves a
European tip which the waiter snatches up with contempt and says something to Angelo in French; for reply and since his patron is going on,
walking a little faster than ordinary, Angelo merely takes time to reverse
his sound of approbation by breathing outward through his pursed lips
instead of inward.

And now musical with motion Michel also, though it is in the Place
de l'Observatoire that Angelo overtakes his patron, where even then he
still has to trot to keep up. Angelo looks about, his single eyebrow lifted.
"No eat-a now?" he says.

"No," Elmer says. "The hotel."

"Otel?" Angelo says. "Eat-a first, eh?'

"No!" Elmer says. His tone is fretted, though not yet harried and
not yet desperate. "Hotel. I've got to retire."

"Rittire?" Angelo says.

"Cabinet," Elmer says.

"Ah," Angelo says; "cabinet." He glances up at his patron's concerned, at once very alert and yet inwardlooking face; he grasps Elmer
by the elbow and begins to run. They run for several steps before Elmer
can jerk free; his face is now downright alarmed.

"Goddamn it, let go!" He cries.

"True," Angelo says in Italian. "In your situation, running is not
what a man wants. I forgot. Slow and easy does it, though not too slow.
Coraggio," he says, "we come to her soon." And presently the pay station is in sight. "Voila!" Angelo says. Again he takes his patron's arm,
though not running; again Elmer frees his arm, drawing away; again

Angelo indicates the station, his single eyebrow high on his skull, his eyes melting, concerned, inquiring; again he reverses his sound of approbation, indicating the station with his thumb.

"No!" Elmer says. His voice is desperate now, his expression desperate yet determined. "Hotel!" In the Garden, where Elmer walks with long harried strides and Angelo trots beside him, twilight is gray and unsibilant among the trees; in the long dissolving arras people are already moving toward the gates. They pass swiftly the carven figures in the autumntinged dusk, pass the bronze ones in solemn nowformless gleams secretive and brooding; both trotting now, they pass Verlaine in stone, and Chopin, that sick feminine man like snow rotting under a dead moon; already the moon of death stands overhead, pleasant and affable and bloodless as a procuress. Elmer enters the Rue Vaugirard, trotting with that harried care, as though he carries dynamite; it is Angelo who restrains him until there is a gap in the traffic.

Then he is in the Rue Servandoni. He is running now, down the cobbled slope. He is no longer thinking *What will people think of me* It is as though he now carries life, volition, all, cradled dark and sightless in his pelvic girdle, with just enough of his intelligence remaining to tell him when he reaches the door. And there, just emerging, hatless, is his landlady.

"Ah, Monsieur Odge," she says. "I just this moment search for you. You have visitors; the female millionaires American Monson wait you in your chamber."

"Yes," Elmer says, swerving to run past her, not even aware that he is speaking to her in English. "In a minute I will—" Then he pauses; he glares at her with his harried desperate face. "Mohsong?" he says. "Mohsong?" then: "Monson! *Monson!*" Clutching the portfolio he jerks his wild glare upward toward his window, then back to the landlady, who looks at him in astonishment. "Keep them there!" he shouts at her with savage ferocity. "Do you hear? Keep them there! Don't let them get away. In a minute I will—" But already he has turned, running toward the opposite side of the court. Still galloping, the portfolio under his arm, he rushes up the dark stairs while somewhere in his desperate mind thinking goes quietly *There will be somebody already in it. I know there will* thinking with desperate despair that he is to lose Myrtle twice because of his body: once because of his back which would not let him dance, and now because of his bowels which will give her to think that he is running away. But the cabinet is empty; his very sigh of relief is the echo of his downwardsighing trousers about his legs, thinking Thank God. Thank God. Myrtle. *Myrtle.* Then this too flees; he seems to see his life supine before the secret implacable eyeless life of his own entrails like an immolation, saying like Samuel of old: Here I am. Here I am. Then they release him. He wakes again and reaches his hand toward the niche where scraps of newspaper are kept and he becomes utterly immobile while time seems to rush past him with a sound almost like that of a shell.

He whirls; he looks at the empty niche, surrounded by the derisive whistling of that dark wind as though it were the wind which had blown the niche empty. He does not laugh; his bowels too have emptied themselves for haste. He claps his hand to his breast pocket; he becomes immobile again with his arm crossing his breast as though in salute; then with a dreadful urgency he searches through all his pockets, producing two broken bits of crayon, a dollar watch, a few coins, his room key, the tobacco tin (worn silver smooth now) containing the needles and thread and such which the cook had given him ten years ago in Canada. That is all. And so his hands cease. Imbued for the moment with a furious life and need of their own, they die; and he sits for a moment looking quietly at the portfolio on the floor beside him; again, as when he watched them fondle the handgrenade on board the transport in 1916, he watches them take up the portfolio and open it and take out the picture. But only for the moment, because again haste descends upon him and he no longer watches his hands at all, thinking Myrtle. Myrtle. *Myrtle.*

And now the hour, the moment, has come. Within the Garden, beyond the dusk and the slow gateward throng, the hidden bugle begins. Out of the secret dusk the grave brazen notes come, overtaking the people, passing the caped policemen at the gates, and about the city dying where beneath the waxing and bloodless moon evening has found itself. Yet still within the formal twilight of the trees the bugle sounds, measured, arrogant, and sad.

H. E. Francis

Her

HIS shack was on a small knob of land that bulged into the narrow finger of the crick. On land the Catholic and Protestant cemeteries separated it from the township, and one road, which wound lengthily around the water's edge, connected him with the village. But the buildings were just across the water and they seemed to bob scarcely out of reach. The largest was the hospital, situated at the very rim, facing his shack. Nights, it was a collection of ordered stars clustered double by being thrown down into the water and shimmering like a handful of silver fire. But days, it was a serene beige, not too obtrusive, comfortingly close in fact. You felt the people, even when you didn't see them.

He looked away from it, into the sink, and decided he wouldn't shave yet. And he neglected making the cot he'd slept on every night this week, set up in the kitchen almost a year ago New Year's, when the Ladd boy dropped in and got drunk and couldn't make it out the kitchen door standing. The bedroom door was closed, and he was not hungry enough to drive himself to the stove.

He went out into the six o'clock morning. The dew sparkled in the early light as if the water, crept in by night, had fled back and left markings everywhere. Between the grass blades the Long Island sand looked covered with a fine wet silt. The whitewashed tubs were thick with geranium leaves, and their pungent earth-scent hovered almost alive over them. He stopped and stared out across the thickening bushes. Down under, farther in the woods that hid the house from the road, they'd be rich with blackberries this summer because they weren't as exposed to the preying birds. He heard them heralding the morning everywhere. Distantly, white as a ghost, a gull floated down behind the trees and led

his eyes to the front lawn, which lay like a road, continued by the morning sun, that spanned the water to the hospital. The sun was up full and
the dead eyes of the hospital acquired a sudden morning wetness, as if
they were opening to life. The sight quickened his pulse and a new movement came into his legs. They wanted to go somewhere, and he was not
sure where to direct them.

He looked for the rabbits, but they were not on the lawn this morning. He thought, listening, he heard them in the underbrush, but he knew
better. It was the welcome sight of them that greeted his eyes every
morning in this weather; and he'd gone so far as to set out nibblings—
against *her* wishes, of course. ("You'll have them coupling all over the
place. Then what'll we do? We'll be overridden by the things." Though
she always meant, really, "Do what you think.") The pan was untouched. He hoped they were not far. They'd be getting into the Bartons' fields across the road, down toward the beach, and that wouldn't do.
He felt a mild propriety about the rabbits. The Bartons would be coming
to him to shoot the critters. She knew he'd never do that. She always
told them so too, though they tended to discount what she said, which
made her say it all the louder. When he confronted her with it, she said,
"You don't have to marry me to give me authority. Marriage is just
clothes. You know that. And clothes are phony dignity. When you have
to wear clothes for dignity, you've got none." *She* told him. "Oh, let's
don't talk about getting married. You're satisfied, aren't you?"

He picked up a shovel and chucked it against the house, too loud
perhaps—it must have scared the chickens, because when he went into
the coop, they clucked warily at arm's length from him. He took out
fourteen eggs, but did not go back into the house—he merely set the basin
outside the back door. The door didn't sag anymore—all winter it had
been tight, added insulation to the house, and she'd got him to make re-
placeable screens as subs for the winter windows so that they'd have more
air in summer and more light in winter.

He thought he'd go into town with Jessie Tull, when he came for
his eggs, rather than bike in. That would be a couple of hours yet. Besides, she'd be sleeping this early and he couldn't bring her home until
ten or so at least, the doctor said. He was rather glad she insisted they
didn't call the children—hers. She'd a few dollars put away and they
were vultures enough to hurry over on the next ferry and make him
feed them for as long as they could get away with staying. She knew it
too. She'd not have it—and, *he* made it plain to her, neither would he—

the sponging part of it. Though he'd be glad to send for them. Insisted, in fact. "Vultures," she said, that's all—which meant *no*. So now they'd have their usual quiet together. She had gained ten pounds in this country—the salt water, the hardy life, and the summer sun had done a job. But her attack of gallstones. . . . He saw her stumble, so it looked anyway, grab her side, and go down on her knees. Not praying. He knew better, but it looked that at first. When he ran, she threw up one arm to him, propped herself against the sawed-off oak stump, and laughed, "It's all right, you old fool. Don't look so worried." She got away with it—calling him that: "old fool." He *was* too. Sixty-eight. It was the Suffolk County joke this year—*thirty-nine and sixty-eight, plug her now, it's getting late*, they sang. But when people met her in person, they kept their mouths shut—the sight of her set them back, *he* could tell you.

He'd picked her up in Connecticut in a neighborhood beer parlor— in New London, where he'd gone on a weekend excursion rate to see his son Timmy—he wouldn't forget that day, a hell of a battle with Tim and his wife over Beverly Wilkes. They always called their mother by her maiden name as if he'd never married *her* either. "What the hell you arguin' about a dead woman for?" he cried. "Jesus! I was glad to get rid of her. She was just like you, Timmy, all mouth and every bit of it in use twenty-four hours a day." That started it. "She's *my* mother," Timmy cried. "You've got no right—" "She was *my* wife, fool that I was, I'm the only one who has rights, and if you'd known her for long, you'd find she was no mother to her own bleeding son. She'd have been just as glad if I'd tossed you to the garbage man when she had you, that's the mother *she* was. And I've no shame saying it either. There's truth in this world and not much more, I'm here to tell you."

The argument drove him to the tavern—a bunch of locals gathered for good fun—and there he saw Billie, a thin bird of a woman, frail but with a good solid head, firm cheek bones—high and proud they were— and a feathernest of the finest silk-gray hair, cut clean as a young boy's, falling with one wave over her forehead; it hung almost between her eyes but she wouldn't cut that.

"I suppose she's just a bitch out for your pocketbook," Tim said to him as he packed, with the whole damn clan behind, belching ugly words at him.

"Pocketbook! A measly government pension—you call that money, do you?" The last goddamn time *he'd* set foot in New London. Relatives! As ugly as warts from toad's piss, that's what.

"You own your own house—and how do we know what you've stashed away all these years. You made enough painting all that time, God knows."

"Not for you I didn't!" They wouldn't forget how he slammed *that* door.

Whether she wanted the house or not, *he* couldn't believe it. The thing that made him so sure—and they learned it too; she wasn't for secrets—was that she wouldn't marry him. "That way I'll be free to go when I want, or when you want me to. That'll show them. They think you can't care about anyone, they think you can't get old and still live whole, do they? Well, we'll show them. Yes," she added, "don't tilt your eyes at me, Hulse Williams. I said *old*. You *are*. That's the first step. Admit everything. Then live." She set about cleaning out the bachelor dust, dirt, crud and scud, the years of his life since Beverly Wilkes—twenty at that—and showed him the raw skin of the place he'd built himself all those years ago. What his kids didn't know, and she did, was that the house wasn't his at all—it was sold to the Knights years before and he had a life lease to caretake the fields around. They had the last laugh on the whole lot of them in New London.

The city was straight across the Sound—he faced the direction, his back to the hospital, and smiled at the rift between. Back, it was nearly a perfect calm, only faint ripples suggesting any life to the water, but the day was vibrant, the crickets were as inevitable as breath, and the clear ride of sound over the water doubled the bird voices. They were always best from the water—farthest off, yet clearest heard. And it was a good morning for a catch. She might like a good soft-shell crab for her supper. A treat. They were much too expensive at the Barge, one-fifty each, and not half so good as his own caught ones.

Plenty of time before Jessie was due. . . .

He got his net from the shed, and the oars and locks, set the boat up, unmoored it, shoved it out, and leaped in. It glided stilly through the water, and he headed in along the tall border grass where the crabs were apt to be scutting for prey. On the far side, beyond the sand dunes of a thin, populated sandbar, a car started and moved like a black beetle down the road. For a while he drifted, letting the boat still itself and chafe the grass quiet as a human whisper, while his eyes scouted ahead where the water was clear and untouched by the stark, blinding sun. He pulled the oars in and let one hand trail in the water for an instant. Cold. It made the life bolt in him, and he laughed inside. At such moments he felt his blood was all salt water and the grass was growing right out of him too.

And then he saw a crab—unmoving; and the boat too was almost unmoving—fortunately its shadow was behind and that gave him the edge over the crab. He shook the net so it hung loose of the rim, poised for one instant, and with an almost silent plop, plunged it in deftly, turned, scooped . . . caught! He dipped it back to wash the mud and grass strands free, drew it in, and dumped. Not one, but *two* crabs. And soft-shells at that. "Billie!" Tea for two! He laughed and rowed ashore vigorously, hot when he got there. He left the bucket with a bit of water in it hard by the boat.

By the time he put away the net, oars, and lock, he heard the car come up the drive—and for a minute it frightened him: he hadn't shaved, and what would she think of that, with all his time too?

"Jessie?" he called from out back.

"How come you don't know better than that?" Alton, the milkman.

"Godamighty," he said. "Alton, it's you."

"Every damn morning of the year except Sundays. What's so new about that?"

"I caught me two crabs. Mating they were. Must have thrown me off," he said.

"Imagine that," Alton said. He waved from the truck. "So long."

"Watch that drive," he called. "It's lined with glass." His morning joke—it was what Alton waited for. After that, Alton gunned.

In the kitchen he took his dark brown jacket off the rack and brushed it, then set it back up on the door hook. The only thing in the place without dust, she'd say. He'd fooled her this time, however—it was almost spotless, except her room—theirs. She could take care of that—he had shut the door to keep the dampness out. It'd be good and dry for her, he told himself, and then he went off to shave. It was still cool enough so his hot breath made a living vapor on the glass—he liked that. As a kid, he painted pictures on the steamed-up windows. He started a letter now, but knew it would vanish by the time *she* saw it. There! Shaved and shining is my love. He laughed aloud, and outside like an echo, distant, entering the woods, a warning horn resounded. In a few seconds, Jessie drove up.

"Come on, you old coot," he said.

"Not so old I couldn't do a skinny twig like you in."

"You just try it."

"Sit down. Or you get the eggs while I climb into a shirt. Guess you know where the boxes are by now."

"That's what I like—good old American independent businessmen."

"What do you expect for fifty cents a week?"

He looped the tie, slipped into the jacket. Jessie was out front. He locked the door, hooked the outer storm door, and started for the car himself when the phone rang.

"Let it ring," Jessie said. But he wouldn't. "Might be somebody for eggs. They run out sometimes. I have to bike over. Won't be a minute."

He had trouble—the storm door wasn't tight on its hinges yet, and the key didn't seem to fit the lock right on the inner door. He made it in time—just. He had to ask twice, "Who is it?"

Jessie waited, dark against the sun, and he couldn't see the hospital because Jessie was in the doorway.

"Oh," he said. The sunlight behind Jessie was bright and it glared in his eyes so that he turned, and for a minute the closed door to the bedroom was soothingly soft.

"How's that?" he said. "I don't understand how it could happen. . . . Only last night—"

He waited quite a while, and Jessie stood still, and then Jessie must have moved out of the doorway because a flood of light fell to the floor, threw the door clear so that he could see the lines firm and dark and sharp like a lid.

"You mean you didn't get all the stones out?"

A vigorous wind blew the curtain up on the window facing the woods and the green leaves swayed like underwater seaweed against the sky.

"All but one? It took only one, then. . . ?"

He nodded at the answer.

"No. You call McCorquedale's parlor—they'll take care, they know what to do. You know. Yes."

He hung up.

Jessie stepped in. He stared up at Jessie. It was quite noisy—there was a shrill call over the water, and the sound of cars filtered in from the town.

"I think I'll just stay here," he said.

"Okay," Jessie said. "I'd better be going."

Still, he stood there.

"You want anything?" he said.

"No."

"I'll have the car all day," he said.

"I just want you to get your ass out of here, Jessie."

"Okay. Hulse." He turned and went out. In a minute the car started again, droned down the driveway, and was smothered in the distance.

He took off his coat and tie and hung the coat on the rack and the tie on the doorknob. The sun was very bright now and it glared on the walls and on the door—he could see the sharp, dark lines in the wood, the age of it—coated and covered but still visible—and he stared deep into it. There was dust between the cracks. He raised his hand and touched the knob and thrust the door open hard.

"You said you'd go on someday," he cried. "Okay, well go—go then!"

The room had a musty smell, but it was gone in an instant—the wind poured in like sea and rippled the bedspread and the curtains and the faintest flurry of dust was clutched by the sun.

Then he turned and went outside. The sun was stark, blinding—it seared the leaves with a golden sheen; and he wandered out to the edge of the water, where the boat was. He didn't see the bucket until he stumbled against it. Then he kicked it, the crabs scrambled out—"Git!" he cried, and he couldn't see what his feet were doing; he heard the momentary *sqush*, and saw the other crab streak over the edge and plop into the water. Near his foot the first one flailed its thin claws in silent motion.

Across the crick the full sun struck the hospital, and the windows glittered like early morning eyes that gazed sightless out to sea.

Ernest J. Gaines

Robert Louis Stevenson Banks,
a.k.a. Chimley

ME and Mat was down there fishing. We goes fishing every Tuesday and every Thursday. We got just one little spot now. Ain't like it used to be when you had the whole river to fish on. The white people, they done bought up the river now, and you got nowhere to go but that one little spot. Me and Mat goes there every Tuesday and Thursday. Other people use it other days, but on Tuesday and Thursday they leaves it for us. We been going to that one little spot like that every Tuesday and Thursday the last ten, 'leven years. That one little spot. Just ain't got nowhere else to go no more.

We had been down there—oh, 'bout a hour. Mat had caught eight or nine good-size perches, and me about six—throw in a couple of sackalees there with the bunch. Me and Mat was just sitting there taking life easy, talking low. Mat was sitting on his croker sack, I was sitting on my bucket. The fishes we had caught, we had them on a string in the water, keeping them fresh. We was just sitting there talking low, talking about the old days.

Then that oldest boy of Berto, that sissy one they called Fue, come running down the riverbank and said Clatoo said Miss Merle said that young woman at Marshall, Candy, wanted us on the place right away. She wanted us to get twelve-gauge shotguns and number five shells, and she wanted us to shoot, but keep the empty shells and get there right away.

Me and Mat looked at him standing there sweating—a great big old round-face sissy-looking boy, in blue jeans and a blue gingham shirt, the shirt wet from him running.

Mat said, "All that for what?"

The boy looked like he was ready to run some more, sweat just pouring down the side of his round, smooth, sissy-looking face. He said: "Something to do with Mathu, and something to do with Beau Boutan dead in his yard. That's all I know, all I want to know. Up to y'all now, I done done my part. Y'all can go and do like she say or y'all can go home, lock y'all doors and crawl under the bed like y'all used to. Me, I'm leaving."

He turned.

"Where you going?" Mat called to him.

"You and no Boutan'll ever know," he called back.

"You better run out of Louisiana," Mat said to himself.

The boy had already got out of hearing reach—one of them great big old sissy boys, running hard as he could go up the riverbank.

Me and Mat didn't look at each other for a while. Pretending we was more interested in the fishing lines. But it wasn't fishing we was thinking about now. We was thinking about what happened to us, after something like this did happen. Not a killing like this. I had never knowed in all my life where a black man had killed a white man in this parish. I had knowed about fights, about threats, but not killings. And now I was thinking about what happened after these fights, these threats, how the white folks rode. This was what I was thinking; and I was sure Mat was doing the same. That's why we didn't look at each other for a while. We didn't want to see what the other one was thinking. We didn't want to see the fear in the other one's face.

"He works in mysterious ways, don't He?" Mat said. It wasn't loud, more like he was talking to himself, not to me. But I knowed he was talking to me. He didn't look at me when he said it, but I knowed he was talking to me. I went on looking at my line.

"That's what they say," I said.

Mat went on looking at his line a while. I didn't have to look and see if he was looking at his line, we had been together so much, me and him, I knowed what he was doing without looking at him.

"You don't have to answer this 'less you want to, Chimley," he said. He didn't say that loud, neither. He had just jerked on the line, 'cause I could hear the line cut through the water.

"Yeah, Mat?" I said.

He jerked on the line again. Maybe it was a turtle trying to get at the bait. Maybe he just jerked on the line to do something 'stead of looking at me.

"Scared?" he asked. It was still low. And he still wasn't looking at me.

"Yeah," I said.

He jerked on the line again. Then he pulled in a sackalee 'bout long and wide as my hand. He rebaited the hook and spit on the bait for luck and throwed the line back out in the water. He didn't look at me all this time. I didn't look at him, neither. Just seen all this out the corner of my eyes.

"I'm seventy-one, Chimley," he said, after the line had settled again. "Seventy-one and a half. I ain't got too much strength left to go crawling under that bed like Fue said."

"I'm seventy-two," I said. But I didn't look at him when I said it.

We sat there a while looking out at the lines. The water was so clean and blue, peaceful and calm. I coulda sat there all day long looking out there at my line.

"Think he did it?" Mat asked.

I hunched my shouders. "I don't know, Mat."

"If he did it, you know we ought to be there, Chimley," Mat said.

I didn't answer him, but I knowed what he was talking about. I remembered the fight Mathu and Fix had out there at Marshall store. It started over a Coke bottle. After Fix had drunk his Coke, he wanted Mathu to take the empty bottle back in the store. Mathu told him he wasn't nobody's servant. Fix told him he had to take the bottle back in the store or fight.

A bunch of us was out there, white and black, sitting on the garry eating gingerbread and drinking pop. The sheriff, Guidry, was there, too. Mathu told Guidry if Fix started anything, he was go'n protect himself. Guidry went on eating his gingerbread and drinking pop like he didn't even hear him.

When Fix told Mathu to take the bottle back in the store again, and Mathu didn't, Fix hit him—and the fight was on. Worst fight I ever seen in my life. For a hour it was toe to toe. But when it was over, Mathu was up, and Fix was down. The white folks wanted to lynch Mathu, but Guidry stopped them. Then he walked up to Mathu, cracked him 'side the jaw, and Mathu hit the ground. He turned to Fix, hit him in the mouth, and Fix went down again. Then Guidry came back to the garry to finish his gingerbread and pop. That was the end of that fight. But that wasn't the last fight Mathu had on that river with them white people. And that's what Mat was talking about. That's what he meant when he said if Mathu did it we ought to be there. Mathu was the only one we knowed had ever stood up.

I looked at Mat sitting on the croker sack. He was holding the fishing pole with both hands, gazing out at the line. We had been together so much I just about knowed what he was thinking. But I asked him anyhow.

" 'Bout that bed," he said. "I'm too old to go crawling under that bed. I just don't have the strength for it no more. It's too low, Chimley."

"Mine ain't no higher," I said.

He looked at me now. A fine featured, brown skin man. I had knowed him all my life. Had been young men together. Had done our little running around together. Had been in a little trouble now and then, but nothing serious. Had never done what we was thinking about doing now. Maybe we had thought about it—sure, we had thought about it—but we had never done it.

"What you say, Chimley?" he said.

I nodded to him.

We pulled in the lines and went up the bank. Mat had his fishes in the sack; mine was in the bucket.

"She want us to shoot first," I said. "I wonder why."

"I don't know," Mat said. "How's that old gun of yours working?"

"Shot good last time," I said. "That's been a while, though."

"You got any number five shells?" Mat asked.

"Might have a couple 'round there," I said. "I ain't looked in a long time."

"Save me one or two if you got them," Mat said. "Guess I'll have to borrow a gun, too. Nothing 'round my house work but that twenty-gauge and that old rifle."

"How you figuring on getting over there?" I asked him.

"Clatoo, I reckon," Mat said. "Try to hitch a ride with him on the truck."

"Have him pick me up too," I said.

When we came up to my gate, Mat looked at me again. He was quite a bit taller than me, and I had to kinda hold my head back to look at him.

"You sure now, Chimley?" he said.

"If you go, Mat."

"I have to go, Chimley," he said. "This can be my last chance."

I looked him in the eyes. Lightish brown eyes. They was saying much more than he had said. They was speaking for both of us, though, me and him.

"I'm going, too," I said.

Mat still looked at me. His eyes was still saying more than he had said. His eyes was saying: We wait till now? Now, when we're old men, we get to be brave?

I didn't know how to answer him. All I knowed, I had to go if he went.

Mat started toward his house, and I went on in the yard. Now, I ain't even stepped in the house good 'fore that old woman started fussing at me. What I'm doing home so early for? She don't like to be cleaning fishes this time of day. She don't like to clean fishes till evening when it's cool. I didn't answer that old woman. I set my bucket of fishes on the table in the kitchen, then I come back in the front room and got my old shotgun from against the wall. I looked through the shells I kept in a cigar box on top the armoire till I found me a number five. I blowed the dust off, loaded the old gun, stuck it out the window, turnt my head just in case the old gun decided to blow up, and I shot. Here come that old woman starting right back on me again.

"What's the matter with you, old man? What you doing shooting out that window, raising all that racket for?"

"Right now, I don't know what I'm doing all this for," I told her. "But, see, if I come back from Marshall, and them fishes ain't done and ready for me to eat, I'm go'n do me some more shooting 'round this house. Do you hear what I'm saying?"

She tightened her mouth and rolled her eyes at me, but she had enough sense not to get too cute. I got me two or three more number five shells, blowed the dust off them, and went out to the road to wait for Clatoo.

George Garrett

The Confidence Man

THE motorcycle, flaring a roar of sound behind its improbable, tilting forward rush, was the first sign of the change. Through years the summer visitors to Gulfport had become accustomed to the spectacle of Miss Alma, prim on her bicycle, twisting in and out of the shiny herd of traffic on the main street, Palm Boulevard, and precariously descending the slight slope down to the wharf where the fish market used to be. There she'd dismount, carefully lock her bicycle, and be seen, a slight gray-haired woman in a high-collared cotton dress, moving among the tall tanned fishermen, boys with their eyes still squinted against the shifting winds and the shiny brass of the waves, awkward and heavy-footed as ducks on dry land. There amid the clatter of unloading, the sagging nets hoisting the squirm and silver of the catch from the boats, the coarse laughter, the rich odor of the deep sea, she'd be like a thin ghost edging her way to examine, haggle, poke, and finally buy a single fish for dinner. She was the only person in the world still allowed to market right there where the boats came in instead of uptown at the Fish Market. Nobody had the heart or the inclination to tell her that long ago all that had changed. Would it have made any difference if they *had* told her? Not a bit. She'd stiffen and go right on about her business. She'd buy a fish and one of the fishermen would produce a paper bag from somewhere and write the price, still the same price, on it with a black grease pencil. She'd open her formidable purse, rummage, count the money out. He'd pocket the coins and, more than likely, tip his hat.

"Thank you very much, Miss Alma," he'd say as if she had conferred a special favor on him by the purchase.

She'd mount her bicycle and pedal away. The summer visitors found it very amusing. It was almost absurd enough to make up for the fact that she was anything but helpless when it came to renting the summer cottage she owned along the beach. She made them pay for the privilege of renting beach cottages in her town with a fine view of her ocean. When it came to real estate, not the least, most subtle variation in the national economic structure escaped her attention.

Miss Alma lived in a fine old Florida house, long, high-ceilinged, rambling, with only a bit of the roof visible above a green jungle of pines and palms and live oaks, and with ragged shrubs like wild beasts crouching on what had been a lawn. You passed the driveway with its peeling signboard, *Capt. T. R. Drinkwater, Esq.*, but you didn't go in. If you had business you conducted it in a paintless lean-to at the edge of the driveway that looked like a child's lemonade stand. Which in fact was what it was. When The Old Fraud died, Miss Alma made it her office.

"Didn't I build this myself?" she'd holler. "Shoo! children. Shoo!"

Sure enough she had built it. She had sat there, longer than was respectable some said, selling lemonade to passers-by, unsmiling, condescending, until her mother died and she was busy from then on leaping about the house like an acrobat to the raging commands of the captain. That he was mad, that he had never been to sea as the captain of anything, tugboat or Titanic, did not lessen the authority of the myth he had found for himself, believed in with all his heart until, at last, even Gulfport accepted it without question. You could hear him and he *did* sound like a foghorn in foul weather. You might have seen him then on the sidewalk, leaning down as if he were bucking the breeze of a gale, rolling-gated in the plenty of space that cleared without a whisper or the raising of an eyebrow in front of him no matter how crowded the time or the day, talking to no one but himself. To be in the real-estate business! To be a seaman condemned to the parceling out of little pieces of dry land to a flock of ridiculous spineless figures in piratical costumes who thought the Gulf of Mexico was something to look at, for children to splash brightly in, to cast a fishing line or to sail on, safe and clumsy in their rented boats —rented from him—cramming the pure calm of the bay with the cursed diagonals of their sails! It's no wonder there was a strong odor of bourbon whiskey in his wake. No wonder the children followed behind, shrill and active like a flight of gulls. And naturally everybody said, "Poor Alma."

Yes, no one was ready for the motorcycle. That day the fishing boats churned into the little bay, the tourists assembled with cameras, and the gulls coaxed with bleak cries overhead. One or two heads might have turned casually to the place where the road comes into view to see her strict, indignant pedaling. Then they heard the motorcycle. It careened into sight, skidding on the curve, a lank man in a straw hat holding the longhorned handlebars, and behind him, clinging to his waist, unabashed, Miss Alma, her skirt misbehaving in the wind and her laughter as naked and shrill as a girl's. They were so still they might have been a photograph themselves, those tourists with cameras, when the motorcycle shot onto the dock, came to a screeching halt. The tall man rolled down his pants legs, took off the goggles he'd been wearing, cocked his straw hat at a wry angle, and, openly, for all the world to see, bought two nice bluefish while Miss Alma, breathless still from the wild ride, held his motorcycle for him. The fisherman even had to make change for him. When he walked back to her with the paper bag, the taps on his heels clicked arrogantly on the dock. He rolled up his pants legs again, revealing red silk socks and a wide garter. He put the goggles on, adjusted them, pulled his hat far down over his ears, and stamped down on the starter. And they were off in a coughing growl, propelled out of sight at unbelievable speed, never even slowing at the curve.

It was the fisherman who spoke first.

"He's from Georgia," he said. "I can always tell a Georgia accent."

"Pocket full of money. Did you see all those bills?"

"I didn't know Miss Alma had any family in Georgia."

"As far as I know, she don't," someone said. "Anyway, that fellow don't have the Drinkwater nose."

"Might be on the Cawley side."

"Doubt it."

It wasn't long before everybody was concerned about poor Miss Alma. It didn't take long to figure out what *he* was up to. What if he *did* have such fine manners, would move aside for a lady on the sidewalk with even the subtle indication of an old-fashioned bow, tipping his straw hat high and wide!

What if he had an alligator wallet crisp with the money he was quick to spend everywhere, for flowers, for a bottle of wine, for a Brownie camera and several rolls of film, for a box of fine linen handkerchiefs, initialed? If his summer suits were neat and clean, creased to perfection, if his pointed tapping two-toned shoes gleamed with white and brown where they ought to, there was nevertheless no doubt that he was an opportunist.

Larry Thompson, the plainclothes policeman, patted his stomach and noted that this Mr. Hunter from Atlanta, Georgia, was a type well known to him.

"You can see him by the battalion at most any race track," he said.

"I expect if you was to turn him upside down and give him a fair shake there'd be a regular shower of ticket stubs."

"It's a shame," everybody was saying, "to see a sweet, lonely, eccentric woman like Miss Alma taken advantage of."

At any rate, whatever was being said, there he was all smiles, bug-eyed in goggles, Miss Alma likewise smiling, zooming around the countryside on the devilish machine. They were seen together. They appeared together one fine day on the beach. Who can honestly remember seeing Miss Alma on the beach? But there they were with a bright umbrella and a striped beach ball that bounced like a joyful planet above the clear bells of her laughter. Oh, yes, and she had been heard whistling, both of them whistling what might have been most any tune as they lunged past baffled spectators in lean profile on the motorcycle.

"I'll keep my eye on that fellow," promised Everett Meriwether, the lawyer. If something—something that we all expected—happened, he'd know first. He would have had a hard time if he meant this literally. They were all over the county. They were seen bidding at an auction, right in the midst of the tourists. Someone with a pair of binoculars and the time to use them swore he saw the two of them heeling along in a swift white tack in a catboat on the bay.

"It's dangerous for a woman of middle age to carry on that way" began to be the sentiment among the women.

This seemed to be confirmed by what happened at the El Tropitan nightclub. They were there too, all right, the report was, starting the evening with cocktails and rock lobster dinner, oblivious of any eyebrows. They stayed on for an evening of it, and he became expansive, hiring the orchestra to play a medley of waltzes for her, having their picture taken a half-dozen times, ordering the tall, ice-packed, colored drinks that put the bartender into a frenzy. They laughed and he waved his hands grandiloquently, his diamond ring flashing in the light, as he told her stories. He tried on her glasses, made faces for her, and they sang loudly and off key without much provocation. It might, they said, have gone on marvelously forever if she hadn't slipped and, head over heels no less, fallen with a memorable clatter in the midst of the dance floor while he was teaching her the samba.

It was at this point that Lawyer Meriwether decided to step boldly forward. He arranged for a little talk with Mr. Hunter. And so, they say, the two of them sat in Meriwether's office above the bank, the lawyer peering behind thick lenses at his prey, trying, in all fairness, to conceal his stern distaste. They talked for a while of this and that, feeling their way like crabs in a wavering submarine light. This gentleman from Georgia spun his fine straw hat like a gypsy's tambourine on his index finger while he spoke a little and listened more.

"About Miss Alma. . . ." Meriwether finally began.

"The flower of the state of Florida," Hunter interrupted.

"That may be. There may be truth in that," the lawyer said. "She is my client, however, and I have the duty and pleasure of protecting her interests."

"I should say so," Hunter said.

"Now, Mr. Hunter, you've been most kind to the lady during this summer season. . . ."

"I've done nothing at all."

"On the contrary. You've squired her around. You've offered her a kind of joy and pleasure she's usually been deprived of by virtue of her position in town."

"Really, I have done nothing at all," Hunter said, modestly enough, staring at the sharp points of his shoes.

"It isn't often that a woman of middle age has the good fortune of an admirer years younger than herself."

"What are years, after all?" Hunter said in a whisper. "Alma has the spirit of a thoroughbred."

Meriwether winced at the allusion to the race track and bore down.

"And where will it all be at the end of the summer season?"

Hunter smiled broadly, triumphantly, spun the hat like a potter's wheel on his finger.

"Who knows?" he said. "Who can tell?"

"I'll be frank with you," the lawyer said. "I don't know for sure what you're up to, but I know you're up to something and I mean to tell you that I intend to protect my client."

"Indeed!" Hunter said, rising, tipping a parody of his sidewalk bow. "I can't say I thank you for your concern, though I thank you enough for being honest with me. Honesty is not to be despised, never, not even when its advocate is no gentleman."

So in a crisp huff he was gone, and Meriwether was left to consider, puzzled, the neat rhythm of the tapped heels as they clicked down the hall. He spun his swivel chair around and looked through the window as Hunter, stiff-backed as a cadet, bowed his bow for the ladies, smiled his smile, and mounted the waiting motorcycle—so indignant, it seemed, at the suggestion that his motives were not wholly honorable, that he forgot to roll up his trousers or put on his goggles.

Meriwether decided to give him a week before he approached Miss Alma on the delicate subject. A week was too long. By the time he'd dressed in a dark suit and slicked down his hair and was walking up the quiet dust of the driveway to call on the lady, the other one, irresponsible, yet shrewd as a cat, had vanished into thin air. The lawyer arrived at least in time to console. He sat stiffly in the living room, vaguely afraid of the close fragility of old things around him, and listened to the sad, inevitable tale of how the confidence man had roared away on his motorcycle, his alligator wallet bulging with new money—not all of it, of course, but all that had been hidden even from the lawyer's knowledge in a copper pitcher for years and years going back to the days of the lemonade stand.

"It was money that I had secreted from Father and from you as well," she said simply.

He decided he would have felt better, more at ease, if she hadn't been so tearless, rational, unperturbed (the women would say, and do, *unrepentant*). She asked him not for pity, not even advice. She was just telling him what had happened.

"I'm sorry, Miss Alma, very sorry."

"Sorry? Why, Everett, what is there to be sorry about? I was duped out of my money by a clever and charming man. Oh, he certainly was *that*—not clever I mean, not terribly clever—but charming, oh, yes, in his own way, quite a charming man."

"Well, we'll certainly catch up with him sooner or later."

"I think not," she said, standing up. "I rather hope not. That makes me feel a little sad. What would a man like Mr. Rodney Hunter, if that *is* his name, do in jail?"

"Do you know," she said, "it's going to be a little difficult to go back to my bicycle again. There was such a breeze and such a sound. There was so much speed on the motorcycle."

"The bike's a lot safer," he said. "You're more likely to get where you're going even if it takes a little longer."

"Oh, yes," she said. "But not nearly as much fun. I may even buy myself a motorcycle. Do you know how to drive one, Everett? Could you teach me? Have you ever been on one?"

"No ma'am," he said quickly, and he hurried away down the still drive.

Gary Gildner

Sleepy Time Gal

IN the small town in northern Michigan where my father lived as a young man, he had an Italian friend who worked in a restaurant. I will call his friend Phil. Phil's job in the restaurant was as ordinary as you can imagine—from making coffee in the morning to sweeping up at night. But what was not ordinary about Phil was his piano playing. On Saturday nights my father and Phil and their girlfriends would drive ten or fifteen miles to a roadhouse by a lake where they would drink beer from schoopers and dance and Phil would play an old beat-up piano. He could play any song you named, my father said, but the song everyone waited for was the one he wrote, which he would always play at the end before they left to go back to the town. And everyone knew of course that he had written the song for his girl, who was as pretty as she was rich. Her father was the banker in their town and he was a tough old German and he didn't like Phil going around with his daughter.

My father, when he told this story, which was not often, would tell it in an offhand way and emphasize the Depression and not having much, instead of the important parts. I will try to tell it the way he did, if I can.

So they would go to the roadhouse by the lake and finally Phil would play his song and everyone would say, Phil, that's a great song, you could make a lot of money from it. But Phil would only shake his head and smile and look at his girl. I have to break in here and say that my father, a gentle but practical man, was not inclined to emphasize the part about Phil looking at his girl. It was my mother who said the girl would rest her head on Phil's shoulder while he played, and that he got the idea for the song from the pretty way she looked when she got sleepy. My mother was not part of the story, but she had heard it when she and my father were younger and therefore had that information. I would like to intrude further and add something about Phil writing the song, maybe show him whistling the tune and going over the words slowly and carefully to get the best ones, while peeling onions or potatoes in the restaurant; but my father is already driving them home from the roadhouse and saying how patched up his tires were and how his car's engine was a gingerbread of parts from different makes, and some parts were his own invention as well. And my mother is saying that the old German had made his daughter promise not to get involved with any man until after college, and they couldn't be late. Also my mother likes the sad parts and is eager to get to their last night before the girl goes away to college.

So they all went out to the roadhouse and it was sad. The women got tears in their eyes when Phil played her song, my mother said. My father said that Phil spent his week's pay on a new shirt and tie, the first tie he ever owned, and people kidded him. Somebody piped up and said, Phil, you ought to take that song down to Bay City—which was like saying New York City to them, only more realistic—and sell it and take the money and go to college too. Which was not meant to be cruel, but that was the result because Phil had never even got to high school. But you can see people were trying to cheer him up, my mother said.

Well, she'd come home for Thanksgiving and Christmas and Easter and they'd all sneak out to the roadhouse and drink beer from schoopers and dance and everything would be like always. And of course there were the summers. And everyone knew Phil and the girl would get married after she made good her promise to her father, because you could see it in their eyes when he sat at the old beat-up piano and played her song.

That last part about their eyes was not of course in my father's telling, but I couldn't help putting it in there even though I know it is making some of you impatient. Remember that this happened many years ago in the woods by a lake in northern Michigan, before television. I wish I could put more in, especially about the song and how it felt to Phil to sing it and how the girl felt when hearing it and knowing it was hers, but I've already intruded too much in a simple story that isn't even mine.

Well, here's the kicker part. Probably by now many of you have guessed that one vacation near the end she doesn't come home to see Phil, because she meets some guy at college who is good-looking and as rich as she is and, because her father knew about Phil all along and was pressuring her into forgetting about him, she gives in to this new guy and goes to his hometown during the vacation and falls in love with him. That's how the people in town figured it, because after she graduates they turn up, already married, and right away he takes over the old German's bank—and buys a new Pontiac at the place where my father is the mechanic and pays cash for it. The paying cash always made my father pause and shake his head and mention again that times were tough, but here comes this guy in a spiffy white shirt (with French cuffs, my mother said) and pays the full price in cash.

And this made my father shake his head too: Phil took the song down to Bay City and sold it for twenty-five dollars, the only money he ever got for it. It was the same song we'd just heard on the radio and which reminded my father of the story I just told you. What happened to Phil? Well, he stayed in Bay City and got a job managing a movie theater. My father saw him there after the Depression when he was on his way to Detroit to work for Ford. He stopped and Phil gave him a box of popcorn. The song he wrote for the girl has sold many millions of records and if I told you the name of it you could probably sing it, or at least whistle the tune. I wonder what the girl thinks when she hears it. Oh yes, my father met Phil's wife too. She worked in the movie theater with him, selling tickets and cleaning the carpet after the show with one of those sweepers you push. She was also big and loud and nothing like the other one, my mother said.

Patrick Worth Gray

Too Soon Solos

I was a little late, so I took the steps leading down into the club two at a time. Roger was already there, slamming his drums and scowling at them, while Al noodled around on his scarred old bass, thrumming a minor, African-sounding pattern. George was drooping on his bench, staring at the keys, his lazy belly touching them, but Mike was standing up, tense, squinting at me.

I let the door bang behind me and walked slowly to the bandstand, trying to conceal my heavy breathing.

"Well, Skoodge," Mike said, "thought us poor peons were going to have to get along without our star tonight."

"Ahh, blow it out, Mike," I said, settling into my chair and unlatching Madge's case. "A guy'd think this was the MJQ, the way you rave."

"You're five minutes late," he said. "Five times four men means twenty minutes you wasted!"

"Yeah, yeah, you can multiply, so can rabbits," I said, lifting Madge from her case. "Gimme an E, George?"

George hit the note and I started tuning Madge, even though she didn't need it. Everybody was studying their instruments like they'd never seen them before, the way they always do when Mike and me get into it; well, I was sorry I was late, but I couldn't tell Mike that—his head would be swollen up bigger than ever. Leader, okay; dictator, no.

I quit pretending to tune her and looked out at the dance floor, dim as the Pit, even in this early evening, so you couldn't see what pale drinks you were getting, but kind of nice all the same, right then. Later on it would fill up with cigarette smoke and perfume so that it actually got kind of hard to breathe up on the stand, but right now the air was clean, just a hint of nicotine-whiskey staleness under it. I breathed it deep into my lungs, wishing I could have it for midnight when I'd need it.

The bartenders were straightening their bottles and glasses, and small clinking noises came floating up to us. I hit my treble strings, using just a little vibrato, and small clinking notes sneaked out of my amplifier toward the bar. The new bartender jerked around and stared.

"Hey, they're not supposed to have any booze till midnight," he hollered.

The other bartenders laughed.

"That's not bottles, that's just ole Skoodge," one of them said. "He's a mockingbird on that guitar."

The new man gaped at me, shaking his head, so I made Madge meow at him and he jumped six inches. They all laughed and we might have gone on that way for quite a spell, but Mr. Merriam came in just then and those bartenders really started moving around. When he sat down at the bar, two of them ran into each other, trying to serve him first. He ordered a vodka Collins like always, lit one of his dollar cigars, and leaned back, watching us.

Mike had been glaring at me all this time, and now he put something extra into it. I grinned at him and ran some diminished chords down Madge's neck; he raised his trumpet and blew a chorus, slow and easy this early, and then I gave it a single-string treatment. George came in, lazied through the verse, and we all hit the last chorus hard, Roger beating his traps like they were his unfaithful wife, Al squeezing high notes out of his bass, and even fat George keeping up. Mike ended on high C, even though he knows that isn't good for your lip without warming up first. He made the impression on Mr. Merriam he wanted to, though, because the old boy snapped his fingers through that last chorus and smiled icily at us before going off and shutting himself into his private office up front.

"Whew, should of warmed up first," Mike said, fingering his lips.

"Yep. You should of," I said, "but don't worry, you got old man Merriam's blood pumping on that last chorus." I did a pretty good imitation of a fast ragged heartbeat on my sixth string and Mike finally grinned at me. He has a good smile, when he uses it.

George was giggling over on his bench, but shut up when Mike glared at him.

We started running through our repertoire of moldy figs—old standards that no one listens to any more, ideal for dance music. Mike kept riding George, making him take solos on every tune and pretty soon the fat little guy was panting. So the next moon-June ditty we got into, when Mike hollered, "Take it" at George, I turned up Madge's volume and laid down a walking bass. Then I slipped clusters of sweet and sour notes between that bass, making them short and straight. When I had run out of boogie ideas, I stayed in the same key, only changed to discord bass and turned the volume down, and spun out a single-string melody I had been thinking. I kept it simple, but I put in the greasy-spoon meals, the windowless rooms, and the talking to yourself. I slowed near the end and struck a few soft chords that, because of what had gone before, hung together and shimmered like rain on Sunday in a strange new town.

I don't know how long I played; I never know when Madge and me are trying to explain something, but she was warm when I finished, her dark brown wood glowing like a woman's well-brushed hair, and her body humming with those last chords.

Al leaned toward me.

"Man," he said, "Skoodge, I wish I had a record of that. That's what music should be."

"Yeah," Roger said, frowning at his high-hat. George sat hunched on his bench, trying to play the melody before he forgot it.

"Well, it's too bad we can't go through life making beautiful music together," Mike rasped, "but the fact remains that we have to play what Mr. Merriam wants, so let's quit dreaming!"

We started rehearsing again, me not looking at Mike. We knew all those cornball arrangements by heart, and the joint was still innocent of customers, but Mike was scared of Merriam, so we ran through them, looking at the music but not seeing it.

Finally Mike put his trumpet down and we took a break. This was what I'd been waiting for. I hustled into the kitchen and Vince, the cook, poured me a cup of coffee.

"You-all soundin' pretty good," Vince said.

"You must mean that soul music Skoodge played," Al grumbled, sitting down with us. "There's as much difference between it and that trash we usually play as between prime and hamburger, Vince."

"Well, I don't know music, but I—" Vince began.

"—know what I like," Al and me finished it for him. He grinned.

"You boys too picky," he said, "always wantin' to get poetical up there. Not that I didn't like your solo, Skoodge, 'cause I did, but people nowadays want to dance, not listen."

Mike blew Assembly and we stood up.

"Two customers must of come in," Al said.

"The coffee was good, Vince," I said.

"But my opinions weren't, huh?" Vince asked, grinning again. "Well, see you-all 'round midnight. Got some nice fresh shrimp in today."

We shoved through the wide, swinging port-holed doors; several couples were sitting at the little round tables. Mike was frowning at us, as usual, so Al and me smirked at him, also as usual, and took our time about getting up to the stand.

The couples moved out onto the floor when Mike lifted his trumpet and started the verse of a standard. The evening had begun. We played thirty-minute sets and rested five; about ten o'clock I caught myself nodding and wished I'd drunk more coffee. I looked over at Al and his eyes were almost closed. Maybe we looked like we were transported with delight over our own music, but I doubt it.

We moved into the "St. Louis Blues," giving it a society treatment; you know, no guts—just notes. After we ran it through a couple of times, we were ready to go on to the next ever-popular, but Mike stood up, so we all vamped, waiting.

He took the mute off his horn, pointed it at the crowd, and cut loose. All of a sudden, it was a blues—hot and swollen, uncombed and crying, running around the room and scorching the paint. Al and me looked at each other, wondering. Our safe-and-sane leader seemed to have popped his cork. I followed the line of his horn out through the dancers, most of them just watching him now, and saw at the end of the line the girl he was playing to. I pointed Madge at her, and Al gave the girl a thorough once-over before he nodded knowingly.

This girl was a cut above the ones Mike was used to. Long golden hair swirling about her bare white shoulders and dark burning eyes dominating her pale face, she made it hard to notice the boy she was dancing with, except as a kind of tuxedoed background.

Mike was really pouring it on now, his horn blasting, then growling low, suggesting dark smoky things. The girl maneuvered her escort near the stand and then she watched Mike, her mouth open a little, showing pink softness.

The boy she was with began to blush as he realized Mike was playing straight to her, the trumpet throbbing softly now, pleading. Mike ended with a little run that left his solo unresolved, like a question. The girl just stood there, staring at Mike with those big eyes, not hearing it when everyone applauded.

While Mike's last note still quivered in the air, Madge and me moved in. I don't know what made me do it; I just know that Mike's solo was good, it was a kind of blues, but it wasn't the "St. Louis Blues." So Madge and me explained our idea. Like, I imagine St. Louis is the same as any other town—full of streets that tire you out, people that put you down, and jobs that make you feel nowhere, so Madge and me looked at them, but we also looked at catfish with hushpuppies, Sunday afternoon street-car rides, grandmothers with parasols and chubby pug dogs, and the love of a man for his woman on Monday morning when the weekend is gone and her face is naked. I put all that in, or at least I thought I did, but when I got through, the couples were dancing again and only a couple of old ladies clapped politely. Al looked at me and shrugged.

It was midnight and we stood up, trying to unkink our muscles. Al and me trudged back to the kitchen. Vince had our shrimp ready, so we dug right into them and the sour-cream potatoes, cole slaw, garlic toast, and lots of hot black coffee. We ate silently and were through in a few minutes.

"Thanks, Vince," I said. "I feel a little more human now."

"I heard your blues," he said. "I liked it—it was kind of this kitchen and me. I mean, I guess you know what I'm sayin'."

"Sure, I know," I said. "I'm glad you liked what I was saying."

Al shook his cigarette pack and a couple popped up. I reached over and grabbed one.

"Yeah, Vince and the old ladies knew," he said, lighting my cigarette, then his. "You might as well give up, Skoodge."

I nodded. Suddenly my plate looked disgusting, and I carried it over to the dishwasher.

"No, Skoodge should play like that sometimes," Vince said. "You can't eat hamburger all the time."

"Hey, you changed your mind, huh? You didn't talk like that before," Al said.

"Yeah, guess Skoodge changed my mind for me. He made this kitchen look better," Vince said slowly, and then grinned. "I'm a pretty good cook," he said, sticking out his chest.

"Oh, oh," Al said, giving Vince a friendly punch in the shoulder and winking at me, "we'd better get back to the stand—his head's gonna swell up so big it'll mash us against the stove."

"Yeah," I said, punching Vince on his other shoulder and feeling better about the world.

"You guys quit pickin' on me," he mock-whined and pushed us out.

But then we were in the middle of the customers, and I felt lousy again. As Al and me made our way through the tables, I saw why no one had understood anything Madge and me had said. They were too busy stuffing themselves with food and liquor and each other—and that's why Mike's solo had gone over so good; it was just another thrill they could gobble and not think about.

We climbed up on the stand and I saw that the blonde was sitting at a ringside table by herself. She had ditched the kid somehow, and now she was just sitting at that table and staring at Mike like he was Christmas, and him showing his best profile to her, his black hair gleaming glossily under the spot. I was very aware of my cowlicks.

"Well, here we go again," Al whispered before he went back to his bass, "a new chapter in the life of the poor man's Casanova."

I grunted, sat down, and ran progressions on Madge until it was time to play those enduring popular ballads again. Somehow I made it till three, and then went back to my fourth-floor room and tried to go to sleep and finally did.

The next night, she was there at the same ringside table, gazing adoringly up at Mike. He played to her all evening, the trumpet wailing and panting. The customers loved it. After a while, it got so Mike would sit with her during breaks. She would light his cigarette and then put it in his mouth, thus saving his fabulous breath.

"That's a pretty nice girl hanging around lately," Al said to him one evening.

"Yeah, she's all right," Mike said carelessly. "One of these college broads—all right below the neck, if you know what I mean."

He laughed at Al and stared at him.

"I know what you mean," he said. I kept busy with Madge.

That's all I did, the next month—played Madge. I didn't even go back to the kitchen on breaks. Vince was kind of hurt, but I couldn't leave the stand. That would have meant not seeing the girl, and I had to watch her all the time, from the corner of my eye. I told myself it was stupid, that any girl dumb enough to fall for Mike's line wasn't worth thinking about, let alone stewing over, but I didn't pay any attention to myself. She was what I had dreamed about a thousand nights in those tiny rooms in shabby hotels. Madge was real good about it and waited, knowing that the course of true love never did run, and that something would give.

So, one Tuesday night, it did. Our first break, the blonde was all smiles, waiting for Mike to favor her with his company, but he walked past her like she was part of the woodwork and kept going straight toward a big redhead sitting across the room. It looked like somebody had stepped on the blonde's face and twisted his heel. But she didn't cry. I figured she would leave soon, and she did get up, but only to move to a back table where it was darker.

She was in every night the rest of that week, too, a little paler than usual but holding herself very straight and not drinking much. Mike spent every break at the redhead's table, drooling down her neck like Count Dracula or something. The blonde was careful to watch the stand during these breaks, and of course I watched her.

Even though she had been dumb enough to fall for that no-good Mike, I kind of admired her control. Most of Mike's conquests would have made a scene with the redhead or at least come up to the stand and cried on our shoulders, but this blonde sat there growing paler each night and drinking a little more, not doing anything like that. It began to get on Mike's nerves a little; he couldn't even twitch up there on the stand and play hot choruses to the redhead because the little blonde's smudged eyes made him too guilty.

One night, he had all he could stand of this silent treatment, I guess, because after the midnight break, he signaled to me to take over. I took the lead and strung out the verse of the first number, watching the crowd. Sure enough, here came Mike, dancing with the redhead. She couldn't dance too good, but that didn't matter to him; she could dance good enough for his purposes. They weren't really dancing when they came past the blonde's table, anyway; it was more like a grade C movie seduction. They stayed there, wriggling around right in front of her, until she sobbed and buried her head in her arms, her long golden hair fanning out on the table like whipped honey.

I missed a note and the people not staring at the blonde looked at me. The band staggered to a halt on whatever rubbish we were playing, and I switched off Madge's vibrato. I didn't know what I was going to play, but I knew I didn't want a throbby soap-opera effect.

So I started, just a ballad bass and a few four-string chords, just picking around until I found what Madge and me wanted to say. I found a progression I liked but pretty soon what I was trying to explain broke free of that, and we were soaring. Yeah, flying through the air like a bird, a big free bird, and telling the people that this is the way to live, to get off the ground and let the wind clean your feathers—stay out of those barns and coops. Man was born free, we said, and he puts his chains on by himself, nobody forces him. If he'll take the chance of setting his own course and doing his own flying, he may get lost, he may go hungry, he may perish and the flock caw over his foolishness, but at the very least he will have seen things they never saw, he will know there's more to life than getting and gorging, and he'll leave this place knowing that he alone is responsible for his end, and not a bunch of cluttering busybodies who hollered "Left!" and "Right!" at the top of their voices all their lives to cover up the fact that they didn't know which way to go.

I realized that I was getting too complicated, so I stopped and sat there, disappointed like always because I had said so little of what I felt. The little blonde sat up, squared her shoulders, and left her table.

"Excuse me, please," she said politely as she brushed by Mike and the redhead. She came on up to the stand.

"I'm fine now, thank you very much," she said to me and I bobbed my head at her. She swept on out of the club, smiling at Vince as she left. He was standing in the kitchen entrance, looking at me. So was everybody else. They had all quit dancing and were gawking at me.

I scowled at the stupid clods, and they burst into applause! They kept on clapping and clapping and I just sat there, clutching Madge to me and wondering what was wrong with them. Finally Al stepped over to me.

"Take a bow, Skoodge," he whispered. "The jerks got it, man. Your ole sermon got through to them!"

So I stood up and they hollered louder, some of them pounding on their tables. I held up my hand and they quieted down, expecting me to play some more.

I tried. Madge tried, but I couldn't give her any directions when I didn't know where I was going myself. All of a sudden, I was out there with those people and we were too small for what we had to do, and we were scared of the dark. I was just whistling in that dark now, and the people knew it. Slowly they started dancing, while I led the guys in a hit parader.

When the break came, I put Madge in her case and ducked out the back door. There was a bus for Mobile at two o'clock, and I was going to be on it.

I was pitching the last of my socks into the suitcase when I heard a knock at the door. I opened it and Al stepped in, bending over a little to keep from scraping his head on the tattered ceiling.

"This's a small room you got here, man," he said.

"Yeah, but it won't bug me much longer," I said. "I'm cutting out for Mobile."

He asked why, but I couldn't tell him. I couldn't find the words to tell him that I didn't have that much to say, after all, that people should listen to me, and that I was ashamed of having set myself up as knowing something more than the dumb crowd. I was dumber than they had ever been. A man who don't understand that he is pretty much the same as everybody else has got a lot to learn, I wanted to tell him, and I was on my way to try and learn it. But I couldn't tell him, he wouldn't have understood; he was still up there thinking he was something special. So I left him standing there, his long stooped shadow moving against the wall in rhythm with the swinging of the naked light bulb, his face wry with unanswered questions.

Donald Hall

The World Is A Bed

1.

IT was not until his early thirties that William Bolter understood what the world was. Thereafter he remained secure in his understanding for twenty years, with a confidence approaching complacency, until one afternoon it fell away from him like leaves in a windstorm from a dying tree.

He was thirty-two when he discovered that the world was a bed. If we lead a life of sexual adventure, he decided, we move in a great dance, for our lovers have had lovers and their lovers have had lovers also. Going to a revival of *West Side Story*, or to a gathering of the American Society of Statisticians, we see *her*, and *her*, and *her*. He resolved that we are all episodes in the lives of each other; we are a directory of flesh, and though we have not reclined with X or Y or Z we have touched women who have had affairs with men who have had affairs with X and Y and Z: the world is a bed.

When an affair began, William liked to tell the story of the summer he was sixteen, and the first woman. Of course it did not do to blurt it out; no one enjoyed the notion that she was one of a series. Yet on such occasions he always wanted to tell the new woman about her predecessors—he reminded himself of obese people who spend dinner time in anecdotes of famous meals—and he learned how to go about it: when the alert skin subsided into dampness, when each leaned back to smoke, he would ask her, as if he stumbled on the thought, about the first time she had made love. Usually it was far enough back to be made light of. When she finished her story he had license to tell his own.

2.

In June of 1945 Bill Bolter turned sixteen, a promising student of mathematics on a scholarship at Cranbrook Academy outside Detroit, and living with his parents. Besides mathematics there was the violin, dreams of composing and conducting, of becoming another Baumgartner to conduct his own compositions. He would have concentrated more on his music if he had not worried about the opinions of his classmates. With a diffidence common among adolescents—he told himself, when his old teacher sighed over his apostasy—he cared for the opinions of people dumber than he was; they accepted his presence when he swam a leg in a medley, but addressed him *Hey, fruit* when he walked with his violin past the Arts Academy, the Milles fountain, and the staid oaks, over the bright lawns to his teacher's quarters. It was this diffidence that kept him from returning to the music camp at Interlochen in 1945, where he had spent the previous two summers on a scholarship. This summer he practiced at home, continued his lessons, studied the calculus in a desultory fashion, took a girl named Beverly to the movies, and read mystery stories. He was bored. When his mother told him about the chance to visit the Balfour Festival on Cape Cod, he was quick to take it.

Mrs. Hugh Fitzroberts was a large lady in her late forties who had befriended his mother, in the thrift shop where his mother worked, and had heard about William's musical abilities. Mrs. Fitzroberts was wealthy, his mother told him, and a patron of the Detroit Symphony, some of whose members spent their summers in the blue air of Balfour. Her husband, on the other hand, was known to care more for balance sheets than for the finer things, and would remain in Detroit aiding the war effort while Mrs. Fitzroberts rented a cabin with two bedrooms near the concert shell, for the two weeks at the beginning of August, and it would be nice to have the boy for company.

They sat up all night on the coach to New York, the Wolverine, when not even the Fitzroberts name could swing a berth. At first the tall older lady attempted to interest him with intelligent questions, but when they had both slept a few hours and awakened disheveled and grubby, their dignities fell away; Mrs. Fitzroberts became "Anne" and William "Bill," and they ate cheese sandwiches as dry as newsprint. At New York they made their connection for Boston where they transferred to a local, and as they approached the Cape her nervousness started. She became suddenly silly, he thought, skittish as a girl, reminding him of middle-aged men around soldiers—falsely friendly, laughing too much, guilty.

He discovered why. Waiting at the station was a ponderous man, older than she was, who occupied a chair in the Detroit Symphony hidden among woodwinds. They took each other's hands, and Mrs. Fitzroberts glanced back at her companion—her *cover*, he realized—with something like panic: there was something she had neglected to mention.

For the next fortnight, Bill saw little of Mrs. Fitzroberts, who never explained herself and never appeared at the cabin, and although he was shocked he was also pleased. It made him feel sophisticated; he found it a relief to be left alone in a new and handsome place with his music. In the mornings he practiced Beethoven, usually on a quiet patch of beach too rocky for bathing and out of range of sea salt. For a while even the natural world seemed to approve; the salt grass waved in his honor, and the cattails kept time like the batons of a thousand conductors. Afternoons he attended rehearsals of the visiting quartet—they were working through Beethoven, as it happened—and daydreamed himself a great performer. At night there were concerts in the shell near his cabin.

And there were girls—dozens of young women and few young men. Girls waited on table, flocked together in boarding houses, played flutes and violas, took notes during rehearsals. Most of them were older than he was—eighteen, twenty, twenty-three. He walked in a grove of young women, lush and warm and possible. He had lunch with one girl, went to a rehearsal with another, ate supper with another, took a fourth to the concert and afterwards walked the beach with her and kissed. To each of the girls he pleaded his plea of bed. A few of them confessed to being virgins like him; others warded him off lightly. He suspected that they felt awkward about taking a sixteen-year-old seriously. And when each of them refused his proposal, Bill was quick to abandon her, for it meant he could pay suit to another. Every night he went home feeling rejected and relieved.

There was no competition at all. The only young men at Balfour at the end of the war were crippled or homosexual. (Bill discouraged the attentions of a thirty-year-old piano teacher.) So he dated a girl with a good figure and big teeth who played the cello. He swam on a Sunday with a bank president's daughter and with a Smith graduate he drank illicit beer in a coupe she drove while her brother was in Europe. For a time he lost interest in music: he was too tired in the mornings to practice. Yet after ten days of frantic dating he had not gone to bed with anyone. When he caught sight of Mrs. Fitzroberts, looking younger every day, irony saturated him.

Slowly he became aware of the girl in the red MG. Not many students had brought cars to Balfour, because of gas rationing. On the one night in the coupe, he and the Smith girl counted the miles that they drove. But the tall black-haired young woman whirled in her red MG through the small streets, parking beside the only expensive restaurant in town. Several of the girls mentioned her, annoyed at the ubiquity of the red MG. Then late one morning—Balfour almost done—he paused when the MG parked at tennis courts in front of him. The tall girl leapt out and took up singles with an older woman who clerked at the hotel. The girl wore a short tennis dress, the skirt fluted like a Greek column, and her legs were long, smooth, strong, luxurious. She leaned forward to wait for service with an intensity that looked omnivorous.

The next day, he came to the tennis court at the same time, and brought a racquet, and hit balls against the backboard while the girl with the red MG played tennis with the older woman. When they finished, and her companion walked away toward the hotel, he approached the tall girl. She smiled at him, and he noticed the wedding ring, and he asked her if she would like to practice with him; when they were tired she drove him back to his room. He asked her if she would play again tomorrow, and she asked him about his music, and she told him that her name was Margaret Adams Olson but everyone called her Mitsy. Her husband, Allen, was an army captain in the Pacific, Intelligence, and she was twenty-four. She came from Seattle, and after the war she and Allen would settle nearby in Allison—"like June Allyson with an i"—where the Olsons owned the bank, which was like owning the town. Her music was strictly amateur, she said. She was here because she was bored.

The next day they played and had lunch and met for the Mozart at night, and afterwards walked on the beach and talked. He asked her how she had gas for her car and she laughed and showed him a wad of A coupons clutched in an elastic band; her father took care of that. If your husband was overseas, Mitsy said, and there was nothing to do, why not have some fun? Last year had been rotten, really rotten, she said, because her great-aunt was sick with cancer, right in their house, and they had to take care of her until she died. Then she told him about her husband, and their courtship in college, and how her husband was a dilettante at the piano, and they had met at a concert, a soprano visiting Seattle, she couldn't remember which one. And all the time she talked, animated and charming, he thought only of thighs blooming beneath a white linen skirt.

Gulls flew in circles over their heads; he squinted to watch them as they circled, and imagined for the moment that the gulls were spying on them.

Bill asked her if there had been other boyfriends, wanting to keep her close to the subject, and Mitsy laughed as she told him: yes, yes, that was what she had lived for at college—because her father had always been too busy to pay attention to her—and really she had been terrible. She had been cheerleader her freshman year, because it was a way to meet upperclassmen and football players, and for her first three years she had dated every night, somebody different every night. She was booked for dates three weeks ahead—she told him, and her eyes were brilliant—and on weekends she had two dates a day. Sometimes three.

He felt embarrassed that she might see the effect her words had.

The day before the festival ended, they played tennis again, the third day in a row. For two nights he had slept irregularly, but conjured up her strong, firm, welcoming body, and then drifted off into small patches of sleep, only to wake dreaming erotic dreams. Today again Mitsy wore the fluted white tennis dress, and Bill was so full of her he could not play at all. He was lovesick, he told himself, "sick with longing." After a set which he lost 6–0, she asked him if he was not feeling well, and he agreed that he was not, and they drove together in the red MG back to her hotel. In the lobby everyone scurried about, looking serious and giddy at the same time. They would have lunch after Mitsy changed her clothes. As they waited for the elevator, they heard the hotel's P.A. system telling them that, on account of the surrender of the Japanese, the evening Shostakovich and Prokofiev had been canceled, replaced by a ceremony of memorial and celebration.

He felt shocked—as if Captain Olson might walk through the door and take her away from him. She was jumping beside him, saying "Allen! Allen!," and then she dropped her tennis racquet, hugged him, and kissed him on the mouth. And before she let him go and fell back laughing, he felt with astonishment her tongue push through his lips and twist for a moment against his tongue. Then the elevator took her away.

At lunch they decided that the memorial service was not for them. They listened to the gaiety around them and felt separate from it. "They don't really mean it," Mitsy said.

He was scornful. "They've seen movies of Armistice Day."

She suggested they have a picnic on the beach, in celebration. She would collect a basket of food, and tonight while the other people were at their service, they would sit on the beach and drink wine.

She picked him up at five. His heart pounded as he sat beside her, sneaking looks downward where her gray slacks tucked inside her thighs and made a V. She had visited the delicatessen, bought cold chicken, paté, tomatoes, cole slaw, potato salad, and wine—two bottles of prewar French wine; he tried to memorize the label, but the French dissolved when he looked away from it.

Bill sat near her on the blanket, and in a moment her knee was touching his thigh, and he could feel nothing else. She opened the wine, and out of Dixie Cups they toasted the end of the war. They nibbled at this and that, then confessed that neither of them felt hungry. After a pause in the conversation, after a drink which inaugurated their second bottle, he said, "You know all those dates, all those boys at college . . ."

He waited so long without continuing his question that she said, "Yes?"

". . . did you sleep with them?" he asked. When he heard himself he felt how naïve he sounded.

Mitsy laughed. "Not with all of them, Bill," she said. "Not even with many of them. Some. A few."

He felt jealousy rise in him. "Didn't your husband mind?"

"He was one of them," she said. "He went with other girls too. Why are you asking me?" she said. She sounded friendly.

"Because I want to go to bed with you, too," he said.

She patted his shoulder and smiled pleasantly. "But I can't," she said, "because I'm married and I love my husband."

"I'm a virgin," he said. He felt himself looking depressed. "I'll get a whore."

"Don't do that," she said. "Don't be silly. There are lots of girls who would sleep with you. I'd love to, except for being married, I mean happily married."

Bill fell silent then, with anguish; and alongside the anguish he felt something like cunning. He dropped his head on his chest. He heard her take another swallow from her Dixie Cup. Then Mitsy swiveled toward him on the blanket. He felt her arm extend around his shoulders, squeezing. He still looked down, keeping his eyes closed. Then her finger lifted his chin, and he felt her lips on his. This time her tongue went in his mouth right away, and stayed there, and he felt his penis rise rigid against his tight underpants and his khaki trousers. With his hand he touched her breast, or the sweater over her breast, and she moaned and moved so that their thighs pressed against each other.

"I can't," she said. "I can't. Not now."

He said nothing but put his tongue in her mouth.

As they kissed, her hand swept slowly from his knees to his shoulder, pausing near his waist. Then her hand squeezed him through his clothing.

"Oh, God," she said. "I give up. Come on. Come back to the room."

That was all there was, when William told the story later, except for things that she said, lying with him on top of the sheets in her room. "It's all right," Mitsy said, "because I love Allen so much." And when they first touched, naked, leg to leg, thigh to thigh, breast to breast, her long hair dangling against his shoulder she said, "This is your first time. Feel it—the *skin*."

The next day Mrs. Fitzroberts appeared again, looking slimmer and younger and not formidable at all, and wept, packing her bags. He should be weeping also—he thought to himself—but when he tried looking morose he felt silly and broke out in a grin. He hinted to Mrs. Fitzroberts about what had happened, and she patted his shoulder. She said that love was the most important thing in the world—the only thing. As they waited on the porch for the taxi that would take them to the station, among crowds of other visitors standing in front of cabins with suitcases, he wondered how many of them had risen from quick beds. Then a red MG swooped down the road, as he had expected it to do, and Mitsy leapt out, shining and untouched, and kissed him long and hard, in front of all the people, then drove away, and he did not see her again for thirty-five years.

3.

In 1965, in early autumn, William went to a cocktail party in Manhattan. He had lived there a dozen years, teaching mathematics to graduate engineers, with a specialty that earned him consultancy fees. His host introduced him to a Mrs. Dodge, the host's sister, and Mrs. Dodge answered his routine question by saying that she lived in Allison, Washington.

He asked her if she was acquainted with a Mrs. Allen Olson.

Mrs. Dodge's smile turned artificial. "Yes," she said, "but I'm afraid she's too grand for me." They both laughed, and his host interrupted and introduced Mrs. Dodge to someone else.

So Mrs. Dodge was jealous of her. On the twenty-year-old snapshot of Mitsy Olson, clear in memory, he tried to impose various "too grand" enlargements, a gallery of Helen Hokinson ladies. None of the images endured. From time to time, over twenty years, he had been curious to see her; now he felt the curiosity again. How strange to hear of her a continent away twenty years later. But the world is a bed, he reminded himself. He had encountered again a woman of the past; it made a connection even with Mrs. Dodge.

At this time in his life, everything that happened seemed to make such a connection. William had married in his senior year at Michigan, too young, and had remained faithful for five years, doing his Ph.D. and beginning to teach. Then there was an episode with a graduate student, and another with a colleague's wife met at a conference. For a year or two he hurtled from affair to affair—inventing late department meetings, conference weekends, Saturday committees—and gradually realized the grandeur of sexual association. He shuffled in the giant dance, and mathematics suffered, but he had known for some years that he would never be more than competent. And music, which his wife did not enjoy, dwindled to an excuse for absence: he went so far as to invent a string quartet in Detroit which practiced Wednesday evenings, often until two or three in the morning.

This extravagance was interrupted when he fell in love, divorced his wife, and married again for six months a young woman he loved and could not abide. When he divorced again he took his job in New York. Cautious of love, finding comfort in variety, he lived in his flat on Ninth Street a life of promiscuous harmony—revisiting old girls sometimes, always with two or three to telephone if he was lonesome—and he searched continually at parties, in bars, at concerts, at the Museum of Modern Art, for the faces of women he would add to his long encounter, as they added him to their own. And many times, as he lay in bed with a new woman, the light from Fifth Avenue faint through the curtains, he told them stories of his sexual life and sought from them stories of their own. He told about his initiation at Balfour, and the first woman whose skin he had touched.

Tonight he glanced over the party to assess the crowd, then moved from group to group with his glass, drinking little, listening to conversations. There was a pretty blonde woman, early thirties, with the animation of the newly divorced. He passed her over; he wanted no tears. There was a young woman, beautiful if overly made-up, surrounded by a shifting group of males and no women at all. Someone identified her vaguely familiar face; she reported local television news, and was supposed to graduate to a network. There would be no tears with that one! . . . but there would be nothing else either. The men would mill about her all night, making little jousts of jokes and attention, and at some point she would glance at her watch, speak of a morning deadline, and disappear leaving the men to each other. William found himself seeking out a tall and pleasant young woman, long legs and large glasses, pretty hair, who was eager to laugh with him. After half an hour of talk, he suggested that she find her purse. She did not protest.

As they were leaving he looked for his host and found him standing with Mrs. Dodge who was very drunk. "Your banker's bitch,"—she said to William, twisting the word—"no one is good enough for her. Holier than thou. I wish she'd fall off that deck and break her goddamned neck."

4.

In 1980 at fifty-one he looked forty, they told him, and when he shaved each morning he tested the flattery out. Although his hair was thin, it was black, and he had grown a burly moustache; with handball and diet his waistline remained what it had been at sixteen. His life had not noticeably altered for twenty years, and he took pride in his life, especially as he saw his friends turn fat, alcoholic, diabetic, frightened, and old; one or two had the bad luck to die. It was true that sometimes he was bored. It was true that the prospect of old age depressed him, and when he allowed it to surface, loneliness felt heavy in his chest. It was true that his love affairs, which he continued to enjoy, had become repetitious. William boasted to his male acquaintances that he had discovered a three-part solution, a relationship partaking of music at its most mathematical. In this solution he kept one love affair beginning, one at a summery peak of attention, and one diminishing into silence. The trick was never to allow two to occupy the same phase, or to allow any moment without resource.

It was boredom, not need for money, that led him impulsively to accept a summer teaching job at the University of Washington. Within a week he had found a young woman who moved in with him for the summer, perhaps a dangerous departure from his three-part invention, but undertaken with forethought. He had begun to suspect that he would marry again—perhaps at sixty, perhaps even closer to retirement. And he had not lived with a woman for twenty-odd years.

Two weeks after his arrival, he found Allison on the map, and on a free Friday morning drove for an hour past hills and rivers and water-falls through great stands of timber. For the first time in years he felt dazzled by the natural world, almost elated with the grandeur of vista and swoop. Maybe this joy was a good omen for his journey. He re-minded himself that returns were always foolish—Mitsy might not be there, might not even be alive—but he *was* curious. The girl in the red MG, the first woman of his life, the social snob of 1965—he speculated on what he would find. He would find a woman fifty-nine years old! Then he remembered his own age, and the boredom of his present life made him shudder as he drove. Perhaps he was coming to the end of a thirty-five-year adventure; how appropriate, then, to revisit the first woman.

He entered the streets of the small town, *Class of 80* spray-painted on the water tower, and found the name listed in the phone book. When he telephoned from the drugstore, a maid's voice told him that Mrs. Olson was out but expected home soon. William represented himself as an old friend who preferred not to leave his name because he wanted to surprise Mrs. Olson. He took directions, parked beside a redwood car-port, and walked past a border of irises toward the low modern house. His heart pounded as he rang the bell in the bright morning. Mrs. Olson was changing her clothes, and he waited in a large Japanese living room. Long windows gave onto a deck that looked down a gully to a stream. There was money in the room, well-employed and inconspicuous. Three paintings on the wall were signed with a name he could not read.

When she walked in, he entertained for a moment the illusion that she had not changed at all. She stood straight and firm, her black hair tied back. Then he saw, as if a film pulled away and he looked behind it, that her face was everywhere finely wrinkled, with dark creases under her eyes and at the sides of her mouth and a trembling looseness under her chin. She was fifty-nine—and remarkable. Her hair was dyed and her figure was trim, her legs a little knobbed with veins faintly blue under her tan. She reminded him, in fact, of Mrs. Fitzroberts.

"Yes?" she was saying. She looked at him firmly, *grand*.

"William Bolter," he mumbled, and gave her his hand. "We knew each other in 1945," he said. "At Balfour. When you had the red MG . . . We played tennis." She looked as if she were trying to remember. He kept on: "V-J Day, Mitsy."

"Oh," she said, and looked pleased, and then flushed lightly with a

look that he remembered. "No one calls me that now," she laughed.
"*Margaret*," she pronounced, mocking her own dignity. "I've thought
about you. I've wondered so often what . . . My goodness!" She laughed,
and again thirty-five years disappeared for a moment. "Really," she said,
"I didn't think you would remember me."

He laughed. "Of course I remember you, and I remember June
Allyson."

He told her what he was doing in Seattle, and that he had abandoned the violin because you could not serve two masters, and he told
her how remarkably unchanged she was. She told him about her life in
Allison, about her two grown children, a granddaughter. There was a
child who had died. She told about a return to Balfour, the changes
there, not for the better. . . . She gave him sherry. She would like him
to meet her husband, she said, but he would not be home until late; would
he please stay for lunch? She left the room to speak with the cook.

When she returned he asked her, "Who did the paintings?"

She looked pleased again. "Gilbert Honiger," she said. "He's a friend
of ours. He lives on a farm west of here." She refilled their sherry glasses.
He told her about meeting the woman from Allison at the New York
party, without repeating the conversation, and she wrinkled her nose
faintly when he pronounced Mrs. Dodge's name. Fair's fair, he thought.
He liked her style better than Mrs. Dodge's.

Then he began to reminisce about the old summer, and she seemed
happy to join in. He remarked that, over the years, he had come to think
that artistic festivals had as much to do with art as checker tournaments
did. He was going to tell an anecdote about a Balfour conductor, but
she interrupted. "That's what Gilbert says," she said, and made a gesture
toward the paintings. "He went to Santa Cruz one summer for something
and walked out the second day." The delighted look was on her face
again—and he knew that Gilbert was her lover, and felt a regret he could
not justify.

Lunch was an omelette with Wente Brothers Grey Riesling and a
salad. They talked lightly and it was pleasant but he began to feel irritation and loss. He mocked himself for expecting grand opera. They emptied a bottle of wine and she pressed a buzzer on the floor and the maid
brought another. He drank several glasses. He spoke lightly of his two
marriages. Feeling mildly flirtatious, he let her know that he had not
lost interest in young women; he mentioned the girl in Seattle, who was
twenty-four.

He noticed that she had stopped drinking; he kept on. Annoyed that she revealed less than he did, he talked without pausing. He had kept up with contemporary music, and liked it; she had followed it less, she said, and didn't like what she heard. He found himself lecturing, as if he were in a classroom, and the more pompous he knew he sounded, the less he could stop, while her smile grew fainter and more distant. He began to feel angry with her, this smooth social creature, Margaret not Mitsy, who had once clutched him on a beach in Massachusetts. Irritated, he began to be insulting about people who were unable to hear anything later than Stravinsky, and he watched her smile turn cold.

Then again he saw through her dyed hair, back to the luxurious twenty-four-year-old hair of 1945, spread on the pillow of her hotel room the night they stayed together. He wanted urgently to be closer to her, to force her to acknowledge that old closeness, to break through the light graceful surface that she wore to protect herself. Yes, he wanted to make love to her again, and he thought of pulling her up from her relaxed chair and kissing her. Instead, he said, "Gilbert is your lover."

"What?" she said. He watched her cheeks grow red.

"Gilbert is your lover," he said. "The world is a bed. Everybody is everybody's lover. What does it matter? It doesn't matter." When he saw her flush he realized that he was drunk and babbling. "I mean"—he stumbled on—"it's none of my business what you do; I mean I understand . . . The world is a bed."

She was looking down at her plate. After a pause she said, "If Betty Dodge told you that she is a liar . . ."

He shook his head. "She didn't say. I understand about these things."

She laughed. "You understand . . . Why do you say something so stupid? I haven't seen you for thirty-five years and I've been perfectly decent to you. Gilbert is homosexual and has lived with someone named Harold for twenty years. Harold is dying now. I spent the morning with him . . . It was such a beautiful morning. Maybe you noticed . . . if you notice anything. I sat in the bedroom with Harold who didn't even know I was there and watched the sunlight coming through an oak Gilbert transplanted there twenty years ago. The sunlight kept getting into Harold's eyes and bothering him until I pulled the shade. What do you *understand*?"

A sense of his own ridiculousness rose to his cheeks and burned below his eyes. "Oh," he said. "Oh . . . I'm sorry . . . It was foolish . . . I was trying . . ." He could not think how to explain.

"*The world is a bed*," she quoted. "That's what you like to say, isn't it? Of course it is. The world is a bed and someone is always dying in it. Have you ever sat with someone dying? My daughter died when she was sixteen."

"I'm sorry," he said. He stood up. "I'm very sorry. I hate to be stupid..."

"I suppose that changed my life more than anything else did." She stood up also. "But most people turn more serious when they are older..." She looked past him out the windows where the deck hung over the gully. He understood that she was no longer addressing him. "But some people stay children and when they die they are still children. Harold was like that."

"I'm sorry," he said again, "I'm sorry." Then, as if it would explain things, he blurted, "You were the first woman I ever made love to."

"And you were the last man I went to bed with," she said, "except for my husband. Oh, you idiot. You were a sixteen-year-old boy named Bill, sweet, and I was lonesome. I suppose I used you to make myself feel powerful, the way I did at college... and for you of course I was a prize to bring back to school, like a trophy you won swimming. But you were decent enough back then. Now you are an old fool full of self-importance because you still take young women to bed with you. What a life."

He went away quickly, then. Driving back to Seattle, he was arrested for speeding and charged with driving under the influence of alcohol. Later his colleagues wondered why it upset him quite so much.

Barry Hannah

Ride, Fly, Penetrate, Loiter

MY name is Ned Maximus but they call me Maximum Ned.

Three years ago, when I was a drunk, a hitchhiker stabbed me in the eye with my own filet knife. I wear a patch on the right one now. It was a fake Indian named Billy Seven Fingers. He was having the shakes, and I was trying to get him to the bootleggers off the reservation in Neshoba County, Mississippi. He was white as me—whiter, really, because I have some Spanish.

He asked me for another cigarette and I said no, that's too many, and besides you're a fake. You might be gouging the Feds with 32nd part maximum Indian blood, but you don't fool me. I only got to the *maximum* part when he was on my face with the fish knife out of the pocket of the MG Midget.

There were three of us. He was sitting on the lap of his enormous sick real Indian friend. They had been drinking Dr. Tichenor's antiseptic in Philadelphia, and I picked them up sick at five in the morning, working on my Johnny Walker Black.

The big Indian made the car seem like a toy. Then we got out in the pines, and the last thing of any note I saw with my right eye was a Dalmatian dog run out near the road, and this was wonderful in rural Mississippi—practically a miracle—it was truth and beauty like John Keats has in that poem. And I wanted a dog to redeem my life as drunks and terrible women do.

But they wouldn't help me chase it. They were too sick. So I went on, pretty dreadfully let down. It was the best thing offering lately.

I was among dwarves of the spirit over in Alabama at the school, where almost everybody dies early. There is a poison in Tuscaloosa that draws souls toward the low middle. Hardly anybody has honest work. Queers full of backbiting and rumors set the tone. Nobody has ever missed a meal, everybody has about exactly enough courage to jaywalk or cheat a wife or a friend with a quote from Nietzsche on his lips.

Thus it seemed when I was a drunk, raving with bad attitudes. I drank and smiled and tried to love, wanting some hero for a buddy: somebody who would attack the heart of the night with me. I had worn out all the parlor charity of my wife. She was doing the standard frigid lockout at home, enjoying my trouble and her cold rectitude. The drunkard lifts sobriety into a great public virtue in the smug and snakelike heart. It may be his major service. Thus it seemed when I was a drunk, raving with bad attitudes.

So there I was, on my knees in the pebble dust on the shoulder of the road, trying to get the pistol out of the trunk of my car. An eye is a beautiful thing! I shouted. An eye is a beautiful thing! I was howling and stumbling. You frauding ugly shit! I howled.

But they were out of the convertible and away. My fingers were full of blood but it didn't hurt that much. When I finally found the gun, I fired it everywhere and went out with a white heat of loud horror.

I remember wanting a drink terribly in the emergency room. I had the shakes, and then I was in another room and didn't. My veins were warm with dope, the bandage on. But another thing—there was my own personal natural dope running in me. My head was very high and warm. I was exhilarated, in fact. I saw with penetrating clarity with my lone left eye. I felt darkly with the dead one.

It has been so ever since. Except, my brothers and sisters, the dead one has come alive and I can see the heart of the night with it. It throws a grim net sometimes, oh kindred, but I am exhilarated.

Nowadays this is how it goes with me: ride, fly, penetrate, loiter.

I left Tuscaloosa—the hell with Tuscaloosa—on a Triumph motorcycle black and chrome, the color of Jimi Hendrix, our dead genius brother of the guitar. My hair was long, leather on my loins, bandanna of the forehead in place, standard dope-drifter gear except for the bow and arrows strapped on the sissy bar. No guns. Guns are for cowards. But the man who comes near my good eye will walk away a spewing porcupine.

I left in the morning when only a few of the dwarves were starting their cars, another bright chance to slaughter the imagination.

The women of this town could beg and beg, but I would never make love to any of them again. The women will grow old and puke on the smell of their men—soap and rotting coward's money. They will see in the smoke of some midnight, when the beer is warm, that it has all been fatuous and chicken and mean, and they will throw themselves back on the bourgeois couch, shrieking with denial until their own tepid spit drowns them. Nothing is left but the religion of the dry blasted vagina.

Thus it seemed when I was a drunk. I was thirty-eight and somewhat Spanish. I could make a stand in this chickenhouse no longer.

Now I talk white, Negro, some Elizabethan, some Apache. My dark eye pierces and writhes and brings up odd talk in me sometimes. Under the patch, it burns deep for language. I will write sometimes and my bones hurt. The black eye claws the marrow for expression. When I need money it goes crazy. The eye will itch and get redder where it was, and it will give me such a view of myself that I cannot support it without hurling myself on a fresh scene. The eye and I know that at the lowest baseline truth it is not with me because I was stupid and drunk in the wrong place.

It will set a pair of binoculars in front of me. You utter miserable ass. These are for some sober, smoothcheeked, handsome champion. Now see what that banal romance has cost you, whiskey pig.

I believe heavily in destiny at such moments, else I go insane.

I went in a bar in Dallas before the great ride over the deserts that I intended. I had not drunk for a week—an awesome Spartan's monument of my thirties. For a while I took some water and collected the past. I thought of my books, my children, and the fact that almost everybody sells used cars or dies early. I used to get so angry about this issue that I would drag policemen out of their cars. I fired an arrow through my last wife's window, hurting nothing but the cozy locked glass and disturbing the sleep of incubated grown children. Then there were the brief stays in the nuthouse and the jail, where you get a view of fatheaded sober idiots "just doing their job" that will curl the fist in your heart permanently.

It was then I took the leap into the wasteland, happy as Br'er Rabbit in the briars. That long long, bloated epicene tract "The Waste Land" by Eliot . . . the slideshow of some snug librarian on the rag . . . was nothing, unworthy, in the notes that every sissy throws away. I would not talk to students about it. You throw it down like a pickled egg with nine

Buds and move on to giving it to the preacher's wife on a hill while she spits on a photograph of her husband.

I began on the Buds but I thought I was doing better. The standard shrill hag at the end of the bar had asked me why I did not have a ring in my ear and I said nothing at all. Hey pirate! she was shrieking when I left, ready to fire out of Dallas. But I went back toward Louisiana, my home state, Dallas had sickened me so much.

Dallas, city of the fur helicopters. Dallas—computers, plastics, urban cowboys with new "ideas" and wolfshooting in their hearts. The standard artist for Dallas should be Mickey Gilley, a studied fraud who might well be singing deeply about ripped fiberglass. His cousin is Jerry Lee Lewis, still very much from Louisiana. The Deep South might be wretched, but it can howl.

I went back to the little town in the pines near Alexandria where I grew up. I didn't even visit my father, just sat on my motorcycle and stared at the little yellow store. At that time I had still not forgiven him for converting to Baptist after Mother's death.

I had no real home at all then, and I looked in the dust at my boots, and I considered the beauty of my black and chrome Triumph 650 Twin, 73 model, straight pipes to horrify old bores, electricity by Lucas, Prince of Darkness, hee. I stepped over to the porch, unsteady, to get more beer, and there she was with her white luggage, Celeste, the one who would be a movie star, a staggering screen vision that every sighted male who saw the cinema would wet the sheets for.

I walked by her and she looked away, because I guess I looked pretty rough. I went on in the store—and now I can tell you, this is what I saw when my dead eye went wild. I have never been the same since.

The day is so still it is almost an object, a clear rock. The rain will not come. The clouds are white, burned high away.

On the porch of the yellow store, in her fresh stockings despite the heat, her toes eloquent in the white straps of her shoes, the elegant young lady waits. The men, two of them, look out to her occasionally. In the store, near a large reservoir, hang hooks, line, Cheetos, prophylactics, cream nougats. The roof of the store is tin. Around the woman the men, three decades older, see hot love and believe they can hear it talking 'round her ankles.

They cannot talk. Their tongues are thick, like baby raccoons in a fetal sac. Flies mount their shoulders and cheeks, but they don't come near her, her bare shoulders eloquent above her sundress. She wears earrings, ivory dangles, and when she moves, looking up the road, they swing and kiss her shoulders almost. The heat ripples about but it does not seem to touch her. She is not of this place and there is no earthly reason.

The men in the store are still rather stunned. They have forgotten how to move, what to say. Her beauty. The two white leather suitcases sit on either side of her.

"My wife is a withered rag," one man suddenly blurts to the other.

"Life here is a belligerent sow, not a prayer," suddenly responds the other.

The woman has not heard all they say to each other. But she's heard enough. She knows a high point is near, a declaration.

"This store fills me with dread. I have bleeding needs," says the owner.

"I suck a dry dug daily," says the other. "There's grease from nothing, just torpor, in my fingernails."

"My god, for relief from this old charade, my mercantilia!"

"There is a bad god," groans the other, pounding a rail. "The story is riddled with holes."

She hears a clatter around the counter. One of the men, the owner, is moving. He reaches for a can of snuff. The other casts himself against a bare spar in the wall. The owner is weeping outright. She will not look around at the clatter and the distress.

The owned spits into the snuff in his hands. He thrusts his hands into his trousers, plunging his palms to his groin. The other man has found a length of leather and thrashes the wall, raking his free hand over a steel brush. He snaps the brush to his forehead. He spouts choked groans, gasping sorrows. The two of them upset goods, shatter the peace of the aisles.

The man with the leather removes his shoes. He removes a shovel from its holder, punches it at his feet, howls and reattacks his feet angrily, crying for his mute heels.

"My children are lowhearted . . . fascists. Their eyebrows meet! The oldest boy's in San Diego but he's a pig! We're naught but dying animals. Eve and then Jesus and us, clerks!"

The owner jams his teeth together, and they crack. He pushes his tongue out, evicting a rude air sound. The other knocks over a barrel of staves.

"Lost, oh lost!" the owner spouts. "The redundant dusty clock of my tenure here!"

"Ah, heart pie!" moans the other.

The woman casts a glance back.

A dog has been aroused and creeps out from its bin below the counter. The owner slays the dog with repeated blows of the shovel, lifting fur into the air in great gouts.

She, Celeste, looks cautiously ahead. The road is still empty.

The owner has found some steep plastic sandals and is wearing them, jerking, breaking wind, and opening old sores. He stomps at imagined miniature men on the floor. The sound—the snorts, cries, rebuffs, indignant grunts—is unsettling.

The woman has a quality about her. That and the heat.

I have been sober ever since. I have just told a lie. I have been sober but I have been drunk with the dark eye.

At forty, I am at a certain peace. I have plenty of money and the love of a beautiful redhaired girl from Colorado. What's more, the closeness with my children has come back to a heavenly beauty, each child a hero better than yours.

You may see me with the eyepatch, though, in almost any city of the South, the Far West, or the Northwest. I am on the black and chrome Triumph, riding right into your face, a man not quite on the earth—in fact shaken by, what shall I call it, terraphobia.

I sing along with our dead electric black brother Jimi Hendrix, and I play the accelerator with my right hand like he played the guitar.

Ride. Fly. Penetrate. Loiter.

Or I will see you in the next world.

Don't be late.

T. E. Holt

Apocalypse

> Thou canst understand, therefore, that
> all our knowledge will be dead from the
> moment the door of the future is closed.
> —*Inferno* x:106–8

IN the gorge the echoes faded. I found myself listening, hoping there would be no voices. For a minute or so—it may have been ten—we waited. I could hear the kitchen clock tick.

When the silence in the room became intolerable, we both stood to go.

The slate steps down into the gorge were buried in snow, and we stepped carefully, taking turns. The cold dimmed our flashlights, leaving us only the light of the sky to tell wet slate from ice. When we reached bottom and walked out onto the frozen stream, the light lay pale around us. Tonight's wreck had joined the others without a sign. There was no fire. Through the sound of water under ice, we listened, and heard nothing.

I could feel Ellen shiver. She told me once, after we had climbed back home, that she is afraid to let me come down here alone. She worries that another car will fall. As I put an arm around her—tried to, but in our parkas the gesture turned into a clumsy shove—I looked up to the rim of the gorge, where our house stands. There the road turns sharply down toward the bridge, and the safety barrier has long since broken down.

It was a mistake to look. No cars (the night was soundless): only the hard angles of the rocks, and the bare trees threading the sky. The night was bitter cold, clear and moonless. Before, a night like this would have burned with stars, and the sky seemed infinitely far away. This night, I saw four, six, seven stars swimming, awash in a faintly luminous haze that lowers, night by night.

Ell caught me staring and pulled at my arm. She dragged us stumbling over rocks hidden in the snow to where the new wreck lay, broken-backed on the stream side. Its engine had spilled out in a single piece, hissing into the ice. Glass glittered everywhere. We bent to a place where a window had been. Inside were six bodies, all fallen on their heads. Their arms were tangled, as if still gesturing.

Last night was Sunday. I had lost track of the day until, as we were half-way up the stairs, Ell asked if I had remembered to wind the clock. She has asked me this every Sunday night for seven years. It used to irritate me.

It is an heirloom, the clock. It was my father's, and his father's, and the story goes that it has been around the world ten times: a great, gleaming ship's chronometer. When I was young, my father would—rarely—consent to show me its works. I would dream about them, sometimes, in the conscious dreams that come before sleep. The gleam and the motion, and the oddly susurrant ticking merged with my pulse and my own breathing to whirr me into sleep.

At an early age I conceived the notion that the clock was responsible for time. I remain superstitious about keeping it wound, and have never let it stop since the day I inherited it, still ticking. When I opened its back that day, I was surprised how my memory had magnified its works: the springs and cogs occupy no more than a quarter of the massive, largely empty casing. I use it to hide spare keys.

Last night, when Ellen asked if I had remembered to wind the clock, I stopped on the stairs, and without a word turned back down. I felt her eyes on my back, and felt ashamed at my own carelessness.

In life I was the editor of a small science quarterly. I read widely in the literature, and so for ten years or more I was forewarned. But some part of me always believed that the world written up in the journals was imaginary. It never touched me: there were no people in it. It was an elegant entertainment, nothing more. This world—the one we live in—was real, and there could be no connection.

Can I understand what is happening? No, nor can I imagine the hour that launched it, some sixty thousand years ago, from the heart of the Milky Way. I can only tell myself facts: since I began this paragraph, it has moved two million miles closer. The words clatter emptily about the page. I only know that when it emerged last June—a faint gleam, low in the summer sky—the world changed.

Part of me feels certain this cannot be, that all of us are in a dream, a mass psychosis: the second week of January will come after all, and we will waken, grinning at ourselves. The other part of me feels the emptiness in those words.

There is a quiet over the land. We drive often now—gasoline is plentiful once more—in the hills outside the town, past farmsteads that could have been abandoned last week, or ten years ago. The livestock have broken down their fences. Cattle, horses, pigs stand in the road, root in the ditches. I saw a goat standing on a porch, forefeet up in a swing-chair, staring abstractedly into the distance. I wonder where the owners of the animals have gone, if anyone still feeds or waters them. I worry for them, should the snow lie deep this winter, and the ponds ice over.

We stop at the grocery store, and the quiet has penetrated there, too, a chill emitted from the frozen foods, the dearth of certain products. The aisles are quiet, but there is no serenity in this place. Out in the countryside there could be something like serenity. I think when I am out there that my intrusion has shattered the peace, this edginess I feel will depart with me, and the pigs will lie down again in the road and sleep. Here in the supermarket, every selection asks us: This large? How long? For what?

The pet-food aisle is empty. A man had hysterics there this week; we could hear him across the store. Everyone looked up, checked his neighbor, and looked down again.

When we found him, he was standing sobbing by his cart, his face gleaming in the fluorescent lights. I wanted to make him stop, but when I laid a hand on his shoulder, he wheeled.

—Do you have any?

I shook my head and offered a package of cheese.

—No. He sleeved his nose. —Do you have any *cats*?

I tried to move him toward the dairy aisle, but he shrugged my hand away.

—It's not *fair*, he howled. —She's just a *cat*.

The last word made him blubber again. At the end of the aisle I saw Ell, looking diminished, mute—one of the frieze of strangers gathered there. I could not meet her eye.

Suddenly furious at him, I dragged him away, wanting to slap him into silence. Instead I pushed his cart across the back of the store, where he lapsed into a sullen calm. I pulled from the shelves anything I thought a cat might eat: marinated herring, heavy cream, Camembert. With each, I gestured, as if to say—She'll like this; there, that's my favorite; isn't this good?—until his flat stare unstrung me, and I led him to the checkout.

I had been down to the bridge, watching the sun go down across the valley. The lake is icing early this winter; the town was sunk in blue shadow. Below me, the gorge was already dark.

The deck of the bridge is an open steel grid. I hate to look down through it: the trees, foreshortened, look like bushes. I came home and found Ellen gone.

I thought at once of the gorge. In the darkening hall I stood and listened to the kitchen clock, and wondered how long I could wait before going to see. Then the door behind me opened, and she entered, swathed in her old, over-large winter coat. She looked as if she had walked in from an earlier year. She looked so familiar—and everything familiar now looks strange—I could not catch my breath and only nodded. —The roads are getting terrible, she said, bearing down drolly on the last word, balancing on one leg as she took off her boots.

When she caught the expression on my face, she laughed. —Were you worrying about me?

My appetite diminishes each day, as I awake before dawn and pad about the house, too restless to start writing. The time required to toast a slice of bread seems too long. Were it not for Ell, I would no longer cook at all. I am wasting, I know: my face in the mirror shows its bones clearly now in the morning light. But Ellen grows. She eats with an appetite she never had before, and seems taller, broader of hip, and of shoulder and breast as well. It suits her. Her face retains its graceful lines, and somehow her cheeks are still indented beneath the high, Slavic bones. Her eyes, too, are still hooded, guarded above the strong, straight bar of her nose.

She has stopped wearing her glasses. She focuses as best she can on the empty air above her lap. What does she see? I have not asked. I watch her, and try to guess. Sometimes she looks up—suddenly, as if she has seen something marvelous—her mouth opens, and I catch my breath.

The telephone system still works. I hear a tone when I lift the receiver. It sounds mournful now, this fabulously complex network reduced to carrying nothing but this message of no message, this signal that says only that it's ready to send. Our phone has not rung in weeks, nor is there anyone I call: I cannot imagine what there is to say. Some numbers I try no longer respond: the weather, dial-a-joke, dial-a-prayer. The number for the time survives, telling the ten-second intervals in its precise, weary voice.

Tonight I was alone in the kitchen, washing dishes. Something was rotting in the trash. For a long time I failed to recognize the smell (my sinuses are bad this winter), or even that I was smelling anything at all. Something was wrong. What had I done? I worked faster, scrubbed harder, but the feeling grew. What had I done? When I finally recognized the smell, my guilt and anxiety changed abruptly into anger. It had been Ellen's turn to take out the trash. I was certain of it.

When I found her, she was in the small upstairs room that still smells faintly of the coat of paint we gave it in the summer. She was sewing again; the light was bad. She looked up as I entered, her glasses on the table beside her, straining to focus on what I knew she could see only as the pale blur of my face. Her eyes still struggle to see at a distance; the effort gives her the look of a worried child. It is the expression that gazes out of the few early snapshots she still has.

That look stopped me in the doorway. I tried to slow my breathing, reminding myself that, without her glasses, she could not see the expression on my face. I pretended my grimace was a smile, walked over to her, and turned on the lamp. She smiled back and returned to her work, presenting me the part of her hair. I stooped, kissed it, and quickly left.

Out in the cold, the smell from the trash was thinner, almost fragile among the smells of wood smoke and snow as I walked past our stuffed and sealed garbage cans, through the hedge to the neighbors' drive. Their house has been dark three weeks. They left their car, which I use as a temporary dump. I would use their house, if I could bring myself to try the door. Their car is starting to fill, and even in the cold stinks dangerously, but it will be enough.

We fought the next morning instead. I had thrown something away—a magazine, the last number of a subscription that expired in November—before she had finished with it. She complained, I snapped, she turned and left the room. The fight continued as a mutual silence that went on throughout the afternoon. When I could no longer bear the rising tension, I brought her a cup of tea. She was reading in the upstairs room—the light was bad again—and when I set the tea beside her, she did not look up.

As I turned to leave, she cleared her throat. —I was afraid you were going to go through the trash.

I turned, and she was smiling at me over the brim of the cup. —I wouldn't have wanted it, you know. It would have stunk. Her smile broadened as she spoke, but before she could sip the tea, she was crying. I tried to comfort her, and felt ineffectual as I always do, at a loss for words. I patted her back, and wondered at the empty sound.

The same dream has come to me these three nights. It starts in a scene I cannot forget, two faces I still see when I close my eyes. They were the first to fall into the gorge. We found them at first light, the car absurd among the boulders. The twin stars in the windshield told us what we would find inside. Perhaps it was the shock of finding them still so young, so peaceful behind the shattered glass, that reverberates now in my dreams: they looked asleep, their faces almost touching.

In my dream they wake, they speak to us, and as they tell us their story, weep—whether for each other or for us I cannot say. As they speak, their words live, showing us their last moments: the guardrail flying away, the slow, looming tilt of the far wall, and then the rocks uprushing. On the seat beside me, Ellen hovers at the corner of my eye. There is something I must tell her, but before I can speak, there is a noise, and then silence, which continues for a long time.

Ell wakes me. —You were crying.

Sitting up in the cold room, by the pale light the curtains cannot cover entirely, I turn and tell her the words the dream would not let me say. But as I speak, Ellen grows smaller, the room lengthens, the distance between us grows and still she lies only just beyond the farthest stretch of my arm. My voice make no sound. Her lips move. Each object in the room is isolated, meaningless, and I think, this is the end, it has happened, and Ell diminishes still farther, contracting to the one clear point in the deepening gloom.

When I finally awake, the world is still, and Ellen still beside me.

Her face relaxes every night, so that by morning the angles and the lines have vanished, her nose is round and freckled, and her lips are parted.

Every morning the urge to clutch her, shake her awake, almost over-powers me. I want to ask her something—just what, I still can't say. But this morning, as every morning, I let her sleep. The aching in my chest ebbs slowly, and the daylight grows around us.

At the neighbors' back door I looked in the curtained window: dishes in the sink, a dinner for four spread on the table. One of the chairs lay on its back, legs up in an expression of helpless surprise. The door swung open as I pressed, and a burst of hot, fetid air swept past me. Dinner had spoiled, filling the kitchen with a high, wild sweetness. The temperature inside was so hot the air seemed gelid: sweat burst out on my face. From the basement I heard the furnace roar. To leave in the middle of dinner seemed unremarkable; but why turn up the heat? I stopped amid the ruins of the meal, stooped and righted the chair. As I bent, I saw in the far doorway another leg stretched out on the floor, and beyond it a room where nothing was right.

I am afraid I understood. I could deduce—I could not stop myself from observing—the tools they had used, and how. Who must have gone first. Him last. But more than that I am afraid I knew exactly how they felt, as the moment came on them over dinner, and they rushed—in some terrible parody of joy—into each others' arms.

I locked the door behind me, and wondered how long I could keep this to myself.

There is a sound that comes at dawn. I have never heard it. I wake in a room full of echoes, holding my breath, and lie beside Ell sleeping, and watch the light change in the room. I cannot escape the sense that I have missed something important. But as the light grows, the room around me is utterly ordinary.

I rise from the bed, the cold floor at my feet telling me again I am awake, the world is real. Through a fragile silence I inspect each room, and everything is as we left it. But in each room, the objects I find—the chair with the book face down upon its arm, my binoculars on the win-dowsill—seem to be holding a pose, waiting for my back to turn. Only the kitchen clock confesses, filling the room with the catch and release of its cogs. In a distant, unconscious way I hear the sound of water flow-ing in the gorge, whispering dimly. The falls are almost frozen over.

I wring back the curtains, snap up the shades, flush the rooms with light and nothing moves. In the kitchen I heat the kettle to a scream, bang pots, and overcook the oats. Upstairs, Ell is moving slowly; she showers, the pipes shudder and groan, the wind picks up outside. In the feeders, finches hiss and flutter, fighting for a perch. A dog lopes hip-deep through the yard, barking bright blue clouds of breath at the tree-tops, where four crows cling to the waving limbs. They flap and caw, caw a senseless monody. Over all of us, gray clouds pour ceaselessly into the east.

The wind has blown for days. I wonder how much longer it can blow before the country west of us lies in a vacuum, and dogs and crows, finches and clouds freeze solid, and the trees' metallic branches thrill faintly against the stars. I have dreamed this. I have been dreaming of the stars as they once were, as I will never see them again, unless there is after all another life after this one, in a cold and airless west.

I woke again this morning among the booming echoes. Through the window I saw the morning star, failing, dim in the sick gleam that made my hand a skeleton on the curtain. Between my ribs my heart was thunderous in its hollow, ticking off the seconds of the dawn.

A restlessness took me out of the house today, on a final, senseless errand. I took the car downtown to fill its tank, though I have nowhere left to go, no errands left unrun.

As I coasted down the long hill into town, I noticed that the odometer was less than ten miles from turning over. This fact—this string of nines rolling up under the quivering needle—loomed before me much larger than I wanted it to. The windshield hazed, and the large, familiar hands that held the wheel seemed not my own. They are older than I noticed them last—the skin is drier, nicked with scars I don't remember, and a gold band glints at one finger.

As I came down the block I saw a banner over the pumps. Free Gas it read, in hand-drawn black. The sign sighed and billowed in the breeze, but nothing else moved: the pumps were deserted.

By the time I stopped the car, I was almost laughing, glad to have my mood broken by this sorry joke. I have given over too often to self-pity: it is only a car. Through the glass, still decked with offers of anti-freeze, I saw the owner dimly, seated at his desk, and thought I saw him smiling.

Gasoline spilled from the neck of the tank. The trigger gave a dull clunk and went limp.

The door to the office was locked; the knob rattled loudly in my hand, but the figure smiling by the open cash drawer did not move. I stooped to peer through the glass. He sat upright, his mouth and eyes wide open.

I took a winding route back home, through the empty streets. Not everyone is dead: as the sun set, windows lit in many houses. The people at the power station are still at their posts. I drove past every drugstore I could think of, and every one was empty, dark. On some of them, the doors stood open; others had their windows smashed. The street by a liquor store glittered and flashed. I drove home wondering, what are they waiting for?

I could not think of an answer.

At the sound of my key in the lock, Ell pulled open the door, rushed at me, and grabbed my shoulders. As I thought horribly of what could be wrong she was saying—Where have you been? and, I was sure, and, where were you?

I couldn't speak. We did not fight. Normally, in such a case, we would, and eventually would understand. I couldn't. There was something on my tongue, even now I cannot say what, only that a fear of speaking welled up once again and stifled me. When she ran weeping from the room, guilt stabbed me, but I could not explain. I walked upstairs and closed the study door, sat here at my desk for a long time before turning on the lights.

The morning is bright. Outside the house the icicles are running, and water echoes loudly in the drain. Fresh air stirs the curtains, breathing in at the window opened for the first time in months. The January thaw has come, but a few days past the turning of the year, rushing as if to make the time. The air is piercing, fresh and sweet. It buoys me with an indiscriminate urge to do something—nothing I can name. It speaks tongueless, as varying and monotonous as the water in the drains. The fresh air blows past my ears, whispering promises of spring.

When I came down from my study after our fight, Ell was reading in her accustomed chair, her feet tucked underneath her legs against the cold. She looked up, angry and compact. I knew she would not speak— that it was up to me. But what was there to say? A minute passed, drawn out into a wire that tightened between us. I wanted to flinch—to run away. But where was there to run?

From where I stood in the doorway, her face seemed a shield held out against me. But in the curve of her lower lip, I saw a trace of motion, a sustained, suppressed tremor. It told me something of what she must have felt when I did not come home—and what she must be feeling now. I understood the offering of her face then, the cost it exacted as the minutes wore on and the muscles of her neck grew tired, quivering. I met her eyes, and the intensity of the look that met me seized me out of vagueness into something solid, here and real.

At that moment the lights flickered, and my heart leapt with an animal despair—dumb, and damned so. The lights went yellow, faded slowly to orange, red, and as the darkness closed in around us, I saw in her face—motionless still, and pale—the same mute despair, and then it was dark.

We found candles in the kitchen. By their light we made love upstairs, in a bed piled high with blankets. The clock beside us was stopped at a quarter to, and the candles held at bay the sky's sick light. We were awkward. I could not remember the last time we had broken the unspoken agreement that for months has kept us from each other.

A silence this morning disturbed me as I stood, awash in morning light, at the kitchen sink. Something was missing. I listened, until I realized that what I missed was the sound of birds at the feeders: the crack and scatter of the seeds, the whirr of wings—the ungainly thud of the jays. I wiped steam from the windows. Every feeder hung deserted, full of seed, shuddering gently in the wind. I watch, and no birds come. Hours have passed, and I have not seen or heard them yet.

Perhaps they know. Perhaps some message came to them. I hope so. I hope that, even now, someone in a Southern kitchen is wondering at the chickadees, the juncoes, the titmice, and the nuthatch, upside down, inspecting some unnaturally sweet and tender fruit.

There had been another wreck. Both of us stayed seated long after the booming died away. The falls have frozen over at last; no sound rose to fill the silence. We sat throughout the afternoon, as the light faded and the sun went down for what must have been the last time—a dull, dim, red extinction. It disappeared and left behind a sky as blank as if the constellations had been destroyed. Perhaps they have. The moon rose soon after, waning, gibbous, sick in a sea of spoiled milk, and still we sat.

Ell rose, groaning a little with the effort it takes her now to stand.

She shuffled out to the kitchen. I heard her fumbling in the drawer where the candles are, rattling hollow objects for a time that stretched out far too long. I couldn't bear it. When she returned, her face alight, I stood abruptly, unable to look at her.

I think she knew, as I walked out the door, that I was not going to the gorge.

The streets lay deep in snow, and as I drove down the steep and winding road that ends in the bridge across the gorge, I lost control, fishtailed out onto the span sideways for the rail. Someone laughed as I spun, the railing moving wrongway by the windshield; then I was stopped, turned sideways in the middle of the bridge.

I got out of the car, stepping out onto the steel grid. Wind whistled up at me. I looked down through the deck; a dozen dark shapes lay at the ends of scars scraped in the snow. I walked to the western rail and looked out over the valley where the gorge opens and falls finally into the lake. On the far hill shone a constellation of kerosene and candles, flickering dimly across the miles. Down in the town, a brighter glow grew into a blaze of buildings burning at the center. On the north wind came no sound, no smell of smoke, only the wind.

In the southwest, a dim glow, as the sunset faded into the ashen light of the sky. No evening star.

Then I was driving, fast again, swerving around curves I had never seen before, headlights doused. I remember nothing until three deer stood and faced me in the road.

Then there was light, shining in my eyes. They lifted me by the shoulders, headfirst through the window of my car although I clutched the wheel and cried. I saw a tire turning, spinning slowly in the air.

Then there was light again, and warmth, a chair, and hands rubbing mine and feeling up and down my arms and legs, voices asking—Hurt? Talk?—a voice whispering—Shock.

They put my fingers around a cup, where heat thawed feeling out of numb nothing. Something hot trickled down my throat, buoying me out of myself.

And the first thing I saw was a tree, standing in the corner, shedding its needles on the floor. I thought: I missed Christmas, and: it was all a dream. The room solidified: a kitchen, plank floor, wood stove, iron washstand, water heater in the far corner. Warm light and the smell of kerosene. A man in coveralls, about my age, but the lines in his face had cut more deeply, the hand with which he slid the teacup back across the table was a farmer's hand, old already. As he watched me critically, I reached out to take the cup, and flushed.

—You're not the first, he said.

I nodded, unable to explain.

He nodded back, indicating my hand. —You're married.

I nodded again.

—Alive?

Again.

The man paused, looked away from me, and cleared his throat. —Do you want to go back?

I feel tears on my face. My voice makes no sound; the room seems to expand around me, leaving me in darkness. It is too late for words.

I heard a chair move, and felt a hand on my shoulder. —I'll go warm up the truck.

The man did not return. I heard an engine catch, roar, and settle into a rapid idle. A woman, in a faded print, and herself worn thin enough to show the pulse at her temple, a tremor in her jaw, each bone and tendon of her hand, sat around the corner of the table. She reached out to touch the tabletop before me, paused.

—Your wife alone? Her voice was hoarse.

—I wondered what she might mean, and looked around the room. Through an open door I saw three children all alike in dingy pastel pajamas, staring back at me.

—We let them stay up late tonight, she apologized. —When we talk about it, they don't understand. But they like to stay up. We wanted to *do* something for them. She looked at them, and whispered—Do you know what I mean?

I stood abruptly, caught myself with a hand on her shoulder and staggered into her lap. Embarrassed, she gave me her thin arm, and, biting her lower lip, led me to the truck. There she whispered to her husband, and with a shy glance at me, kissed him long and urgently. Then we were gone.

The road was drifted deep where snow had blown across the fields. The clouds had broken before the rising wind. The moon burned bright at our backs, the only thing in the ghostly sky. It shone unnaturally bright. I felt it pushing, as it brightened by the minute, behind us.

The man drove fast, his need for haste twice mine. Deer were everywhere. They stood in silent groups of twos and threes beside the road. Smaller shapes, writhing in the headlights, fled before us. Overhead, darkness dotted the sky, flitting from horizon to horizon as if the graves gave up their dead. The face of the man beside me was taut in the dim green light of the speedometer. He swerved to miss something that froze before us—a skunk—and silently drove on.

He turned on the radio, tuned from static to a voice beseeching to the sound of running water, then fire, then large masses breaking, waves upon a shore, marching feet, applause, a voice explaining, violins, a chorus shouting, a man singing

> *Froh, wie seine Sonnen fliegen*
> *Durch des Himmels prächtgen Plan.*

He switched it off. —Last night there was hymns, down from Canada. You could tell it was hymns, even in French.

One road to the city was blocked by fire: black against the flames, men and women were dancing, singing, in tuxedos and gowns, diamonds flaming like stars.

The bridge from the north was destroyed.

The way from the south was blocked by a creature I cannot describe.

The door was unlocked. It opened into the dark hall, and I stepped in. I stood in the doorway, seeing no reason to shut the door behind me. The house was as cold as a crypt, and—I knew without having to ask—as empty. I wondered where she had gone, where she would be when the time caught her. I hoped the time would find her ready. I would never be, and saw no reason to wait, not any longer.

I went to the kitchen and pulled the stool up to the sink, and fumbling open the casing of the clock, I found the vial that I had hidden the night we fought. Not all of the drugstores had been closed that evening. I am more coward than I seem. I stood on the stool, the vial warming in my palm, and tried to remember something I had forgotten. The silence in the room was complete: my pulse seemed to surge out to the walls and return. The clock at my ear was silent.

She reached up and took the vial away. —I poured it out. It's just food coloring now.

How foolish I was to think anything would remain hidden. She helped me from the stool, stopping me as I started to fall. Her hair was cold, smelling of the outdoors. For a long time we were silent. For the space of half an hour, nothing mattered.

Then she moved, reached up a hand to touch my face. The light of the moon had brightened abruptly, as if a window shade had snapped up. As the light and silence grew, I felt the spell that has kept me speechless breaking. But when I bent to her ear and started to whisper, she placed her hand gently over my mouth and held it. I understood: there is nothing to say.

We stood together in the growing light, the thunder rumbling in the distance, drawing nearer, and I shrugged away impulses that no longer had meaning—to speech, to fear, to sorrow. I felt laughter growing inside me. Certainly she was laughing. At the window, moonlight poured in.

Ellen spoke. —Is there anything you want?

—Yes. The words came easily. —I want to finish something.

And at the door of this room, she left me. —I'll call if I need you.

Little remains. She is calling. The moon burns still brighter with each passing second, leaves my hand too slow to record, to report. I must end now.

But before the end we will speak once more, of everything that matters: of the brightness of the moon; of the birds still flying dark against the sky; of the man who brought me here; of the hours that she waited; of what we would name the child; of the grace of everything that dies; of the love that moves the sun and other stars.

Mary Hood

Manly Conclusions

HIS wife, Valjean, admitted that Carpenter Petty had a tree-topping temper, but he was slow to lose it; that was in his favor. Still, he had a long memory, and that way of saving things up, until by process of accumulation he had enough evidence to convict. "I don't get mad, I get even," his bumper sticker vaunted. Fair warning. When he was angry he burned like frost, not flame.

Now Valjean stood on the trodden path in the year's first growth of grass, her tablecloth in her arms, and acknowledged an undercurrent in her husband, spoke of it to the greening forsythia with its yellow flowers rain-fallen beneath it, confided it to God and nature. Let God and nature judge. A crow passed between her and the sun, dragging its slow shadow. She glanced up. On Carpenter's behalf she said, "He's always been intense. It wasn't just the war. If you're born a certain way, where's the mending?"

She shook the tablecloth free of the breakfast crumbs and pinned it to the line. Carpenter liked her biscuits—praised them to all their acquaintances—as well as her old-fashioned willingness to rise before good day and bake for him. Sometimes he woke early too; then he would join her in the kitchen. They would visit as she worked the shortening into the flour, left-handed (as was her mother, whose recipe it was), and pinch off the rounds, laying them as gently in the blackened pan as though she were laying a baby down for its nap. The dough was very quick, very tender. It took a light hand. Valjean knew the value of a light hand.

This morning Carpenter had slept late, beyond his time, and catching up he ate in a rush, his hair damp from the shower, his shirt unbuttoned.

He raised neither his eyes nor his voice to praise or complain.

"You'll be better at telling Dennis than I would," he said, finally, leaving it to her.

She had known a long time that there was more to loving a man than marrying him, and more to marriage than love. When they were newly wed, there had been that sudden quarrel, quick and furious as a summer squall, between Carpenter and a neighbor over the property line. A vivid memory and a lesson—the two men silhouetted against the setting sun, defending the territory and honor of rental property. Valjean stood by his side, silent, sensing even then that to speak out, to beg, to order, to quake would be to shame him. Nor would it avail. Better to shout Stay! to Niagara. Prayer and prevention was the course she decided on, learning how to laugh things off, to make jokes and diversions. If a car cut ahead of them in the parking lot and took the space he had been headed for, before Carpenter could get his window down to berate women drivers, Valjean would say, "I can see why she's in a hurry, just look at her!" as the offender trotted determinedly up the sidewalk and into a beauty salon.

She was subtle enough most times, but maybe he caught on after a while. At any rate, his emotional weather began to moderate. Folks said he had changed, and not for the worse. They gave proper credit to his wife, but the war had a hand in it too. When he got back, most of what he thought and felt had gone underground, and it was his quietness and shrewd good nature that you noticed now. Valjean kept on praying and preventing.

But there are some things you can't prevent, and he had left it to Valjean to break the news to Dennis. Dennis so much like Carpenter that the two of them turned heads in town, father and son, spirit and image. People seemed proud of them from afar as though their striking resemblance reflected credit on all mankind, affirming faith in the continuity of generations. He was like his mama, too, the best of both of them, and try as she might, she couldn't find the words to tell him that his dog was dead, to send him off to school with a broken heart. The school bus came early, and in the last-minute flurry of gathering books and lunch money, his poster on medieval armor and his windbreaker, she chose to let the news wait.

She had the whole day then, after he was gone, to find the best words. Musing, she sat on the top step and began cleaning Carpenter's boots—

not that he had left them for her to do; he had just left them. She scrubbed and gouged and sluiced away the sticky mud, dipping her rag in a rain puddle. After a moment's deliberation she rinsed the cloth in Lady's water dish. Lady would not mind now; she was beyond thirst. It was burying her that had got Carpenter's boots so muddy.

"Dead," Valjean murmured. For a moment she was overcome, disoriented as one is the instant after cataclysm, while there is yet room for disbelief, before the eyes admit the evidence into the heart. The rag dripped muddy water dark as blood onto the grass.

They had found Lady halfway between the toolshed and the back porch, as near home as she had been able to drag herself. The fine old collie lay dying in their torchlight, bewildered, astonished, trusting them to heal her, to cancel whatever evil this was that had befallen.

Carpenter knelt to investigate. "She's been shot." The meaning of the words and their reverberations brought Valjean to her knees. No way to laugh this off.

"It would have been an accident," she reasoned.

Carpenter gave the road a despairing glance. "If it could have stayed the way it was when we first bought out here. . . . You don't keep a dog like this on a chain!"

It had been wonderful those early years, before the developers came with their transits and plat-books and plans for summer cottages in the uplands. The deer had lingered a year or so longer, then had fled across the lake with the moon on their backs. The fields of wild blueberries were fenced off now; what the roadscrapers missed, wildfire got. Lawn crept from acre to acre like a plague. What trees were spared sprouted Posted and Keep and Trespassers will be signs. Gone were the tangles of briar and drifted meadow beauty, seedbox and primrose. The ferns retreated yearly deeper into the ravines.

"Goddamn weekenders," Carpenter said.

They had lodged official complaint the day three bikers roared through the back lot, scattering the hens, tearing down five lines of wash, and leaving a gap through the grape arbor. The Law came out and made bootless inquiry, stirring things up a little more. The next morning Valjean found their garbage cans overturned. Toilet tissue wrapped every tree in the orchard, a dead rat floated in the well, and their mailbox was battered to earth—that sort of mischief. Wild kids. "Let the Law handle it," Valjean suggested, white-lipped.

"They can do their job and I'll do mine," Carpenter told her. So that time Valjean prayed the Law would be fast and Carpenter slow, and that was how it went. A deputy came out the next day with a carload of joyriders he had run to earth. "Now I think the worst thing that could happen," the deputy drawled, "is to call their folks, wha' d'ya say?" So it had been resolved that way, with reparations paid and handshakes. That had been several years back; things had settled down some now. Of late there were only the litter and loudness associated with careless vacationers. No lingering hard feelings. In the market, when Valjean met a neighbor's wife, they found pleasant things to speak about; the awkwardness was past. In time they might be friends.

"An accident," Valjean had asserted, her voice odd to her own ears, as though she were surfacing from a deep dive. Around them night was closing in. She shivered. It took her entire will to keep from glancing over her shoulder into the tanglewood through which Lady had plunged, wounded, to reach home.

"Bleeding like this she must have laid a plain track." Carpenter paced across the yard, probing at spots with the dimming light of the lantern. He tapped it against his thigh to encourage the weak batteries.

"She's been gone all afternoon," Valjean said. "She could have come miles."

"Not hurt this bad," Carpenter said.

"What are you saying? No. No!" She forced confidence into her voice. "No one around here would do something like this." Fear for him stung her hands and feet like frost. She stood for peace. She stood too suddenly; dizzy, she put out her hand to steady herself. He could feel her trembling.

"It could have been an accident, yeah, like you say." He spoke quietly for her sake. He had learned to do that.

"You see?" she said, her heart lifting a little.

"Yeah." Kneeling again, he shook his head over the dog's labored breathing. "Too bad, old girl; they've done for you."

When the amber light failed from Lady's eyes, Valjean said, breathless, "She was probably trespassing," thinking of all those signs, neon-vivid, warning. He always teased her that she could make excuses for the devil.

"Dogs can't read," he pointed out. "She lived all her life here, eleven, twelve years. . . . And she knew this place by heart, every rabbit run, toad hole, and squirrel knot. She was better at weather than the almanac, and there was never a thing she feared except losing us. She kept watch on Dennis like he was her own pup."

"I know . . ." She struggled to choke back the grief. It stuck like a pine cone in her throat. But she wouldn't let it be *her* tears that watered the ground and made the seed of vengeance sprout. For all their sakes she kept her nerve . . .

"And whoever shot her," Carpenter was saying, "can't tell the difference in broad day between ragweed and rainbow. Goddamn weekenders!"

They wrapped the dog in Dennis' cradle quilt and set about making a grave. Twilight seeped away into night. The shovel struck fire from the rocks as Carpenter dug. Dennis was at scout meeting; they wanted to be done before he got home. "There's nothing deader than a dead dog," Carpenter reasoned. "The boy doesn't need to remember her that way."

In their haste, in their weariness, Carpenter shed his boots on the back stoop and left the shovel leaning against the wall. The wind rose in the night and blew the shovel handle along the shingles with a dry-bones rattle. Waking, alarmed, Valjean put out her hand: Carpenter was there.

Now Valjean resumed work on the boots, concentrating on the task at hand. She cleaned carefully, as though diligence would perfect not only the leather but Carpenter also, cleaning away the mire, anything that might make him lose his balance. From habit, she set the shoes atop the well-house to dry, out of reach of the dog. Then she realized, Lady was gone. All her held-back tears came now; she mourned as for a child.

She told Dennis that afternoon. He walked all around the grave, disbelieving. No tears, too old for that; silent, like his father. He gathered straw to lay on the raw earth to keep it from washing. Finally he buried his head in Valjean's shoulder and groaned, "Why?" Hearing that, Valjean thanked God, for hadn't Carpenter asked *Who?* and not *Why?*—as though he had some plan, eye for eye, and needed only to discover upon whom to visit it? Dennis must not learn those ways, Valjean prayed; let my son be in some ways like me . . .

At supper Carpenter waited till she brought dessert before he asked, "Did you tell him?"

Dennis laid his fork down to speak for himself. "I know."

Carpenter beheld his son. "She was shot twice. Once point-blank. Once as she tried to get away."

Valjean's cup wrecked against her saucer. He hadn't told her that! He had held that back, steeping the bitter truth from it all day to serve to the boy. There was no possible antidote. It sank in, like slow poison.

"It's going to be all right," she murmured automatically, her peace of mind spinning away like a chip in strong current. Her eyes sightlessly explored the sampler on the opposite wall whose motto she had worked during the long winter she sat at her mother's deathbed: *Perfect Love Casts Out Fear.*

"You mean Lady knew them? Trusted them? Then they shot her?" Dennis spoke eagerly, proud of his ability to draw manly conclusions. Valjean watched as the boy realized what he was saying. "It's someone we know," Dennis whispered, the color rising from his throat to his face, his hands slowly closing into tender fists. "What—what are we going to do about it?" He pushed back his chair, ready.

"No," Valjean said, drawing a firm line, then smudging it a little with a laugh and a headshake. "Not you." She gathered their plates and carried them into the kitchen. She could hear Carpenter telling Dennis, "Someone saw Gannett's boys on the logging road yesterday afternoon. I'll step on down that way and see what they know."

"But Carpenter—" She returned with sudsy hands to prevent.

He pulled Valjean to him, muting all outcry with his brandied breath. He pleased himself with a kiss, taking his time, winking a galvanized-gray eye at Dennis. "I'm just going to talk to them. About time they knew me better."

She looked so miserable standing there that he caught her to him again, boyish, lean; the years had rolled off of him, leaving him uncreased, and no scars that showed. He had always been lucky, folks said. Wild lucky.

"Listen here now," he warned. "Trust me?"

What answer would serve but yes? She spoke it after a moment, for his sake, with all her heart, like a charm to cast out fear. "Of course."

Dennis, wheeling his bike out to head down to Mrs. Cobb's for his music lesson, knelt to make some minor adjustment on the chain.

"I won't be long," Carpenter said. "Take care of yourselves."

"You too," Dennis called, and pedaled off.

Carpenter crouched and pulled on his stiff, cleaned boots, then hefted one foot gaily into a shaft of sunset, admiring the shine. "Good work, ma'am." He tipped an imaginary hat and strode off into the shadows of the tall pines.

A whippoorwill startled awake and shouted once, then sleepily subsided. Overhead the little brown bats tottered and strove through the first starlight, their high twittering falling like tiny blown kisses onto the wind-scoured woods. It was very peaceful there in the deep heart of the April evening, and it had to be a vagrant, unworthy, warning impulse that sent Valjean prowling to the cabinet in the den where they kept their tax records, warranties, brandy, and sidearms. Trembling, she reached again and again, but couldn't find the pistol. Carpenter's pistol was not there.

Not there.

For a moment she would not believe it, just rested her head against the cool shelf; then she turned and ran, leaving lights on and doors open behind her, tables and rugs askew in her wake. She ran sock-footed toward trouble as straight as she could, praying *Carpenter! Carpenter!* with every step. And then, like answered prayer, he was there, sudden as something conjured up from the dark. He caught her by the shoulders and shook her into sense.

"What's happened? Babe? What is it?"

But she could not answer for laughing and crying both at once, to see him there safe, to meet him halfway. When she caught her breath she said, "I was afraid something awful—I thought—I didn't know if I'd ever—"

"I told you I was just going to talk with them," he chided, amused. She gave a skip to get in step beside him. He caught her hand up and pointed her own finger at her. "I thought you said you trusted me."

"But I didn't know you were taking the gun with you . . ."

Angry, he drew away. Outcast, she felt the night chill raise the hair on the back of her neck.

"I didn't take the damn gun! What makes you say things like that? You think I'm some kind of nut?"

"But it's gone," she protested. "I looked."

And then a new specter rose between them, unspeakable, contagious. For a moment they neither moved nor spoke, then Carpenter started for home, fast, outdistancing her in a few strides. Over his shoulder he called back, edgy, unconvinced, "You missed it, that's all. It's there." He would make sure.

She ran but could not quite catch up. "Dennis has it," she accused Carpenter's back.

"Nah," he shouted. "Don't borrow trouble. It's home."

When he loped across the lawn and up the kitchen steps three at a time he was a full minute ahead of her. And when she got there, Carpenter was standing in the doorway of the den empty-handed, with the rapt, calculating, baffled expression of a baby left holding a suddenly limp string when the balloon has burst and vanished. The phone was ringing, ringing.

"Answer it," he said into the dark, avoiding her eyes.

Judith Hoover

Proteus

THE curtain falls, the house lights go up, and the performance is over. If the audience hesitates, if it takes just a few seconds for their attention to turn back to themselves, you have mastered them. If, in that hesitation, there is a jolting surprise and flash of unfocused anger, you have successfully deceived them, Stefan Mira: they will come back again and again but they will not forgive you.

Stefan takes the portrait of Madame Henriot and a self-portrait of Van Gogh with him to every new city, to every new hotel room; he believes he could not sleep if they were not constantly watching him, if, when he turned over in the strange bed and opened his eyes, he could not be assured of seeing them. He carries them himself, wrapped tightly in brown paper and bound with yellow string, and won't let the cabdrivers or the bellboys or the porters take them from him. On the train he buys two seats: one for himself, one for the paintings. The public applauds his eccentricities because he is a celebrity and a foreigner.

For the stage he uses the name "Proteus." He has awed his audiences by transforming his body into unthinkable shapes, by seeming to expand to the size of a giant and then squeezing into a child-sized coffin. He has changed his facial features to resemble any volunteer from the floor who will stand on the stage beside him, man, woman, or child, and has, at the end of each performance, appeared to melt like a warm wax doll into a puddle on the floor.

Now Stefan is sitting uncomfortably on a train leaving Pittsburgh. This is where his father had come, and looked, and then written his mother to tell her yes, there was work for him in America and yes, it was good work. This is where his mother had brought him and his sisters and

[196]

the baby, crossing the Atlantic on the crowded deck of the *Kaiser Wilhelm*; the baby had died from exposure on the way. When they had arrived in Pittsburgh on the train from New York City and his mother saw the blackened buildings, streets, people, sky, and thinner, blackened husband she had refused to get off the train. His sisters had cried while Stefan and his silent father struggled with his mother, finally lifting her down the steps of the train onto the platform and holding her there until the train departed and she stopped fighting. She did not speak to her husband for the first two weeks of her life in America, did not look at him until he told her he would buy tickets for the train and boat home as soon as he made enough money. When he said this, sighing the soft Czech words and staring down at her brown shoes on the wooden floor, she took his hand and accepted America as prison and home. She died three years later, just after Stefan had finally persuaded her to let him teach her English.

The train follows the river outside of the city, into the farmland. Last night after the performance, when Stefan was reaching for his suit in the closet, he had uncovered the hiding place of a small boy. He had a thin, pointed face and black hair, and Stefan had not been surprised when the boy had asked in Czech for his autograph. He smiled and wrote "Proteus" on the wrinkled scrap of paper the boy offered him. It is not unusual for children to approach him with their notebooks, autograph books, or pieces of paper, but this was the first time any of them had gotten all the way into his dressing room without being seen by one of the guards. Stefan smiles again remembering the boy's shaking voice and frightened eyes; he hopes he did not disappoint the boy by showing himself capable of wearing a black suit and tie as easily as a stage costume. "You are the greatest magician in the world," the boy had said in Czech. "I am not a magician," Stefan answered in English, but the expression on the boy's face did not change; he did not understand the language.

Stefan had led the boy from his dressing room through the maze of two-dimensional props and rows of hanging costumes as far as the stage. From there he had pointed the way out. He never enters the stage after a performance; he never looks past the thick, dark curtain after a show. Once in the early part of his career he had gone back to talk to one of the directors who had summoned him, just after he had removed his makeup. In what had become instinct he had turned at center stage to face the audience—the silence—the darkness—the rows and rows and two balconies of empty seats—the loss of his audience—the recognition that people came to see him perform, or did not see him at all. . . . He had begun moving backwards, his hands reaching behind him until they touched the folds of the heavy, immobile curtain, then ran to his dressing room, paced from closet to mirror to closet and—because he needed to do something and because he could think of nothing to do—he had begun reapplying his makeup.

From his window he can see lines of wire fence surrounding farms of white barns and white farmhouses. He measures the speed of the train by how solid the blur of wire looks, the blur closest to the tracks. His father had promised his mother he would quit the mill and buy a farm as soon as he made enough money. Yes, yes, she had nodded, her long brown arms stretching wet clothes across a line: I will wait. She had always allowed her husband his dreams; he came home from the steel mill with his match-book opportunities—excited, planning, promising—waving his blistered hands in the air as if conjuring dreams into existence. At least once a week he swore to quit his job after the next paycheck. They would have a farm, he would buy a store, he would become a salesman and wear a new gray suit, he and Stefan would start a newspaper for the Slavs who couldn't, or wouldn't, read the American papers, he and Stefan would build a shop and make and sell furniture, he and Stefan would join a construction company and in a year buy their own machinery and start their own company.

Young Stefan accepted each new dream as though the preceding ones had never been mentioned, had never been heard. He was willing to wonder at these untouchable lives without expectation of more than that wonder. He had learned to watch his mother's face for the degree of possibility of each scheme his father presented to her; when she sat back and nodded silently, her most common signal, he knew he could accept without hope, without disappointment.

The cows are lying down in the fields: it will rain soon. Even that is not magic, Stefan thinks. He hopes the rain is coming from the west, behind the train; he hopes the train is the faster. He closes his eyes, attempts to be more comfortable in the seat but fails, looks up quickly at the brown-covered paintings across from him, then sleeps.

"You are the greatest magician in the world," a small boy is telling him, repeating it louder and louder. "You are, I know you are." But he is speaking English and Stefan cannot understand him, though he knows by the wonder on the boy's face what he must be saying. He thinks he must be the boy's father because they are in the yellow kitchen of the old house outside of Pittsburgh, or the kitchen of the older house in Moravia. He sees a woman in the corner whom he does not recognize but knows she is his wife; both wife and son have thin, pointed faces and black hair and Stefan realizes that they resemble him, and then that they are mocking him, putting their hands on their hips at the same moment he does, both copying his expression of annoyance at what the boy is saying. "I told you never to say that in this house," he reprimands the boy, and wife and son echo his Czech statement with an English one. Stefan turns to run out the door but finds he can only move very slowly, his feet almost too heavy to lift, and he panics at the way he must strain to pull them from the floor. He looks up quickly and sees his wife and son are in front of him again, sees that he has not been able to turn away from them, that he has been trying to run towards them and not out the door at all. The woman now is putting on some sort of mask; when she has fit it to her face Stefan sees that it is a mask of Madame Henriot, but there are holes for eyes and mouth and the woman's own are showing through, making Madame look malicious instead of beautiful. Stefan watches the boy raise his hand to his ear, sees him laughing at him now while his eyes are still large with wonder. He tries to look down or away or to close his eyes but he cannot and he tries to stop the terrible slow running but he has no control and he sees his son has a knife in his hand and is beginning to saw off his ear and Stefan tries to tell him to stop but cannot open his mouth and just as he reaches them just as he is about to touch them he sees that they are no longer there and he is holding his own bleeding ear in one hand and falls slowly down trying to tear the mask of Madame Henriot from his own face. But it only grows tighter, pressing into his skin; there is no hole for the mouth for him to breathe and he is choking, the mask burying itself into his face.

The jerk of the steel brakes wakes him. Looking out his window he sees a wooden platform without shelter and a man standing alone in the rain. The engine slows down just enough for the man to step aboard, the whistle screams, and the train moves on.

Stefan is wiping the sweat from his forehead with a white handkerchief when the conductor opens the door of his compartment and ushers the man in. He does not look at Stefan but hands the conductor his ticket and takes the seat next to the paintings. The brim of his wet hat hides his forehead and eyes; he leans back into the seat and appears to be trying to sleep.

The appearance of the man disturbs Stefan; a musty smell has begun to fill the compartment and the windows are becoming frosted with steam. Stefan can see no part of the man's body which is not covered by clothing; even his hands are curled in gray gloves. Puddles are forming around the black shoes and drops of water drip rhythmically from the wide brim of the hat onto his chest and lap. There seems to be enough water soaked into the man to flood the entire compartment, the train itself.

Closing his eyes, Stefan tries to sleep again. His dreams do not frighten him because he can never remember them, though he has had this same one, with variations, many times. But the presence of this new passenger with his warm smell of soaking clothes and skin makes Stefan uneasy, afraid to close his eyes before the man.

"You are the magician Proteus, aren't you?"

His voice is deep and rumbling, and he does not look up at Stefan. The water is still dripping from his hat.

"I . . . yes. But I have never been billed as a magician."

The new passenger seems undisturbed by the last remark, though Stefan has found people are usually aroused to question or deny it. He still does not move, and is silent for a while. Opposite him Stefan shifts his position to stare out the window, after waiting expectantly for the man to ask or say more. The rush of the fields outside makes him dizzy, his eyes tired, and he must constantly wipe the window clear of steam.

There is a movement, and Stefan's eyes are jerked from the wet fields to watch the shoes of the new passenger scrape back beneath the wooden seat, the knees pull slowly back towards the folds of the jacket, the back unbend and extend from waist to chest, the shoulders spread, the neck uncurl, and chin stretch into the air. Now the movement is stopped, or held back; there are seconds of hesitation, Stefan holding his breath, when the new passenger finally releases a long sigh of whistling air and the movement flows down from chin to shoes to refold his body like a wave receding.

He lifts his head and slowly opens his eyes, eyes yellow and large, the whites a lighter, dirtier shade of yellow, as if bruised.

"I have seen many of your performances." He speaks slowly; Stefan is staring back at the eyes which stare into his, does not even notice the mouth moving, the nose or the shape of the face.

"I have had occasion to be in many cities at times when you were on the stage. Oh yes, I have been a member of, I would think, most of your audiences. A salesman: I'm a traveling salesman." Here the man pats the brown suitcase on the floor between his legs, but Stefan does not look down, will not look away; he is relaxed staring into the yellow eyes, and the man calmly returns the look.

"Watches: wristwatches, pocket watches, watches on ornamental pins for ladies, watches with compasses on the back, any type and style of small timepiece you can imagine. I like to claim that my motto is *I sell Time*. Not such an inaccurate statement, I think. These watches do, to some degree, encapsulate Time, don't you think? Contain it? And, in a sense, they give a form to Time: a body, if you will. A man who owns such a thing might be able to persuade himself that he controls Time—winding or refusing to wind the mechanism as he chooses."

As he speaks, the man feels for his suitcase again, and raises it to his lap; he reaches into a pocket of his wrinkled jacket and brings out a single key. With his last statement he opens the suitcase and presents its contents to Stefan, who blinks his eyes and looks down.

There is a cacophony of syncopated, disharmonious ticking as the lid is raised and at least a hundred timepieces are visible to him. Gold and silver flash even in the dim sunlight coming in the window, gold and silver chain and ornament sparkle like the pirate booty of a treasure chest.

"Hm, yes: I sell Time," the man says proudly, watching the expression on Stefan's face change from amazement to interest to the look of a man captured and seduced by an enemy. He closes and locks the suitcase, then places it on the floor between his legs.

The steam whistle blows loudly and the brakes begin to scrape against the iron wheels; peering out the window to left then to right, the new passenger grabs the handle of his suitcase and opens the door of the compartment.

"Well, my stop here," he says, speaking rapidly, sharply now. "You're probably going on to the city: Philadelphia? New York? South to Washington? I'll be in each of those places before two weeks are over. We'll meet again, Mr. Proteus; no doubt of that, no doubt of that." The door slides shut and Stefan hears the squelching sound of the wet shoes hurry down the corridor. He clears a small space on the steamy window and waits for the man to step from the train to the platform, but when the machine moves forward again no one has jumped off. He watches for a long time after the platform is out of sight, then decides that the man must have left from the other side of the train. This stop was like the last one, where the new passenger had boarded: a single raised platform without shelter, a dirt road disappearing into the fields of corn or hay, no city or town visible from the tracks.

From nowhere into nowhere is no place of business for a traveling salesman, Stefan says to himself. The window is defogging by itself now; the warm, wet smell becomes less noticeable.

A parade? What makes me think of a parade?

The image in Stefan's memory becomes clearer and stronger as he stares at the steam-muted windows, and just as his hand touches the pane to wipe it clear the image snaps sharp and he remembers.

He remembers that he was standing in the kitchen in the old house, his mother was cooking, and because there was a great noise of bells, band music, laughing, and shouting he was wiping the steam from the kitchen windows to look outside. His mother scolded him for smearing the windows she'd have to wash—no, *he'd* have to wash them, he'd smeared them—before the guests came to supper.

"What would they think, our only friends in America?" his mother had asked him, biting down on the foreign word "America."

He remembers next that he was outside and that his father was with him, explaining what a parade was by saying "There's a circus at the far end of it, past the post office," and then explaining what a circus was by saying "where the parade stops."

And then he was at the circus past the post office, seeing so many things that had to be explained but weren't; his father dashed straight to a small purple tent with silver stars and moons sewn onto it, and they went in—"to see the future," his father said. They entered the purple tent with only one candle on a round table in the center when it needed at least five streetlamps, he thought, in a row inside that tent, because that old woman sitting at that round table looked like someone he would want to be able to see clearly, someone whose every move he would want to be able to watch carefully.

He stood behind his father, who sat down at the table opposite the old woman, and over his father's shoulder watched her squinting at them both. His father reached out his hand and she grabbed it—Stefan jumped forward against the table to grab it back from her, but his father caught him and said that it was all right, that this was how she was going to tell him the future. Stefan ran out of the tent.

He turns his head from the window and looks at the two paintings covered in brown paper on the seat across from him. "I am not a magician," he says aloud.

What I do is not trickery, or deceit: it is pure physical ability. I have never performed a "stunt": what I do is the result of . . . not triumph over the limitations of the body, but the discovery that there are no limitations. I have expanded my body to the height of a man two feet taller than I; I have contracted my muscles until I am the size of a nine-year-old. And I do not yet know the limitations: how much taller or smaller I am capable of teaching myself to become.

Yes: teaching. The body must learn that it is not restricted, it is not imprisoned within the dimensions of tape measure or yardstick. How do I know that I cannot teach my body to become larger than this Pullman compartment? If I try and cannot, it is because I have failed, not because it is impossible.

There is no "gift of magic" in this: it is talent, it is skill. It is a triumph over space if they insist on billing it as a "triumph" over anything. . . . And time . . . it is a triumph over time as well. Because I have given it form.

A porter slides open the door of Stefan's compartment and announces that the dining car is now serving lunch.

A parade of passengers begins a clumsy, bumping march down the aisle toward the dining car. As it moves past Stefan's compartment individual faces peer in at him now sitting alone; a careless, automatic curiosity, thinks Stefan, watching them. Just as they will carelessly, automatically grow old: thoughtlessly resigned to process. None of them will ever wake up one morning, none of them, to find to their astonished discomfort that they have become much older than they believed they had. There will be no privilege of surprise allowed them.

I will not wait to be changed.

Moving along with that monotonous march of the passengers is a man who smiles and tips his still-dripping-wet hat to Stefan as he is pushed past the compartment. Stefan jumps up and shouts "Wait!" but the forward motion of the line of bodies has already carried the salesman far down the aisle. Sliding open the compartment door Stefan tries to step out and squeeze into the line, but is pushed back and aside by arms and voices yelling. He keeps his eye on the familiar hat floating fast to the front of the car and finally pushes himself out into the aisle; finding no room to get past anyone in front of him, he can only wait until the open space of the dining car allows him to search for the man there.

The dining car is crowded with passengers in gaudy holiday outfits or wrinkled traveling clothes, who shout in auctioneer voices for their lunches, who fight for a cup of muddy coffee. Stefan scans each face, but the salesman is not there; he retraces his steps down the aisle, emptied now, looking through the glass of each compartment, but the salesman is not in any of them. He returns to his own compartment, to his uncomfortable seat, and stares at the brown-covered paintings until, exhausted but resisting calm, he falls asleep.

The man carries his suitcase filled with Time across the sand to the edge of the ocean, and stands. It is dusk, the horizon is swallowing the sun, and the tide is pulling the sand from under his shoes, already and always heavy with warm saltwater. His jacket is wrinkled across his bent shoulders, the weight of the suitcase stretches the fingers of one gray glove, the brim of his hat curls limply over his forehead. Slipping with the sand, he sighs and lifts his head, and steps slowly into the water until the bottom of the suitcase in his hand is gliding heavily along the tops of the waves.

As he walks farther and farther into the water the waves swell and crash higher and higher onto the sand, as if there is barely enough space in the ocean to easily contain the weight of the tired god's body, and its age, or as if his return has stirred a boundless ecstasy.

James Lewis MacLeod

The Jesus Flag

IF God, in cursing Lot's wife, had turned her into a pillar of sugar, instead of salt, Mrs. Wilhelper would have fit the bill. With her tight bun hairdo and squat body resembling a bush, she was five feet three inches of sweetness as determined as a dump truck. She had two sayings—"Too Sweet for Words" and "Perfectly Marvelous"—which she unloaded on every aspect of the universe as relentlessly as a manure spreader covering a green field.

"Clara's just Too Sweet for Words," said Mrs. Wilhelper to her daughter, Mugsie. They were seated at an imitation early-American breakfast table under a large still-life of fruits. Stirring her breakfast coffee with a plain-patterned silver spoon engraved *W*, Mrs. Wilhelper regarded Mugsie.

"Don't you think so, dear?" she asked, adding as if there might be room for misconstruction, "Clara's just too sweet for words?"

"Ummm," said Mugsie. Long ago she had outgrown the desire to scream, to strip off her clothes, to run around the table at the banality of her mother's conversation. This was probably the millionth and first time she had heard the same views expressed in the same words, yet she had adopted an almost predestinarian fatalism about the whole thing. She had learned to let her mother clank on, assuming agreement, until her view of the universe was exhausted.

Mugsie was not an unattractive girl with her straight red hair and bright brown eyes; however, she dressed severely, purposely out of fashion. She had been christened Estella Carolina, but her father, who had hoped for a boy, called her Mugsie. It fit, even though she was a girl, for her mind was as hard as any man's.

The girl was educated and teaching school at a branch of the state university ten miles away. Mrs. Wilhelper realized that her daughter was an intellectual but always treated her as if she were normal. The daughter repaid the compliment by treating Mrs. Wilhelper as if she were human.

"Clara's a nut, but, at least, she's interesting," answered Mugsie. With that she rose briskly from the table, pecked her mother on the cheek, and grabbed a briefcase from under the table; her flat heels ground efficiently and speedily out of the room.

Mrs. Wilhelper's friends said Mugsie was on flame for knowledge. This was merely Southern rhetoric but it affected Mrs. Wilhelper strangely. She had a vision of a dry haystack going up in flames, a loss to nobody but cows. What Mrs. Wilhelper wanted was grandchildren, yet she was not one to stand in the way of talent. She dismissed the misfortune of Mugsie from her brain, concentrating on the silver spoon with the *W* on it that Clara had polished so beautifully.

Clara loved to work. She dressed herself in a long white apron to go about cleaning with the love of an artist.

"Work for the night is coming," Clara would say brightly to Mrs. Wilhelper as she sat on the porch. Mrs. Wilhelper thought of herself in the old tradition of being a lady. A lady was decorative, ornamental, useless, closely identified with the beatific vision whose chief duty was to sit and be admired.

Clara had no such views. She was the late Mr. Wilhelper's sister, recently come to live with them, and she had no intention of letting work lie on her hands. She had polished the Victorian sideboard in the dining room with a mixture of beeswax and yellow oil until the sideboard fairly shone. She had aired the mattresses, beat the rugs, ironed the linen, and the day before had just finished polishing the silver, including the spoon with the *W* that Mrs. Wilhelper was holding admiringly in her hand at the breakfast table.

Mrs. Wilhelper admired the virtues of Clara. She preferred to overlook the social vices, of which there were a number. Clara was a religious fanatic. Mrs. Wilhelper had seen her in operation once.

Clara had stood tall (six feet), erect (she had been trained by a Victorian mother), dressed in black linen topped by a cameo (the cameo had belonged to Mr. Wilhelper's mother) by the orange and green neon sign of Metcalf's Clothing Company on the corner of Main Street and Greene. Against her leg there was propped a briefcase in which she dipped to pull out tiny pocket Bibles, offering them to passers-by.

Holding out the tiny Bibles she asked, "Have you found Jesus?" as if religion were a game of hide-and-seek.

If the passers-by had found Jesus, she thrust the Bibles into their hands telling them, "Then this will help you on your way."

If the passers-by had not found Jesus, she said, "It's all here. The path of salvation. Take it. Read about it. Take it."

She would thrust the Bibles into their pockets if the passers-by would not take them in their hands.

Mrs. Wilhelper had considered thrusting Bibles, or anything for that matter, into strange men's pockets as obscene, but of course she was too much of a lady to say so.

If this had been all, Mrs. Wilhelper would have thought nothing of it. Plenty of families were under the domination of hard-lipped, religious-minded old women. But this was not all. The clincher was the Jesus Flag, an original idea conceived by Clara and, as far as Mrs. Wilhelper knew, practiced only by her in the civilized world.

Clara had originated the flag as a signal to let Jesus know a soul was falling from grace so that He might rescue the perishing. She waved it in dire circumstances when she felt the aid of Jesus was vitally needed. Having called Christ's attention to the sinner in peril, Clara, more or less, considered her work done.

"I don't do a thing," said Clara piously, stroking her white apron, "grace saves and grace alone."

The flag was known all over the state. When the governor had made a commencement speech to the graduating class of the State University, Clara had risen up and waved the flag right there—right there, Mrs. Wilhelper thought, right there, pointing specifically in her mind to an imaginary scene so that she could work up a hotter indignation.

Mrs. Wilhelper was glad Clara had been married (even though she had had no children) so that the Wilhelper name had not been in the papers whose headlines generally ran: "Auntie Appeals to God to Save the Governor."

The picture in her own paper, her own paper, the *Union-Times*, had shown Clara standing on a chair beside a puzzled young man in a mortar board hat whose tassel obscured his nose. She was holding the flag in both her hands like a classical statue of Victory or something Greek.

The flag was a green cross on a red background with John 3:16 embroidered in black beneath the cross. Clara had designed it herself.

Mrs. Wilhelper sometimes wondered if Clara knew the modern value of publicity, but generally decided she was too unworldly to know the modern implications. People said it cost the governor plenty. The opposition had circulated underground pictures of Clara and the flag with the caption underneath: "Pray for the State Under J. P. Gilmore." It seemed to have no effect on Clara.

Mrs. Wilhelper put the silver spoon with the *W* back on the table, groaned inwardly, and got up to go sit on the front porch. Lately she had become fond of an old wicker chaise longue at the end of the porch in the shade of an oak tree. She could count on Clara's coming down to do the work.

"Making myself useful as well as ornamental," Clara would say briskly.

"Darling, you're too sweet for words to do all this," Mrs. Wilhelper would say as she watched Clara grab a brush to scrub the porch.

"Work's good for the spirit," Clara would respond happily digging into an offending black path on the shiny surface of the paint.

That evening the mother, the aunt, and the girl sat on the front porch to enjoy the sunset. The aunt sat in a captain's chair, painted white, commanding a view of the pasture in front of the house. Her straight back, hands carefully folded in her lap, gave her an almost royal silhouette. The girl sat in a wooden rocking chair, painted green, next to her aunt. Mrs. Wilhelper lay in the chaise longue by the oak tree.

"Isn't it a perfectly marvelous view," said Mrs. Wilhelper referring to the sky in the process of sunset as the pattern of the oak tree fell across her legs, its intricate shadow promising a grotesquely Celtic day after night's unyielding cancer had eaten light away.

"Striking," said the aunt, as the hard yellow sun folded the sky into a brilliant coarse texture, and the white clouds spun themselves into ragged cones of orange cotton, resembling cotton candy sold at county fairs.

"Pleasant," said the girl. The statement was generous for her. She was not given to growing weak over sunsets.

Mrs. Wilhelper noticed the generosity of the statement. Though she was as dedicated to sweetness as a Vestal virgin, she was nobody's fool. She was sharp in a shrewd, earthy way. Noticed things.

The girl had spent an unusual amount of time with her elders since the aunt had arrived. If the mother had been the sole occupant of the house, the girl would have been inside, reading a book, flaming for knowledge. The mother wondered what had happened to the flame as she shifted uncomfortably on the chaise longue, trying to get her legs back in the shade of the tree and away from an unusually vital last shot of the sun before its departure.

The girl, swaying gently in the green rocker, was burning—even consumed—with curiosity about the Jesus Flag. She dared not ask directly. Manners forbade it and she had horrifying visions of what a direct attack might set off. A revivalistic retaliation. A Puritan Sermon. A Shouting Methodist. So she said politely, "The world situation seems to be getting worse."

"Yes, I think they'll have to drop the bomb eventually," said the aunt.

"Don't think about it," said the mother.

The flag did not appall Mugsie as it did her mother; if anything, she felt it added color to the world. She had the intellectual's delight in eccentricities coupled with the intellectual's desire to analyze them. She wanted to see how, when, and under what circumstances Aunt Clara flew the Jesus Flag. She did not often have the opportunity to examine so unusual a curiosity, abnormal psychology not being her field.

Moving the green rocker gently back and forth on the porch in the soft solemnity of the night, she felt disappointed there had not been even one sign of evangelism so far. Vaguely she had relied on the horrors of the world situation, the atrocities so faithfully recited each night over television, to spur so religiously sensitive a soul as her aunt to fly the flag.

Perhaps, the girl reasoned as she stood up from the rocker to bid them good night, her aunt felt Jesus was already informed of the state of the world by modern communications methods, whereas the aunt worked on an individual basis among the unpublicized.

The girl's bedroom consisted chiefly of books and a bare four-poster bed. Her mother had done her best to make it feminine and she had done her best to make it sexless. Lying down on the bed, which she had carefully de-chintzed, she arranged the white pillows beneath her head to settle down to consider the problem.

She would have to force her aunt's hand.

The more she thought about it, the more determined she became. It was not an irrational desire. If push came to shove, she could rationalize it in the name of science by submitting a report to the psychology department.

Poking the white pillows to make a more comfortable gap for her head, she began to recite in her mind all the horrors she could think of to spur the old lady to fly the flag. It was not difficult, for she had a naturally tough mind, yet she was not unkind enough to wish to shock her aunt too deeply.

She decided to start gently, playing the campaign by ear. Having decided, she got up to turn the lights out so she could undress. She preferred to turn the lights off to undress rather than deprive herself of the night breezes by shutting the blinds.

The next night the round mahogany dining table was set formally with a silver epergne in the middle of the table directly beneath the crystal chandelier. The first layer of the epergne was filled with ferns, the second layer with white roses.

The three of them sat around the shiny centerpiece. The mother was in the hostess' position, the girl in the man's position, the aunt in the middle.

"Isn't this salad just perfectly marvelous," said Mrs. Wilhelper drawing out the words into breathy loops of airy contentment. She was especially proud of the salad. She had made it herself out of grated cabbage and topped it with a yellow syrup swimming with cinnamon. The rest of the food—a pie, a soufflé, a grilled steak—had been prepared by the aunt.

"Delicious," said the aunt, who had acquiesced in the matter of the salad.

"Appetizing," said the girl, eyeing the yellow mess suspiciously, its turgid liquidity demanding moral effort. She fastened her eyes resolvedly (she knew her mother would object) on a white rose (she knew there was a worm in it) and determined (in the name of science) to begin.

"There was a rape yesterday," she said.

She interpreted the ensuing silence as nonbeing awaiting being and described the rape vividly, including a pair of bloodstained rayon panties that, under laboratory analysis, would clinch the case for the prosecution lawyers, until the mother squealed from the hostess' position, "Not at the table, dear, not at the TABLE."

The aunt munched on as contentedly as a cow. When a low-flying plane shook the house, drowning all conversation in the rattling of the chandelier, jolting a rose from the epergne onto the mahogany table, the aunt asked to be caught up on the backwash: "I missed the part about the panties," she said, poking for further information.

The girl gave it again in detail. Nothing happened, but the question showed the aunt was amenable, involved, paying attention.

Like a good fisherman, Mugsie, having baited the hook, determined to catch the fish. She placed her eyes carefully on the white rose and began casting with tales of beatings. The aunt's serenity on beatings warmed her to consequent murders. The aunt's tranquil acceptance of murder stymied the girl momentarily. She regarded the worm in the white rose and was caught up in perversion.

"Homosexuality is very prevalent today," said the girl.

"Anyone we know?" said the mother.

"I wonder why the Apostle Paul was against it," said the aunt, as if she were ignorant. The girl told her descriptively. They had homosexuality with the soufflé, incest with the steak, and sodomy with the pie, disturbed only by the mother's periodic yappings of, "Not at the table, dear, not at the TABLE," as if it were all right to wait until they got into the parlor.

"I knew a case in '05," said the aunt, carefully manipulating the last cherry from her plate onto her fork and finishing up her pie.

It was useless. There seemed to be nothing under the sun that could shock the aunt and no perversion she was unacquainted with. The girl summed this up as the result of the aunt's having lived in boarding houses where the atmosphere was morbid, the caliber of the gossip notorious.

Awaiting the hostess' signal to rise from the table, the girl moved her center of attention from the white rose to her mother. Mrs. Wilhelper, in a kind of trance, had taken a handful of ferns from the epergne and was making a wreath arrangement of the spidery green skeletons on her plate.

When they finally rose from the table, the light of the chandelier caught the silver centerpiece, and the girl noticed her aunt's cleaning had left no black paths of dirt unexplored even in the most creviced parts of the highly chased ornamentation.

"That was a perfectly marvelous meal, Clara," said the mother as the group passed a red velvet love seat in the hall on their way to the porch.

"Yes, and think, just think, of all the people starving in China," said the aunt piously, as if she were giving an invitation to the girl for a further recital of horrors.

"Just think," said the aunt again.

"Not now, love," said the mother who thought she had had as much as she could take.

"But just think," protested the aunt as the mother hurried on her way past the group to the chaise longue, as if there were a disease sitting on the love seat in the hall.

The girl decided to overlook the bid to discuss the Chinese. She had a mental picture of starving Chinese children groaning on the ground, each weighing thirty pounds, their tremendous heads with eyes slightly askew stuck on very small bodies like concentration-camp pictures which, the girl felt, would greatly satisfy her aunt.

She began to wonder just who had been hooked at the dinner table and if her aunt were not profounder than she had heretofore considered.

That night in her bedroom the girl lay on the four-poster bed with the two pillows propped sturdily under her head, considering the aunt from various angles like a prism held up to the sun of her mind. For stability in the middle of her mental readjustments she fixed her gaze steadily on one of the bedposts which had a carved pineapple at the top.

She considered her aunt's having a highly original mind which she, the girl, would discover. The thesis of the original mind would certainly explain a lot. It would explain not only the absurdity of the flag, but her inability to be shocked, her resolute desire to face the plight of the Chinese, her familiarity with murder, her acquaintance with sex perversions.

The girl remembered that the aunt had not brought up the sex perversions, as she had the Chinese, but the girl did not blame the aunt for not dwelling on them, since she was born in the nineteenth century.

The pineapple assumed gigantic proportions in the girl's mind as she groped towards a picture of a completely untrained, undisciplined native mind realizing its existential situation. She could see her aunt in an absolutely shaking essay which she, the niece, would write.

She could see the essay now: "Educated by herself, her untrained mind nevertheless groped with the great problems of our age. Natively realizing her existential situation of futility, her flag became her chief contribution to the absurdity of the universe. Her expression of it in Judeo-Christian terminology is merely the recognition of the limited symbolism in which her experience had to move."

This theory clarified much. On one hand her aunt might be a self-educated folk genius paralleling in the intellectual realm what Grandma

Moses did for art, her name ringing eternally in the halls of fame of primitive Americana. On the other hand she might belong in an institution.

The girl's eyes followed the straight line of the bedpost from the pineapple down to where the wood met the sheet. She had to plumb her aunt's depth.

On consecutive nights after dinner the three of them took up their positions on the porch. The aunt, hands carefully folded in her lap, sat in the captain's chair. The girl sat in the green rocker. The mother lay in the chaise longue by the oak tree trying to keep her legs out of the sun.

"I was reading an article by Turgenev," said the girl.

"By who?" queried the aunt.

"Did I remember to turn the hose off?" asked the mother.

The girl, moving in the solemn rhythm of a summer rocker, threw out names like sparks hoping one would catch fire. She ran out Malraux, Gide, Dostoevsky, Dante, Fiske, and Darwin like a Greyhound bus caller hinting beyond the mereness of names to some existent reality waiting expectantly for the traveler. She gave a brief survey of current intellectual thought. She gave up when she found out the aunt had never heard of Freud, though, in probing the aunt's existential situation, she did strike a spark in telling her Kafka's tale of the boy who metamorphosed into a roach.

The aunt hung on every word of the roach story. Every night beneath the orange cotton sky the aunt, hands carefully folded in her lap, royally erect in the captain's chair, would wait for a lull in the conversation.

"Now tell us the roach story, Mugsie," she would beg.

The girl had the feeling she was telling a child a favorite bedtime story that could be repeated endlessly. Since the girl had decided the aunt was as shorn of intellectuality as a sheep, she couldn't decide whether her interest in the roach was traceable to a dirty mind or the right instincts in an untutored one.

The aunt particularly liked the part where the boy turned into a roach. The girl, ceasing rocking, would tell it in words she felt the aunt could understand. She dramatized it for further effect upon the peasant mind. She would open her large brown eyes wide, screw down the corners of her mouth, and say histrionically, "And he woke up and found he was a ROACH."

The aunt's bright little eyes would blink appreciatively like a child's when the wolf was mentioned in "Red Riding Hood." The girl, unmoving in her rocker, would smile bravely. The mother in the chaise longue looked nauseated.

The girl concluded the aunt must be like a child and simply enjoyed a delicious state of terror as greatly as children enjoy scrawling "I am starving to death slowly" on the cellar wall in red paint to symbolize blood.

Dismissing the aunt's original mind, the girl resumed her old position of trying to get the aunt to fly the flag. The rocker continued to be her battle station every night for assaults upon the captain's chair which remained immovable, unshaken, occupied. The chaise longue was a bystander in agony, yet the mother remained fixed in it, constantly redistributing herself to keep her legs out of the sun and in the shade of the oak tree.

"Nietzsche says God is dead," the girl said.

"I've seen quite a few corpses in my time," the aunt volunteered as if she had strength to face it.

"I thought He rose," said the mother.

The girl pointed out to the aunt in a carefully chosen vocabulary of two to three syllables that God was dead, morals foggy, the world an open wound, capitalism a failure, nationalism a disease, patriotism a vice. She broached the idea of a Black Mass, but found her aunt was a Baptist.

As the summer passed, the girl, each night swaying rhythmically in the green rocker, made a discovery. She had started out to shock the aunt, but the result was she had expressed herself so fully that now she felt comfortable with the aunt as with no one else. She dismissed as nebulous the idea of the aunt's ever flying the flag again. She now used the aunt for therapy and began to enjoy her home as never before.

Every evening the group would take their stations to watch the sunset, and the girl, her eyes like obscene yellow lights whose motored passion rapes the night, would address the captain's chair: "I am reading a man who is a silly, ignorant, stupid ass," she would declare, spitting out the words in carefully enunciated contempt.

"Really?" the aunt would say, her ears perking up like those of a fox hearing the distant yapping of a dog pack.

"A jackass," the girl would say flatly.

"You don't mean it," the aunt would say in a tone implying she would be delighted to have it proved.

"The hell I don't," the girl would say in the tone of an officer gathering his men for assault.

"Now, dear," the mother would say, hoping to shut her up though she knew it was useless. The two were as made for each other as fire and straw. For her sins she had to watch the combustion nightly, though it was true nobody forced her to stay in the chaise longue.

When the summer ended, they all went into the parlor.

The girl became harder and more well-defined as if she were aware error emerged from preciseness and truth through definition. Her eyes solidified to rock, piercing the coverings of ideas as easily as a man's lusting eyes piercing skirts to evaluate the living mysteries therein. She toughened into a tartar and gained a reputation.

Soon the girl was giving a series of lectures that terrified the state, the old lady accompanying the girl on her drives to the various small towns where she lectured. The mother did not accompany them, explaining, "I'll just stay here and enjoy peace and quiet for a change."

The girl had a black 1963 Chevrolet with red upholstery. The aunt sat on the right front seat always clutching her black leather handbag with the tulip clasp which, the girl knew, but no longer cared, contained the Jesus Flag. They were two hours from Doomsboro, where the girl was to lecture, the aunt looking calmly out of the window.

They passed a general store with a red Coca-Cola sign, two brick houses, and a Sinclair gas station. After the gas station there was a herd of cows in a green pasture. The aunt watched the cows, seemingly unaware that a brown and white cow was defecating, or, perhaps, unaware that the brown and white cow should do anything else.

Next to the cow pasture the realization came to the girl like a bolt of lightning out of her subconscious, where knowledge had lain passively for months generating energy. She could not conceive of her own stupidity. Insight flashed into her brain and she felt it was illuminating her entire body, yet she drove on, moving the gears from fourth into third and back again as straight-faced and solidly as any Indian.

She saw her aunt's innocence crawling out of a pit so depraved her own world view was merely titillating. She saw her serenity was not betrayal but the last word in acceptance of a view as stark and straight as from the pineapple to the sheet. That her aunt had been a master psychologist squeezing her like a pimple till the pus and core shot out.

The girl passed a white Cadillac convertible and looked slyly at her aunt, who was studiously regarding the remains of a dead dog by the roadside. Pressing the accelerator efficiently, firmly on the floor, she ironed out the tremors in her voice as sleekly as a good maid turning a wedding gown.

The aunt, noticing a sudden spurt in speed, transferred her eyes from the dead dog to the niece.

"What are you gonna lecture on tonight?" she asked, gently sharp in a tone like a harpsichord speaking of rabbits eating grave grass in the moonlight.

"Think I'll reaffirm man's basic position; stress hope, that sort of thing," said the girl's voice smoothly normal.

"Sounds like your mother," said the aunt metallically.

"Mother's pretty sharp in her own way," said the girl sanctimoniously.

By the time they neared the outskirts of Doomsboro, the Jesus Flag had been flying for thirty-eight minutes. The girl had timed it on her watch. Iron-armed, the aunt held the flag out of the right side window to catch the breeze the car was creating as it moved along its path. The tulip-clasped handbag had fallen on the floor and was a black splotch on the red floor upholstery.

The aunt's black-linened arm out the window was as stiff, long, and straight as a poker. If the girl skimmed anything, the arm would be broken. She couldn't risk passing the little green Volkswagen trailing a battered hearse in front of them. The black Chevrolet, chromium gleaming, fell into line at thirty miles an hour behind the Volkswagen and the hearse, while a red '55 Buick came up behind to tail them into the city.

The girl was not unconscious of the scene they were creating, yet there was no sense of amusement in her. She was driving, grim-faced and glorious, through the South Carolina countryside in a procession resembling, on the left, a part of a funeral; on the right, a parade in which people waved flags ridiculously behind hearses. In this way she would enter the city to the acclamations of jeering adolescents. She was determined neither to stop nor to veer.

Jack Matthews

The Burial

Moses Beno

It come to me right away, like a smell or a far-off sound you been hearing for a long time, and all of a sudden there it is. Like thunder over the hills or a wind picking up from off the river or a coming out of the woods up north. It was just a hour or two before supper.

Only this, it come from the river. I was out there a hoeing corn, with my head down and my back straight, but not thinking of nothing but them little wild pea vines and such that grow like spider webs around the young corn stalks. And then it was I straightened up, just to rest my back a second and maybe wipe the sweat out of my eyes and from offn my forehead; and there it was, silent as a snake, a coming straight for the little landing where I keep my rowboat, but where they ain't room for nothing bigger.

But it was a coming, anyway. The air was so still that the smoke didn't hardly lift at all from the river, but just kind of laid there on the water downstream, where the boat was a coming from.

And then, right after I look, I could hear the chug of the engines, and it was like that chugging sound, it made me realize that they was headed straight for my little dock, like they meant to ram it right up into the bank. They wasn't no body on the deck, even though it was a hot evening, like I said, and right in the middle of July.

Yes, I knew it then. They was something wrong. And I laid my hoe down and went into my house, where my wife said, "Why are they coming here?" and I said, "That is what I mean to find out."

And then she said, "Why are you taking down your gun?" And I told her I meant to have it in my hand in case I needed it. Then she just looked at our infant child in the crib, the way a woman will do, because

[217]

it is the nearest thing to her heart. And right away after that, she looked at our boy, and said, "You keep your self right here inside," and he was just a staring at her with his eyes wide open, and he said, "I will."

They was both scared. I could tell. Because it was not right for a steamboat, a big riverboat like that, to turn from its course in the channel and head toward that little dock I made eight or ten years ago out of locust posts and whipsawed walnut boards. It was not right to see no body at all a standing on the deck and a waving their hand, the way they will sometimes do way out in the channel, even, if they see you a hoeing corn or slopping the hogs.

No, it was something else, and I knew it from the start, like I have been saying. And maybe my wife and boy, they knew it too.

They did not do anything as crazy as I thought they was going to do. They did not come right up to my dock and they did not get their-selves stuck in the mud bottom.

What they did was stop about sixty or seventy feet from shore, and then it was I saw the first sign of life. It was the Captain, with his Captain hat on, but otherwise in shirtsleeves. He come out on the deck and he just looked at me a minute, where I was standing in the path with my gun cradled in my arm.

He didn't say nothing, but went back inside; in a minute they was four men that come out with him on to the deck. They was riverboat men, you could tell that. They wasn't gentlemen and they wasn't pas-sengers. You could tell that. It didn't look like they was any sign of passengers at all, but then you couldn't really say, because whoever was on board that steamboat, why they was keeping theirselves inside. What-ever the reason was.

Then one of the crew members, he pulled a tarpaulin off something that was a laying there on the deck in front of the wheelhouse, and they was no mistaking what *it* was. It was a coffin. Somebody had hammered it together with some kind of cheap wood. It looked like yellow poplar from where I was a standing, there up the bank a ways.

The four of them got busy and lifted it up and carried it to the edge of the deck, and then they unlatched the side of the boat, what they call the gunnel, and I saw what they was a planning to do. They was a planning to bring that coffin a shore. And when I saw that, I knew what else they had in mind. They had it in mind to bring that coffin up the path, right on past my house, and take it to a little graveyard that lies about a quarter mile up the path, where it meets the road. I don't know how he knew it, but that Captain knew they was a graveyard there, and he knew this was where they had to land if they was a going to bury some body in it.

I did not move. I stood there and just looked at them while they unloaded that coffin into a rowboat, and then got in the rowboat and rowed theirselves to my dock. After they had first looked at me, they didn't wave or nothing, and they didn't look at me again. Now, you know that is not right. That is not the way people are supposed to act, unless they is something wrong.

While they was a rowing up to my dock, I just moved slow and quiet down toward them a little bit and the minute the Captain put his hand on one of them locust posts at the end of the dock, I said, "Take your hand off that post."

The Captain, he didn't move. He just lifted his face and looked at me. He was younger than I expected, with little bitty eyes that looked like he was tired to death.

"Get yourself back to the boat, and take that thing with you," I said.

The four crew members just sat there and looked at me, like they didn't care one way or another, even if I shot them dead, one by one. The Captain, he looked a little bit that way, too. He cleared his throat, like he was getting set to say something, but he didn't. And now he wasn't a looking at me. He was staring at his hand that was still holding on to that locust post at the end of my dock, and keeping the boat from drifting off. He was studying that hand, like he did not understand it.

"You heard what I told you," I said. "Get your hand off that post and take that thing back to the steamboat with you, and get yourself out of here."

The Captain, he did not move his eyes. He was still a looking at his hand, and he said, "We have got to bury this man. He died last night. He was one of my crew."

"You will not bury him here," I said.

Then he looked at me and said, "We don't want to bury him here. We want to bury him in the graveyard."

I lied to him and said, "They ain't no graveyard here."

"Well," the Captain said, "I happen to know that they *is*. I have been to it, and I know."

"They ain't no graveyard within five miles of this place," I said, lying once again.

"I know they is," the Captain said.

"Are you calling me a liar?" I said.

"No, but I am saying they is a graveyard up that path, up there by the road. Because I have seen it."

"I could blow your head off for calling me a liar," I said.

The Captain nodded and said, "Yes, you could do that, but then there would be two bodies to bury in that graveyard up there."

For a minute, I just looked at him, and he looked back at me, and then I nodded, deciding to let it drop.

"Well, you still can't land," I told him.

"We don't want to bury him on your property," the Captain said. "I think you should understand that."

"I do understand," I told him. "And I understand something else. I understand what it is you have got in that coffin."

"It's only the body of a man," the Captain said. "Surely, they ain't nothing wrong with that."

"No, they is more than the body of a man that you have in there," I said. Because now I was sure what it was. I had heard the talk up and down the river, and every body was afeared that it was a coming back, any day now. I don't mind saying that I was afeared too. And had been for a long time at the thought it was coming.

"Nothing but a dead body," the Captain said with a tired look on his face and shaking his head.

"No, they is more than that," I said. "And I am not going to let you bring it ashore and carry it past my house to the graveyard. Because my wife and two children are in that house, and I will not let that thing get near them, because I know what it is."

"Aren't you a Christian?" the Captain cried suddenly. "Don't you understand that you can't refuse to bury the dead?"

"You take him on up the river," I said. "You can bury him at Hockingport, or even Parkersburg. But you can't bury him here, because I am not going to let you."

The Captain had let go of the post, and I had not even noticed. Now, the boat was floating free of the dock, but not one of them was making a move to row back to the steamboat.

"You know," the Captain said, "that if we wanted to do it that way, we could go on back to the boat and get ourselves some guns, and we could by God bring this coffin ashore and bury it the way it should be buried."

"You would have to bury more than one," I said. "If they was any of you left to bury the others."

The Captain, he stood up in the boat and pointed his finger at me like he was a preacher, and he cried out in a loud voice. "Do you know what you are doing? Do you?"

"I know what is in that coffin," I said. "And I intend to protect my own."

"It is a dead man, and that is all," the Captain said.

"It is a dead man, but that *ain't* all," I said. "Are you ready to swear that the body in that coffin is the body of a man who died in a knife fight? Are you? Are you prepared to swear he was killed with a pistol? A rifle? Was he hit over the head? Did he die of old age? Did he die of a cough? Did he?"

The Captain, he was sitting down again, and the boat was just drifting a little to the side, almost to where it would go into the weeds and mud of the shore. The crew members had not moved a muscle since we had started arguing. They might as well have been dead theirselves.

"At least, you are not a liar," I said. "At least, you are not ready to swear he died of anything but what you and me both *know* he died of. I will tell you something, I almost knew it the minute I saw you coming to the shore. They is talk all up and down the river, and people are afeared. So you take that thing and put it back on your boat where it belongs, and you take it up river to Hockingport or Parkersburg or even Pittsburgh or hell, for all I give a damn. But you are not going to bury it on my land, and you are not a going to carry it up past my house with my wife and children in it on the way to that graveyard."

When I said this, I lowered my gun so that it was pointing right at the Captain's face.

For a minute he sat there, looking up the barrel of my gun, like maybe he wouldn't care a lot whether he died or not. Then he just nodded and said a few words to his men, and before long, they was a rowing back to the steamboat, as slow and sad as they had left it only a little while before.

I don't care. A man has the right to protect what is his. A man has the right to protect his home and his family. They wasn't about to bring that thing, with what I knew was inside it, up past my house. Never. Not as long as I could hold a gun and keep them away.

Edward Clark

The first case along the river was at Chester. They was a Dr. Hibbard who come and looked at him. He was a steamboat man that took sick and they brought him into Chester, and they called this Dr. Hibbard, who come and examined him, and said the words that no body wanted to hear. Yes, it was cholera.

Dr. Hibbard, he started home through the woods on his horse after doctoring that steamboat man. In the middle of the woods, he took sick hisself all of a sudden, so that he could hardly move. But he got off his horse and took a dose of calomel, and laid right down beside the road and went to sleep. When he woke up, he felt better, so that he could climb back up on his horse and return to his home. This was in July. The doctor recovered.

Yes, they was several other people in Chester who took ill, and most of them died. Fear rode on the wind and it walked in the summer heat. Van Weldon, a coffin maker, went every where and helped out, but he never got sick. John Ware, a harness maker, died of it; and so did William Torrence and a boy named Bosworth and a man by the name of Horton.

This was in 1834, the year of the great epidemic along the river. But what I have to tell you happened the year before, and it has to do with a man named Moses Beno, up the river some twenty to thirty miles, in Meigs County, who I never actually met, but who I know about and still dream about ever now and then. I will never forget him and what he did and the way he did it, as long as I live. No, I never met this man Beno, but I listened to him talk, just that one time, and I will never forget it.

I was a crew member of a steamboat that plied its way up and down the river in them days. Oh, it was early, and a long time ago. Mad Ann Bailey had been dead only seven or eight years. They used to talk about seeing her on the porch of her cabin, smoking her pipe and telling about the Indians she had killed. And they was still Indians around, too. Some was married to niggers, and some was married to white people. Why, they wasn't no telling who them people up in the little valleys was, or who they come from. Some people talked about a clan up the Hocking Valley a ways that come from Thomas Jefferson's black maid, and carried Thomas Jefferson's blood in their veins.

But it is not them I wish to tell about. It is the man named Moses Beno, and what I seen one evening in the summer, when the cholera talk was just a starting, and people was afraid like it was the Devil after their souls.

Back in them days, if you saw smoke a coming out of the woods, it was almost as likely smoke from a campfire as from a cabin. Oh, this was a wild valley, at that time. And I was still a pup, just barely a year on the river, and I couldn't have steered that boat down the deep channel past Gallipolis without running it aground.

One of the boys on the boat got sick one night. He was a drinker, oh, about seventeen or eighteen year old. Not much older than me. I think his name was Jenkins or Tompkins. Something like that. I hardly had nothing to do with him, and when he didn't show up for his watch, why we just thought maybe he was sick from drinking. But it wasn't that.

And when they found him dead in his bunk, ever body on board that boat knew what it was. There was no mistake. And no body said nothing to no body else. And no body stepped out on the deck, even, unless you had to keep the old boat a going and you was a crew member.

The Captain, he got all of us who wasn't a standing watch together, and he said, "Boys, I think you all know what this is that has struck down one of our members. I think there is no doubt in any body's mind. But I am not going to say the word, and I am going to ask you not to speak that word, neither. If any body on this boat finds out that a crew member died last night, you tell them it was delirium tremens, because every body knowed that boy was a bad drinker."

Then the Captain just stood there a looking at us, and not saying a word, until we all felt sort of uncomfortable, like we was thinking evil thoughts, or something.

But the Captain, he hadn't finished with us. And what he said was that we was going to land at a place only five or six mile up river, where he knowed they was a graveyard near by, so we could bury the corpse right away, the sooner the better, and yet give it a decent burial in a real Christian graveyard, instead of just digging a hole and dropping it in the ground like a dead dog or cat.

Well, we didn't none of us say nothing to no body. I am right certain. But do you know, we didn't have to. Because every body knowed what it was, but they didn't say nothing neither. No sir! There wasn't no questions asked because no body had any doubts. What they did was all stay inside their cabins, where some of them prayed and some of them quietly wept and some quietly got drunk. Some did all three, but there wasn't no body left to care one way or the other, because the hand of Death, it had been laid on our hearts, and each man was left a wondering if he would be next to catch it and die. The truth was, the cholera was some thing awful to behold and terrible to contemplate, because a strong man could catch it and die in a few hours, whereas a little infant might catch it and not die at all. There was no telling one way or the other, and that was one thing that made it seem even worse, because it was beyond human understanding, like the judgment of God Hisself, or maybe even the Devil.

Whatever awaited us, we did not know. Like he said, the Captain turned toward the shore a few miles up the river, and we could see a little log cabin there on a knoll and a man standing at the top of the bank, a holding a rifle cradled in his arms.

We anchored a little ways off the bank, and loaded that coffin into a rowboat. I was one of them that rowed it right up to the little dock there, and I saw every thing that happened, and heard every word that was spoke.

Yes, this was the man named Moses Beno, and he was a spectacle to behold. Why, he must have been seven feet tall and as skinny and knobby as a thorn tree. He was hairy and bearded, like he had been stranded on some desert island some place but had never been found. One eye was bleached like a fish scale, and the other was black. The afternoon sun was almost exactly behind his head so that he looked like he was wearing a halo of wickedness while he stood there on the bank and defied us with a rifle in his hands.

Yes, this was the man Moses Beno, and he was crazy. You could tell. It showed all over. He was dressed like a river rat, but he talked like a preacher, and he talked about that little log cabin like it was a palace, and about his family like they was all dressed in robes and wearing crowns, while he stood out there and protected them.

Nothing the Captain said would move Beno. He was liable to shoot the first man that set foot on the dock. That's what he said. "The first man that sets foot on that dock will get his damned head blowed off." He said it calm and steady, like he was talking about the weather. His voice, it was low and quiet, like he was almost a hoping you would not hear, so he could go ahead and shoot you dead if you disobeyed his orders.

They was nothing to do. We turned around and took that corpse about half a mile up the river, where we landed again and just dug a grave on the bank and dumped the coffin in it.

By now, the Captain was drunk, and so was one of the boys who dug that grave with me. I was not drunk, because I did not believe in whiskey and such.

Yes, the Captain read the service above that fresh grave, and he cursed as much as he prayed. Some body had told him Beno's name, and he spoke it like he was a speaking of a snake or the Devil hisself.

And it is true, Moses Beno was an evil, uncharitable, and un-Christian man.

Next year, the cholera epidemic hit the river for sure, and whether you believe it or not, I am going to tell you something: Moses Beno was the only one who come down with it in all that long stretch between Gallipolis and Hockingport, and he died like he was plucked by the hand of God.

I can't help it, whether you believe it or not.

But such is the Judgment of God, and don't you forget.

Calvin Beno

To the best of my memory, he never once spoke my name. And I don't think he ever looked at me, either. At least, I can't remember the way *he* looked, exactly.

But then he was the tallest man in the county, people said. He was so tall he was almost a freak. He was blind in one eye, and as skinny as a flag pole. So all them early memories have to do with him moving around so far above me, I can't hardly believe he saw the ground.

I do remember his smell, though. His clothes, they smelled sour all the time, from sweat and the sawdust of green wood, I suspect. He did not trust people. My Momma said if he went to town, why people would point at him when he walked past, and little children would sometimes cry. He had a long beard and long hair, and people said he was a mad man. Momma said he bought this land way back from the road, down on the river, to get away from other people. The only one he trusted was Momma. Maybe because she was scared half to death of just about every body, including him. All her life she walked with her hands folded in her apron, a staring at the ground like she didn't deserve to rise above it. And he never noticed me at all, like I just said.

Yes, I remember that day well. It was hot, and I was in the cabin, which was most always cool, because it was under two great big beech trees that would sometimes drop their little nuts a pattering down on the shake roof when the wind blowed at night.

Momma saw the steamboat first. Daddy was out in the garden, a hoeing the sweet corn.

Some times the river boats would blow their horns out there in the channel when they come by. Daddy never lifted his hand to wave, but some times he would stop and watch them, to be sure they went on by. I never had no body to play with, and Momma said I would talk to myself in whispers all day long.

She didn't talk, and neither did he. My infant brother, Ned, was too young to know any thing at all. This was in 1833. It had to be, because it was just one year before the cholera struck. I remember it pretty well. It is maybe not the first memory I have of life on this earth, but it is the first memory with almost all the details of a picture. It is the first memory that happened to me in a way that I was part of it. So that what happened that day, or what *begun* to happen, was about me, in a way.

That was the first time ever that a river boat turned around and started to come right toward us. Momma said, "Oh Lord!" and I was so excited that I wet my pants, right there in the cool house where I stood a looking through the doorway and watching what Momma was a watching.

"Oh, Lord!" she whispered, and I was so scared at seeing that boat turn around and start toward us that I was peeing down my pant leg before I even knowed I had to pee. I remember that terrible sweet warm feeling down my leg even today, and the thought makes me want to roar like a wild beast.

When Daddy come in, I was afraid he would see what I had done, and I was afraid he would maybe kill me. Like they said he done a tanner up river before he come down here and built our place all alone by itself.

But he didn't look at me no more than he ever did. He just went up to the fireplace and he got his gun. Momma, she asked him what he was doing, and he said something. I don't remember what, exactly.

And then he went outside and stood on the bank above the little dock, a waiting for the river boat as it got nearer and nearer.

Momma told me, "You keep your self right here inside," and I said, "I will."

Both of us stood there and watched him. The Captain of the river-boat put up an argument, but Daddy would not let him bring the coffin ashore. It was the coffin of a man who had died of cholera, right there on the boat. They wanted to bury him right away, because they knew what it was, and they were afraid.

Yes, he knew what it was, too. He knew danger when he saw it. Because he had spent his life distrusting strangers and other people, and he could sense when danger come near, the way it did that day.

You could tell them riverboat men was mad. But they could not get past Daddy, because he would not budge to let them by.

Afterwards, he kept on a saying, "What was I supposed to do? Was I supposed to let them come ashore and poison us?"

He read the Bible after that. Most people thought he could not read, but it was just that he could not write anything, except for his name, of course.

But he sat there a reading the Bible, moving his lips with the words, for hours at a time, it seemed. All that winter, sitting by the fire, he read and read, while Momma sewed or cooked or carded wool. She did not hum or sing. There was no music of any kind in our house. It was as silent as the grave. That is the way I remember it always was.

Yes, I remember it all. I remember what he said it was, that he was out there coming between the poison of the world and us. He said it with his glazed eye fixed on Momma, and his mind lying somewhere behind that eye, fixed on the truth of what he was saying.

"Do you think it could be any thing else," he said, "that would make me keep you here where it is safe?"

No body said, safe from what. No body asked. Mother would not have crossed him with a word, not even a question. I would not have said any thing, for I was as afraid of him as of the world he talked about.

The next summer he died of the cholera. He did not say it, but he might have thought he was coming between it and us again. Standing somewhere off in his mind, like it was as real as a cornfield, and they was this steamboat that come ashore like death, and he held up his gun and said, "No, damn it, you can not pass."

Mother, she has been dead almost a half century now.

But Ned, he is still alive, and so am I.

I sit on the front porch of a summer evening, and I look out and I think of that old time. It would be good if there was a place, like they say Heaven is, where I might see him again and watch him a while, and try to figure him out.

Or maybe it would be hell. Who could know? I surely do not.

Yes, some think his death was a judgment. Nobody could rightly argue against such a thought. But by God, you do not have to believe it either. Such an idea is too handy. I have learned that things just don't work out that easy and clear. Do you say I can't bear witness, because of the love a child naturally has for his father? Why, I didn't hardly know that man; and as for love, why, when I try to remember him, I realize that you might as well try to love a tree or a river.

No, love don't have nothing to do with it. Truth don't either. And God doesn't have nothing to do with it. None of the things you can name.

What it was, and maybe this is all you can say, is that there was this man who stood up there on that day and kept the steamboat men from carrying a diseased corpse past our house. Then he died a year later, from the very disease he was afraid of.

All you can say is he come between something out there and the three of us, Mother and Ned and me. What he saw from inside his head, no body can say. What he was thinking when he was a laying there dying, no body can imagine.

Something was buried and festering in his memory already, when it first started. He learned to fear some thing, yes, and no body will see it like he did. But you can hold the world off only so long, and then it will come a knocking at your door.

He stood up there and held them off with his gun. For a little while, at least. Hell, he probably wasn't even *thinking* of *us* at the time.

That is all you can say.

Samuel Reed

My grandfather Beno had an old brother named Moses. There is a story that I have heard my father tell about him many a time. It is sort of a family legend.

What it is, there was a terrible cholera plague that hit along the river one time, way long before the Civil War. Great Uncle Moses lived right on the bank of the river with his wife and three children. Two girls and a boy. They say he was a big man, six and a half feet tall and wide as a barn.

Anyway, there was a steamboat coming up the river one day, and he looked up from whatever it was he was doing and saw that they were coming out of the channel, headed right toward his place.

It was like right away he knew what they had in mind. He'd gotten the word from somebody that the steamboats were just full of the plague. Just crawling with it. In fact, people believed they were carrying it up river from the Mississippi, all the way from Memphis and New Orleans. And maybe they were right. Who can tell?

Whatever the truth of the matter, Great Uncle Moses wasn't having any of it. Several people had died during the night on the steamboat, and the Captain wanted to land and bury them on his property, right there on the bank, as soon as possible, so the damned stuff wouldn't spread any further. You can understand how he felt.

But like I say, Moses Beno wasn't having any of it. No sir, not for one minute. He picked up his gun and held them all off, alone. The story is, he didn't actually fire at any of them when they tried to bring the first coffin ashore, but he discharged a shot and put a dimple in the water right beside one of the oars, and that was enough to discourage them from coming any closer.

I imagine he could reload about as fast as you or I could take a shell out of our pocket and slide it in the chamber of a single shot. Well, maybe not quite that fast, but almost.

Anyway, the interesting thing was that the cholera came back next year, just as bad, and he was the only one in the whole area who came down with it and died. They say it hit pretty bad downriver toward Cincinnati, and various other places. But not in Meigs County.

Great Uncle Moses had only one eye. I think Dad told me that he'd lost the other one when an old musket blew up in his hands while he was still a boy. That old black powder was treacherous stuff, and sometimes they'd make guns that *nobody* would know how strong the breech on it was.

That was years ago. They buried the corpses from the steamboat just upriver a piece, out of sight around the bend.

I suppose the old man thought he was in the right.

Funny, my calling him an old man. Because according to the genealogical research I've been doing, he couldn't have been over twenty-eight or twenty-nine years old when he died. But people grew up fast in those days, and aged fast.

At the time, people naturally considered his death a retribution. You can see how they would.

Ted Adams

Somewhere over there on that knoll, there used to be an old log house. Grady Weldon told me the story when he was in his nineties, about a year before he died. His memory was sharp as a tack, and when he'd look out at you from those little blue eyes of his, you knew you were in the presence of a smart old man who had a lot of good stories to tell.

Like I say, he's the one who told me about the man who lived in that old log house. It was way back in the days before the Civil War, when they had cholera plagues along the river. One day, a steamboat tried to land to bury some passengers that had just died.

But this old farmer went out there on the bank with his rifle and held them off, made them take their corpses and bury them downriver near Gallipolis, in a regular graveyard.

The story is that the plague hit anyway, and in another month he was dead, along with his whole family. Wiped out.

I've often thought of that story. I've often stood here and gazed at that spot and tried to imagine what the cabin looked like then, and the river beyond.

Several people knew about it, and it's even included in one of the local histories, I forget which one. George Trice says it didn't happen here, but upriver a couple of miles, at the big bend. But I'll take Grady's word for it; that old man knew his local history, and of course he was nearer to the time it happened. Probably he had even known some of the people who could remember the event first hand. Even though it was a long time ago, about 1840 or 1845.

Like I say, I often think about that story and about the kind of man it would take to hold off a whole steamboat full of frightened, hysterical people. Obviously, he had a lot of courage, and thought he was in the right. Maybe he was.

At the time, people thought he got what was coming to him, refusing Christian burial to so many people. God, they must have died like flies when that damned business started!

I don't remember whether Grady ever did mention the name of that man or not. If he did, I've forgotten.

But it's quite a story, if you think about it. And I'm convinced that's exactly where he lived, right over there. You can sort of make out where there was a clearing at one time. Grady said there was even a dock down there on the river, where the steamboat tied up that day.

Yes, there are a lot of stories hereabouts. Many of them forgotten. A lot of life has been lived in this valley, and sometimes you can almost feel it, like a gentle breeze you hardly notice, and wonder about all the strange things that have happened through the years, right here, right in this place.

Naomi Shihab Nye

The Cookies

O N Union Boulevard, St. Louis, in the 1950's, there were women in their eighties who lived with the shades drawn, who hid like bats in the caves they claimed for home. Neighbors of my grandmother, they could be faintly heard through a ceiling or wall. A drawer opening. The slow thump of a shoe. Who they were and whom they were mourning (someone had always just died) intrigued me. Me, the child who knew where the cookies waited in Grandma's kitchen closet. Who lined five varieties up on the table and bit from each one in succession, knowing my mother would never let me do this at home. Who sold Girl Scout cookies door-to-door in annual tradition, who sold fifty boxes, who won The Prize. My grandmother told me which doors to knock on. Whispered secretly, "She'll take three boxes—wait and see."

Hand-in-hand we climbed the dark stairs, knocked on the doors. I shivered, held Grandma tighter, remember still the smell which was curiously fragrant, a sweet soup of talcum powder, folded curtains, roses pressed in a book. Was that what years smelled like? The door would miraculously open and a withered face framed there would peer oddly at me as if I had come from another world. Maybe I had. "Come in," it would say, or "Yes?" and I would mumble something about cookies, feeling foolish, feeling like the one who places a can of beans next to an altar marked *For the Poor* and then has to stare at it—the beans next to the cross—all through the worship. Feeling I should have brought more, as if I shouldn't be selling something to these women, but giving them a gift, some new breath, assurance that there was still a child's world out there, green grass, scabby knees, a playground where you could stretch your legs higher than your head. There were still Easter eggs lodged in the

mouths of drainpipes and sleds on frozen hills, that joyous scream of flying toward yourself in the snow. Squirrels storing nuts, kittens being born
with eyes closed; there was still everything tiny, unformed, flung wide
open into the air!

But how did you carry such an assurance? In those hallways, standing before those thin gray wisps of women, with Grandma slinking back
and pushing me forward to go in alone, I didn't know. There was something here which also smelled like life. But it was a life I hadn't learned yet.
I had never outlived anything I knew of, except one yellow cat. I had
never saved a photograph. For me life was a bounce, an unending burst
of pleasures. Vaguely I imagined what a life of recollection could be,
as already I was haunted by a sense of my own lost baby years, golden
rings I slipped on and off my heart. Would I be one of those women?

Their rooms were shrines of upholstery and lace. Silent radios standing under stacks of magazines. Did they work? Could I turn the knobs?
Questions I wouldn't ask here. Windows with shades pulled low, so the
light peeping through took on a changed quality, as if it were brighter
or dimmer than I remembered. And portraits, photographs, on walls, on
tables, faces strangely familiar, as if I were destined to know them. I
asked no questions and the women never questioned me. Never asked
where the money went, had the price gone up since last year, were there
any additional flavors. They bought what they remembered—if it was
peanut-butter last year, peanut-butter this year would be fine. They
brought the coins from jars, from pocketbooks without handles, counted
them carefully before me, while I stared at their thin crops of knotted
hair. A Sunday brooch pinned loosely to the shoulder of an everyday
dress. What were these women thinking of?

And the door would close softly behind me, transaction complete,
the closing click like a drawer sliding back, a world slid quietly out of
sight, and I was free to return to my own universe, to Grandma standing
with arms folded in the courtyard, staring peacefully up at a bluejay or
sprouting leaf. Suddenly I'd see Grandma in her dress of tiny flowers,
curly gray permanent, tightly laced shoes, as one of *them*—but then she'd
turn, laugh, "Did she buy?" and again belong to me.

Gray women in rooms with the shades drawn . . . weeks later the
cookies would come. I would stack the boxes, make my delivery rounds
to the sleeping doors. This time I would be businesslike, I would rap
firmly. "Hello Ma'am, here are the cookies you ordered." And the face
would peer up, uncertain . . . cookies? . . . as if for a moment we were

floating in the space between us. What I did (carefully balancing boxes in both my arms, wondering who would eat the cookies—I was the only child ever seen in that building) or what she did (reaching out with floating hands to touch what she had bought) had little to do with who we were, had been, or ever would be.

Joyce Carol Oates

Ballerina

ON that enormous darkly gleaming wing, years ago, the figure was dancing. Legs, arms, torso, the arrogant tilt of the head: a dreamlike precision that could not be dislodged by the wind or the constant spray of snow and cloud. Georgene could hear nothing, but there must have been music. The figure was dancing to music, quite clearly. Each of her movements was measured, and unspeakably beautiful. She rose on her toes, she lifted her arms, bent only slightly at the elbow and again at the wrist, as Georgene stared helplessly. A pause, a long dramatic pause, and then a sudden spin: the eyes in that pale angular face catching Georgene's for a half-second before the head whipped smartly around.

Someone was nudging Georgene. But she did not dare turn away from the window.

The dancer, the ballerina, in her black leotard, her silk slippers, with her dark hair pulled back severely from her face and fastened at the nape of the neck, her figure spare and lithe and confident, unhesitating; oblivious of the wild gusts of snow that rushed across the wing; oblivious of the danger. Her control was absolute. Each movement of her body, each subtle inclination of her head, was so graceful that Georgene could only watch transfixed. Didn't she understand the danger. . . ? But perhaps there was no danger . . .

Now in a series of slow tight turns the ballerina was moving out to the tip of the wing, into the deepening mist. She grew fainter. She was disappearing. Her head turned but Georgene could no longer see her face.

"No," Georgene whispered.

She had become, herself, a figure made of stone. Sitting hunched in her seat, her fingers squeezing one another hard. Her lips pursed, and her chin tucked down into her throat. Rigid, apprehensive. Something was going to happen. She could not call the ballerina back but if she concentrated hard enough . . . if she stared without blinking . . . without allowing herself to breathe . . .

"Georgene," her mother said nervously, "your father wants—"

But her father was already leaning across her mother, to give Georgene a poke in the shoulder. "I said I'd like that magazine now. You aren't reading it. Pass it over."

Georgene turned, smiling her perplexed blurry smile. The smile was usually worthless—it often maddened her father, and even her mother—but in the past year she had come to rely upon it, both at school and at home.

"You haven't been reading it," her father said, taking the magazine from her lap. Involuntarily Georgene's fingers clutched at it but her father did not notice; he slapped it down on his own knees. "You've been staring out the window for the past half-hour."

Georgene continued to smile, frightened. Her mother squeezed her hands, which were damp, and very cold. "She's afraid," her mother said, "this is only her third or fourth time in the air. And—"

"It's her fifth time," Georgene's father said. He was leafing through the magazine impatiently, turning the glossy pages one after another. "She isn't afraid, she's just putting on an act. Preparing for the big sympathy appeal to my parents. Right? Just like you. But she's less subtle than you."

"Don't be afraid, hon," Georgene's mother said, squeezing her hands again quickly, and then releasing them. "There isn't any lightning, you heard what the pilot said, and the sun is shining in Miami. And anyway it's useless."

Georgene's father laughed in appreciation. He did not look up from the magazine; he had paused to read the caption beneath a large gorgeous photograph of a Mediterranean sunset. "It certainly is," he said. His voice had grown abstract but it was as forceful as ever. "We're all in the hands of Allah. Or is it hand? Hand. Of Allah."

Years ago, it was. December 21. The last day of Georgene Terrill's childhood.

The shortest day of the year, and the longest night.

But the sun was shining hotly on her grandparents' balcony on the tenth floor of the Biscayne Towers. The sky was a clear hard turquoise blue, the ocean was bluish-gray, obscured in filmy yellow-toned clouds at the horizon. Georgene's mother complained happily of the sun: she put on her white-framed sunglasses with the smart squarish lenses. Georgene's Aunt Janet turned her canvas chair about and stretched her legs, which were pale and rather short, and threaded with pink veins. She wanted to go back to Indianapolis with a tan, she said. Even if it only lasted a few days.

The sun shone on the balcony floor, on the handsome black and white tile; and on the dozen hanging plants Grandmother Terrill arranged; and on the big wooden bucket of poinsettias. Georgene leaned over the railing, which was white, and unusually wide; it felt very solid. Though they were high above the ground—overlooking an oval swimming pool and a small grove of palm trees—Georgene did not think they were in any danger. There was no wind, it was really a summer day. They had left the snowstorm behind them over the Atlantic, hours ago.

Georgene's grandfather brought out his binoculars for her, and showed her how to adjust them. Everything was wonderfully clear and sharp: the wide stretch of beach, the sunbathers lying on their towels, the half-dozen swimmers, the tall spindly palm trees with their ragged browning leaves. There were gulls on the beach, fighting over something Georgene couldn't make out. And those big ungainly melancholy-looking birds, pelicans. And those tiny quick-running birds she had liked so much last year: sandpipers. Their name sprang to her lips and she said it aloud, pleased: "Sandpipers."

"Don't hold the binoculars over the railing, Georgene," her father said. "You're liable to drop them and they're very expensive."

Georgene had not been holding the binoculars over the railing, but resting them on top. She moved them an inch or two back, however, to be safe.

"Put the strap around your neck," Grandfather Terrill said. "Like this. Now they can't fall."

Georgene imagined she could see something at the horizon. A long low finger of land. Is that Spain across the ocean, she wanted to ask her grandfather, could you get to it in a sailboat. . . ? But she knew the question was a stupid one so she remained silent.

The Cuban woman in the white dress that fitted so snugly across her big hips came out, carrying a red plastic tray. Her name sounded like Garda. There were drinks for everyone: tomato juice with a twist of lemon for Grandmother Terrill, tonic water and lemon for Grandfather

Terrill, a tall foam-topped glass of beer for Uncle Peter, white wine for Aunt Janet, martinis in squat green glasses for Georgene's parents, ginger ale for Aunt Margaret, Mrs. Stein (who was a new next-door neighbor of Georgene's grandparents: evidently Mrs. Morrill had moved away or died), and Georgene. At first Georgene thought the drink was all right, then her tongue caught the flat metallic taste. Diet ginger ale, not real ginger ale; the kind her grandmother drank. Georgene swallowed a mouthful and set her glass down on the railing. "Thank you," she murmured, but of course the Cuban did not hear. Either you were always supposed to thank servants, or never supposed to; Georgene had been scolded in the past but could not remember which was correct. Fortunately her father was talking loudly with the others and took no notice.

He was not yet angry about the ballet lessons, though Georgene's mother had told her, when they were unpacking, that he knew: Grandmother Terrill had told him. But he hadn't yet acknowledged the gift—it was Georgene's grandparents' main gift to her, this Christmas—to Georgene. When he did acknowledge it, it would probably be casually, while they were doing something together. In this way he had announced to her the fact that they would all be flying down to Miami Beach to spend ten days with his parents; when Georgene had been seven years old he had happened to mention, quite casually, that she had *almost* had a baby brother—but something had gone wrong and so her mother was very sick and would have to rest when she came home, and Georgene mustn't bother her. One time they had been going down in the elevator of the apartment building, the other time they had been unpacking groceries in the kitchen, laughing and making a game of it. Georgene's father told her important things without warning, at odd unpremeditated times, so she had to be ready. He smiled his handsome half-smile, he backed away. He didn't like to explain anything; he never answered questions. Georgene had learned never to ask but her mother still did, occasionally, raising her voice and following Georgene's father if he left the room. I don't care to be interrogated, Georgene's father would say.

They were discussing Grandfather Terrill's doctor problem.

He had started out with one doctor; no, really two if you counted the internist Marks. ("You'd better count him," Grandmother Terrill said. "A bill came from his office just the other day.") But the side-effects of the drug were so awful, he'd lost faith in the whole business and started over again with a youngish doctor from California named Lilliard. Then in three weeks the same wretched thing again. . . .

They lowered their voices. Aunt Janet exclaimed softly: "Oh poor Daddy, *does* it? I mean . . . I didn't know."

"I wrote you in a letter," Grandmother Terrill said. "I'm sure I did."

"No you didn't, Mother," Aunt Janet said. "You really didn't."

"Do you feel that way right now?" Uncle Peter asked. "I mean—at this very moment?"

Grandfather Terrill paused. Then he said, with a harsh little laugh: "No, not at this very *moment*. Not at this very *moment*."

Georgene knew, though she was not supposed to know, that her grandfather had something called Parkinson's disease. She had overheard her mother telling a friend, on the telephone. A perfectly dreadful disease, her mother had said, half-angrily, but Grant refuses to discuss it, he skimmed through his mother's letter and handed it to me and said, What can you expect, my poor father's getting on toward eighty, and he was gone all night, came home at ten in the morning, sick to his stomach in the hall, and still wouldn't talk about it to me, and naturally we have to go down there again this Christmas though you'd think *last* Christmas would have been enough and they wouldn't ask us again. . . . No, I don't think it's fatal. I mean right away. The worst things aren't, you can count on that.

"Well—you're looking very good," Georgene's mother said, running her fingers through her short curly hair, nervously. "That wonderful tan, and I really don't notice any tremor. . . ."

"There isn't any. It's all in his imagination," Grandmother Terrill said. "Since Dr. Lilliard it's completely under control."

"I fell down five times in one week, back in August," Grandfather Terrill said with a sardonic laugh. He raised his glass of tonic water and drained it, sucking noisily at the ice cubes. "It's a funny thing, falling down. Children fall constantly. But they're closer to the ground, you know. And it must not surprise them all that much. Though of course it hurts."

"Children's bones are more resilient," Georgene's father said. "They don't snap—they bend."

"That's a silly thing to say," Aunt Margaret murmured. "Sometimes they do snap."

"What do you know about it?" Georgene's father said.

"What are we talking about?" Aunt Margaret said.

"You *are* looking good, Daddy," Aunt Janet said. "This was the smartest thing you and Mother ever did, coming down here. I mean—

could you imagine a more beautiful view? And the building is so clean and so quiet, it's so well maintained. . . ."

Everyone agreed. Mrs. Stein was asked her opinion and she agreed. Before her husband's death they had lived in a smaller building, on one of the waterways, yes it had been a condominium too, but not nearly so well maintained. Half the palm trees were dead, the pool wasn't kept clean, the security couldn't be trusted. She had moved to Biscayne Towers, she said, because she couldn't bear living in the other place alone. There were one-bedroom condominiums here, and the view was much more dramatic. She hadn't a serious complaint.

"Security *is* good here?" Aunt Janet said, looking from Grandmother Terrill to Grandfather Terrill. "I mean—it certainly *looks* safe. It looks like a fortress."

"What's safe, these days?" Grandfather Terrill said with a shrug.

They discussed the weather in Florida. Should they ask Garda to serve lunch now, or bring out another round of drinks. Was it a good idea to eat outside. (The sun was still shining but there were clouds, a darkening bank of clouds, in the east.) Dade County politics, the Colombian drug traffic, Uncle Peter's father's brokerage on Water Street, inflation, oil, gasoline, the weather in Indianapolis ("It turned cold Labor Day," Aunt Janet said, "and it's been downhill ever since"), the weather in Chicago (where Aunt Margaret taught at the University), the weather in New York ("Shitty," Georgene's father drawled, and Georgene's mother said, "Oh—not bad so far, but it's only December"), St. Croix Port, recession, tax-exempt bonds, the disappointing season on television, the death of Grandmother Terrill's oldest sister, in Portland, Oregon ("Well—you know the poor thing was *very* bad off, every time I visited she said, Pray for me, Elvira, I want to die, and she *wasn't* just talking, and in the casket she looked so peaceful you wouldn't believe it"), Georgene's grades at the Hayes School, Georgene's orthodontic work, Georgene's new haircut (her mother had taken them both to Bloomingdale's, to the beauty salon, for these *very* short cuts—and maybe Georgene's was a little too short—her eyes looked so big, her cheekbones were so prominent—but of course it would grow out).

Georgene's mother was wearing a jumper made of blue denim, and a long-sleeved red cotton shirt, and leather sandals. She laughed frequently. She appeared to be enjoying the visit a great deal. From time to time she reached out, snapping her fingers, and Georgene's father supplied her with a cigarette; she was "cutting down on her smoking" right now. Georgene could see that she was the prettiest of the women—far prettier than Aunt Margaret, even—though it was always said of Margaret that she was a "striking woman." (She was six feet tall, as tall as Georgene's father, and had his dark, rather narrow face, but there were sharp lines on her forehead, and she seemed to be squinting a great deal this afternoon, as if she found the sunlight unpleasant or was disturbed about something. She taught art history at the University of Chicago, she had published a book on Renaissance caricature, and she spent most of her summers in Italy and Greece; but Georgene's father had said of her, once, that it hadn't done much good, had it? Georgene did not know what her father meant.)

Georgene's mother, a cigarette slanted in her mouth, tried to fluff out Georgene's hair with both hands. "Well—in two weeks it will be all right," she said. "It will look just fine."

"A skinned rat," Georgene's father said. "My baby's a skinned rat."

He smiled at Georgene, hunching forward.

"Oh Grant—what a thing to say," Aunt Janet murmured.

"An ignorant thing to say," Aunt Margaret said sharply.

"My baby's a cute little funny-faced mouthwatering skinned rat, aren't you?" Georgene's father said, winking at her. "The kind a big dog— a Doberman pinscher—would love to gobble up. Because she's so mouth-watering. Aren't you?"

Georgene giggled. Then stopped. Sometimes her father tickled her roughly, to make her squeal, especially in front of company; sometimes he rubbed her head hard, making her scalp pull. Sometimes he turned away from her abruptly because, in his words, she was a poor sport who couldn't take a joke—exactly like her mother. She stared at him, wondering what he wanted: should she giggle like a much younger child, or should she pretend to be huffy, or even talk back to him—because sometimes he liked that, he applauded her spunk. He laughed with one corner of his mouth, his cheek dimpling. And gave her an affectionate little pinch as he heaved himself to his feet.

"Onward and upward," he said gaily.

"Where are you going, Grant," Grandmother Terrill said, "Garda's got lunch practically on the table. . . . You're not going to make yourself another drink, are you?"

"Yes, Mother, I am going to make myself another drink," Georgene's father said, raising his voice prankishly, in imitation of his mother, "but I am also going to place a call to New York. An important call. A business call. Do you object? I'll make a note of the toll charge and pay you before we leave."

He went inside, and Georgene's mother jumped up to follow him, and the others began to talk animatedly, so that no one could hear them quarreling. But perhaps they were not quarreling. A moment later Georgene's mother returned to her chair, flushing, managing to smile, and said, "Grant's always involved in so many things. . . ."

Mrs. Stein asked Grandmother Terrill a question about one of her hanging plants.

Uncle Peter asked Grandfather Terrill about an old business partner of his who had retired and moved to Miami Beach a few years ago. "Oh him—that one!" Grandfather Terrill said contemptuously. "Worth two-three million at least, and do you know he dresses like a pauper? No woman to look after him, not even a housekeeper, he says it's too much trouble and he doesn't care what he eats, he sits with the blinds drawn watching soap operas on television. The sun hurts his eyes, he says. We invited him over for dinner and he said yes, then at the last minute called and said he couldn't make it, no excuse offered. I tell you he's a pathetic case. He's *depressing*."

"Is Mr. Greenspan really worth that much money?" Uncle Peter asked.

"Who isn't, these days?" Grandfather Terrill said with a shrug of his bony shoulders. He was watching Garda set the immense wooden salad bowl on the table.

"Does Grant know about Georgene's ballet lessons?" Aunt Margaret asked Georgene's mother. "I mean—that Mother and Daddy want to pay for them?"

"Yes, of course," Georgene's mother said, lighting another cigarette and waving the smoke away.

"Is it going to be all right?" Aunt Margaret asked.

Georgene was looking through the binoculars again, scanning the beach. Up and down the beach behind the condominium, and the high-rise building to the left, and the building beyond that. She wanted to laugh because they were talking about her, right in front of her; her body twitched as if she were being tickled. ". . . I know how badly she's been wanting lessons," Aunt Margaret said in her low quizzical voice.

"Of course it's going to be all right," Georgene's mother said. "Why wouldn't it be all right?"

"This Miles Greenspan," Grandmother Terrill said with a little cry, "you *can't* imagine! We met him at the deli one morning, looking woe-begone and haggard, in rumpled clothes, not shaven for a day or two, and his pockets were stuffed with checks from the morning's mail—he owns a number of apartment buildings, you know, on Long Island, and office buildings too—he had checks for, I don't know, $15,000 stuffed in his pocket from a single mail delivery—and all he could say was the market looked bad, and he hadn't gotten a letter from either of his sons for a long time! Isn't that pathetic?"

"I didn't know he was worth that much money," Uncle Peter said.

"He doesn't take care of himself," Grandmother Terrill said, shaking her head. "He just doesn't eat right. But what can you do? He says his heart is heavy and he doesn't have the energy any longer for conversation. We wanted to introduce him to Hazel here, but. . . ."

Mrs. Stein laughed sadly. "Oh Elvira, I don't *think* so."

"Grant seems to have lost more weight," Aunt Janet was saying to Georgene's mother. "I assume it's deliberate? He's as lean in the waist and hips as a teen-age boy."

Georgene's mother did not reply at once. Then she spoke slowly and carefully. "He's been working hard lately; they've been making him fly out to Detroit once a week, which he hates; he hates Detroit. All to sell some damn cars. . . . He's under pressure constantly. In his work, you know, most men are exhausted by the time they're forty. I mean, their ideas are exhausted. They burn themselves out."

"It's funny to think of Grant as forty years old," Aunt Margaret said with a little half-smile. Her cheek dimpled like her brother's.

"Forty?" said Grandfather Terrill. "*Forty?*" He let his jaw drop and wriggled his overgrown grizzly eyebrows. It was one of his jokes so Georgene prepared to laugh. "You mean my youngest child is *forty years old?*"

Everyone laughed except Georgene's mother, who glanced uneasily at the opened French doors. Mrs. Stein pressed a cocktail napkin against her forehead, giggling so that her shapeless fallen breasts quivered. She wore a bright pink cotton shift and several strands of beautiful pearls. Frequently her eye moved to Georgene, and she smiled in a queer cringing hopeful way, as if she and Georgene knew each other; but Georgene did not respond. She could not determine whether she was shy, or simply indifferent.

"Since when did my youngest child celebrate his fortieth birthday?" Grandfather Terrill said in a booming voice. He had had only tonic water to drink, but he was pretending to be slightly intoxicated. Mrs. Stein giggled helplessly and patted her damp forehead.

∽

It was a time of truce, a time of cease-fire. A convalescence as well, as dramatic in its own way as the quarreling. For Georgene's parents had had one of their fights not long before. Wild, flamboyant, noisy, tearful, with doors slamming, chairs shoved against walls, suitcases packed (and triumphantly unpacked: Georgene's father had snatched her mother's bag from her and opened it, dumping the contents on the floor), broken glassware and china, screams and accusations and threats. An alabaster lamp that had belonged to Georgene's grandparents was smashed, a pewter candlestick holder was thrown so hard at the dining-room wall it left a deep gouge. Georgene wandered through the apartment, afterward, noting the destruction. She estimated that it was no worse than usual.

This fight had begun on the first of December. Georgene, prematurely watchful and "adult" at the age of eleven, made a tiny black mark on her calendar, to record its onset. It was to last approximately five days, if one counted not only the physical abuse and the shouting but the hostile aftermath as well.

Georgene's father disappeared. Georgene's mother made telephone calls, locked in the bedroom with a bottle of scotch.

And how is everything at home, Grandmother Terrill always asked Georgene in secret, at the start of a visit, and of course Georgene always said, Everything is fine, Grandma. For she *was* an adult, more or less.

Don't ever tell tales, both Georgene's parents warned. But they need not have warned her.

Ah, look at you! Georgene's father said with a fond sad smile. He ran his fingers over her scalp, he squeezed her shoulder. Perhaps it was because she whined and pleaded so frequently about taking ballet lessons. (The mania began the Christmas before, when the mother of a classmate at the Hayes School organized a small theater party for her daughter's birthday, and took the girls, including Georgene, to see a performance by the Bolshoi troupe. Georgene had never experienced anything like it: she could talk of nothing else for days. After that she managed to acquire a dozen books on the ballet, she watched every televised performance, she begged and pleaded with her parents, usually unsuccessfully, to be taken to the ballet or modern dance or to be allowed to go alone.)

Ah, but look at *you*! her father said, cupping her chin in his hand.

His cheek dimpled with a melancholy half-smile. Don't you know it's hopeless, my little friend? By which I mean—hopeless! You're certainly tall enough but you have no natural grace, your legs and arms are bony rather than thin, you're not pretty—I couldn't bear the prospect of anyone seeing you tottering about on your toes! My God, how sad. How very sad. All the homely little girls in New York City and their sheepish fathers. . . . I suppose you think it's play? It would be fun? You have no idea of the hours and hours of work—practice at the bar—physical pain, suffering—

I know what it's like, Georgene said. I'm not afraid.

You *don't* know what it's like, her father said.

Yes I do, she muttered, I know all about it, I've read everything you can read. . . .

Pirouettes and spins and tottering about on your toes! Georgene's father said, shuddering. My God, I couldn't bear it, it would be so *sad*.

You wouldn't have to watch, Georgene said. You would never have to watch.

But I couldn't resist! I'd have to come to a recital, wouldn't I, or whatever they might be called—dance school performances? I'd have to sit in the audience, cringing, while my poor daughter made a fool of herself on stage.

Georgene's eyes filled with angry tears. She turned away so that her father would not see.

And last but not least, he said irritably, turning her around to face him, last but not least is the expense, my silly little friend! About which you haven't thought, have you? Have you?

He shook her and shook her until her teeth rattled in her head.

After that he surprised her in her room, "cavorting about" as he called it. The photographs of dancers on her walls, the big photography books, bought at discount prices, lying opened on her bed, her little plastic bedside radio turned to a classical music station. Sad, he sometimes murmured, leaning in the doorway, as she turned away shamefaced, or ran to hide in her closet. Sad, he told Georgene's mother at the dinner table, but harmless, for even children must get through the day somehow, I suppose. (Georgene's mother, who might have hurried back to the apartment at six o'clock or later, only a few minutes before Georgene's father arrived, would be bright and breathless and agreeable and oddly deaf. Yes, she would say, yes I suppose so, it *is* harmless, I'm glad you don't mind.)

When Georgene was younger her father sometimes caught her talking and humming to herself, and this did disturb him. Only crazy people do that, he said. Do you know what happens to crazy people? Georgene discovered that it was less offensive for her to talk to a doll or a stuffed animal—though it was still a mistake, of course, if her father was anywhere near. Babbling, chattering, carrying on like a little maniac, Georgene's father complained to her mother, can't you discipline her at all? I'm gone most of the day. . . . I feel so helpless. . . .

One rainy Sunday morning while her parents read the *Times* in the living room, Georgene stared out the kitchen window at the dreary wet vista of buildings and roofs and television antennae and chimneys, and suddenly she saw, on a distant roof, the figure of a dancer: a ballerina. She watched as the figure danced lightly across the roof, turning, pirouetting, spinning, her movements effortless, her body in complete control. How gracefully she danced, and yet her limbs were hard with muscle: she was not nearly so frail as she appeared. Georgene watched, transfixed. Of course the figure was not "real." She knew that. Yet it seemed to exist apart from her; she could not direct its movements or even anticipate them. It was important that she remain motionless, and hold her eyes open, not blinking more often than was necessary; it was important that she show no emotion, not even surprise.

The telephone rang in the other room and someone went to answer it and when Georgene looked out again the ballerina had vanished.

But of course she appeared again, usually at unexpected times. While Georgene sat in her desk at school, daydreaming; on the Fifth Avenue bus; when she was in the shower; sometimes even at meals, if she was facing a window. It was ironic that she might stand for long minutes at a time at the high living-room windows overlooking the street, trying to summon the dancer to appear on the rooftops across the way, without success; doubly ironic that, one afternoon at dusk, while she was staring helplessly at nothing at all, her father should come up behind her and say, frightening her with his closeness, Now just *what* are you thinking?— *what* daydream is so fascinating?

There was angry talk for a while of divorce. Then of separation—a few weeks apart, a little distance—so that, as Georgene's mother said, she could breathe again. But then of course, as always, there was a reconciliation. Georgene's father went away for a day or two, and then returned; or Georgene's mother went away, taking her along, sometimes to a friend's apartment and sometimes to a midtown hotel (We don't

want everyone knowing our business, Georgene's mother said furiously),
once to the apartment of her "special friend" Mr. Hewitt, whom Georgene had never seen before but whose voice she recognized from the
telephone: but that visit did not work out because of Georgene's behavior. (She sulked, she would not be charmed by Mr. Hewitt's kindness. She thought his pretense of interest in her—her schoolwork, her
liking for the ballet—was condescending and patronizing.)

The fights, the three or four days of hostility, the reconciliations.
Georgene noted them on her calendar—for she *was* a precocious child,
and her father could not be blamed, she often thought, for disliking her—
and saw that they constituted a pattern, and that the pattern emerged
every seven or eight months. Of course Georgene's father's work affected
it—he was sometimes particularly bad-tempered when he returned from
Detroit; and Georgene's mother's relationship with Mr. Hewitt (who
could also be, it seemed, bad-tempered); and whether the street was being
repaired out front; and the weather; and telephone calls—often mysterious, often late at night—for Georgene's father. The trip to Miami Beach
appeared to have triggered a fight several weeks early, Georgene thought,
possibly so that the reconciliation—the truce, the cease-fire, the "honeymoon"—would last through the first few days of the vacation. At such
times Georgene's parents were courteous with each other, even solici-
tous, as if one or the other had been gravely ill, in danger of dying: it *was*
a sort of convalescence. Georgene was scolded if she spoke loudly or
moved clumsily; she was often instructed to "make things easier for her
mother in the kitchen"; she had to change from her school uniform into
a nice dress, for dinner, so that her father wouldn't be distressed by her
appearance. During the period of hostility she could expect to be treated
with exaggerated care: her mother took her to the ballet, to movies, out
to dinner; her father might even pick her up after school, in a cab, and
take her out for an impromptu excursion—a museum visit, a hike through
the park, Mexican or Turkish or Thai or Russian dinners in odd parts of
the city, even a dance performance (though not ballet: he claimed to hate
ballet). She was hugged, she was wept over, she was cherished. Separately,
both her parents would frame her face in their hands, and stare at her, and
say, after a long painful moment, that they hoped she would understand,
someday—they hoped she would forgive them. She had learned to remain
quite still at such times, and to say nothing. For this mood, like the others,
would soon pass.

After the reconciliation, however, Georgene was unprotected: her parents did not want to attack each other yet, and so their nervous energy had to have an outlet, they had to be vexed with someone, had to explode at someone's clumsiness or stupidity or insolence. At such times her mother would lose her patience suddenly, and say, Oh it's hopeless—and hurry out of the room sobbing. Her father would find fault with her posture, her speech, her answers to his questions, her manners at the table, her appearance. During this phase it was a bad idea to bring him her report card, for a string of *A*'s was dismissed with a curious heavy sigh and a remark she could not interpret (I see the road you're set upon, it's one I know well, both your Aunt Margaret and I took it, and what good has it done—?); single *B+* was the subject of an hour's interrogation.

She was unprotected, and wisely cautious. She said little, she held herself still, kept out of her father's way. The fragile courtesy between her parents was, she supposed, a good thing—it should last as long as possible. In the cab bringing them from the Miami airport to her grandparents' home Georgene's mother had been chattering away about the sun and the blue sky and the palm trees and the water, how generous it was of Grant's parents to invite them down, and Georgene had known her mother was pretending—her voice tripped and rattled prettily at such times, she gestured a great deal with her hands—and she had known her father knew, and was sitting silent in the front seat, his head turned away. They were less than ten minutes from Georgene's grandparents' home: the tension was considerable: at any moment her father might turn to face them and begin shouting. So Georgene reached out to touch her mother's hand, impulsively. Just to touch it. And her mother stopped talking, and looked at her, startled, frightened—and the dangerous moment passed.

〜

And then at lunch everything was shattered.

There was a quarrel, and of course it was Georgene's fault, and her father said something no one would ever forget. Georgene did not quite understand it—that understanding was not to come until years later— but he saw from the others' expressions that he had said a very terrible thing; at last he had said something no one could forgive.

It was addressed to his parents, but primarily to his father. After he had disciplined Georgene at the table (she had had a great deal of difficulty getting some tiny bones out of her mouth, midway through the meal of cold salmon), and Aunt Margaret had criticized him for persecuting his daughter, and he had told Margaret to go to hell—what did she know about children; and of course Georgene's mother intervened, and Grandmother Terrill, and Grandfather Terrill said angrily to Georgene's father that perhaps *he* ought to be the one to leave the table, since he hadn't any manners; and for some reason Georgene's father brought up the subject of the ballet lessons and the "emotional blackmail" they constituted, and more words were exchanged, and Georgene jumped up from the table and ran to crouch in a corner of the balcony, panicked, her hands over her ears, and her father said in his loud mock-ebullient voice that meant he was still only mildly drunk—mildly and affably, not in danger of smashing things or striking anyone—that he didn't quite see why his parents were so critical: "After all I did get married. I did what you wanted. What you wanted so badly, though of course you were too coy to be explicit. . . . I did fall in love and all that, with a woman, oh yes with a woman, I did fall in love and marry, mustn't spill seed in the wrong place, kitchee-kitchee-coo, kitchee-coo, Daddy will spank, Momma will have hysterics, yes?—right?"

They stared at him in astonishment. Georgene saw that his face was rosy, his dark eyes liquid-bright, sly and sparkling as if with tears; but there were no tears. He lifted his wine glass, saying, "Now let's have a toast to the next generation—" but Grandfather Terrill slapped him in the face, and the wine glass went flying.

Georgene's father rose from his chair with dignity, and made a mocking bow to his father, his face flushing beet-red; and then he left the balcony. They could hear him inside singing "Kitchee-kitchee-coo, kitchee-coo," and then they heard the door of the apartment slam.

"Age doesn't bring wisdom, only apathy that passes for wisdom," Grandfather Terrill said, hours later.

They had gone down to the beach, all of them, for a long walk. Even Mrs. Stein had accompanied them; she thought it might be "good for her nerves."

Surprisingly windy at the edge of the ocean. And when clouds were blown across the sun it was quite cold.

"You should have brought that sweater along, Georgene, as I told you," Georgene's mother said irritably. "After all this isn't summer. . . ."

They were stooping to gather shells, walking too slowly for Georgene. So she ran ahead. She ran at the edge of the ocean, through the spray, squealing and shouting. Great noisy flocks of gulls rose flapping their wings, there were tangled seaweed and jellyfish-like creatures underfoot, there were mussels oozing out of their broken shells, and giant flesh-colored conches. Someone called Georgene but she ran and ran. Her teeth chattered though she wasn't cold.

The high-rise apartment buildings became motels, the beach grew shabbier, more crowded. Georgene supposed that her father had gone off in this direction and that she might even find him: he might be sitting on a sea wall, his legs dangling, a cigarette in his mouth. He would sight her before she sighted him and call out laconically: Hi there, pal. Perhaps he would be rather subdued by now, and his eyelids would flutter guiltily. He would say: Those lessons, you know . . . those lessons are going to involve hard work. And pain. Your leg muscles, your ankles, your feet. . . .

Georgene shouted and squealed, dashing through the surf. Her heart pounded joyfully. She had won: she had certainly won. Nothing else mattered. She would dance along the sea wall when she found him, keeping her balance by waving her arms; she would show him how graceful she was; or anyway how bold. He would be subdued, sober, his face drawn with fatigue. He would cringe before her, smiling nervously, as he sometimes did—if she dared, she would leap over him.

She thought she saw his figure, up ahead, but it always turned out to be someone else. She had run a great distance from the others and was now in a fairly untended area, behind a one-story motel that had been boarded up after a fire. There were a few sunbathers here, a few children splashing in the surf. She paused, panting. She could see no one she knew in either direction.

The sun came out again, and again the beach pulsed with heat. She climbed to a partly dilapidated sea wall and began walking along its top, her arms extended for balance. She watched her feet, her bare toes, yet held her head back and her chin slightly uplifted; she felt the powerful exhilaration course along her spine, which was so straight and yet so supple, so living.

Graceful, in control. Like this. A dancer, an artist: yes. Like this.

A. B. Paulson

College Life

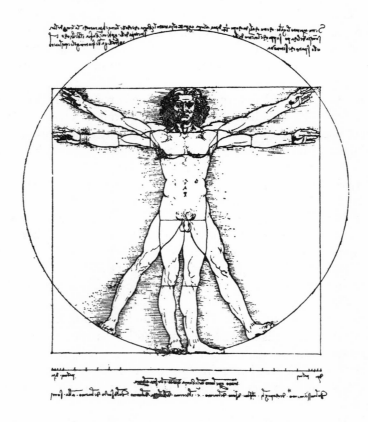

AT the beginning he found himself as usual in the middle.
The Apaches had staked him out, spread-eagle, in the middle
of the Great Salt Flats. They had loosened his necktie, but out of some
perverse respect for his academic integrity they had not removed his

Harris Tweed jacket. Now, as the hot Utah sun climbed toward noon, the rawhide bindings dried at his wrists, tightening to pull the skin over the heel of his hand like a hem, so that to a disinterested observer he appeared to be wearing colorful garden gloves.

"This is not what I expected," said the Assistant Professor to himself, "but then the ambush of expectations is the stuff of—" Of what? Great Romantic poetry? He made the effort, heroic in its own way, of applying what he knew best to his present condition. And what he knew best was how to make up sentences about English literature, how to spin phrases into looping skeins, knotted webs, and networks across whose taut threads the braver of his students might venture a step, testing their own weighty selfhood against the transparent resilience of mere signification.

Apparently displays of one's verbal aptitude were related to articulating how precisely one understood his condition; and this in turn was at once the origin and goal of the Liberal Education: in the end, understanding one's condition would save you. Unfortunately, the Professor's immediate vulnerability involved not understanding, but the refusal to understand what, in the present case, was truly at stake. Anyone else, with a kind of desperate lucidity, would have simply asked: "How am I going to get out of this one?"

Meanwhile the earth turned and the sun climbed higher. It was difficult to ignore the sun. He turned his head from side to side to avoid it, as if posing for a police mug shot. Rolling his eyes around in a casual circle, he could make out in the distance a low line of mountains that evidently ringed the Salt Flats like the open mouth of an undergraduate snoring in the front row of a lecture hall. There was no doubt about it: here he was, a brilliant turquoise sky arching over him, in the middle of it all.

And in the middle, as usual, he found himself at the beginning.

It began the day before with a timid knock at the door of his office in the English department. The Assistant Professor was a student of knocks (hard, hurried, hesitant: all sorts of knocks; oddly they turned out to bear no relationship to the figures whom he subsequently found standing —knuckles poised—out in the corridor), and he set down his copy of *The Midwestern Quarterly* (the issue containing his own recent article, "Ritual Purgation of the Ironic Victim") in order to study the persevering zeal of this knock's timidity more carefully. He had not called out "Come in!" or "Open the door!" because, especially in the case of timid knocks, he was experimenting in urging them toward what he called "the knock-in-itself" or "knocking without hope of entry." After a silence the door slowly opened anyway. Several eyes appeared, arranged vertically up and down the edge of the door. He concluded that some sort of Committee had come to call—the sort of Committee unable to delegate among itself even the rudimentary executive functions.

The Committee filed into his office barechested, wearing black shoulder-length hair, carrying Winchester carbines and rolls of white surgical tape. Except for the elaborately tooled pictographs on their dangling leather loincloths, the savages appeared to be carbon copies of one another. Because he was ignorant of the semiotic codes by which artificial Native Americans might be distinguished from genuine Hollywood extras, the Professor seized on the familiar notion of "Apaches" and cast it like a lasso of identity over his silent visitors.

Rudely, as if they read his thoughts, the Committee grabbed him. As they taped his mouth shut, taped his hands and feet, the Assistant Professor wondered if the phrase "carbon copies" ought now give way to the phrase "Xerox copies," and he regretted for a moment the loss of a nice ambiguity (for with multiple carbons each copy was in fact fainter, less true to the original than the one before).

"Another fraternity prank," he sighed to himself as they carried him out the door and threw him roughly—like a rolled up 9 x 12 rug—into the back of a waiting van. To show them how good-natured he was about such pranks, he had put on a broad grin as they first unrolled their surgical tape. Lying in the back of the van he came to regret this gesture, because he found that his mouth had been taped shut still smiling. Accordingly, beneath the white tape he had been constrained to smile during the entire ride out to a small regional airport; he had smiled as they hustled him aboard a private jet aircraft; he was still smiling when they landed in some far western state, smiled even when they staked him out under the rising sun, smiled when they rudely ripped the tape from his mouth, and (tape gone but muscles frozen in an absurd grimace) had still smiled as the Apaches drove off whooping in their four-wheel-drive Cherokee Jeep.

Now, lying under the blue dome of a Utah sky, he licked the upturned corners of his mouth and said to himself, "What do I have to smile about?" High overhead some sort of large bird was circling the sun. That bird, thought the Professor, is probably perplexed at the incongruity of my condition. The Professor was about to rehearse to himself all the categories of incongruity when he heard the distant sound of an automobile engine.

The car that screeched to a stop in a line with the Professor's right toe was a Ford LTD, and the fellow who leaped from its air-conditioned interior wore sunglasses and a Hawaiian shirt.

"Holy cow! I can't believe it!" the fellow muttered to himself as he stepped hesitantly across the burning Salt Flats.

Relieved as he was to be rescued, the Professor was oddly put off by the fellow's striking resemblance to Julius La Rosa.

"Holy cow!" repeated Julius. "I mean, you know. How you doing?"

The Professor lifted his head and was about to croak a reply—no doubt, as the occasion required, a bitterly ironic one—when he saw his rescuer's face suddenly go blank. Julius had seen the foolish grin on the Professor's face. This halted his advance and he stood still, frowning, biting his lower lip. He turned in a slow circle, surveying the horizon for something—movie cameras perhaps—that would explain what he had unwittingly stumbled into. Finally he took off his sunglasses and wiped his hand across his face to partially disguise an expectant smirk. "Well well, heh heh heh," he said.

The Professor had seen that smirk before. He had seen it most often on the faces of people at cocktail parties. It apparently signified the heightened uncertainty of someone in the presence of a joke he fails to understand. As a rule, the smirk precedes an abrupt exit—usually out to the kitchen for more ice. Those without an easy getaway present a curious phenomenon: unwilling to play the part of that imagined Other at whose expense all jokes are told, they laugh uproariously, and strangely their hollow laughter is infectious, drawing other auditors to a growing circle of hilarity, a generous community of shared understandings, until small smoky faculty apartments ring with choruses of genuine guffaws that bring rare tears of joy to the eyes, drunken wings to the spirit.

Julius, in his Hawaiian shirt, was now backing toward the icy interior of his Ford LTD, whose motor was still running. "Well! Ho ho ho!" he chuckled, as if to say, "I'm no fool." Before he put on his sunglasses he gave the Professor a broad wink of mutual understanding, then slammed the car door and drove off grinning.

The wheels of the car sent up a fine spray of crystalline particles that fell on the Professor's face. There was, he thought, a lesson to be learned from this episode. For one thing, he decided that in the future—if there was such a thing—he would avoid the phrase: "take it with a grain of salt."

Indeed, he had taken just about as much as he cared to take. Now he was ready—not to "give out"—but to "dish it out!" If he had been *had*, then he had *had* it "up to here!" This last phrase (usually accompanied by a flat gesture of the hand toward the neck—as if one had literally been pumped full of an invisible noxious substance) caused the Professor to strain at the bindings that staked him out flat on his back. In a way, after his brief flight of colloquial indignation, it brought him—how do you say?—it "brought him around." What if this is really the end of me? he wondered. If it is the end, then I may as well stretch it out as long as I please.

Accordingly, at the beginning of the end the Professor found himself, as usual now, staked out in the middle of the Great Salt Flats.

When it was past noon he finally submitted to the luxury of asking, "What have I done to deserve this?" The question (with its rather neat reversal of compensating etymologies) required more than a simple answer. What it conventionally required was the dreary process of psychic dredging: a grappling of mental hooks onto the sludge of previously unacknowledged guilt.

Contritely, the Professor began his confession by recalling the petty joke he'd once told at the expense of his junior colleague, Klipspringer, who had the office down the hall. In retrospect it may have been more prudent to have told this joke to Klipspringer's face, rather than behind his back. But in that case it would have not been very funny. This seemed to say something about the difference between being self-righteous and having a sense of humor. Klipspringer, instead of having a sense of humor, was overweight and claimed to be well-read (perhaps because as a graduate student he had made a bundle selling encyclopedias door to door in a ghetto). These days he bustled around the department puffing on a pipe so absurdly long that he'd thrown his neck out of joint lighting it once at a department meeting.

The joke about Klipspringer had started innocently enough: the Professor had merely noted one day in the coffee room that all twenty-four of Klipspringer's scholarly publications were marked by a colon in the title (for example, "Through a Glass Darkly: Window Imagery in *The Great Gatsby*"). That was the joke. Privately, to the Professor, it seemed funnier that eighteen of Klipspringer's scholarly articles were about *The Great Gatsby*. He must read that novel once a week.

Could all this be Klipspringer's revenge? No. Whoever hired those Apaches had real clout at the college. Someone in the Dean's Office, then.

Perhaps a member of the Board of Trustees? Lower down in the ranks it had to be the work of several individuals. Possibly the senior members of the department were trying to give him a hint about his chances for receiving tenure. What if they all were aged Klipspringers fond of colons in the titles of their scholarly articles?

Suddenly the heat of the afternoon sun reminded the Professor that he had gotten off the confessional track. Somehow he had begun by trying to dredge up the thing within himself at fault, but now he was trying to pin the blame on someone else. What if no one were to blame for all this—nothing to blame except the blind ferocity of the Apaches? Worse, what if someone were to blame, but the Apaches had abducted the wrong man? What if it were Klipspringer they were after? Here he was, nearing the middle of his end, and they'd begun with the wrong victim? What would Klipspringer have done in a case like this one? He was ingenious, that Klipspringer. Thick eyeglasses, long-stemmed pipe: he'd find a way to burn through rawhide bindings. That was Klipspringer's genius: to seize upon obvious solutions. Given the choice between publishing or perishing, Klipspringer had published. The Professor on the other hand, champion of the Liberal Education, was constrained to examine both sides of the issue. And as it turned out, in the issue of perishing, the whole point was not to "publish or get off the pot" as Klipspringer snidely maintained, but rather was the twin etymology of the words "perish" and "issue" themselves! Both implied a journey, and in the end, to perish meant to go too far out from the Self—with the hope, perhaps, that in going out one might go through and return in a kind of circle.

Seeing however that he wasn't going anywhere, he decided to try the Klipspringer Method: that is, he strained at the rawhide bindings. Surprisingly one of the stakes—the one at his left ankle—was loose. In fact it was comically loose, hardly driven into the ground. With a grunt he heaved his leg triumphantly to the sun. The crudely whittled peg swung free on its line and wrapped itself around the leg of his Perma-Press trousers. After all this inertia, this absence of meaningful activity, here was something! But what next?

During the next two hours he reached out in all directions with his one free leg. He kicked at the bindings that strung his palms out in a line even with the top of his head. He explored the ground on either side of him, probed and scuffed at the unseen space beyond the top of his head. But the only result of all this restless agility was to inscribe in the salty earth a complete circle around his outstretched body. Afterwards, he lay there panting, all desire for escape gone now, as if in whirling that one leg about in its arc, he'd unwound some vital spring of energy at his core. Between the edge of the circle and the center at his navel, he now knew the utmost limits of his possibilities.

It was late afternoon. About time, really, for his students to show up and save him. This, he realized as the end approached, was what he'd been counting on all along. In the end your students will save you. By sunset they still had not arrived. Clearly something was wrong. Perhaps they had never grasped the subtle thing he wanted to pass on.

The Professor had a theory of education that in its own way was subversive—if only because it tried to extend itself across the temporal (and cash on the line) boundary marked by "commencement" (literally a beginning, but most often an end to one's liberal education). The theory here was not to be too clear about things. In other words, not—in any obvious way—to teach much of anything at all. That is to say, he believed that in ambiguity itself were the seeds that eventually (who could tell when?) would burst, explode like time bombs, in a pyrotechnic display of organic illumination.

The Professor had admitted there were risks here: for example, the risk that his students would only remember him as the fellow who was always a bit confused; or who would recall him as the fellow who referred, not to the text, but to echoes of other texts. (Gosh! they'd say, as if they had a choice, Aren't there better things to do with your life than to sit around and read all the time?) He was on the brink of calling out across the miles to these dear, thickheaded students ("Hello! Hello! Do you read me?") when the Stranger arrived on horseback.

He reined in his chestnut gelding near the Professor's feet and then stared down at him coldly. After several minutes he said, "You poor bastard."

The Professor said nothing. It was a way of acknowledging the justice of the Stranger's remark.

With a creak of old leather, the Stranger tipped back his hat and threw one leg casually over the pommel of his saddle.

The Professor lifted his head off the ground. "Who are you?" he rasped. There was something pathetic in his voice; the old classroom authority in it had nearly vanished for good.

"Me? I'm the Outlaw King."

The Professor considered this: "I didn't know the outlaws had a king," he said. "In fact, given the notion of being 'outside the law' (whether civil law, common law, or ecclesiastical law), then necessarily—" He stopped. This was no time for a lecture. And besides, his heart wasn't in it anymore. He was tired. Weary of talk. Tired especially of this Professorial Self he inhabited—so often long-winded, too rarely attentive.

"Everybody's got a King," declared the Stranger. "For the outlaws, I'm him."

The Professor had to admit that this made perfect sense.

"You draw that circle around yourself?"

"Not intentionally."

"I've never seen that before. You did a good job. Funny how they always leave one stake loose."

The Professor let his head fall back on the sand with a dull thunk. So, his condition had not been unique after all. When he looked up again the Outlaw King was pointing a revolver at him. He'd do the same for any lame animal.

"Don't do me any favors," said the Professor, licking his lips and giving himself up for lost. He'd forgotten about the smile. Faintly, Buddhalike, it was still there. And now he noticed an equally ambiguous flicker of amusement pass across the Outlaw King's face. He looked like a homely version of the Mona Lisa as she holstered her revolver.

The horse was growing restless. "Well," said its rider, "you've got guts. I'll say that much." Then he spurred his horse into an easy gallop, called out "So long!" as an afterthought, and rode east toward the darkening mountains.

◇

Like all real endings, this one came too soon, in an abrupt rush. The Professor found himself under a desert sky full of stars. Small nocturnal animals appeared in the cool evening air and clambered up on his chest, scurried in and out of the pockets of his clothing.

In the end, he didn't protest when a swarm of ants flowed over him and thread by thread carried off his shirt and tie, his Harris Tweed jacket, and his Perma-Press trousers. He was strangely quiet as a cloud of moths fluttered down like moonlight, and when they mounted up again to the stars his J. C. Penney's underwear had vanished. When a pack rat snatched his wallet (containing his faculty I.D. Card) out from under a bare buttock, he knew that all references to the old Self called the Assistant Professor had finally been given up and lost. With a faint smile he realized that beneath his clothes he'd been—like most men—naked all along.

At the end then, naked as usual, he found himself staked out on the Great Salt Flats—except that some small mammal had gnawed away the rawhide bindings, and this allowed him the freedom to explore the interior of his circle. Here and there his fingers discovered secret pockets of moisture in the barren earth. At his touch, growing things sprang up: green ferns, blossoming shrubs, forests of beech and oak. He lay on his back and wandered the valleys of this oasis until he came to a clear pool of still water. There, he bent and stared into its depths. What he saw both fascinated and repelled him. So that at the end, as usual, he found himself.

Fred Pfeil

The Idiocy of Rural Life

> The bourgeoisie . . . has thus rescued a consid-
> erable part of the population from the idiocy of
> rural life.
> —Marx and Engels, *Communist Manifesto*

A patient stoical man, the Farmer waited through his work into the evening, until after washing up out back, rubbing the cold spring water over his face and hands, before he walked into the kitchen of the white frame house and asked his wife: You seen them cars outside there today?

Sure did, said the Farmer's Wife, a worrier, from the stove. Often—as now—her pale eyes were shadowed with a vague anxiety, and her thin lips quivered white as she turned to look at him.

Whole afternoon, she said. I was out there peeling apples for this pie—she nudged a thumb to where it sat on the counter, round and brown—and just looked up and there they was.

He nodded. Then walked in unhurried strides, his face impassive, past her and out of the kitchen and through the small living room, where he brushed the gauzy curtains of a front window aside with one large hand. Fifty feet away, across the yard, the cars still moved up the road, chrome glinting, glass glaring like moving shields in the stark heat of this strange dry spring.

Still there? his Wife called behind, wiping her hands in her apron.

The Farmer let the curtain drop, turned his head in profile to her, nodded. He raised up and went over to the maple rocker they had bought the year before from Sears, sat down in it, and began to unlace his boots.

Probably some folks gettin together up on Old Saddleback for some kind of do, he said, glancing at her haunted eyes. I wouldn't pay no attention to it. Chances are it don't amount to nothin at all.

While they sat at the kitchen table eating pork, okra, pie, the traffic noise reached them as a slight constant roar, like the sound of a distant plane. Afterwards, while she picked up the dishes, he went in to watch TV. At this hour, in his time zone, the Farmer had a choice between *Welcome Back Kotter* and *Little House on the Prairie*. Being a farmer, he chose the latter, though tonight it was a rerun he had seen during the regular season. In this show a deadly blizzard attacks Walnut Grove, the small town in Kansas near the Ingalls family farm, trapping beautiful children, clothed in attractive homespun, in the little wooden schoolhouse. Michael Landon, with his dark curly hair, his boyish yet resolute face, rescues them and leads them home, in the middle of the nineteenth century and the days of the frontier.

By the time she came in the show was over. Outside, the cars must have turned their lights on; a pulse of muffled light swept through the windows regularly.

He watched her look around the room, eyes drifting from grandfather clock to pole lamp to the old armchair where he sat—everything, thanks to the headlights, strange. When her eyes met his she started to talk.

Gettin low on a few things, she said. Oughtta get to town pretty soon.

Fine, he said. Anytime.

You still thinkin you're gonna have to go see Boles this year? she said.

He scraped his hand across the stubble on his chin and watched the TV. *Baretta* was starting now. Don't know, he said. Depends on what they want for seed and fertilizer. Pretty soon, we'll see.

He watched the beginning of the episode. Tony Baretta is chasing a flashy black pimp down an alley of the city. Then he heard her strained voice.

I don't like the idea of this kind of thing goin on when you're not here, she said. What if one of them cars was to stop and somebody come right in here?

When he turned and smiled at her, crow's-feet formed in the corners of his gray eyes. Well, he said, I guess the way they're goin now, car behind that one'd smash right into the back of it, now wouldn't it. Then there'd be hell to pay.

Her tight mouth opened, released a high squealing chitter which ceased abruptly, even as he joined it with his own guffaws. She stared at the window, at the sweeping lights, rubbing her fingers around and around on the arms of the rocking chair until, rising, he stepped over and rested a work-worn hand on her thin arm.

Just don't you worry, honey, he said. It ain't goin to keep on; and it ain't no business of ours.

The air is thick, rich gold with the dust of hay as the old robust farmer and his strapping sons climb down from the hay wagon and tractor and walk—tired, dusty, happy—homeward through the mown field to the white frame house on whose front porch they sit and are regaled by the old farmer's comely wife, age oddly indeterminate, bearing gold bottles of Miller's beer as someone sings "When it's time to relax, one thing comes clear, if you've got the time, we've got the beer," while the farm family raise their bottles to their lips in the gold air.

The Farmer woke at the first music of the GE digital clock radio, rose and dressed to the Farm Report—*Alfalfa, 43; Oats, 40; Soybeans, 72; Wheat, 59; and in Poultry*—as his wife still tossed and rolled in restless sleep. Then he heard the noise from outside, and remembered.

So he stepped out without his customary coffee, and walked over the soft dew-fresh grass until he stood at the edge of the drainage ditch not more than two yards from them, watching them snap past. The string of cars stretched into mist on either side. On the right, towards Saddleback, a few red taillights winked a glow through the last of night, caught in the trees.

The Farmer looked across the road, at the shed with his own car and the wheat field beyond, powder-green in the wet air. It needed fertilizer, extra water soon. How the hell was he gonna get across to it?

He lowered as if to an invisible chair, hands braced on his knees, so he could glimpse, blur after blur, the occupants of the cars. Hey, he said—first in a soft call, finally in a hoarse shout—how the hell you expect me to get across here to my field? How the hell you expect me to get across here to my field?

When he realized nobody heard him the Farmer stood, wheeled around, and walked past the house to the barn, where he fed the chickens and milked the cows, holding his face as still as theirs, calming down. In all the hen boxes there were only three eggs.

By the time he came back out the sun was a good inch free of the horizon, and his wife was outside, her back turned to him, standing by the front corner of the house watching the cars pass, a pale shape tipped with the brown of her hair. Slowly, heavily, he walked up to her, dreading the fear he would find on her face.

But when she turned, he was surprised to find her looking far less frightened than he'd counted on. You picked up anything on them? she said.

For a second he thought of telling her about the bottom field, how they were blocking it; but if she did know there was no use repeating it, if not there was no use getting her upset. No, he said.

A light, elusive smile crossed her smooth face. What kinda cars they drivin, she said.

He looked. The fog had burned away so he could see maybe forty from the rise on the left to the hill on the right, where they went up into the woods: station wagons, compact cars, medium-sized models, sporty compacts and sports cars, family and luxury sedans, coupes, convertibles and luxury automobiles . . .

Well, he said, all kinds, I guess. He scratched his head, sneaked another quick look to the side: No trucks . . .

She grabbed his arm, turned him straight ahead again. No, she said, staring fiercely. The *makes*.

He looked; and, as the day's first real heat touched his head, saw that they were Fords.

Against black we see first one ordinary watchband, then a dazzling host of them, of shapes, sizes, elasticities, and light tones; and the urbane yet concerned voice of a skilled announcer asks how we would like it if we lived in a country where we could only buy just that first kind of watchband and no other, some unnamed other place under the oppression of the lone watchband, only one thing to buy, instead of here where you can pluck out of the glittering heap of watchbands the very one that is right for only you before you line up at the register to pay. This ad is a public service of the Ad Council, a "nonprofit" organization headed by representatives of United Airlines, General Mills and General Foods, ITT and IBM, General Electric, etc., etc.

Soon the day was starched with heat; in the west meadow where the Farmer went, choosing to mend fence, the heat stood breathing close and sour in his face as he strung, stretched, clipped wire, pounded a few posts deeper down. Yet he made it all day without so much as going in for lunch, scrutinized only by his own idling cows jostled together under the meadow's few trees, stopping only to slap at sweat bees.

Late in the afternoon, he propped the spool of wire on one shoulder, swung the sledge from his free arm, and started back across and down the ridge that sloped to his barn, house, and the dirt road beyond. The second the cars came into view he could see how much they had slowed down; to twenty mph anyways, and still no end to them in sight. And he could see, framed by the two oaks in the front yard, the tiny figure of his Wife.

She was, he found once he was all the way down, sitting close to the spot where he'd hunkered that morning to yell at the cars. All day plumes of dust must have drifted from the road to the lawn; dust lay in a dull brown all over the grass, over her aproned lap.

Her face was rapt; her brown, normally troubled eyes remained fixed and calm; rather than follow each car out of sight, she let them fill and refill her field of vision, like someone thirsty drinking glass after glass. When at last she turned to him her eyes looked yellow; for a second he was afraid she did not recognize him.

Ever notice how Ford makes their cars animals? she said, and pointed a finger like a gun at the road: Pinto; Mustang; Bronco; Thunderbird.

Above his head he heard a high breeze shiver the oak leaves. Shoot, he said, and snorted. How bout Torino? You heard of a animal called Torino? You know of a animal named LTD?

The Farmer and his Wife stared at each other with dull angry eyes.

You been sittin out here all day, he said. I suppose you know how I'm gonna get over there, tend that goddamn wheat?

Her mouth grew a slow, sly smile though her eyes did not change. They'll let you through, she said.

How you know? the Farmer said as once more sweat broke out on him, as though hot water had been flung on his face. You been talkin with them? You the one's so scared some one of them'd stop to see you; they stoppin to see you now?

The Farmer's Wife rose, slapping the dust off her apron and house-dress before looking at him again almost in her old way, without the smile. I just think they will, she said. Just a feelin, that's all. Now come on, she said, reaching for his hand. Let's go on in, news is on. They might have somethin to say about all this, you never know.

So he allowed himself to be led in, seated in his armchair; the TV was on, had been on the whole time. While she got supper he watched the news, featuring a farmers' strike. The farmers have their tractors drawn around the Governor's mansion and stand sullenly in flannel shirts, arms crossed on chests. The Governor comes out to speak in a gray suit, white shirt, and tie, and says I will go to Washington; I will tell them that the farmer feeds us all; and a thin ragged cheer floats from the crowd, followed by a commercial for Union Carbide.

She wafted in with two shiny silver trays from which he could discern no smells, flopped a dish towel in his lap, and set one tray on top of it.

There, she said, indicating the content of each bin: there's your crispy chicken leg and thigh, your green peas with pearl onions, your apple brown betty for dessert—

The Farmer looked down at the food, like pictures on TV, and closed his eyes and let a wave of feeling pass over him. You get the same for yourself? he heard his voice say.

Oh no, she said. I got loin of pork.

He opened his eyes and watched her awhile, eating in her rocking chair. She attacked her portions with apparent relish, without benefit of a fork, dipping her fingers in her tray and mouth with her eyes fixed on the TV, an episode of *The Waltons*. John-Boy is upstairs in the Walton farmhouse recording in his journal the events of this episode from the days of the Depression which now begin to unfold, brought to you by General Foods. By Gulf-Western. By Zenith color TV.

Since when you bought this stuff? the Farmer said.

Her thin hand stopped halfway to her mouth, then redeposited a Tater Tot in her tray. Her eyes looked somewhere between the TV set and his chair.

Oh, she was saying, I don't know when. She was laughing now, with that smile on again: All this weird stuff we got goin around now, I just thought we might's well eat somethin new too. How you like it?

Don't know, he said feeling sick with her lie. Ain't yet tasted it. But she had turned her face back to the set.

Sadly the Farmer dipped his head, pinched a chicken leg's gold crunchy crust, and lifted it toward his mouth. Grease like some hot secret spurted through the chicken skin over his hand, John-Boy and Pa on the TV jog the mules across the hill toward home, Pa nodding sagely, and the Farmer heard at that selfsame moment once again the deep-throated murmur of the cars outside, and felt this strange conjunction so—hot skinny chicken, her deception, the cars outside, the pictures on the screen—that his lap trembled beneath the towel, his broad thighs buckled and spread apart, sending kelly-green peas up in the air, brown betty to the floor, soft side down.

Aw, he cried, Hell's bells.

Hey, she said, rising swiftly: don't worry about it, okay? She set her emptied tray down on the floor and came and stood over him; she passed a hand through his short-cropped hair, down the back of his bull neck. I'll get it later, she said. How bout if you and me do somethin different for a change?

He looked down in time to see one of her small feet squash a pea. Like what? he said, voice trembling.

Like go to bed a little early for a change? she said.

Ain't even dark yet, the Farmer mumbled, feeling his face go hot; but already, once again, she had him by the hand and was leading him out of the room, into the bedroom, again leaving the TV on.

What they did then, there in the bedroom with the red sun going down, was indeed different enough from usual that when it was done, while she was all giggly happy, he set his shamed body and mind running toward sleep but did not manage to arrive before her voice, silky, thrilling, reached him one last time.

And we're out of food and practically a dozen other things too, why I can hardly think what all, you just remember now, we go to town first thing tomorrow—you hear?

I hear, he groaned—and fled below the voice, beneath even the slow rolling of wheels outside, so far down he never noticed when she got up from the bed and went back outside, humming in the dark.

The background, brown, textured, woody, suggests a farm or cabin, soft dream of rural interiority. Likewise, the man wears suede tones and conveys in voice and manner a certain sturdiness, though he is not husky enough to be an Outdoorsman, too polished for a Farmer, as he slides across the background (through whose window you glimpse wildflowers? gnarled oak tree in bloom?), moving his calm jaws. He says some people want the lightness of white bread. Others want the firmness of wheat and whole grain. Roman Meal gives you both, he says, showing you gray-brown rugged grains in the iron scoop; flour in a barrel; honey in a jar. Where did the grains grow, in whose field, by what methods; where and how do these ingredients come together to compose the loaf he hefts in

*his hand? And his shirt of raw cotton, open almost to the pectorals—
where and by whom was it made? Who decided he should have black
hair? The Roman Meal people, he says, thought you'd like to know.*

There was just room enough for his car, a Plymouth V-8, ten years
old, to squeeze by the Fords inching the other way on the dirt road. He
drove the mile to the main road slow and cautious, sweat crawling down
his face and dampening the Sears plaid short-sleeve shirt he was wearing
to town. Beside him on the seat, his Wife, cool and dry in some lime slacks
and blouse he had not seen before, began reading aloud from her book.

During barbarous ages, she read, if the strength of an individual declined, if he felt himself tired or sick, melancholy or satiated and, as a
consequence, without desire or appetite for a short time, he became relatively a better man, that is, less dangerous. . . . She stopped reading, peered
over the top of the paperback at him: What do you think of that?

Think of it? The Farmer squinted fiercely at the road, the space the
Fords left him; the morning sun shone hard, straight at the windshield of
the car. Ain't nothin to think of it. Bunch of trash is what it is.

I just knew you'd say that, said his Wife. That's just the kind of
thing you'd say. And it's Nietzsche, in case you're interested.

I don't give a hair of my behind what it is, the Farmer was about to
say; but they had reached the hard road, where he saw a sight that si-
lenced him. In the westward, left-hand lane of the hard road, the Fords
lined up to turn left stretched off to vanishing point; then, in his full
shock, he turned to his Wife and saw her eyes staring off at them shining,
her tongue tracing the line of her lips.

I don't know where you gettin that trash anyways, he said, looking
back at the road and turning the car right, onto the macadam: Neechuh.
People in them cars puttin that trash in your head or what.

Oh *God*, she said. Why can't you just leave me alone? And with
that, poked her nose back in the book again the rest of the way in, inking
in passages now and then with a purple felt-tip pen.

He dropped her off at the Safeway and went to the Agway, where
the fellow told him No he hadn't heard a thing about it. To which the
Farmer replied as how he hadn't really figured it was anything to amount
to anything anyway; just curious was all.

The fellow slapped the sacks he had hauled up to the counter: All
right then. That be all today?

That's all I guess, the Farmer said.

Cash or charge, the fellow said.

Charge, said the Farmer.

The fellow reached down under the counter and went through the slips until he found his. Then he took a stub of pencil from behind his ear and figured on the slip for a while, his round face wadded in a frown, while the Farmer's eyes traveled over the dusty outlines of bags and barrels in the cool dark of the warehouse, thinking nothing, waiting for the calculation to end.

I hate to tell you, the fellow said when he looked up, in a voice without sorrow: You're already over.

Figured as much, the Farmer said quite levelly, looking straight on back at him. Goddamn prices the way they are. He moved a step closer to the counter, so close now his belt buckle touched the wood. Gotta have that stuff, he said.

The fellow's eyes seemed to lose focus, turn watery. You been to see Boles yet this year? he said.

No, said the Farmer. Not yet this year. I'll be goin directly now.

The fellow's mouth knit and firmed, though his eyes stayed the same. All right then, he said. I'll put you down and let you ride. He wrote a few more numbers on the slip and turned it around for the Farmer to sign. I'll be hearin from you then just as soon as you see him, he said.

That's right, the Farmer said, hefting to his shoulder a sack of potash, popping fresh sweat on his brow. Already the fellow was scuttling around the counter wheeling a dolly.

Here now, he was saying brightly, smiling again: Lemme give you a hand there gettin that in the car.

In the parking lot at Safeway he watched a checkout boy watching her cross the asphalt with her bags, bend to stuff them in the back, get in herself, still looking dry and cool; only high on her cheekbones he saw blazes of red.

You gonna go see Boles soon? she said staring out as though to someone on the hood, and lighting a cigarette.

Yeah, he said in a much higher voice than usual. He had never seen her smoke before.

I couldn't buy *half* what we need with what you gave me, she said and puffed, tapping the ash off on the floor. I had to take back half the things *after* they were rung up. *Very* embarrassing, as you can imagine.

I'll be goin directly, the Farmer said.

As soon as they reached the main highway again, he realized his mistake: the Fords, fender to fender, still jammed the right side of the road. Oh Christ, he heard his wife sigh, what a—

He wrenched the Plymouth into the left lane and gunned it as she shouted his name; the car popped, shuddered, raced up the road. Three times before they reached the turnoff cars moving legally in the lane came straight at them and he had to sound the horn as loud and long as he could to send them off the road to the berm in time. But even as his car fishtailed and scudded up the wrong side of the dirt road, not one of the Fords pulled out after him.

He wheeled the car into the shed and shut it off and looked at her taut face. You could have killed us both, she said.

Naw, he said, smiling, feeling good for the first time in days. Not much chance a that.

They crossed between two Fords easily; the line was now still, though the cars all had their engines on. A thin blue haze of hydrocarbons, faint as gunsmoke, reached as high as the first boughs of the oak, and the ditch was strewn with Big Mac wrappers, DQ cups, Coke bottles and cans, though all the car windows were up. The grass beneath its dust blanket had turned a dying yellow.

You mind puttin this stuff away? she said when the bags were on the kitchen table, with a vestige of her old tone. I think I'd like to go and lie down for a bit. She draped a forearm over her brow: It's just so hot.

Yeah, the Farmer said. Sure. He thought of touching her but instead stood looking at his hands until she was out of the room. Then he took all the strange frozen boxes out of the bags—Spinach Soufflé, Turkey Tetrazzini, Cannelloni in sauce, Potatoes au gratin, Lobster Newburg— put as many as would fit away in the freezer, the rest in the fridge, piled the books she had stowed in the bags' bottoms on the table for her— *Critique de la raison dialectique?*—and, after some hesitation, went out to doze himself for a few hours in the known, deep shadows of the barn with the animals.

In less than twenty years, from 1950 to 1969, the number of farms in the United States has declined by half—from 5.4 to 2.7 million. This decline is not due to a drop in agricultural activity, but from the rapid process of concentration of U.S. agriculture into large-scale capitalist enterprise. Thus in 1969 a little over 2 percent of U.S. farms consisted of at least 2000 acres. And these large farms accounted for 40 percent of U.S. farm-

land. At the other end of the scale 23 percent of the farms in 1969 were less than 50 acres, and another 17 percent were between 50 and 99 acres. Taken together, these two groups—or 40 percent of the farms—operated less than 100 acres each and accounted for less than 5 percent of total farmland.

So shortly thereafter the Farmer found himself waking in dark morning beside his sprawled Wife, fallen asleep with the reading light on again, her fingers marking the 246th formulation of the *Philosophical Investigations*; found himself hauling on his overalls and tiptoeing out, turning back only once to let his hand come back and almost rest on her hair, as his eyes lighted on the passage without meaning to; something about knowing someone's pain.

Outside the Fords had their headlights on, each shining directly into the taillights of the next a matter of inches away. The line no longer moved; so the strangely refracted glow, the radiance suffusing the stream, seemed the product of the massed, purring engines of the cars, gas-burning generators of light. Crossing the line this time he had to step up and over a Torino's bumper; the dark backlit outlines in the car did not honk.

Shortly after he had reached the hard road and turned east, darkness began to leak out of the sky. Soon it was the same time he usually got up; he turned on the Farm Report in the car—*Alfalfa, 43; Oats, 40; Soybeans, 72*—and found the litany of prices conjured up his Wife the way she used to be, eyes closing and opening in slow fatigued anxiety as he moved around the bed and dressed. The image held him all the way to the airport, a goodly distance away.

The jet took off into a swollen sun, then banked to the northeast so that he, in a window seat on the right, could see it rising orange and monstrous in the haze of the day before. He thought of that sun shining on his fields all day, of spreading gray fertilizer and hoping for rain, of the way weather worked before the Fords came. But soon the high vibration of the machine he sat in soothed him; gradually he assumed the indifference of an object, as one does in planes, rousing only to eat a yellow square of hot soft stuff he did not bother to think of as eggs.

Hours later, as the plane touched down again and taxied the runway, the Farmer felt a new and general sadness creeping over him as his sense of self returned—a sadness he realized he had been holding back in his mind for a few days now anyway. The feeling something was over, things were changed and would not come back, stuck inside him like a pit in a peach. Still, he told himself, scanning the profile of the gray city as it passed, just have to keep goin on.

So, willful as an animal, consciously blind to the concourse crowds and noise, he forced his way as usual through the terminal, grabbed the first cab he could, shot Boles's address in the cabby's ear like a poem he had memorized and would soon forget.

The cab moved over beltways, expressways, freeways, on- and off-ramps; occasionally the Farmer, staring fixedly out the window, would see a Ford in the clog of traffic, but he tried not to count.

The cab dropped him off downtown at the foot of a giant alabaster building where, Boles had once told him, everyone worked for the same company he did. You see ads for them on TV sometimes, showing couples on stretches of beach or sunsets on wheat fields or sunrise on forests and saying Working to make America stronger, or better, or things like that.

The Farmer took an elevator to the eighty-fifth floor, Boles's floor. It let him off into a magenta room with lime stripes and a slim secretary who said in a voice of cool disapproval, May I help you please?

Like to see Mr. Boles, he muttered, dropping into what seemed to his nervous haunches to be a bottomless chair.

Do you have an appointment, said the secretary, examining a fingernail.

Believe I do, he said, almost inaudibly.

She frowned at him and pressed the intercom. Mr. Boles, she said, there is a gentleman in overalls out here to see you, sir. Says he has an appointment. Then she listened to the button in her ear, said Yes sir, and swiveled in her chair back toward the Farmer with a smile: Yes, Mr. Boles will see you now. Walk right in, please.

Obliged, he mumbled and lurched to his feet, swiping the Harvester cap from his head.

Well, Boles said in the inner office, without rising from his massive desk: Hello again.

Hello Mr. Boles, the Farmer said.

What can I do for you, said Boles.

The Farmer stared at Boles's name and title on the edge of his desk, wrung the cap in his hand, tried to smile; failed. Need some seed and fertilizer money, he said. Plus a little for provisions the next month or so.

He stopped; Boles said nothing; he went on. All I'm askin for, he said—

Boles raised one slim hand, palm out. I must tell you, he said. The answer this time must be no. We can offer you no advance funding this year.

He pressed a button on the console on the right-hand edge of the desk; a map of the earth slid down the wood-lined wall. On the map in various areas emblems of food were stuck. A teapot covered Kenya; soybeans dotted Brazil; a steer head loomed over Central America; a chicken stalked Pakistan; pineapples rested on the Philippines; etc., etc., etc. In his own region the Farmer saw a representation of a milk can and stalks of corn and wheat, but now Boles rose and lifted them off the map.

We're relocating many of the sources of our agricultural supply, he said, and seemed about to replace the stalks and can on their new home.

But the Farmer, to his own surprise, lifted his eyes straight at Boles; and Boles stood still with the little images in his hand. You know anything about these Fords keep comin up my road? the Farmer said, astonished at himself.

Boles frowned, staring off, and slid the emblems into his suitcoat pocket. Fords? he said. Fords . . . No, he said, sliding back into his chair; I can't tell you why Fords. He spoke softly and slowly, as though talking to himself: Although certainly there would be increased traffic in the vicinity I can't tell . . . Fords . . . Fords, you say?

That's right, said the Farmer.

Hmm, Boles said, tossing his head casually back and to the side: Frankly, that worries me. We've got some nice little plans for your part of the country, your neck of the woods, whatever you want to call it—you know, that Saddleback you've got up there is a *very* important hill—and I don't like to hear about a lot of Fords in there, no sir. I don't like hearing about it one bit.

What kinda plans, the Farmer said, amazing himself again.

Across the desk Boles pursed his mouth and looked at him with sharp blue eyes. Then he leaned forward suddenly. Listen, he said. You've been a good tenant, client, whatever you want to call it; I'm gonna give you a break.

He settled back in his chair and swiveled it slightly from left to right and back. The plan is to wait about another month, he said, until you're really low and the stuff's burning up in the fields; it won't rain either, see? Then we come and make you an offer on the whole shebang. And that offer's gonna seem real nice.

His eyes were gleaming; his left-hand index finger shot up in the air: Don't take it. Ask us to make a second offer, maybe a third. I'm telling you this for your own good; you mention it to anyone, I can kiss this job goodbye. But you keep your mouth shut and play your cards right and you won't ever have to farm again, all right?

He jumped up from the seat and bent over the desk with his hand out like a chopping blade. Don't forget now, he said as they shook hands: I'm telling you because you're a good man and for telling me about the Fords. But don't forget to leave my name out of it, okay?

My great-grandfather, recently over from Sweden, is working out of the Wetmore lumber camp, stripping the bark off shag hickory trees. He goes out in the morning with a gunny sack and a short saw and an eight-inch double-handled blade, and comes in at night with the bag full of bark. This is in western Pennsylvania, the northern tip of the Appalachians, 1904. The company pays him so much per pound and sells it to the chemical plant over in Coudersport where they do something with it, he doesn't know what; but the money is good enough that, with the help of my great-grandmother, who cooks for the men at the camp, he will be able to buy a small ramshackle farm in four years' time, up what will be called Farmer's Valley where he will live until his death in 1958.

So on this midsummer afternoon he is working in the forest down a hill towards the Smethport road, metal voices of locusts off behind him, last shade-cool of the woods fading away. Then, he hears another noise, or set of noises, popping and crackling from down on the road. He rests his blade and saw on the sack and walks to the edge of the woods and looks down. On the road, about a half-mile away, is a black box tapered a bit at the front end, moving forward on four wheels mounted on the outside edge of the carriage, trailing great clouds of dust behind it and a thinner, higher plume of smoke, all traveling at least as fast as a good horse at a gallop. My great-grandfather takes out the red print bandanna he bought last time he went down to town and wipes his brow and watches closely, without expression, until the first car he has seen is gone; then he goes back up in the woods to work.

On the way back there were not only the immobile Fords but other equipment, earthmovers, caterpillars scraping, already at work, flagmen everywhere in the dust; it was twilight before the Farmer reached his home again. From the kitchen, where she had left her note, he could hear the livestock calling out back from the barn: hens clucking with hunger and irritation at the cars, cows lowing to be milked and fed. They made at least as much sense as her note, in block capitals, held before his eyes.

THE CONTRADICTIONS IN OUR SITUATION ARE IRRECONCIL-
ABLE. I'M SORRY.
KATE

The floor, table, and counter space were covered with empty boxes with pictures of serving suggestions on their fronts, with spine-broken books whose pages fluttered in the breeze swept through the screen. Could it be about to rain? Boles had told him no. For a minute he thought of going after her, finding the car she was in, even started toward the front door. Then he stopped; it would be easier, after all, this way.

He went out back, pumped some water into his cupped hands, washed his face. Seemed silly to feed or tend the animals, too, if all they were going to do was die. So he let them yell, and walked on past the barn to the south field he'd put alfalfa down in a few weeks ago.

Now, though the first stars had come out, there was still enough light left to show him the bright clean green of the sprouts coming up: the coolest, most beautiful green in the world. He felt refreshed just looking at it; though it too would die. And be paved over? he wondered, idly.

In the middle distance, some two hundred yards away, the Fords on the road were turning on their lights. The Farmer sat down in his field, and felt the warmth of the earth soaking into his body. He reached over, plucked a green sprout from the ground, ate it. Cool green taste filled his mouth, eyes, mind. He ate another. Another. Another. When he had finished the row he obeyed another sudden urge, and lay down on his stomach against the earth.

After a while, a cry rang out of the night—carried over the sounds of insects and cars with the aid of an electrified bullhorn, which helped alter the sound of her voice considerably.

JIM, she called. CAN YOU HEAR ME? I DIDN'T GO WITH THE CARS LIKE YOU THOUGHT.

The Farmer rolled over on his back; the cars' lights were so bright you could find stars only in a small portion of the sky. *Sure*, he thought, somewhere far back in his mind. *Hear you just fine.* His large hands stroked, sifted, patted the warm ground.

SOME OF THEM—US—SOME PEOPLE LEFT THEIR CARS, the voice said. THERE'S QUITE A FEW OF US HERE, ACTU-ALLY. AND IF YOU WANT TO, JIM—

The electric voice went on; but the Farmer no longer listened. In that place back in his skull, a voice still went on saying things like *sure enough, uh huh, yeah, yeah, yeah*; but he had lost the habit of speech. He lay on his back while the voices talked on until finally, after they both stopped, he felt the moment he had been waiting for, with or without knowing it, all along: when, his belly full of warm green stuff, his eyes could see the sparks of light up there and—thanks to the cars—the glow around the edges of the sky like the whole thing was a big TV screen, the world's biggest, which he kept right on watching for a very long time.

Scott R. Sanders

America Is One Long Bloody Fight

> Sham fights would sometimes be gotten up for the purpose of indulging the popular taste for excitement.

WHAT could an old man do to preserve the Union? General Alphonso Roof wanted to know. He rose before the Roma town meeting on seventy-eight-year-old legs. Born in the last year of the Revolution to a man who died fighting the English, wounded at the Battle of Lake Erie in 1813, one arm twisted from an encounter with a bear, his face scarred from Indian fights, eyes squinted from five decades of plowing—the general stood before the people of Pilgrim County like a living archive of their history. If heart were all that was needed, he would fight the rebels before supper. But his body just would not go anymore. Form a Home Guard, then, Judge Luther Day suggested. The audience cheered. A motion was passed empowering the general to do just that.

Enough boys and aged men joined him to form a respectable company. When it was discovered that some of the boys were actually girls in long breeches, General Roof said he would train them anyway, plus any other women who turned up. If the rebels invaded Ohio, he explained, everybody with a stout heart would be needed for defense— and women had about the stoutest hearts he had ever come across.

Since there were barely enough rifles to equip the regular militia, the Home Guard rehearsed for war carrying broom handles and cornstalks. The general did not bother with marching or any of the other rigmarole inherited from Old World soldiering. He taught his recruits how to bush up in a clump of sumac and lay for the enemy with tomahawks. He taught the quickest boys and girls how to steal horses, on the

[275]

chance that enemy cavalry might one day show up. Women and the
sturdiest old men he instructed in the use of bowie knives, which had
been made to his order by a Lebanon Township blacksmith. Into every
house in the county he introduced a tiny sack of poison, to be dished out
to occupying soldiers. Anyone who questioned these bloodthirsty prepa-
rations was told in heated Yankee English that the country had been won
by fighting, made rich by fighting, and would damn well be kept in one
piece by fighting. America is one long bloody fight, he explained, and
don't you ever forget it.

The war kept General Roof alive, right up through Lee's surrender
at Appomattox. By and by he died, without seeing the enemy again, without doubting that a new enemy was there, waiting.

Jesse Stuart

From the Mountains of Pike

"THIS will do the trick, Sal," Pa said to Mom. "Look! See what I've got! This is the deed for the Sid Beverley property. All made ready to sign! I'll show Permintis Mullins something. He'll never outshine Mick Powderjay when it comes to tradin'!"

Pa held the clean unsigned deed for Mom to see. Mom was hooking a rug while she waited for us to return. She didn't look up when Pa held the deed for her to see. She kept on working on her rug.

"What's the matter, Sal?" Pa asked. "This is the deed for that property! Don't you want us to have it? Don't you want to see me buy it? Why don't you back me up like a good wife backs up her trading husband?"

Mom still didn't speak. She kept on hooking her rug while the night wind sang around our house. Wind flapped the loose shingles on the roof. Wind rattled our loose window sashes. We heard it moan through the barren branches of the apple trees in our front yard. Pa wouldn't have any kind of shade but apple trees. He said they were good shade trees and they bore fruit too. Mom couldn't understand this, since we had seven hundred eighteen acres of land in The Valley. We owned all of The Valley but two farms. Permintis Mullins owned seventy-three acres. Sid Beverley owned one hundred and sixty acres. But Sid Beverley had moved from The Valley back to Pike County in the high mountains. And Pa and Permintis had tried to buy him out and he wouldn't sell. Not then.

And what had caused all the excitement was a letter we got at The Valley post office in the four o'clock mail. I had gone to the store for

By permission of the Jesse Stuart Foundation, Judy B. Thomas, Chair; H. E. Richardson, Editor-in-Chief, Department of English, University of Louisville, Louisville, Ky. 40292.

groceries, and John Baylor, who runs our post office and store, gave me the letter. When I saw it was from Sid Beverley I knew the letter must be important. Important to Pa. I rode the horse home in a hurry. Pa was delighted when he read that Sid Beverley said he was ready to sell. Said he was happier back in the mountains where he was born and grew to manhood. Said something about going home to drink the water from the well of his youth and it tasted so good and things like that. How much fresher and better the air was. How much friendlier the people were. The smile left Pa's face when he read where Sid said he was writing Permintis Mullins and telling him too the farm was for sale. Said in the letter he was writing both at the same time. "I'm telling you that I'm writing Permintis," the letter said. "I'm telling Permintis I'm writing you. I know you don't get along too well. But both of you are my friends and I'm ready to sell my farm in The Valley."

When Pa read this he stood a minute and looked into the open fire. That's the place Pa looked when he was in a deep study. And when he looked into the fire he didn't speak to anybody. Then Pa shouted: "Adger, put the saddles on the horses in a hurry." I ran to the barn to saddle the horses. We had a car but in March our roads were impassable. We had to ride horseback when we traveled any distance. I didn't ask Pa any questions. I knew he'd hatched something. After I'd saddled the horses and run back to the house, I heard Mom say: "Don't do it, Mick."

But Pa and I ran back to the barn, led our saddled horses from the stalls. Pa climbed upon Moll's back like a young man. His foot in the stirrup and his other leg high up over Moll's back, he dropped into the saddle and we were off. I followed him. I knew something was in the wind. A big trade was on. He was off to beat Permintis Mullins.

"As fast as we can go to Blakesburg," he said. "Nine miles and an hour and a half to get there. We got to get there before the clerk's office closes. It closes at six. And we've got muddy traveling."

We made it all right. We had ten minutes to spare. But when we asked for the deed, it took more than ten minutes to make it. We were on the safe side now. Jack Willis, Greenwood County's clerk, belonged to Pa's party. Pa had ridden horseback every day and part of the night for one week before the election to help elect Jack Willis.

"Sure, Mick," he said. "I'll favor you. You favored me. I'll never forget you. Got this office by forty-four votes and I think this work you did put me over. Yes, I'll make that deed."

Permintis Mullins rode his horse day and night for you too, I thought. But I didn't speak my thoughts. He belongs to the same party too. And I wondered if Jack Willis wouldn't tell Permintis the same thing if he'd come to have a deed made in the night. I wondered if Pa would think to ask if Permintis had been there before we arrived. Pa never left a stone unturned when he traded. This was one reason Permintis Mullins didn't like Pa. I'd heard Mom and Pa talk on winter evenings when they sat before the fire, how Sid Beverley, Permintis Mullins, and their wives and Pa and Mom had come from Pike County when they were young married couples. How they all worked with each other in the beginning. They were all traders. How they left Pike County where about everybody was a good trader and had all come to Greenwood County where there weren't many land, cattle, and horse traders. They'd heard great stories of the poor traders in this county and they came to get rich. And when Pa got ahead of Sid Beverley, Sid got sick at heart and went back to Pike County. I knew it wasn't the fresh air, the water from the family well he drank when he was a boy, and the friendliness of the people that called him back. It was Pa's doing so much better than he did. It was Pa's getting most of The Valley that hurt him. It was Pa's getting up at midnight and getting there first that beat Sid Beverley.

It was when Pa tried to buy Permintis Mullins' farm that Permintis turned on him. From that hour, Pa and Permintis never stood by one another again. And they never traded with each other. Viola Mullins, Permintis' wife, never came to see Mom again. Permintis' boys, Cief, Ottis, and Bill, never spoke to my brother Finn and me again. The big rift came between us when Pa got enough ahead by his trading to "buy Permintis out." Pa had insulted Permintis. And if anybody on earth knew the Mullinses we did. If anybody knew the Powderjays, the Mullinses did. They knew we had often carried "hardware" pieces. We knew they did too. They knew we had used them in Pike County before we left. We knew they carried them there and had used them too. We didn't want to get into it with each other. How many dead there would have been, would have been anybody's guess.

"Say, Jack," Pa whispered when Jack had finished making the deed, "I want to ask you something. Don't ever mention I've asked you this. But I want a truthful answer right from the shoulder."

"You'll get it, Mick," Jack Willis told Pa. "I won't lie to you."

"Has Permintis Mullins been in here this afternoon?" Pa asked. "Have you made a deed for him for this Sid Beverley property?"

"He's not been here, Mick," Jack said.

"Thank you, Jack." Pa's face beamed with happiness. "I know you'd tell me the truth."

Then Pa pulled a big fat billfold from his hip pocket. He took enough bills from it to paper a small room. He started peeling off the ones with his big thumb to pay for the deed.

"I wouldn't take a penny for that deed, Mick," Jack said. "I know you've made the green lettuce in your day by trading. I know you got more lettuce than I'll ever have working in this office and getting myself elected every four years. But I wouldn't take a penny from you. It's a pleasure to serve you, Mick. It's a pleasure to have you for a friend. You're the greatest trader in Greenwood County. There's never been one as good and I don't think there ever will be."

Pa loved these words. His face turned redder than the cold March winds had ever made it. He looked at Jack Willis and smiled. Jack stood there looking at Pa, a large square-shouldered man, with a clean, folded, unsigned deed in his big stubby hand. Pa didn't insist that Jack take the money for the deed. With the other hand he slipped the big billfold into his hip pocket and buttoned the pocket and kept it there. That's where Pa kept his big money. He kept his "chicken feed" in a little pocketbook in his front pocket.

"Jack, you're a good man and a reliable friend," Pa said. "I appreciate this from the bottom of my heart. Appreciate it more than I have the words to tell you. My wife doesn't like the way I work all night when a trade is on. She can't understand it. But I have often told her if I go first, the one thing I want her and my sons to remember about me is I was a great trader. I want them to remember the grass didn't grow under my feet. That the early bird always got the worm and I was the early bird."

"You're that, Mick," Jack agreed as we left his office.

With the deed in his inside coat pocket, Pa went down the courthouse corridor laughing. His laughter echoed against the stone walls and returned to us, deafening our ears. When we got back to our horses, unhitched them from the posts, and were in the saddles again, Pa said: "See how men respect you, Son, when you do something in life. Boy, I'll make that Permintis Mullins live hard. He'll die when I get that Sid Beverley farm. His mouth has been watering for it ever since Sid went back to Pike. And I don't blame him," Pa shouted as we galloped our horses from Blakesburg. "Sweet meadows, timbered hills, good tobacco ground . . . who wouldn't want it?"

I didn't say anything. I rode along beside Pa.

"I want you boys to learn something from me while I'm alive and trading," Pa said. "You boys don't realize what a great trader I am. And you won't know it until after I'm gone."

"I've loved you for thirty years with all my heart," Pa said as he stood before Mom with the deed in his hand.

"Second to trading, Mick," she said. "I play second fiddle. It's your trading you think about. It's been your life since I've been married to you. All you do is trade and brag about it. Some of these times, somebody is goin' to be just a little smarter than you."

Then Pa laughed as I had never heard him laugh before. He put the deed in his inside coat pocket, pulled a cigar from his vest pocket, bit the end from it with his tobacco-stained teeth, wet the cigar with his tongue. Then he put it between his clean-shaven lips, pulled a match from his hatband, struck it on his thumbnail, and held the flame to the end of the long black cigar. He pulled enough smoke from the cigar into his mouth at one time to send a cloud of smoke to the ceiling. With the cigar in his mouth, he looked up at the smoke, put his thumbs behind his suspenders, pulled them out, and let them fly back and hit him while he laughed, smoked, and listened to Mom.

"You're too proud of yourself, Mick," Mom warned. She had stopped hooking her rug now as she sat there watching Pa walk up and down the room. "You know Permintis Mullins is a dangerous man. You know he's a proud man. When you hurt his pride, you do something to him. He's liable to explode. You know the Mullinses back in Pike County, don't you?"

"And you know the Powderjays too, don't you?" Pa snapped. "You're married to one. We had pride back in Pike County too. And we got it now. That's why I own The Valley. I'll have Permintis Mullins hemmed. I'll own land all around old Permintis. And if he's got any pride left in his bones he'll come to me like a man. We'll set a price 'give or take.' And when he sets the price, I know he can't 'take it.' I'll get it all. What kind of pride do you call that, Sal?"

Pa laughed louder than he did before.

"We've been together thirty years, Mick," Mom said. "Even if you do stay on the road and trade, I want you to be with me a while longer. I just have a feeling something is goin' to happen to you. I don't know what. I do know Permintis Mullins!"

"Not anything is goin' to happen," Pa assured her.

Pa had stopped laughing now. He had taken his big thumbs from behind his suspenders. He didn't blow smoke at the ceiling. He held the cigar in his hand and looked at Mom. Mom didn't often talk to him like this. "We're goin' to have this farm before Permintis Mullins knows what's goin' on. I'm leaving here tonight. Adger is goin' with me. Finn is goin' with us to Auckland and bring the horses back. We're goin' to get that five o'clock train up Big Sandy. We're heading for Pike County tonight. Sid and Clara will be signing this deed for me at about noon tomorrow if the train's on time."

Mom looked at Pa and then she looked at me. Mom didn't know what to say.

"It's the early bird that gets the worm," Pa bragged. Then he started laughing again.

"I've heard you say that so much, Mick," Mom said. "But I'm afraid, Mick."

"Not anything to be afraid of," Pa boasted, as he walked toward the dresser and opened the drawer.

"No, Mick," Mom said, getting up from her chair. And then she smiled. "You don't need that. Not you. Anybody who can trade and make money like you, can protect himself with his big strong fist."

Pa closed the dresser drawer. He looked at Mom and smiled. Then he pulled her close to him with his big arms around her.

"Now you're talking like the little girl who used to love me," he told her. "That's the way I love to hear you talk. That puts the spirit in me. I'll have that farm now or I'll know the reason. Adger, get Finn out of bed. Have him dress and let's be on our way."

When I returned with Finn, Pa was still holding Mom in his big arms. He wasn't acting like the trader now. He was acting like a man in love when he held my beautiful mother in his arms. And I knew why Mom had bragged on him. She didn't want Pa to take his piece of hardware with him. She knew Pike County and she knew Pa. She knew Pa had as much spirit and pride as any man in Pike County. She knew if any man asked Pa to count to ten and then draw, Pa would do it. She knew there wasn't a Mullins of the name who could bluff my father.

Pa squeezed Mom tight and kissed her goodbye and we were off into the night. Finn and I rode old Ned double. Pa took the lead on Moll. It was past midnight. The moon was down. We rode through the mud and the night wind. We rode by starlight. It was four in the morning when we reached Auckland.

"Now, be careful goin' back," Pa advised Finn. "Don't go to sleep in the saddle. Don't get Moll's bridle rein tangled around you and let her drag you from Ned's saddle. Go home and get some sleep."

"Don't worry about me, Pa," Finn replied. "I'll get the horses home all right. I won't go to sleep in the saddle. I worry about you. Up all night and not any sleep. I've had some sleep."

"We'll get a little sleep on the train," Pa told him. "Business is business, you know, and when a deal is hot it's better to forget sleep. There'll be time enough for sleep when I have this deed signed. I'll sleep peacefully coming back on the train tonight. Be sure and meet us here with the horses."

"I won't forget," Finn said as he mounted old Ned.

We stood there in the starlight, not far from the depot, and watched Finn ride away. Then Pa turned toward the railroad station and I followed him. When Pa stood at the window getting our tickets, I just happened to look back and there sat Permintis Mullins. His eyes were about half-closed. He sat there dreaming like a lizard half asleep in the morning sun. I didn't say anything. Not to Pa. I'd let him see Permintis for himself. It made my heart skip a few beats to see him there.

"Here's your ticket," Pa said, looking up at about the same time.

When he saw Permintis Mullins, he froze like my Irish setter, Rusty, when he sees a bird. Pa didn't move a muscle. His big gray eyes narrowed down. When Permintis Mullins awoke from his half sleep with Pa's eyes on him, he jumped up from his seat. He muttered something we couldn't understand. I think he called Pa a bad name under his breath. He sat back down and looked at Pa. Neither one spoke. He knew what Pa was after. Pa knew what he was after. When Pa did move he walked outside the station and I followed.

"What do you know about that." It was hard for Pa to believe. "Do you reckon Jack Willis lied to me?"

"I'll bet he came later and went to Jack Willis' home and got Jack out of bed," I said. "That's how he got his deed. You know he's got one too."

"You reckon he has?" Pa looked strangely at me.

"Think I saw it in his inside coat pocket," I told him.

"Let's get our heads together and do some thinkin' before we get on the train." Pa wasn't laughing now. "Let's get on the same coach so we can watch 'im."

"But Pa, you don't want any trouble with 'im," I pleaded.

"We're not goin' to have any trouble," Pa assured me. "I just want to get close enough to watch him. Want to be close enough to feel any move he makes. Want one of us to keep an eye on him at all times."

"Suppose he's not got a piece of hardware along?" I said.

"I'd a had my piece along if it hadn't been for your mother's soft-soapin' me right before I left," Pa explained. "Even a woman when she loves a man with all her heart is liable to get him hurt. Hurt by a dangerous character like that Permintis Mullins."

Permintis Mullins was a big Pike County mountaineer. He had a clean-shaven bony face. His handlebar moustache looked like a long black bow tie, tied under his nose with both ends of the tie sagging. He wore a big black umbrella hat. He was a big man but he wasn't built like Pa. He wasn't broad shouldered. He was tall. He had long arms and big hands. He was long legged and wore tight-fitting pants that bulged at the knees. Permintis had the eyes of an eagle. They were beady black eyes that pierced when they looked at you.

"When we get off this train at Bainville, let's make a run and get the first taxi," Pa suggested. "Take it all the way to Sid Beverley's. It's just three miles from the railroad station. I've been over that road many a time."

"You make the plans, Pa, and I'll follow 'em," I said.

"All we want to do is beat old Permintis there," Pa whispered.

When the train pulled up, we stood there waiting for Permintis. I happened to turn around and he was standing behind watching us. "Come on, Pa," I said.

And Pa followed me onto the coach. When we walked in and got a seat in the smoker, Permintis followed us. He sat on the other side of the aisle just a little behind us. When he sat down, I saw the deed in the inside pocket of his unbuttoned coat. Maybe it was my imagination, but I thought I saw the prints of a holster on his hip. I was sure he'd brought his hardware piece along.

When breakfast was called and Pa and I went to the diner, Permintis followed us. He sat about the middle of the diner. Pa and I got up in the front corner so we could talk.

"He's goin' to Sid Beverley's sure as the world," Pa said. "I wonder when he got that deed. We were the last ones in Jack Willis' office before he closed. After the way Jack talked to me, I don't believe he would get out of bed to make a deed for that scoundrel."

"But he voted for Jack too, Pa," I said. "He belongs to our party and he rode day and night the last week of the election to help Jack

Willis. I understand he says he elected Jack. Said his work gave Jack the extra forty-four votes."

Pa couldn't believe it. He couldn't believe we were on the train eating breakfast in one end of the diner and down midway sat Permintis Mullins. All of us heading for Sid Beverley's place on Wolfe Creek.

After breakfast we went back to our seats in the smoker. Strange, but Permintis finished his breakfast same time we did. When we sat down, Permintis had to walk past us. Pa scanned him carefully.

Just before noon, about the time we reached the border of Pike County, Pa got up to light a cigar and stretch his legs. Permintis got up too. He stood up and watched Pa, though he didn't speak. And everybody riding on this coach watched the strange actions of Pa and Permintis.

When the conductor called "Litchfield" Pa stood up again.

"Bainville's the next stop," Pa whispered. Then Pa walked out into the aisle while the train stopped. Permintis got up too. Pa walked in the opposite direction since he was a little shy of Permintis. Then we heard "all aboard" from outside. Pa walked back to our seat and sat down. He was so restless he couldn't wait. He didn't like Permintis Mullins' black eagle eyes trained on him all the time either. When Pa got seated the train was moving again.

"Where's Permintis, Pa?" I said, looking back.

"Men's room, maybe," Pa said, puffing on his cigar. Then, Pa looked back. "Do you reckon he got off this moving train?"

"There he goes, Pa," I shouted as I looked from the window. "He's running down the street."

"Let me off'n here," Pa screamed, jumping up.

"But the train is moving now, Pa," I said, holding him by the arm. "You can't get off. Not now."

"We're tricked," Pa shouted.

Everybody started looking at us and the conductor came running and grabbed Pa by the arm. "What's the matter with you?" he asked Pa. "Are you trying to commit suicide? You can't leave this train when it's moving like this."

"But that scoundrel," Pa screamed, shaking his head. "That Permintis Mullins! He's tricked me!"

"What fellow?" the conductor asked. "What did he do? Relieve you of your wallet or something?"

"Not that, Conductor," I said. "I'll explain it to you. He and my father are here to buy the same piece of land down in Greenwood County and it's owned by Sid Beverley on Wolfe Creek. The other fellow got off at Litchfield and is trying to beat us to Wolfe Creek. We're on this train and can't get off before Bainville. Which is closer to Wolfe Creek, Litchfield or Bainville?"

"Bainville, of course," the conductor said, smiling at Pa. "It's only three miles from Bainville to Sid Beverley's on Wolfe Creek. It's thirteen miles from Litchfield to Sid Beverley's. I know this country well. I live in Litchfield."

"Can we get a taxi in Bainville?" Pa asked.

"They'd laugh at you if you asked for a taxi there," said the conductor as he looked over his bright-rimmed glasses at Pa. "Bainville's not big enough to support a taxi."

"Can Permintis Mullins get one in Litchfield?" I asked.

"He can't get one there either," the conductor said.

Everybody on the coach had become interested in our problem. They listened when the conductor talked with us. There were whispers from one end of the coach to the other. And there was much laughter which Pa didn't like. His face got as red as a ripe sourwood leaf. The fire died in his cigar. Pa put it in his mouth and chewed the end. When the conductor left us to call the next station, Pa and I hurried to the end of the coach.

When the train stopped, we were the first to get off. "Taxi! Taxi!" Pa screamed. Somebody laughed at Pa. "Can I get somebody to drive me to Sid Beverley's on Wolfe Creek? I'm in a hurry." There wasn't any bidding. Not a single bid.

"Come, Adger," Pa shouted. "Not any time to lose. We've got to hoof it! We can beat him if we hurry! I know the way! Come on!"

We started off. I never saw Pa move like he was moving now. He threw the cigar down. I hoped, as we trotted along down the muddy road, somebody might come along with a wagon and pick us up. I wondered how Permintis was going to cover his thirteen miles if his road was as muddy as this one. And I hoped it was.

"Now is the time to beat Permintis," Pa grunted with a half breath. "Pray for a ride and keep going. Let's strike while the iron's hot. Early bird . . ."

"He's got thirteen miles of this muddy road," I grunted. "We've got three. . . . We can beat 'im . . ."

"But we lost time on that awful slow train," Pa stammered, for he was short of breath. "Permintis pulled a fast one."

After one mile on this muddy road, we stopped. We didn't talk, to save our breath. We doubled time on the second mile. We reached the mouth of Wolfe Creek. Then we crossed the bridge.

"Back to my homeland," Pa grunted. "Changed so I don't know it. Not my homeland any longer. The Valley . . ." And Pa stopped talking, saved his breath, and increased his speed.

When we turned the first big bend in the Wolfe Creek road, Pa stopped. "Yonder's where Sid lives," he moaned as he wiped streams of sweat from his face.

As we hurried the last quarter mile, our breath coming short and fast, we saw three men come from Sid's big log house. We stopped short when we saw them get in a car. They started driving toward us. To our surprise the car pulled up close beside Pa, who was spattered with mud, and stopped.

Permintis rolled the window down and stuck his head out. "Would you like to have this, you old land-hawg?" Permintis shouted, holding up a paper for Pa to see. Then, he laughed slyly as he pulled his head inside and rolled the window up. The driver gunned the car.

Pa was stunned. We stood there in silence looking at each other and at the car as it moved slowly along, flinging two streaks of yellow clay into the bright March wind from the rear wheels.

"Wonder if he got that farm?" Pa said, breaking our silence as Permintis' car crossed the Wolfe Creek bridge and was out of sight. "Let's go see what happened!"

Sid Beverley, six feet five inches tall, and a big man for his height, opened the door when we walked onto his porch. His frosted crabgrass-colored hair was ruffled by the March wind. His blue eyes sparkled.

"Welcome home, Mick," Sid greeted Pa. "Welcome, Adger! Back to the land of your people. Come in! I've been waitin' for you all mornin'! Permintis told me you were on your way!"

We walked into the house, where Clara took Pa's hand. "How is Sallie, Mick?" Clara asked, but Pa didn't answer her.

"I come to buy that farm from you, Sid," Pa said, turning to Sid.

"Well, the early bird always gets the worm, Mick," Sid told Pa. "You've traded enough to know that!"

"It beats all I ever heard tell of," Pa grunted as he wiped streams of perspiration from his red face with a big blue bandanna. "Do you mean that Permintis outsmarted me?"

"Call it anything you like," Sid said calmly. "Permintis telegraphed the Sheriff of Pike County to meet the train at Litchfield with a car, a notary public, and a witness for a land deal."

"That scoundrel," Pa shouted as he shook his fist in the direction Permintis had gone.

I looked at my father as he stood there before Sid Beverley. The light that had always been in his eyes when he was about to make a good trade was gone. And then, I remembered how many times Mom had warned him that someday an earlier bird would get the worm.

Barry Targan

The Editor of A

> and whatsoever Adam called every living
> creature, that was the name thereof.

BUT that the view was from the twenty-ninth floor of the Kremer Building, this might have been the office of a philologist, a linguist, an old grammarian in an ancient and grand university where the rooms, in fact or musty legend, were named for distinguished (if forgotten) dead, where the walls were half-wainscoted in dark, time-stained oak, and amber sherry stood ready by in cut-glass decanters upon convenient sideboards waiting for the scholars of Trinity at Cambridge, say, to take their gentle ease from their sweet, exquisite labors.

Across the entire large wall opposite the windows from which he could look out upon the anachronism of Weehawken and Hoboken and to the heavily freighted ships being tugged slowly into their greasy berths—opposite that view, tightly stuffed shelves of books, learned journals, facsimile copies of manuscripts and incunabula, and string-tied bundles of unbound proof sheets tiered up to the high ceiling, and then books and journals and sheets sloughed off as rock breaks off a mountain into fan-shaped talus slopes onto the floor and out into the room. But it was a workable clutter. Symington could find with reasonable effort in the scree of words the exact mound and its source in the shelves for recent work on Urdu reconstructions, perhaps, or for the most immediately relevant disputes about the advisability of using the schwa in describing the dialects of late-period Indo-European.

And like a ballast to it all—to the wall, the office, his life—the ranks of the important and lesser dictionaries stood firm and stalwart and irrefutable, the fundamental magma: all of the Websters from Noah to the Third International, the Century's superb volumes, the four great books of the *Dictionary of American English*. Littré's venerable *Dictionnaire de la Langue Française*, the *Thesaurus Linguae Latinae*. Greek, Italian, Middle English. More. And, like majesty itself, Murray's *Oxford English Dictionary*, all its sublime volumes and supplements. Near to this, the *curiosa*: John Bullokar's start, Cockeram's earnest efforts, Blount's slight glossary. Fenning, Coles, Phillips, Kersey. Dr. Samuel Johnson's still worthy and splendid arrogances in their two original folio volumes, their leather bindings powdery. Others.

And Minsheu. *Ductor in Linguas* or *Guide into the Tongues*.

Among Symington's favorites, certainly John Minsheu stood first, this rogue, this buccaneer, this impecunious, improvident, brave, and flaring genius. For Symington, himself a maker of dictionaries—more exactly an etymologist, a patient archaeologist of derivations and meanings—he could relish Minsheu's astonishing accomplishment, his dauntless enthusiasm, his adventurousness. Particularly that.

Symington had had no comparable adventures, not nearly. He had not traveled through plague-y and bandit-ridden Europe on a lame mule to Paris, Heidelberg, Bologna, Rheims to search out the merest particle and twist of utterance. Symington had not gone hungry for his craft and subtle art, had not fled printers and their legal judgments in desperate poverty, had not debated Shakespeare and Jonson and Donne to their faces. Symington had not instructed the fabricators of the King's Bible.

Minsheu's work was first published in 1617, a full-blown attempt at an explanatory and etymological study of English with meanings in ten other languages. Ten. Egregiously wrong, brilliantly right by fits and starts, of all the works of this kind from the past, *Ductor in Linguas* alone was still importantly consulted by the present. In his brief prefatory remarks he acknowledged "greate debtes, impossible for me ever to pay." He meant the pounds, shillings, pence that he had somehow stolen, lied, and cheated for through his determined years. But Symington had thought prettily that Minsheu's "debtes" were now paid many times over by those who had labored after him—like Sam Johnson, who also missed meals for the price of foolscap, and Noah Webster, who mortgaged his house to meet his costs, or Clendon, who watched the bailiff cart away the volumes of his life's work to make up accounts.

And Symington thought of Minsheu now as he looked out across the river at a ship being bent in out of the channel by the small attending tugs butting and charging at the ship like terriers herding a great cow into its manger. He had returned from his talk with Ferguson, and now he was looking out at the familiar scene and thinking of how Minsheu must have lived his life along a constant edge of adversity and disappointment, an edge so thin that no step could be calculated safely enough and only the courage to move at all, and quickly, could sustain him if anything could. Simply the going on. Symington held on to the thought. That was important to him. Exceedingly.

The ship in the river slipped out of the grasp of the tugboats, the bow swinging slowly away from the wharves and back into the river. Perhaps the tug bearing against the bow had lost power, or the river, which was tidal, had unexpectedly surged as the outward running tide quickened. The ship swung and bore down sideways toward the next wharf and another freighter, tied up and vulnerable, unloading there. The loose freighter would crash against it. Or else trap the tug between and crush it.

Symington watched. He thought of the cargo. What had cast these vessels, these men, into this danger? Bananas from Honduras? Nickel from Mozambique? Pernambuco wood from Brazil? He thought how out of materials the imagination is bred to find a form in action.

The second tug raced around beneath the stern of the drifting freighter and rushed at it, its own stern churning down deeply into the river as its bow rose up against the freighter. Still the heavy drift continued, but more slowly. Then the three ships held, not a hundred feet from the moored boat, balanced against the river and their own displacement, and at last the freighter was inched incrementally back and up to its proper dock and secured. Quickly the tugs moved off after another ship waiting in the roads.

There, Symington thought, was the difference between an act in time and out of time, the difference between events and remnants, the difference between Minsheu and himself. He turned from the drama at the window as from a proscenium stage, as if away from illusion. All illusion henceforth. And yet back to what reality?

If there could be anger at least, a cleansing draught of fury and not this simple aridity like an aftertaste. But there was not. Nothing. Only Ferguson's words and the memory of the falling, the plummeting down. The terrific wind and the idea of the terror.

What Ferguson had told him first was that the company had decided at last to begin the work that it had debated for two full years,
perhaps not unreasonably for such a venture, the making of a dictionary
of this magnitude, a dictionary to stand in the history of the language
itself. Such a dictionary would invite—demand—intense scrutiny and the
inevitable comparisons, and thus the prestige of the company would be
put at stake, ventured to some degree. Until now the company had concentrated upon the lucrative area of college dictionaries and the generally
popular ubiquitous desk-type volumes, often paperbacks nowadays. And
there, in that area, it had grown dominant and rich by its competency
and an efficient sales force.

But the company had always been uncomfortable that it could not
presume upon some mighty lexicographic base. It did not matter, of
course. The work on the college dictionaries was as exact and thorough,
as respected, as any other work that the staff might now be expected to
do. Still, that proud factor was an important element in the two-year-
long deliberations, but the risk to the company's reputation (and perhaps thereby to its sales) was decided to be worthy, the triumph of
creating a great dictionary the sweeter for the chance. That sort of thing.

The second thing Ferguson told him was that he, Ferguson, would
be the most senior editor. But Symington would not be a senior editor
at all. Nor the chief etymologist. He would be the editor of a letter, the
letter *A*.

He and Ferguson had met at the University of Chicago in graduate
school. They had gotten there just too late to have studied with the im-
mortal Craigie himself or to have worked directly on the *Dictionary of
American English*, which had been compiled at the university, but they
had come close enough to the sun and its system of disciples to have fallen
into the orbit. They graduated as scholarly linguists, journeymen if not
yet fully masters of the arcane, just as linguistics was becoming academi-
cally fashionable. They might have expected jobs and futures in that
direction, but it was towards dictionaries that they had been forever
turned.

Ferguson got there first, immediately, a job at once in publishing,
while Symington went off to teach for a time and to spend a postdoctoral
eighteen months in England, most of it either in the British Museum or
at Oxford, sifting through the tailings of the mother lode out of which
Murray's dictionary had come. Then Ferguson had called him, put him

in his place, and set him in his motion, which he had maintained from then to now. They had stayed good friends, *intensely* friends, the way people stay sealed forever when the first weld is quickly made in the early heat of mutual discoveries of trust.

It had always been this way. Ferguson would always tell the truth. Immediately. So when Symington asked him why, as chief etymologist of the company, he would not now be made either a senior editor or the chief etymologist of the great lexicon, he knew that Ferguson would tell him, and that Ferguson would be right, as he had always been right about his, Symington's, career. Right the way a good trainer or manager can be better aware than his subject, can have a perspective that the subject cannot. And Ferguson did have that, did understand lexicography—*dictionaries*—as he did not. All that he knew was etymologies. And this is what Ferguson told him, which was, of course, what he did know about himself but had never *bothered* to know until he was told. As now. And etymologies were not enough.

"The senior editors and the chiefs of section don't even get near words on a project this size. Not these days. They organize. They administer. They write cajoling letters to contributing editors. They defend their budgets to the comptroller. They make excuses for falling off schedule. They kick ass. Yes, and they communicate with computers. They have conferences with programmers who don't even speak English. It's like being in New Guinea, for all that. You speak FORTRAN or BASIC or SNOWBALL THREE. Imagine that, Sy, someday constructing the etymology of SNOWBALL THREE."

"I'm not ignorant of the process, you know. I've been here over thirty years, you'll remember. I have, you know, worked on dictionaries recently. Successfully." But Symington was not good at the tone he wanted here.

"No," Ferguson said. "No, Jimmy, you're not, really. You've made etymologies. But that's all, really."

"That's *not* all."

They both let that settle.

"Do you want to be a senior editor?" Ferguson asked. "Do you want to be the chief etymologist?"

It was not a question but an offer. If Symington said yes, then Ferguson would do it. They looked at each other across their years and met in Ferguson's accurate assessment.

Ferguson said, carefully, "Look. All that's happening is that you're not getting what you never wanted."

It was a marvelous statement. Symington nodded. To move into a major editorship now would be a mistake. He would be unhappy, soon cut off from his research. Unmoored. Adrift.

And, indeed, none of such things had ever mattered to him. He had never had ambitions larger than those his work had provided for him, the ever-fining rearticulation of old languages, the digging up and delicate piecing together of verbal shards into vessels of languages increasingly remote, languages about which few cared and upon which little of importance was determined or depended. He was like an astronomer studying the light of stars that had disintegrated in eons past.

To Symington his ambition had been to do his work excellently; to him his work was like the solving of small aesthetic problems. For all the hurrahing at the professional conferences about the importance of etymological achievements to psychology, philosophy, or communication theory, Symington could not make such connections, saw himself closer, rather, to the abstract mathematician working out the permutations of a personally invented configuration, closer to the chess scholar examining *Alekhine vs. Capablanca, Cuba, 1931*, closer to the composer developing the harmonic gradients of an inverted theme. It had all been as limited and as satisfying as that. For language made itself, Symington had come to believe after thirty years, and its past, like any past, did not matter at all. The past was airy thinness, and only the present was flesh.

But in this moment in Ferguson's office he had fallen as if through a crack in his life. Ferguson's announcement had broken something open, cracked a pane in the crystal dome of his life, and he had fallen through like an accident. And then, sitting across from Ferguson's thin-legged table-desk, he had tumbled and clawed at the cold, dark air streaming by. He must stop this, this plunge into terror. Terror? He could not understand what was happening, could not believe his feelings even as he believed them terribly, believed in the cold wind blowing by and through him. He shook.

"What is it?" Ferguson said.

"I don't know." The shaking increased. The wind blew more fiercely, swirling now and roaring, a roaring that filled his head until his head felt tight and swollen to bursting. The terror pulsed through him in spasms as accurate and high as waves in a precise storm.

"Sy? Jimmy? What is it?" Ferguson reached across his desk and took his hand. "Sy?"

"I don't know," he said. "I . . . don't know." And then he said, desperate to stop, to find a handhold, a ledge, a bearing in the tumult at least, or any direction, "S. Let me do S. S instead of A. Let me do the greatest letter." He said *greatest* and not *largest*, and he would remember that later.

But that embarrassed them both. Ferguson let go of his hand and sat back.

"*A* is enough to do," he said.

Excellent, Symington thought. Yes. *Enough* to do. Yes. Ferguson was as loyal to language as he was to him. Ferguson would not condescend to either. Good. Symington nodded. The falling had stopped. The wind, the terror, the roaring. Only the cold stayed and this taste in his mouth like dry wood.

"Yes. *A*," he said.

"The editor of *A*," Ferguson said.

And now, here where he had ever been between his blocky rampart of words and his window over the river, he must contend with what had happened, must understand what had swept him, this shriving wind, for what has once happened is forever possible, and he must know if he had fallen through his life forever. Or had what happened been simply the result of an adrenal shock, an overreaction to Ferguson's news, a reaction to a disappointment that looked at first like a failure and thus a threat against which his body had defended? It was a plausible enough explanation, but Symington disdained the endocrine explanations of life. If he stepped back from illusion, it would have to be to a reality greater than the reductions of enzymes and hormones racing in the blood; for mind, he never doubted, was not simply synaptic patterns in the brain.

Then what was it?

He scanned the dominion of his knowledge and grew supple in his endeavor, warmed and loosened by it. Reality. He considered expertly. The cold was gone. He did not expect to find any more than men had ever meant by it. Reality enough. But it was a vast word, and he examined its evidences closely. 8. *Philos.* a, he concluded:

something that exists independently of ideas concerning it.

Yes. That was his condition. 8. *Philos.* a.

The indictment was sharp and ironic and yet satisfying. He would have to live with that. But there would be no more terror, no painful spasms of cold fear and confusion. He would be done with that at least. Through the small rent in his life, the momentary rip, he had touched briefly the Logos, the mystery, the whirlwind, had touched it slightly but enough to have felt it tear at his mind sufficiently to know of the fathomless passion that he had escaped or missed or maybe even lost carelessly decades before, or more likely had never had any claim to at all— this cosmic blare in which men lived that Adam had been called upon to name. And Johnson and Webster and Murray and even Blount.

And the divine Minsheu.

But not himself.

Robert Taylor, Jr.

The James Boys Ride Again

This song it was made
By Billy Gashade . . .

A great opportunity has at last come the way of Billy Gashade. Sitting at his dressing table, the thick and beribboned crinoline billowing from his corseted waist, he holds the telegram before him, reads and reads it again: *New melodrama opening. Jesse James Betrayed. Want you for the grieving widow. Promise of long run, agreeable profits for all concerned. Notify undersigned as soon as convenient within 48 hours of receipt. Bunnell. Olive Street. St. Louis, Missouri.*

Convenient? He'll wire his acceptance posthaste. Out of the crinoline, loosed from the stays, he sees himself already in St. Louis, once again walking the streets of that great Western city, strolling along the levee of the river of rivers. The women, why there's nothing like a Western woman, so artlessly guileful, graceful in mirth and in grief abandoned. There was a woman once that wore a pistol strapped around the waist of her velvet gown, in one breath recited the poetry of Lord Byron, in the next spoke to the virtues of Jesse James. The Wild West? Railroaded, corralled. Custer dead, the Sioux subdued. This is 1882, son.

Comes a knock on the door.

Please enter.

John Jessup, red in the face, breathing heavily, steps into the room.

Billy, it is your mama. She says she's dying. She says John, go get Billy. Says she's got last words and she wants you to hear them!

How has he come to this. Ain't it strange, ain't it a little mad. A young man, a boy, he watches for the posters that announce the time of the min-

[297]

strels. He languishes in the stuffy parlor amidst crystal figurine and plaster statuette. Gilt-edged volumes rest tight in their shelves and smell like flesh as it begins to sweat. Dark walls. Heavy drapes brushing the floor. A scratching, a scurrying, as if small animals live in the walls, something smaller than mice that might ease through one of the narrow cracks near the baseboard and proceed to do harm.

Father clears his throat, strikes a match on his heel. Mother's gown swishes. She smells like a gardenia, her small feet in boots of smooth leather, edging from the hem of her silks as she steps into the room.

Brown streets, bleak skies. He would be elsewhere, but where? The puddled roads of Cincinnati lead only to the knobbed hills of Ohio and Indiana. Across the Ohio River is Kentucky, more trees, more hills, gray bluffs giving way to grayer mountains. Strange people live in that direction—people who, according to Mother, want nothing to do with the civilized world, live little better than savages in rude cabins on rocky mountainsides. Why? They have no place else to go to. They are unsuited, they are ignorant, they are degenerate.

There is a better world, she tells him, holding him to her smooth bosom, the dark silk soft as skin. No, Father says, the world ain't as we would like it to be. It don't yield to our fantasies, son. We must take it as we find it. The toughest amongst us survive. Pity the rest.

Slender, frail, sickly, Billy lies in his parents' bed, covered with heavy quilts and scratchy blankets, his mother's hand on his forehead. No minstrel show for him this year! His father in the tall-back chair close to the wall, near the door, breathes heavily, rubbing his palms on his trouser-legs. It is not that Father would not come closer. Papa merely shows restraint. I must go, he says finally, standing, his pink hand already turning the doorknob. There's work to do. Mother does not appear to notice when the door downstairs is slammed. He loves you, she says. You must understand that your father loves you. You are his son, his only son.

The other son, who would have been a year younger than Billy, dies before taking his first step. He is named Christopher George and is buried *Our Dearly Beloved Son Sorely Missed* in the graveyard of the Presbyterian Church. After that come daughters, four in rapid succession, Esther, Emma, Mary Elizabeth, Alice. Mary Elizabeth comes to resemble her mother, with the same flashing brown eyes, the pale hands, the languishing graceful movements. Esther looks like Papa, has his long parabolic nose, his cinnamon-colored and peanut-shaped eyes, his ponderous gait. The others—Emma of the auburn hair, little Alice of the dark ringlets, the lace collars, the flushed cheeks—seem early to find their own molds. Emma sits in the parlor in the dim light of dusk and strums melodies on the dulcimer Father has made for her. Alice takes up embroidery, stitches elaborate designs on the hems of her drab skirts, whorls of violet or lavender, indigo or rose-red, crescents of robin's-egg blue.

Billy reads novels in the shadows. Come here, Billy, says Esther. I want to show you something. She whispers through a crack in the door. Papa is at the bank, of course, and Mother braves ice, in the sleigh calling on an ill friend. It is the day after Christmas, and snow lies smooth among the fragile trees, not melting, hardened by icy winds from the north, the roads silvering in the pale sun. The holidays! All the morning he has listened, from his father's big chair in the parlor, to the footsteps and occasional laughter of his sisters above him. Chores done, he has chosen a volume from the flesh-smelling shelves, opening the glass carefully. Shall it be Walter Scott or Fenimore Cooper? He passes over the commentaries on Calvin, on Knox, the concordances and the prayer guides. Scott it shall be. *The Heart of Midlothian.*

Come here, Billy. I want to show you something.

Open the door and she's gone. An empty hallway, dark and cold. But the sound of her footsteps on the stairs, and then: Oh, no. You'll not see. It's too late now. But it isn't. She's brought him forth from Jeanie Deans and he will not go back until he has seen what she has to show him, damn her soul. He swiftly ascends the stairs. Esther, let me in. What is it I'm to see. He puts his ear to the door. If there is motion, why then it is brought off quietly. He can hear nothing. He listens hard. *Boo!* It is Esther. She has come up behind him, clapped him on the shoulder. A strong grip.

It isn't fair!

Shh . . . it is too, you'll see. First you have to say the password.

I don't know the password.

That's why I'm here. It's—— And she whispers in his ear a word he thinks sounds like *Damascus.*

Damascus! he says. Then he hears the laughter behind the door, but it opens and Esther pushes him into the room. In spite of the dark, he sees the reason for it. They have hung blankets back of the curtains.

Damascus! Esther says, and suddenly the candles are lit, the sisters all in a row before him, Emma, Mary Elizabeth, and Alice, each with a candle, Esther remaining by his side, her fingers clasping his frail arm.

Happy Birthday! Alice cries.

Happy Birthday, the others echo.

It's not his birthday. His fourteenth birthday has been duly noted, adequately celebrated, three months previous, in the fall of the past year—streamers hung from the ceiling, a cake consumed, a Bible presented. Now they laugh, these sisters of his. Esther wears his father's long black frock coat, his stovepipe hat, stands tall in his boots, his vest, his cravat expertly tied.

You don't look like him, he tells her, lying. You don't look anything like him.

I don't *mean* to. I mean to look like myself and nobody else.

You look foolish.

I feel fine.

Father will be angry if he finds out.

I don't care!

Billy, says Emma. We have made up a play.

Yes, says Alice. And we want you to be in it.

We want you to be—

Hush! says Esther. I'm the one to tell.

Tell then.

All right. We have made up a play.

He knows that.

We told him that.

Hush! Sit down, Alice. Not another word, Emma.

I haven't said anything, Esther.

I know, Mary Elizabeth. You're the smartest one.

I get to be the grandmother. That's why I'm smart.

Esther folds her arms across her chest. She paces in the center of the room. The others sit still, watching her. They are children, after all. Dutiful. Obedient. Properly chastised. Mary Elizabeth smiles at him, the very image of his mother, though only for an instant before once again she looks at Esther. Alice frowns with great severity, and Emma closes her eyes, her hands clasped in her lap. In the candlelight her auburn hair shines beautifully. It looks like fire, he thinks, all that wonderful color in motion. His own hair, grown long and brushed diligently, would look like that. Feverish, his skin slick with sweat and his mother beside him laying another blanket on, he remembers Emma's hair in that candlelit room, the volume and motion of it, the calm sheen, the pure flame of it. *Emma! Pray for me, Emma! Strum a melody for me on your dulcimer. No more blankets, Mother!*

She sleeps. He sits beside the bed. Her face is calm and white. Across from him Esther, sobbing softly, dabs at her eyes with a lace-edged handkerchief. Her grief, he feels, comes late, but is altogether proper. He will save his weeping for later, only proper, though were he woman! Ah, put a brave face on it, Billy Gashade. Sit still, stoic in your hard chair. Emma will not come, not all the way from St. Louis, nor Mary Elizabeth from her safe tomb next to Father in Ohio. Only Esther, Esther of Washington Heights, late of Long Island, large Esther, Mrs. George Brooks, matronly in her thick skirts, her powerful stays, her hats tall and turbanlike.

Where is Glory? Bring me my Glory.
She's out in Missouri, Mama.
Where's Billy then?
Right here, Mama. I'm Billy. And there's your Esther.
Where's my Glory?
She's far away, Mama.
Is that Esther?
Yes, Mama.
Billy?
Yes, Mama.
And your father?
He's dead, Mama.
Thank goodness. Are you sure?
Yes'm.
It is a comfort to know that. A small comfort.

Esther weeps into the handkerchief. He remarks the length of her fingers, the breadth of her wrists, remembers her in her father's frock coat frowning, pacing the floor of that upstairs bedroom, dark with the shutters locked, the heavy drapes closed. She strikes a match, lights a candle, another, hands one to him, lights another, hands one to Emma. *You are the bearers of the light.*

His mother rests. Esther, her eyes dry now, stands, walks slowly to the window, her figured silk rustling. She pull back the drapes, and the dim winter light flickers, makes a long rectangle that crosses the floor and touches the foot of the bed.

What is that?

Can she have felt the light? No, it is something else, a complaint pushing into her dreams, some old intrusion. How is it that we grow to this? Father leads him through the crowded sidewalks of Cincinnati, his boot heels sounding on the damp planks like pain itself, the routine pain of our lives, a steady thudding followed by brief stillness, and all around you the others, the tall and burnsided men, the derbied and the mustachioed, the sheltered and the decorated bodies stepping, thudding, scraping through their lives. Melodrama of grief, dreary routine of remorse! Billy, Father says, it is a hard world that awaits you. He knows, does Billy, he knows. His mother's better world lies out there beyond the street lamps, throbbing in its soft globe. Hasn't he been walking towards it all his life? And is this where she has led him, is this what she has had in mind all along? Yes, yes.

Billy, Esther says, returning to the bedside opposite him, do you remember how it was? Do you remember the long days, Emma and her dulcimer, Mary Elizabeth and her grace, little Alice's red cheeks when she ran in from the cold, asking for Papa? Papa, she called, here's sweet Alice asking for you.

Hush. She's sleeping.

She's sleeping. She won't be disturbed, dear brother, by what I have to say to you.

You've said it, Esther. What you have to say, you've said before. I've heard you. I've listened long and well.

You've not listened. You've not heard. You hear your own voices.

Nonetheless I hear.

When I speak to you, it's as though you are elsewhere.

I hear you.

I say again. Your father loves you.

He is dead.

His love is alive. It was a loving life Papa led.

You would believe it. It's his life he's given you. It's my life he wants.

That's not my voice you're hearing, Billy Gashade.

The voice of reason.

The voice of an actor. A minstrel's voice.

Let *her* speak. Let our mother speak her mind.

She can't speak, Billy.

I hear her.

She's silent. She's not awake.

She's eloquent. She's heartbreaking. It is her triumph!

When Mary Elizabeth died, she said, Pray for Billy's soul.

I heard.

I prayed.

I said Thank you.

And when Emma ran away, disgraced, Alice set the dulcimer on fire. She'll not be wanting it again, she said, not where she's going.

Alice wasn't always spiteful.

Emma wasn't always a whore.

Our Emma is a dancer, sister.

I know what she is, what she has become.

You know, it seems to me, what you want to know.

Still I know it. I say it.

I hear it. Damacus, sister. Our secret.

You can't blame me for what has happened to us, Billy. You can't blame me for your sorry state, for our Emma's fall.

I feel sorry for Alice, I regret the burning of the dulcimer. I blame no one.

Blame? What is this talk of blame?

His mother has spoken. Her eyes remain shut, but the lips have moved. I'm warm, she says. Who has covered me with these woolen blankets in the dead of summer? Is it you, Glory?

Glory isn't here, Mother. It is not spring yet, certainly not summer.

Is it Glory who is the whore?

Emma is a dancer.

Yes. And Billy a minstrel. Esther a wife, a mother. Lord help us!

I'm only myself, Mother, your Esther. Emma was Father's Glory.

I told him not to call her that. John, I said, she will have an inflated opinion of her worth. She is my Glory, he said. And there was Esther, yellowing in the corner, her hands stiff in her lap, dry, dry Esther, lost in an ill-lit room.

Mama. I am here. In *this* room. Your Esther is here, Mama.

And where is *he*, where is John Gashade?

Mama, Father is dead.

It's my husband I ask about.

Dead. Passed away. Gone from us these seven years.

Then he won't come?

He's gone to his reward.

Ah! Thank goodness. He wanted that so badly. Was it handsome?

Was what handsome, Mama?

The reward. Was it sufficient.

Oh, Mama. It's his *eternal* reward.

I hope it was big enough for him. He had such—cravings.

At any rate, he won't be coming.

I don't want to see him. Tell him I don't care to see him.

She opens her eyes then. Dark they are, dry and clear, astonishingly clear. Esther shoots him a quick glance. It means something—she never looks at him without meaning—but whether anger or pain or reproach he can't tell. It's a brief scrutiny, perhaps no more than that, and then she reaches for his mother, whose hand has arisen from beneath the blankets. It has hold of his wrist.

Bring my son to me. I want a word with him.

She is terribly lucid. How can it be so? Truly it is a miraculous recovery. Her cheeks flame up, her eyes moisten and dart about, her grip of his wrist so strong that he feels nothing in his hand and must beg her to release him.

My life, she says, has been long and hard. I have no regrets. I die a Christian. I will get what I deserve. It will be enough. It will be right. I never cared for my husband, but I did my duty by him. He was not at fault. He was not to my taste. Six children I bore him. Three survive. I have loved each as I have been able, and each has repaid me in kind. All my life I have wanted to love, I have had love in my heart to give. He did not want that love. There was no one to accept it the way I felt I could give it, and so I kept it to myself and grew unkind and solitary, no one to trust. Yet always was this love with me, it was my own, my hope and my despair, my pride, my shame. My own.

She looks at him, takes his hand again. This time she is gentle. Already her cheeks have paled, but there is warmth in her touch, light in her eyes. Her head might have no weight at all, so slight a mark does it make on the broad pillow. She is smaller than he has ever realized, frail as a flower. Lift her to the light and you would see through her.

Esther?

She's in the next room, Mother. You sent her away.

She resembles my husband. Have you noticed?

Yes.

He lost his teeth, one by one. In a month there was nothing left. No false teeth for him! I admired that. But he was much embittered and came to resent me. You are Billy, aren't you?

I'm your son. I'm Billy.

My how you've changed.

I grow older.

Father?

Your son.

Father will not come. Not for the world. He likes his boys best. Esther?

It's Billy.

Is she out of the room then?

Yes, Mama.

Can she hear what I'm saying?

The door's closed. You're whispering. I don't think she can hear you.

It seems to me I'm shouting. Well, listen to me, son. I want you to do me a favor. Will you do your poor mother a favor?

Yes. What is it you want?

When I die—are you listening to me?—when I die I want you to shut my eyes for me. Will you do that? I want no one else to do it. I want you to do it. Don't let *her* now, do you hear me? You do it yourself. Will you promise me?

I promise, Mother.

It is a great relief. Bless you.

I promise.

I did not relish the thought of *her* fiddling with my eyelids. It is a relief to know you will be the one.

I will be the one.

Bless you.

Thank you.

You are the very image of Father.

The Mississippi is as broad as he remembers it, as brown and as handsome, the levee a feverish blur of crate and deck, brick, boot, and parasol. He has traveled by rail, speed a necessity, but looks on the massive paddle-wheelers—their boilers smoking, bows listless in the gentle lap of the water—with great admiration, a kind of envy.

Bunnell is sorry to hear about Mrs. Gashade.

The trunks of lavish gowns and crinolines are carried upstairs to his room by men whose bare shoulders shine with sweat.

Glory has been here, says John Jessup, asking for you.

Bunnell introduces the Ford brothers, who in the melodrama of *Jesse James Betrayed* are to play themselves. They have long hands and wear tight waistcoats and high-heeled boots.

I, says Bob Ford, am the slayer of Jesse James.

There wasn't no need, says Charley Ford, for me to shoot too.

Bunnell, a tall man with burnsides that cover his cheeks sleek as fur, announces that he himself means to play the role of the Bandit King. Frank James will be cast directly.

Glory, jeweled and satined, steps into his room as if the floor were made of gauze that a more careless woman might fall through. In that auburn hair surely resides the power of beauty itself. Sitting just opposite the faintly glowing light, the play of shadows across her face like spirits seeking shape, she holds her hands still in her lap, but for an instant he sees them move, stroke again the strings of the dulcimer, those same hands, the music the same, a chord he's heard all his life, as if, alive as trees, it quivers everywhere in the air.

Did you do as she asked, Billy?

She slept. She woke. Again she slept. When she woke, she did not speak except to call me Father, Esther Mother. This went on for days. I did not forget my promise, but the last sleep marked the last waking.

And so there was no need?

No need, Emma.

Then tomorrow I dance.

Tomorrow I take my womanliness to the stage.

I let my body move to the song my soul hears.

I wed myself to the martyred outlaw.

Walter S. Terry

The Bottomless Well

SINGLE file they walked down the rocky trail that he had not traveled in thirty years—not since he was Carol's age. Carol followed a few steps behind him while Mike, Carol's shadow, placed his tennis-shoed feet deliberately where hers had been.

"How much farther is it, Daddy?" Carol said in the measured tones of her solemn adolescence.

David looked around at her, seeing the brisk movement of her bare legs under a body thinning out but still retaining a residue of little-girl plumpness.

"You tired?"

"I wish I had a horse," she said.

"Let's rest," Mike said with his eight-year-old's directness.

The children selected rocks on either side of the trail and sat.

"Horse," David said. "Are you still on that horse kick?"

Carol drank from her canteen. "I'd take care of it," she said solemnly. "Feed it."

"Living on a mountaintop is not the same as living on a farm," David said. He pulled a flashlight out of one hip pocket and a half-full bottle of beer out of the other. He used his thumb to remove the pressed-back-on cap. He sat drinking the beer and looking out into the mountain forest. *It won't carry me*, he thought. *I should've brought the flask.*

But Grace had been worried-worried-worried, as usual. ("Surely you don't need to drink on a hike with the *children*.") He didn't bother to remind her that his drinking was deliberate, calculated, and always under control when he wanted it to be. (It's no worse than any number of other things that we bribe our senses with in an effort to make life more bearable. Why don't we give them *all* up: coffee, cigarettes, rich foods . . . copulation?)

"We could keep it in the garage in the wintertime," Carol said. "When you build it, I mean."

David glanced sharply at her to see if he could detect any hint of innuendo in the "when you build it." Her face was inscrutable.

I wouldn't put it past her, he thought.

If he had slowed down in his initially ambitious house-building project it was because every human machine must slow down as it approaches its death. He was on the brink of forty, not a golden thirty-two as he had been when he had started the project. He was flat tired; and the spirit of adventure and personal accomplishment in the beginning had given way to a drudgery that he found increasingly difficult to force himself to.

"Horse," he muttered. "Carol, every twelve-year-old girl in the world wants a horse. It's tied in with their sexual development."

"Daddy," she said evenly, "I just want a horse."

"What's 'sexy devilment'?" said Mike, chewing a leaf.

David laughed. "Good paraphrasing, boy."

"You wouldn't understand," Carol said quietly.

"I don't," he repied. "What's 'parapraising'?"

At Flint Arsenal, in the valley and beyond the town, a static test rocket rumbled. David listened, automatically counting off seconds, trying to determine which one it was. The sound ended abruptly.

He shrugged. *Whatever it was it didn't blow up.*

He arose, shoving the flashlight back into his pocket and pitching the empty beer bottle into a clump of bushes. He belched, wryly twisting his face at the memory of a rebellious stomach. "We'd better get going if we want to see this hole in the ground."

They started down the trail again. His mind turned to things he *should* be doing—like installing the kitchen cabinet doors. *Grace has been waiting six years, with her groceries showing. . . . Hell, I should be hiking with my daughter and son; I haven't got around to that either. I can't remember the last time, or even if there was a last time. First too busy, then too tired.*

He thought again of the left-behind flask: instant energy; instant optimism; fountain of youth. He wished fervently for a good stiff optimistic drink of deliberately calculated bourbon.

The trail took a sharp turn to the left, becoming steeper. At the end of the turn Bottomless Well came into view. David saw that there were the remains of a barbed-wire fence around the site and, nearby, a small stone house that the CCC had built, so he had heard, back in the thirties. There once had been plans to build an access road to the site and make it a public attraction. The plans had for some reason fallen through and only the fading ghosts of human meddling remained.

The opening of the "well" proper, essentially a vertical-running cave, was at the center of a large depression in the ground, a sinkhole. There was an old theory that the well extended all the way down through the mountain and connected with great limestone caverns under the town of Garth at the mountain's foot. In support of this theory was the legend of the duck that had been dropped into the hole, reappearing a week later much ruffled but alive out of Garth Spring, which flowed under the town and out at the bottom of the hill on which the town was built.

However, recent exploration by local spelunkers had failed to find the legendary passage, and they had drily reported the cave's bottom to be some three hundred feet into the rocky bowels of Buena Vista Mountain.

David extended his arms in warning as they approached the funnel-shaped depression. The walls of the funnel descended at a forty-five-degree angle to the dark opening of the well.

"Take it very easy," he said. He had forgotten what a treacherous thing this hole in the ground was. The mouth of the crater was roughly circular and perhaps sixty feet across. The well opening at its bottom was more irregular in shape and about twenty feet across at its widest point. Someone had rolled a hickory log across the opening—not too long ago, judging by its sound appearance. David guessed that the log had been a part of the spelunking activity; certainly, without it, it would be hard to imagine what they would have secured a line to. Other evidence of activity at the site was a set of crude dugout steps leading down the earth bank of the funnel to the near end of the log.

David picked up a small stone and pitched it toward the opening. After a prolonged silence, there was a faint *clink*, another silence, then another *clink*; after that it was difficult to tell whether you heard anything or not.

"Moses!" Mike whispered. "It must be a thousand feet deep!"

"Bottomless," Carol said.

David glanced at her, wondering at the solemnness of this little person he had sired. He could never help suspecting a precocious sardonic-ness, or at least satire, in her consistently restrained manner and speech.

"The folks who went down there say it's about three hundred feet." David addressed the remark to Mike. "Down. Then a short tunnel to the side."

"The length of a football field," Carol said, as if to herself.

"I'll take you down," David said, "but one at a time. I couldn't watch both of you at once." He gazed at them, almost selecting Mike first out of spite. "You first, Carol."

"All right."

"Mike," David said, "you stand *right there*. Don't you move until we come back up."

"Yessir."

They had to duck through the barbed wire to get to the steps leading down. David went first, keeping his body low and backleaning, insisting that Carol do the same. At the log they stopped and cautiously peered over into the chasm, with their hands on the end of the log for support. The walls of the hole, though generally sheer, were broken at irregular intervals by narrow, rounded ledges of stone. The flashlight beam was able to probe only a feeble distance into the darkness. David picked up a pebble and tried to direct it so that it would miss the ledges and free-fall as far as possible. As he let it go he counted "one thousand one, one thousand two . . ." He heard a *clink* after about a three-second count. He struggled with some mental arithmetic and discovered to his irritation that he had forgotten how to figure it. *Rotting innards and mossy-brained. It would be difficult to convince anyone that I was ever a paratrooper or that I'm supposed to be an engineer. I don't know that I could convince myself.*

For Carol's benefit he muttered a guess. "Hundred feet maybe. There must be a prominent ledge at about that level."

She gazed silently into the blackness of the hole.

He tried other trajectories and finally counted better than four seconds before the first sound, this time a distant splash.

"About two hundred and seventy or eighty feet if you disregard drag," Carol said, after a moment of silence.

Drag, schmag! Shades of the space age! Yet he could not help feeling an obscure admiration for her, maybe even pride.

"I think we still haven't reached bottom," David said.

"That's possible," Carol said gravely.

"Would you like to try?"

"All right."

She tried several times, but her throwing arm was not as good as her physics.

"Let's let Michael," she said finally.

He was in the process of turning when he heard the sodden cracking of rotten wood and Mike's sharp cry. The fence post that he had been leaning against had suddenly snapped and Mike was plunging down the steep side of the funnel six feet to one side of where David and Carol were crouched. Instantly David launched his body in a horizontal line of motion, striking dank earth flat-out, skidding across and down, even in this paroxysm of motion, outraged, thinking: *My God, I might have known he'd do that.* His hands clutched at the earth and closed on tenuous sassafras roots. His motion stopped coincident with the impact of Mike's body from above. His own body shifted downward with the impact and in slow, creeping motion moved to within inches of the brink of the well. His face was pressed into the earth and his body felt so poised on the edge of further movement that he wondered if he dared speak.

He tried it. "Mike?"

"Dad?" He could feel the trembling in Mike's body, hear it in his hushed voice.

"Get hold of something, boy."

"I'm scared to move."

"Move real slow. Get hold of a root."

"I can't. . . ."

"*Do* it!"

"Dad." Carol spoke as if in the imminence of a snake's strike. "You're mighty close to the hole, Dad."

"I know, I know. I know that. Get a stick, Carol. A strong one. Long enough. Hurry!"

He heard her quick steps up the side of the funnel, soon after heard the snapping of a branch up above.

At least I can depend on her not to get a rotten one.

He felt the faintest shifting of the earth beneath him. "Hurry, Carol!" He still did not dare try to move his head in an attempt to look for her.

"I'm here," she said after a moment.

"Brace yourself good on the log and reach out with the stick so Mike can grab it."

"All right. . . . Here, Mike—*grab!*"

"I . . . can't," Mike said. "I'm scared. . . . Dad?"

"Do it, Mike. You've got to do it."

He felt a slight, tentative movement as Mike extended a hand toward the stick.

"All right," he heard Carol say. "Now the other hand . . . slowly. . . . Got it?"

He felt Mike nod, then felt the boy's weight slowly coming off his body.

"I've got you," Carol said. "You dig your feet in as best you can and I'll do the pulling."

He felt Mike's body complete its departure from his and simultaneously the strained damp earth released from the underlying rock and David went over the chasm's brink in a twisting, arching motion, then falling feet-down and spread-eagle. He hit the first ledge in approximately this attitude but leaning slightly forward so that the impact was distributed fairly evenly along his thighs, belly, chest, and the undersurfaces of his arms. He hit clawing and scrabbling for a purchase on the damp stone. He pressed his body to the stone and felt the final momentum of his fall come to a slithering tenuous halt on the rounded contour of the ledge. It was only when his motion stopped that he was aware of the shrill screams from above.

In his delicate balance on the ledge he couldn't bring himself to use his lungs, from which most of the air had been forced by his flat impact against the stone. Then he could not forestall the reflex any longer. In a raucous inhalation he sucked in air and felt a slight downward shift of his body. He dug his fingernails into the stone, bringing the slithering motion to another perilous halt. His feet in this last movement had left the rock and projected out over the chasm below. His hands had found some small cross-running ridges in the stone, but his fingers already had begun to ache, all the strength of his body, it seemed, concentrated at their stiffened tips.

"Daddy! Daddy! Oh, Daddy, Daddy!"

He recognized through his stunned senses the terror-stricken voice of Carol. He steeled himself for an answering call. He didn't know whether or not he could talk at all or, if he did, whether he could do it without destroying his pitiful purchase on the ledge.

"Daddy!" Now he could distinguish both their voices, and with that he had his first real knowledge that Mike had not fallen too. It at least gave his plight some meaning. He imagined them crawling out on

the log, or venturing upon the treacherous slope of the funnel in an effort
to see him.

"Carol," he said in a hoarse whisper. His fingers remained clamped
to the stone. "Mike? Can you hear me?"

"Yes, Daddy. Yes." They, too, were whispering, as if they were
as aware as he was of his delicate balance on the ledge.

"Carol, don't endanger yourselves. I'm all right. But . . . listen,
honey, Mike, I'm going to need help. Fast as you can."

I don't know, I don't. . . . I couldn't possibly hang on long enough.

"Mike?"

"Yes, Daddy?"

"Mike, do you think you could find your way home?"

"Yessir! I'll . . . find it."

"Listen carefully, boy. Tell Mother to call the spelunkers."

"Cave explorers," he heard Carol say.

"Yes. Tell them your daddy . . . tell them I'm in a deep hole—
Bottomless Well. They know about it. Need rope, climbing equipment."

"Yessir." His voice sounded steady enough under the circumstances.

"Daddy," Carol said, "I can see you. Can you hang on?"

"I don't . . . I don't know. . . . Mike, you hurry. Follow the path. . . .
Carol, you stay here with me?"

"Yes, Daddy, I won't leave."

"Go now, Mike."

"Yessir!" His voice was already receding.

"Carol?"

"Yes, Daddy?"

"Is Mike gone? . . . Tell him to take care, and tell him . . . tell him . . .
that I love him."

"All right, Dad—" Her voice broke off abruptly.

My God, have they heard it from me so seldom.

He thought he felt a slight creeping of his body on the stone and
made a special effort to check his handhold, looking carefully at each
of his fingers in turn. His hands looked spatulate and frog-like on the
rock, the tendons showing through flesh like taut cables. Oddly he was
not afraid, at least at that moment he wasn't. He felt a profound animal
alertness the like of which he couldn't remember having felt since his
combat days. He also felt the beginning of a kind of tender sadness that
he would have found impossible to define.

In the waiting silence he took time to try to assay his position—and his chances of survival. *At least as a paratrooper,* he thought wryly, *I've had some training and experience in the business of falling. It's not as new to me as a lot of other things are.* He calculated, from the feel of the fall and from an educated guess as to which of the preobserved shelves of rock he had hit, that he had fallen twenty or thirty feet. He was most certainly bruised and abraded but, as far as he could tell, unbroken—except maybe for a cracked rib or two.

He turned his thoughts to the almost inevitable *next* fall. Movement upward to a safer and less demanding perch was unthinkable; his first effort would certainly send him plunging again. And yet he was certain too that he could not hang on for the hour or maybe two that it would take for help to come—that is, if it came at all. It was his sad admission that he did not know how much trust he could place in Mike because he had not, as far as he could recall, ever before tested his trustworthiness.

He was suddenly aware of motion on the rock. Focusing his eyes, he saw that it was a small spotted salamander waddling by not three inches from the end of his nose. Fascinated, he watched its progress across the ledge. To the salamander this stone, in this hole in the ground, was a native dwelling, a place where all the vital functions of life were carried out. Here in its home he, David Masters, Homo sapiens of sorts, waged a ludicrous war of survival—an injured, out-of-place animal, clumsy, clinging with desperation to the alien rock.

I wonder how the salamander would do in my *world? No worse than I have—ill-adapted, sick at heart—desperately clinging to unsubstantial things like self-pity, infidelity . . . alcoholism. Yes, there's that too; I would have called it any word but that, but that's what it is.*

He felt the slightest giving of his body on the stone—a concession to gravity, a low coefficient of friction and fatigue.

He tightened his fingers.

It would be nice to know what's directly below, he thought. *I don't remember, or the light didn't shine down that far.*

He thought of the flashlight in his hip pocket. *Go ahead, Dave boy, pull it out and shine it down there where you're gonna be. Enlighten yourself. Go ahead.*

He clutched the stone, letting the first wave of hysteria wash over him and then, recognizing it, putting it aside for the moment.

Perhaps a lucky fall and a kinder ledge down there? . . . Or death. He let himself think about that rationally. Why not? He'd already accepted it. He'd been killing himself for years. The stone could be no less kind in its infliction of death. In fact, it undoubtedly would be more merciful—certainly without rancor . . .

Let go, you idiot! You'll never have a better chance.

"Daddy?"

He curved his aching fingers into the unyielding stone.

"Yes, Carol?"

"I've got a grapevine. I'm going to let it down and swing it over to you."

"Honey, honey . . . Carol . . ."

"It's very strong, Daddy. I had to chop it off at the bottom with a sharp rock."

"Carol . . ."

"Daddy, I'm letting it down. You'll feel it touch your back in a minute."

Tears flowed from his eyes and salted the stone under his cheek. He tried to look up but couldn't complete the effort. He felt something brush his right shoulder like a warm caress.

"Carol—" He choked on the word. "Honey, how have you got it tied?"

"I tried to tie it around the log, Daddy, but it's too thick; I can't bend it enough."

"Carol, honey, don't bother, don't—"

"Daddy, I've got my legs wrapped around the log. I can hold it, I can."

"No, Carol darling. I'd just pull *you* in. Besides, you couldn't possibly pull me up."

"I could hold you till they come."

He tried to stifle his free-flowing tears. *If only I could give my life meaningfully for her*, he thought with hopeless regret.

"No, Carol, I don't think I could let go to reach for it anyhow. Now you pull it on back up, honey."

It seemed he could *feel* the vine receding from him and it made him feel infinitely lonely.

"Carol?"

"Yes?" He could hear the helpless defeat in her voice.

"Thank you, darling. . . . I love you." It was getting easier to say.

Unexpectedly, as if he had been struck a sudden blow from above, his grip failed. He slid off the ledge and fell, essentially in the spread-eagle attitude of his earlier fall. He had no time to resign himself to anything before his extended legs smashed again into merciless stone. He hit differently this time, less flat, taking a large part of the impact on one leg; sharp pain in that leg informed him that he had hit with more damage to himself than before. But again, before sliding over the new precipice, he flattened himself to the rock and brought his motion to a stop. His purchase was somewhat better, more secure, than before, but his strength had been greatly sapped by his previous effort.

"Daddeeeeee!" He heard the wail from above, profoundly regretting the ordeal of terror he was inflicting on her. He laboriously sucked air into his lungs.

"Carol. I'm . . . all right, honey. I'm on another ledge. I . . . might be able to hang on."

"Daddy, I can't see you anymore!"

I know. Much darker . . .

So this is the way it ends. Maybe befitting enough: swallowed up by the boyhood mountain that he loved. . . . Determined he had been to return to gentle Garth and its magnificent mountain—Buena Vista— and on an expansive wooded lot build a fine house with his own two hands and his native intelligence—a house with a fieldstone fireplace big enough to warm a man's soul, and massive oak beams, like security itself, overhead. Then live an active, creative, meaningful life, full of good cheer, with Grace—and with the most wondrous children of their flesh. . . .

And they lived happily never after.

"Daddy?"

He had to think a moment, then gather himself.

"DADDY!"

"Yes, yes, Carol. I'm here."

"Oh." A silence. "Daddy, will you say something every now and then so I'll know you're all right?"

"Yes, honey. I'm sorry. Every minute I'll tell you I love you. Okay?"

"Oh, Daddy, Daddy. I feel so *bad*."

He thought he felt something splash down upon him and momentarily clung to the belief that it was her tears. It was as if she had touched him and he felt less lonely.

He let a delirium wash over him.

Ah, such golden dreams! . . . But he pooped out, got diverted and perverted—overly involved with failure and preoccupied with advancing years; blighted with cynicism, infidelity, mistrust, and nuclearitis. (*At* least I built, I mean completed, the fallout shelter. I finished it, no doubt, because it sickened me. It's typical of my recent attitude and behavior.)

"I love you, Carol," he called up to her.

"I love you, Daddy," she called back.

If we love each other why haven't we shown it? What have we been doing all this time? . . .

A far cry, David, from the Golden Man with his Golden Dream. Where did the degenerative process start? Who knows? It seemed that cause and effect were lost in a hopeless tangle of negativeness. Golden Man, after two wars and much searching, returns to Garth with his Golden Wife to work at the thing he had once been trained to do: engineering. Maybe that was it; maybe there had been too many years and too many other things between the learning and the doing. Maybe some obscure incident he couldn't even remember had conveyed that to him and started a chain reaction of doubt. At any rate, he had failed to secure the feeling of competence and of being respected in his profession. And the lack of those things, which had been a basic part of his plan and a basic part of his need, could have started a pattern of defeat in him that he could never overcome . . .

And Garth. What had happened to his beloved Garth? No longer quiet, no longer a sleepy Southern town, no longer the embodiment of a boyhood memory. It was not even called Garth anymore but names like "Space City" and "Rocketville, USA." Not a town at all anymore, but a madhouse of bustle and outrageous growth and profit and spoilage.

At least that's the way he had looked at it, even if it and its missile business, its dynamic Flint Arsenal, had provided him with the means to return. . . .

Man-o-man! . . . I could use a drink. As he pressed his life-worn flesh to the deathless stone, he thought in another flash of hysteria: wouldn't it be something if I, needing a drink now maybe for the first time in my life, really needing it, have the flask, miraculously unbroken, in my hip pocket . . . and can't get to it. Needing it just like I need that flashlight and both of them a million miles away on my butt. A perverse laughter bubbled in him.

The next fall caught him almost unaware of its occurrence. In midair, as he sank again into the abyss, realization struck him and instinctively he made an effort to control the attitude of his body. He hit jarringly on his legs and his right hip and sank wearily into a broken heap on the new ledge. His senses were dulled almost beyond physical pain and in one sense he was filled with a fatal hopelessness; yet as he felt himself slipping once again over an inevitable brink he clutched the impersonally sadistic rock and, momentarily at least, found a purchase.

Through his shocked senses he listened for sounds from above. *Thank God. I don't believe she even knew about that one.*

"Carol?" His voice floated up through the tube of stone.

"Yes, Daddy." Her voice sounded small and weary—weary beyond her age.

"Carol . . . it is perfectly natural for a girl of any age to . . . to want a horse."

"Daddy . . . don't—"

"You're a good girl, a good person, Carol. You ask for little. You'll have your horse. . . . Tell Mother—"

His senses blackened, and with infinite sadness and regret he slid off into his waiting void, even in his delirious exhaustion clutching for some useful and substantial handhold; and then, not finding it, falling, trying to orient his plunging body into some rightful order of descent . . .

He opened his eyes to a spot of light directly above; bending into the light was a hallucination, then another.

Sudden memory signaled a sharp warning to his brain, spurted adrenalin into his veins. His arms moved like pistons, hands clutching at stone. They found no substance and he knew he was falling again. His body twisted in an effort to gain the proper attitude of falling; sharp pains shot through his legs.

"He's conscious, Ben. Help me hold him."

Reality returned to his brain and, more slowly, to the desperate reflexes of his body.

Conscious? Conscious of what? . . . Oh, yes. . . .

He felt firm hands restraining his arms.

"It's all right, fella. Just take it easy."

In one arm he felt the distant prick of a needle. He looked up at the owner of the voice, a bespectacled face loosely attached to a small wiry body. He slowly let out his taut breath. "So . . . I finally stopped falling." His voice sounded hollow and hardly recognizable as his own.

"You did. It's a fairly broad shelf. Covered with several inches of silt, luckily for you."

Another face leaned out of the shadows. "My hat's off to you, mister. It's bad enough coming down here on a *rope*."

The bespectacled man, apparently a doctor, listened to his chest with a stethoscope.

He nodded. "We'll hoist you up now."

"My family? Grace?"

"They're up there."

His memory leapt. "*Mike?*"

The doctor chuckled. "You mean the new sprint champion of Tuscahatchee County? I don't believe a Sherman tank could remove him."

David and the doctor gazed at each other.

"You're pretty busted up, but as far as I can tell there's nothing we can't patch."

David looked up at the rough circle of daylight above him. He felt an old identity flowing into him like the return of a benevolent ghost.

"Doctor," he said, smiling with a new inner bearing that was at once profound and risible, "what's it like on the outside?"

The man smiled back at him. "You'll soon be finding out."

"Doctor," David said, "you can say that again."

David Wagoner

Wild Goose Chase

THE fields of corn stubble in the flat river valley had been half flooded
by a week of storms, and though it wasn't actually raining at the
moment, it was going to. He could taste it, smell it, and feel it coming,
even inside the car as they drove slowly along the zigzagging humpbacked
macadam road between barbed-wire fences, past groves of black cotton-
wood and red alder, then into the stubble fields again.

Suddenly he slowed, stopped half on the weedy shoulder, ran his
window down, and focused his field glasses. He said, "Four shovelers,
two cinnamon teals, and a lesser scaup."

Leaning nearly into the driver's seat with him, she used her own less
heavy glasses while he pressed backward to make room. "*Five* shovelers,"
she said. "Three females. And a bufflehead."

He looked again at the shallow fifty-foot-long temporary pond in
the middle of the field, knowing she would be right.

She said, "Aren't they beautiful."

He nodded, agreeing genuinely, but her voice had in it the soft edges
of reverence she kept strictly for the animal kingdom, and an old uneasi-
ness stirred in him. He'd never heard her speak that feelingly and be-
nevolently about any human being, including him. He hoped it would
be a healing day for a change. She almost always felt better after looking
at anything wild, preferably not through cage bars, and even though this
was duck season and her main enemies in life—killers of animals—were
out in red-faced force all over the state, there had been enough No Hunting and No Trespassing signs for the past mile to make her feel reassured.
They hadn't heard a shotgun go off for half an hour.

The open window had chilled the car in a hurry, and with her unspoken agreement he rolled it up and began driving again, going slow, letting his eyes flick from the leafless wild rosebushes to the tops of split-cedar fenceposts to the silhouettes of tree branches against the gray sky and back down to the pools in the next field, the restless scanning of a bird watcher.

He saw it first—the Canada goose standing by itself in the two-inch stubble, not dabbling in the nearby pond, but rigid, oddly alert, more like a decoy than a real goose. At first, he didn't put into words what seemed wrong about it, just knew it, and he found himself wishing she wouldn't see it at all.

"Canada goose," she said, the way some women mentioned the names of famous dress designers or prize dahlias. But she turned uneasy almost as quickly as he had. "It's wounded."

He didn't contradict her right away. While she rolled her window down to use her glasses better, he stopped the car half on the road, idling, and began hoping no damage would be noticeable, no blood, no disarranged feathers, no wing-crooking. He let her do the inspecting.

"I can't see anything," she said. "Let me use yours."

He unlooped his stronger glasses and handed them over. "It's probably all right," he said without enough conviction in his voice. The trouble was the bird shouldn't have been alone: it was very ungooselike behavior. He waited.

"I still can't see anything. Turn off the engine."

He switched off the ignition to reduce the slight jiggling the motor always gave to a magnified image.

After staring for a few more seconds, she said, "What's it doing alone?"

He let out the breath he'd been holding. "Maybe it's waiting for a friend."

"They mate for life like eagles. Where's the mate?"

"Maybe it's immature." But even with the naked eye he could see the plumage was fully developed, the neck, head, and bill as black as they would ever be, the breast fully rounded, so he wasn't surprised when she didn't bother to answer.

"We've got to go see," she said.

He didn't bother to ask why. It wasn't necessary to hear, again, about his moral responsibility in matters like this. Their house through the fifteen years of their marriage had been a combination zoo, pet store, veterinary clinic, and pet cemetery, and he personally had undertaken the private burial services of water turtles and land tortoises, four kinds of lizards, a woodpecker, a rabbit, three tropical songbirds, a raccoon, a weasel, a mountain beaver, and other creatures which he had momentarily and mercifully forgotten, some of which they'd found injured, some acquired sick from careless shops or grateful owners, all given a clean, warm place to die.

So he opened the driver's door without protesting and slid out, clicking it shut, snapping his parka against the cold breeze. "He's watching. One false move, and he'll be heading back to Canada."

"Prove it," she said through her open window. "Make a false move."

All his moves felt false: the tug at his Irish tweed hat, the stomping to make sure his feet hadn't gone to sleep in his rubber hikers, the sidling away from the car so the goose could get the full benefit of his manshape. He tried to *will* the goose to fly, but it stayed put, staring, fifty yards away beyond the wire fence. He shouted, "Hey!" at the gruffest, most intimidating pitch of his voice.

"Don't scare it!" she said.

"I thought that was the idea." But the goose hadn't budged. Moving along the fence for a slightly closer look, he wondered whether it might not be a newfangled plastic decoy after all.

The car door opened and closed quietly behind him, and he turned to see her unfolding their old red-plaid car blanket, giving it a tentative shake.

Trying to forestall what she obviously had in mind, he said, "Take a better look at it. It's holding both wings in tight. Not a hitch. It's standing on both feet, and it's alert."

"We can take it to the Wild Bird Clinic."

"Now let's just back up a minute," he said. "Do you have any idea how strong a wild goose is?"

"A wounded goose isn't as strong."

He turned his back to the breeze, hunching his shoulders. "A wounded wild goose is even more irrational close to human beings than an unwounded wild goose. We'd do it more damage than it's already had. *If* it's wounded."

"It's wounded. I can tell."

"How?"

Immediately he wished he hadn't asked, and instead of replying to her silence with *It takes one to know one* or some other hazardous, flip remark, he turned to the barbed wire, set one boot hard against the lowest strand, grabbed the second wire between barbs, pulling it taut as a bowstring, and managed to duck through without damaging himself or losing his hat or even looking particularly awkward—more from luck than experience. Turning, he held out his hands for the blanket. "Let me do it," he said. "If it can be done. You've got good slacks on."

But she held on to the moth-eaten red wool, clutching it close as if for comfort. "No, I'm coming too."

"Take a look at that mud."

"I know what mud looks like, and I know what a healthy Canada goose looks like. Hold the wires for me."

He spread the gap again, helping unsnag the blanket when it caught briefly, and watched her skim through with the dancer's agility she'd never lost, in spite of the year-old operation in which she'd lost so much else.

"Thank you very much, sir."

Instead of reacting to her mock formality, he looked toward the goose, hoping all this bustle and activity had sent it into its short takeoff scamper, but it had only waddled a few yards and was keeping its right eye on them in full profile. The ground between the long rows of stubble was mucky, even here in a relatively well-drained area, and he glanced ahead to the swampier patches with depressed resignation. "Somebody's going to get hurt trying this," he said.

"Something's already hurt." She began a slow stalk of the goose, ex-aggerated by the need to pick her boots all the way out of the upper layer of mud before she could put them down again.

"Have you ever caught anything in a blanket?" he said. "Besides me and your feet?"

"Don't talk."

The bird, leaner-necked and more agile-looking than a domestic goose, was watching them intently—a little insanely, he thought, and cer-tainly with no hint of welcome. "It doesn't like the look of us, and I don't blame it."

She made clucking noises he'd heard farm women use when scatter-ing scratch, but the goose gave no sign of interest in becoming domesti-cated. With its long neck up straight, it began a steady waddle at an oblique angle away from them. She stopped, he stopped, and after a few more waddles the goose stopped, still watchful. "If it could fly, it would've flown by now, so it *is* wounded," she whispered.

"All right, suppose it is. This is posted land. It's safe. They spend most of their time on the ground anyway. They don't want to be flying all that goosefat around twenty-four hours a day. Let it make a living around here. On foot."

"It's *not* safe. There are dogs and foxes and farmers."

"There's probably a farmer right now aiming a .30-30 at us from his hayloft. We're in his posted cornfield, stalking a game bird. We've got a shorter life expectancy than the goose."

"You're just quibbling because you want to get out of it."

The goose was standing equidistant between them and a stand of brush-filled alders, and beyond that—if he had his local geography straight—was the swollen river, only a few feet below flood stage. It seemed unlikely the goose would want to enter the brush, that being poor flying territory for anything larger than a wren or a warbler, and so it was just possible they might be able to corner it long enough to use the blanket. If it was crippled.

Even so, he tried again. "Couldn't we just drive back to a feed store and get a sack of hen scratch for it? Let it build up its strength? Lots of them winter around here. They don't *all* have to go to California." He could see her face souring on the idea, rejecting it, so he let it turn foolish. "Then in the spring when the flocks start coming over again, it can come out of hiding and honk for a mate."

"That's really likely, isn't it," she said. "If you're so scared, go on back to the car and be a coward. Nobody's asking you to stay."

"I'm not a coward." He examined her blue lips as if identifying fieldmarks on a subspecies that could easily be mistaken for a common variety. "Why don't you at least wear that blanket till we catch up with the damn thing, which we won't."

"I'm not cold, and I don't want to spook it by flapping a blanket around."

He wanted to tell her he was being prudent and judicious, as thoughtful of her and the goose as of himself, but it didn't seem worth the effort.

When she started her muddy, clodhoppery walk again, he followed, and the goose headed for the alder thicket, picking up speed when she did, its black legs beginning to scuttle. It unfolded its wings halfway, and for the first time they could see the gap in the scapulars on the left side and the dark wound there, probably a wing shot. The right wing flapped momentarily, but the left stayed half folded while the goose stretched its neck forward and did its best to run.

And its best was as good as theirs across the slippery, puddle-filled furrows.

"Stop it!" she said, either to him or the goose or both.

As he lumbered past her, managing not to fall down, he grabbed at the blanket, ready to take over leadership of the Cause with the enthusiasm of a convert, but she kept hold of one end of it, hauling him back off balance, and by the time they'd recovered, arms out like people crossing ice and the blanket between them like an improvised sail, the goose had gone scooting into the brush, head down and forward, as neatly as a pheasant taking cover.

"Where in the hell did it learn how to do that?" he said, skidding to a halt just shy of the sagging rail fence between them and the alder grove. He expected her to stop too and talk it over with him, to consider the chase ended and to go back, honor intact, both having tried their damnedest to do some good.

Instead, she yanked his end of the blanket away from him, bundled it quickly, and clambered over the fence, knocking the rotten top rail loose, and blundered straight into the thicket, not taking her eyes away from the direction the goose had been headed.

"Wait a minute," he said. "You'll get scratched up." The ground cover among the forty-foot, gray-and-white-splotched alders was a mixture of salmonberry and trailing blackberry, and though it could have been denser, it looked like uncomfortable going. But she wasn't hesitating except when the tough vines and withes caught at her slacks or jacket or the blanket, or when they half tripped her.

Worried about her doggedness and the trouble it might make for her (and therefore him), he scissored his legs over the fence and kept on her trail. Whether it was also the trail of the goose was problematical: he had no idea whether it also had a pheasant's gift for lying doggo or veering unexpectedly.

Raising his voice, he said, "The river's just ahead. For godsake, be careful." Already he could hear its full, steady rush, and even though nearly all the banks in this district were low and she wasn't in much danger of falling in where she couldn't scramble out, the high water was full of snags and other debris, and the currents were more complicated than usual.

Suddenly she stopped cold ten feet ahead of him, frozen like a bird dog pointing. But when he caught up with her, he saw that her eyes—

those gun-metal blue eyes that had used to soften whenever they looked into his—were darting from all the way left to all the way right, saw she was listening hard, and he'd already held still before she hushed him.

They stood together in the middle of the thicket, trying to hear through the increased noise level of the river. She stood slightly bent, as if ready to spring, and he leaned sideways against one of the alders, remembering other times he'd admired the mottled bark up close, the pale-green lichen clinging to it in patches. Even without sunlight, the tall, slim, closely palisaded tree trunks cast an uncanny light. It would have been a wonderful place to sit and think and watch and learn, but at the moment there seemed to be nothing to think about, only something clumsy and dangerous to do, and he felt lost beside her, displaced. A man with an impossible assignment. He thought of kissing her to make up for the sense of estrangement, but her usually soft, sensual mouth was as thin-lipped as one of the lizards she'd tried to keep, whose mucous membranes didn't compromise with the tough exterior by allowing anything as vulnerable as lips.

They heard it at the same time—a brushy scuffling that had nothing to do with the sound of the river—and at first he thought a dog or a raccoon had caught it and they'd all wind up in a catch-as-catch-can free-for-all, everyone a loser. But then he saw the goose struggling to wedge itself through the last patches of salmonberry, catching its half-crooked wings sometimes but churning away with its flat black webfeet.

She ran toward it, her shoulders glancing off tree trunks, stumbled, and fell short, only cushioning herself partly with the blanket, and he saw her face collide with an alder.

He caught up while she was still thrashing to get to her knees, and he tried to touch her scraped cheek and the puffed split lower lip.

Shaking his hands away, she scrambled forward, sometimes on her knees, sometimes on her feet, and he followed her into a shallow grassy clearing at the river's abrupt edge. The goose stood on the two-foot cutbank above the heavily silted, roiling current full of small branches and all the clutter from flooded tributaries, not so much poised there as beside itself. It wasn't used to being chased on the ground, especially not through bushes, and it looked ready to get back to its own kind of territory.

They were only ten feet away, and she said, "Don't let it fall in! It might drown."

"Geese don't drown." He was short of breath and worried about her lip.

"Be quiet!" she said, then took a moment to spit blood.

The goose was still hesitating, and never having been this close to one before, he stared at its wild black eye and the white face-patch, feeling like apologizing for all this harassment. The hunter who'd shot it was probably half shot himself by now in a tavern somewhere, enjoying the exchange of lies with other shotgunners, and he wished the man a bad night and a bad day and weeks more of the same.

When the goose saw the blanket come up in her hands and she made a short rush at it mostly on her knees, it squatted to slide down the bank. Even with her clumsiness, she nearly caught it: one edge of the blanket momentarily covered it halfway, but the goose slid from underneath and went into the water with only a small splash and began paddling downstream.

He saved her from going in too by hanging on to her snagged jacket, then eased her back to a sitting position while they both watched the goose heading out of sight beyond a low-hanging willow branch, not battling the current but using it with an easy skill.

She started weeping silently. "It's hurt."

"It doesn't swim with its wings," he said. "And it's doing what it *wants* to do."

"Except flying." She glared at him. "Right now it doesn't know what's good for it."

He let that pass and offered her his fairly clean handkerchief, but she shoved it aside, spitting more blood. He tried to think of something, anything, to distract or comfort her. "Don't worry. It'll swim ashore at a safe place."

"There aren't any safe places," she said with a contemptuous superiority, like a disciplinarian whose star student was failing in an exam.

And he felt, with a weird certainty, that she would have preferred going down the river, even under it, with the goose instead of staying where she was. Trying to regain some kind of advantage, he said, "I mean, that goose is a survivor. It knows exactly what to do, day or night, one wing or two, on the ground, in the air, on water. It would probably even know what to do in a cage."

"That's not true." She was probing the inside of her mouth with her tongue and spitting more blood, and again she refused the handkerchief as if refusing a blindfold. She said, "I broke a tooth."

He could tell from her look she was turning away from not trusting him and the rest of the world, at least for the time being, and was beginning to concentrate on not trusting her body, the still beautiful body she now considered ugly. He saw on her face a kind of bitter pleasure, and he blinked and half turned from it, wishing he hadn't noticed. She let him help her to her feet, and could see she was going to need stitches in her lip. He felt panicky, inadequate, responsible, compassionate, tired, and raggedly geared up, a bad combination of emotions for the ambulance driver he was going to have to be in a few minutes.

And he knew he would come out of this fiasco looking bad. He'd done something wrong, maybe everything. Or maybe just *felt* the wrong way. She would know what he'd done wrong and would tell him sooner or later and probably over and over. She began to groan rhythmically, and he walked with her through the tangled thicket and helped her climb over the fence. It was drizzling and turning darker as he half guided and half followed her across the empty stubble field.

Leigh Allison Wilson

From the Bottom Up

OLD BLACKBURN's granddaughter, Lorraine, sat on the edge of the bathtub and thumped the heels of her patent-leather shoes against the porcelain sides. Her legs hung like sapling trunks below where her dress hiked up crooked at the waist, and she was busy picking strings from the cotton hem. The morning sun splayed through the bathroom window, caught the reflection of Old Blackburn full in the face while he knotted his tie in the medicine-cabinet mirror, and beveled from the glass onto his granddaughter as if to enlighten them according to age. Swinging the mirror a little allowed Old Blackburn both to knot his tie and, squinting, to watch the child as she pulled little irreparable cockades in the material of her dress. She pulled a six-inch string, staring intently as the cotton writhed up onto her thigh. Then she dropped the thread to the tile floor, where several others already lay curled.

Old Blackburn practiced a benevolent smile in the mirror; when he bared his teeth, his nose drooped like a boll of cotton and the lines of the smile split his jaw like a field furrow. When she left for Nashville all Edna Earl had said was "Just don't beat her to death," and from that minute on that's practically all he'd wanted to do. He stopped practicing. He liked to tell relatives that he received the aquiline features in the family, that he was the product of a buried strain of nobility on his father's side; and with the world falling apart from the bottom on upward, Old Blackburn saw no reason for the noble to smile.

"Are you ready to go?" he said and noticed that his nose was indeed as stern and proud as an eagle's. It seemed to ripple in flight through the dazzle of reflected sunlight. "Are you ready to go?"

"We got showers in Knoxville," Lorraine said. "We don't have no

From the collection of stories entitled *From the Bottom Up*, published by the University of Georgia Press. Copyright © 1983 by Leigh Allison Wilson.

bathtubs. Momma says they carry disease in the shape of spiders." She leaned over and stuck her head in the bathtub and made mewing noises. "Says they carry gangrene." She dipped and slid over the lip of the bathtub, mewing. On the back of her dress two streaks of dull green met in the shape of a great bird flying across the cotton.

"Have you sat in something?"

"I thought I saw a rat," Lorraine said, her voice resounding in the hollows of the tub. "They breed rats in Knoxville, in the sewers where every time you flush . . ."

"What have you sat in, girl?"

"You're feeding a rat," she said.

Old Blackburn picked his coat off a hanger on the back of the bathroom door and held it by the collar as if to wipe his hands on the black polyester. In the mirror he noted the gravity of his aspect, the sharp slash of black tie against white collar, the proud nose above the slit of an unvacillating mouth, riveting green eyes that blinked but never connived or winked. He thought himself the picture of restrained nobility, a last bastion of human dignity. DEATH WITH DIGNITY was the motto of the funeral home and, though he didn't own it, still Old Blackburn drove the hearse, consoled the bereaved with words of unsentimental wisdom, and helped carry the coffin from hearse to gravesite, all the while inspiring the confidence of mourners and gravediggers alike with his calm severity. Old Blackburn was indispensable to the many dignified deaths administered by the Jefferson Funeral Home, and today would crown his achievement. Today they would bury Thomas P. Appleton, former mayor of Jefferson City and beloved owner of Appleton's Drugs, a chain of drug stores that linked half of the state with pharmaceuticals. And half the state would be at the cemetery to watch Old Blackburn drive the hearse slowly forward, parting whole clusters of weeping women and dour-faced men, to stare with not a little relief as he stepped proudly and vigorously from the hearse, his black and white appearance tracing a fine figure under the noon sun. His whole person would scream DEATH WITH DIGNITY to the awaiting crowds.

"Lorraine, sit up and listen to me," he said and shut the medicine cabinet. The sunlight had shifted, had fallen into one pure stream of yellow that flooded the back of Lorraine's head and formed a frowzy halo. "You will take off your dress and put on another. You will do it in five minutes and will do nothing to mess it once you've dressed. Do you hear me?"

"I ain't done nothing but listen since I got here. There ain't nothing to do *but* talk and listen when you're in the middle of nowhere. We got TV in Knoxville."

"Television is the eye of little people, and little people are tearing the world into little pieces. It's an evil, Lorraine, the eye of evil." Lorraine puckered her lips and pulled another string from her dress, looking vacantly toward the door of the bathroom as if in wary contemplation of escape. "You will right now go change your dress. The funeral starts in an hour."

"I reckon he won't mind if we're a little late," she said, snickering into her sleeve, then wiping her mouth on the cotton, "I reckon he can sit tight for a while." She stood up, her dress twisted sideways at the waist, and pranced out of the bathroom.

"I'm no baby sitter," Old Blackburn had said to Edna Earl when she dropped Lorraine off without asking either his permission or his consent, "and I'm no kindergarten service neither."

Edna Earl had just stood there, dabbing pink lipstick on her mouth and champing down on a pink-dappled Kleenex, while Lorraine roamed around his living room, inspecting his collection of glass elephant pieces, grabbing them up and staring them right between the eyes with a look of malice on her face. "What am I supposed to do around here," Lorraine said, and Edna Earl said, "Shut your mouth and sit down please ma'am," and then Old Blackburn wagged his head back and forth, watching a glass elephant disappear in the palm of Lorraine's hand and reappear in little fractions on the wooden slats of the floor. It had taken her three minutes to shatter his piece.

"Papa, it's my chance in a lifetime," Edna Earl said, looking down at the slivers of glass. "I'm the only representative for Knox County in the whole Tennessee convention. Here's her suitcase. I really appreciate it, Papa." She showed Old Blackburn all of her front teeth and two of them bled a faint pink, then she squinted her eyes at Lorraine, saying "I'll wring your neck when I come back. Just remember that." Before he could move Edna Earl was rushing out the front door and waving goodbye; "Just don't beat her to death" trailed after her like a flourish of trumpets, then she submerged into her car and left.

"Will this do?" Lorraine asked. She held the sides of her hem in both hands so that two wings of dark blue material formed under her arms. Flapping her wings she followed Old Blackburn down the hall and into the living room where she let go of the dress and flopped onto a couch, lying stomach-down on the cushions with her arms pointed toward an armrest.

"Up up and away," she said.

"Sit up and be quiet," Old Blackburn said. He pulled on his coat. Even though the cuffs of his shirt hung down two inches below the line of his coat sleeves, giving the appearance of broad white grins on his wrists, the polyester of both was spotless, unfrayed. Old Blackburn conjured an image of a proud but wise country preacher and thought for a second that perhaps he had missed his calling. "Sit up, we have to hurry. There's hundreds of people waiting for us."

He stood by a brown coffee table and picked up his wallet, placing it in the back left pocket of his trousers; then he picked up a set of keys, placing them in the front right pocket; then he picked up a store-bought carnation and planted it in the buttonhole of his lapel. If he had been a preacher, instead of rooting after line leakage for Western Union, he might still be preaching. They made him retire although he had more than once offered his services indefinitely; they gave him a silver watch that broke two weeks later and sent him home. Every month he got a check from the state headquarters and enclosed with it, every six months or so, would be a note that said "We miss you down here, you old rascal" or else "Come see us sometime." But the funeral home picked up on him as soon as he walked in the door—"Maybe we could use a good man like you," Mr. Toad had said. And Old Blackburn strode right into the job with the air of an incumbent governor, telling everybody that he worked for no pay, that money was nothing to a noble man.

"Sit up, sit down," Lorraine said, sitting up, "shut up, get dressed, listen to this, listen to that—I may's well be a hearing aid." Perching, she seemed to vibrate along the cushions.

"You should thank God you're not worse off. There's people in the world without the legs to stand on." Old Blackburn walked to the front door, opened it, and stood there while Lorraine got up from the couch, her face inscrutably pinched around the eyes, and followed him outside. He locked the door, then put the keys back in his pocket.

"Dear Lord," she said. "Now I lay me down to sleep and if I should die before I wake, I pray You Lord to take take take." With a look of surprise she giggled: "Take take take," she said again and skipped down the porch steps.

"You better watch your mouth, miss. People are struck dead every day." If he had been a preacher, he could have saved Lorraine's soul, hundreds of souls, and abruptly he pictured leading great masses of black-robed people into the cleansing waters of a beautiful blue river. He would preach that God helps those that help themselves, that He takes only the great and noble unto Him—no little people—that the Lord giveth and the Lord taketh away. His words would move grown men to tears, and they would follow him out of the rabble and rabidity into the path of a severe dignity.

Lorraine hung on the open door of his Pontiac, rocking it back and forth on the tips of her toes. Beside the car Old Blackburn cocked his hand in a salute, warding off the sunlight, and inspected the weather way off past his neighborhood tract, past the fields of half-grown tobacco, way off to where the mountains crouched against an encroaching wall of black clouds. They were swelled to rupturing, moving in quickly from the northeast; there might be rain on the funeral. He inspected his house to make sure the storm windows were all shut. It was pink brick. Every house in the tract was pink brick, although the front doors and windows got shuffled around from house to house making the row of them look like one face strung in a variety of emotional positions. Old Blackburn's house was in a state of astonishment: two gaping windows stared over a wide front door that warped ever so slightly outward. At last he got into the car and revved the engine, satisfied that all his windows were tight against the rain. Lorraine climbed in beside him and immediately turned on the radio. Old Blackburn turned it off.

"I reckon the radio's a evil, too," she said and folded her arms, looking out her window with a stiff neck. Sunlight streamed in through the front window and formed tiny dull pockets of gold dust on the dashboard. When Old Blackburn backed the car slowly out of the driveway the light veered and struck the front of Lorraine's head, making her hair turn into a glowing nimbus, while he manipulated the wheel in a dim gray shade, his back reared erect against the seat. He drove with a grim authority, the whole car seeming to extend and shape itself under his direction. A mail-order black man in riding britches stood at the end of his driveway and pointed toward the garage with a black crop.

"He looks bored," Lorraine said, letting her neck go loose. She was approximately the same height as the statue. "He looks like his arm's tired." They drove out of the tract, turned onto the main highway, and set off through the farmsteads and the tenant houses with their grubby, spidery children crouched in front on the packed dirt, and on past a shuttered Esso station and a sunken brown barn that had SEE ROCK CITY painted in white on the roof. Lorraine sat and swiveled her head left and right, her eyes flicking over the landscape. Old Blackburn sat as rigid as an ancient boulder.

"I seen a movie just like this," she said. "They had soldiers come and burn it all down."

"I want you to be quiet when we get to the funeral home," he said, "and I want you to stay beside me the whole time." He sat so stiffly that his mouth seemed to be the only movable part, and it moved with a sparse pecking action across the jaw. "There's hundreds of people at the cemetery and you might get lost. You're liable to get taken home by mistake."

"They spared the women and children though. Took them to the city and put them in the sewers to scrub for the rest of their lives. I seen it on the late show."

Up ahead was a gray stoplight, and the road was lined on both sides by clusters of scraggly old buildings. Off in the distance the road continued on into more farmsteads and tenant houses, the pavement cutting a clean arrow through the yellow-green landscape, pointing straight into the welling pregnancy of thunderclouds that were shoved head and belly over the mountains. Old Blackburn turned left at the stoplight, then drove into the parking lot of the funeral home. Except for the modern wing on the south side, the funeral home had a colonial façade and could have been the house of an old and rich and decorous family; the hearses lined up in the lot could have been a fleet of limousines; and the well-dressed undertakers who lounged on the front veranda might have been the family's prodigal sons, lazing away the morning in the coolness of the shade.

For years the policy of the funeral home had been to assemble the parties of the bereaved at the cemetery, then to deliver the coffin immediately before the service began. They maintained that a funeral parade was an indignity to the dead, that it sullied the respectability of the funeral for ignorant or derisive or impassive spectators to watch the mourners drive through town. And Old Blackburn maintained, in private, that it kept the bereaved from wandering aimlessly around the home, impeding an orderly execution of affairs. More than any other place he had ever frequented, he felt at home here. It was dignified.

"Nice place you got here," Lorraine said and got out of the car. She stood with her arms planted on her waist and looked up at the wrought-iron DEATH WITH DIGNITY sign over the back entrance. Little chips of black paint had fallen off it, revealing patches of pale gray between the letters.

"It says 'Death with Dignity,' " Old Blackburn said. "It means we're careful here."

"I can read it. I been reading for a million years," Lorraine said. "Just about exactly a million years." He headed toward the glass door under the sign and held it open for Lorraine, but she hung back, adjusting her dress, then rubbing her nose with two pronged fingers, then craning her neck backwards with her eyes rolled up in her head.

"Does it stink in there?" she asked, her voice catching as a roll of thunder sounded in the distance, resounded against the home, and drifted off into the air.

"Get in here, Lorraine," Old Blackburn said and kept his form as rigid as a well-dressed scarecrow. "If you keep your mouth shut in here maybe they'll think you've got good sense."

"Maybe it's them that's without the sense," Lorraine said. "They're the ones that live in this one-horse town, not me." Snorting, she marched through the door and into the home. Old Blackburn let the door shut by itself behind them and looked over Lorraine's head up the corridor where the gravediggers usually leaned on the walls and spat on the floor and passed around hand-rolled cigarettes that slashed between their lips while they spoke. But there wasn't a soul on the corridor today except for a single black man in overalls who was sweeping the floor at a slow lope. At each step he thrust his head forward, gave the floor a swipe, then retracted his neck, swiping and thrusting and retracting as if any minute he might uncover something of value on the floor. Old Blackburn stood in the middle of his path with his shoulders squared to show he was a man with a mission.

"Where's Mr. Toad, young man?" he asked, pecking the words.

"Mought be downstairs, Blackburn," the man said and continued sweeping. A spray of dust billowed over Old Blackburn's shoes but the man kept sweeping and stabbing his neck as though stuck in neutral in front of a stoplight. "Mought be upstairs and mought be on the porch. Mought be at home with dinner on the table. Don't know."

"You should get a vacuum cleaner," Lorraine told the man. "One of them with the long cords. They'll suck up anything."

"Is that right," the man said and looked at her. "Need me a swimming pool, too, and a goose that lays the golden eggs." He tapped the broom on Old Blackburn's feet until he stepped aside. Then, shifting gears, he went loping on down the hall behind his broom.

"If you weren't so ignorant," Old Blackburn said, stamping his shoes, "I'd think you were touched in the head. He don't need you to tell him what to do." She turned her back to him and looked at the wall, her shoulders drawn up in a little blue square.

"Blackburn!" a thin voice said, preceding a short, thin man in a black suit. It was Mr. Toad, teetering down the corridor with his right hand wiping his face with a white handkerchief. "I want to have a word with you, Blackburn." Old Blackburn drew himself up to his full presence and stood ready for orders.

"Listen, I'm in a hurry. You've got number two today and the funeral starts in thirty minutes." He wiped his face, although tiny globules of sweat popped out on his brow like indelible pink bubbles after each swipe, and he stared at the carnation on Old Blackburn's chest.

"And the other thing, Blackburn: we've been, well, we've been getting complaints about you. I believe this will be your last day with us."

"What do you mean?" Old Blackburn said and squinted his eyes to get Mr. Toad in better focus.

"I mean we've had complaints, attacks even, from the Devotie party. They say you were morbid to them, that you told Mrs. Devotie that her husband was better off dead than alive, that he was deader alive than buried. I can't have my men disrespecting the clients. You've got thirty minutes, I tell you." Mr. Toad turned on his heel and started teetering away, his handkerchief pressed to his face like a giant baby's breath.

"Number two," he said over his shoulder, and then he disappeared.

"Number two," Old Blackburn said, still squinting for focus. The whole hallway seemed to be losing its shape, to be drifting in soft pieces away from the center. But there were still the funeral and the hundreds of people and the hearse with him in it that would part the sea of faceless mourners and his clean, stern, black and white appearance. The hallway came together again and in the middle of it stood Lorraine. As soon as he focused her into the picture she turned sideways, standing there with her arms hanging down close to her sides.

"We've got thirty minutes," he said. "Number two."

Lorraine shrugged her shoulders and stayed put.

"It's the number two is what we've got," he said and walked down the hall toward the door. Opening the glass Old Blackburn glanced behind him, saw Lorraine following him at seven paces with her eyes hooded and sullen, then walked out into the parking lot. He got into the number two hearse and waited until Lorraine got in beside him, head turned toward the window, neck stiff, arms pulled toward the car door. It started to rain, angry sheets followed by tentative patters followed by a steady dull hiss, and he turned on the wipers, watching the windshield go from confusion to half-circled clarity. Pulling in a deep breath that seemed to tighten his back and hold it at attention, Old Blackburn started the engine and pulled out of the parking lot. Except for the coffin proper the whole interior of the hearse was chalk-white leather that gave off a fluorescent glow and illuminated the driving area with a silver tarnish.

"Hundreds of people," Old Blackburn said, "hundreds and hundreds of people," and then, as if his brain had stuck on a difficult problem, he said "Hunnerds and hunnerds a people" a little louder.

They drove into the cemetery and rounded a curve. There, at the bottom of a sloping hill, he could see a tremendous circus tent that seemed to bulge with people, all dressed in black. They swelled past the sides of the tent and strung out across the lawn, dark umbrellas blooming over every head, television cameras rolling here and there in the crowd. Old Blackburn felt something like an intoxicating pride seep into every cranny of his person, felt his muscles tighten and rear back, felt his clothes starch up and grow powerful to see. Guiding the hearse into the outskirts of the shaded people, he kept a look of solidity on his face, his eyes and nose and mouth as stern and proud as stone, glancing only once at Lorraine, silent and unmoving against the door.

An umbrella and the black trousers of a fat man disengaged from the crowd and trotted up to the hearse. The man tapped on Old Blackburn's window with a notebook until he rolled it down.

"We have arrived," Old Blackburn said, solemnly.

"No you ain't," the fat man said and adjusted his umbrella, then pursed his fat lips at the notebook. "The number two party is down the hill. This is the Appleton party, number one."

"But this is my funeral!" Old Blackburn shouted.

"Down the hill and hurry for God's sake, it's raining." Then the umbrella and the fat legs eased back into the shifting, thronging welter of umbrellas and legs. Old Blackburn stared at the drops of water that came through the open window and stained his shoulder. He put his hand on them, making a patch of wetness spread onto his coat sleeve, and he studied it as if it were a scientific experiment. With a little gurgling sound coming out of the pit of his stomach he put the hearse in reverse and backed down the hill all the way to where a little awning covered a small group: four men, three women, and a square hole in the ground. He stopped the hearse beside the awning. The four men opened the back of the hearse and carried the coffin over to the hole, the rain making perverse tears gush down on their grim faces. Still gurgling, Old Blackburn opened his door and got out and stood with his head bared to the rain.

"My own flesh and blood," one woman wailed and her voice drowned through the rushing rain. "My own flesh and blood."

"Hunnerds," Old Blackburn said. The rain was blinding him, and he felt his knees, his back, grow very tired, wanting to return to the ground. A vision of a broken watch loomed before his eyes and behind that telegraph poles stretched on and on, toppling abruptly into a beautiful blue river where robed bodies floated face-down, hundreds and hundreds of bodies. But he wasn't even in the picture. The gurgling sound grew to a mighty surge down the base of his spine, prickly as broomstraw, and he crouched on the grass to stop the flow. The funeral began in front of him but he couldn't see it; blind, he groped around on the grass for something to hold on to.

"Let's get out of here, let's go home." Old Blackburn tried to focus his eyes and at last he could make out Lorraine in front of him, standing with her feet planted firmly on the grass. Between her white legs lay his carnation, mud-smeared, its stem stuck straight in the air. "Please Papaw, let's go home." He held out his hand, groping, the world flashing in and out of focus, and she took it, suddenly looming gigantic before him, and pulled him to his feet.

"Flesh and blood," he said, as if fetching for a forgotten lyric. Lorraine held his hand and tugged him toward the hearse.

"Let's go home," she said. "It's no one here to cry over." And Old Blackburn let her lead him like a child into the hearse, into that white interior, into that place where the dead were dignified.

"Home," Lorraine said.

"Flesh and blood," he repeated, tentatively.

He was just beginning to mourn.

Contributors

LEE K. ABBOTT's second and third collections of stories, *Love Is the Crooked Thing* and *Strangers in Paradise*, are both being released during 1986. *The Heart Never Fits Its Wanting* (1981), his first book, won the St. Lawrence Award. Three times published in *The Georgia Review*, Abbott has also had stories in *The Atlantic*, *Best American Short Stories*, and *O. Henry Prize Stories*. He is associate professor of English at Case Western Reserve University in Cleveland.

MAX APPLE's "My Real Estate" appeared in his first collection of stories, *The Oranging of America* (1976). That book was followed by *Zip* (1978) and *Free Agents* (1984), with *Disneyed* forthcoming in 1987. His stories have won the Texas Institute of Letters Best Fiction Award in 1976 and 1984; *Free Agents* won the Hadassah-Ribalow Award in 1985. Apple has taught for many years at Rice University, where he is now professor of English.

HARRIETTE SIMPSON ARNOW (then Harriette Simpson) wrote "Fra Lippi and Me" in 1937 or 1938—one of a group of stories that she did not initially attempt to publish. Its appearance in *The Georgia Review* in 1979 was its first. Arnow has published several novels, including *Mountain Path* (1936), *The Dollmaker* (1954), and *The Kentucky Trace* (1973). A native of Kentucky, she has lived for some forty years in Ann Arbor, Michigan.

MARY CLEARMAN BLEW maintains strong ties with her native Montana. She is Dean of Arts and Sciences at Northern Montana College, has been an editor of the *Montana Centennial Anthology* (to be issued in 1987), and has served with the Montana Committee for the Humanities. She was a recipient of the Breakthrough Award of the University of Missouri Press in 1978 for her collection of stories, *Lambing Out and Others*.

T. CORAGHESSAN BOYLE is a novelist and short-story writer. His first collection of stories, *Descent of Man* (1979), won the St. Lawrence Award; his first novel, *Water Music* (1982), won the Aga Khan Prize given by *Paris Review*. He has also published *Budding Prospects* (1984) and *Greasy Lake and Other Stories* (1985). A graduate of the Iowa Writers' Workshop, he lives in Los Angeles.

SIV CEDERING is the author of nine books of poems, two novels, and five books for children, and she continues to work in all of these forms. *Letters from the Floating World: New and Selected Poems* (1984) is her most recent publication. Her short stories have appeared in *North American Review*, *Partisan Review*, and elsewhere. She lived for many years in Sweden and writes her poetry in English, most of her prose in Swedish; however, she is now at work on a novel in English.

FRED CHAPPELL, author of six books of fiction and seven of poetry, won the Bollingen Prize in 1985. Earlier awards included the Sir Walter Raleigh Award and the Best Foreign Book Award from the Academie Française. His most recent volumes are *I Am One of You Forever* (a novel) and *Source* (poems). His major work is perhaps *Midquest*, a four-volume sequence of poems published first separately and then in a single volume in 1981. He has taught for many years at the University of North Carolina at Greensboro.

HARRY CREWS's "A Long Wail" was his first accepted and second published story. It was also his *last* published story, as he moved quickly to the writing of the novels for which he is best known: first *The Gospel Singer* (1968) and then seven others, including *Karate Is a Thing of the Spirit, Car,* and *A Feast of Snakes.* Over the past ten years he has written essays for *Esquire* and *Playboy,* many of which are collected in *Blood and Grits* (1979). His autobiography, *A Childhood* (1978), has been widely recognized as a modern masterpiece of the genre. Born and reared in Bacon County, Georgia, he has taught at the University of Florida for more than fifteen years.

PAM DURBAN's first collection of stories, *All Set About with Fever Trees,* was issued last year by David R. Godine. (The title story from that collection also appeared in *The Georgia Review.*) Born in South Carolina, she has lived in Ohio for many years and now directs the creative writing program at the University of Ohio in Athens. Her stories have appeared in *TriQuarterly, The Reaper,* and many other magazines. She has won *Crazyhorse* and Rinehart awards for fiction.

WILLIAM FAULKNER (1897–1962) wrote "A Portrait of Elmer" in the middle 1930's, but it was not published until its appearance in *The Georgia Review* some forty-five years later. The story was subsequently printed in Joseph Blotner's edition of Faulkner's uncollected stories. At the time of its composition, Bennett Cerf of Random House told Faulkner that "Elmer" contained "some of the best writing of yours I have ever seen," but that the story ought to be expanded into a novel. Faulkner received the Nobel Prize in 1950.

H. E. FRANCIS' first book publication was a collection of his fiction, *All the People I Never Had,* translated into Spanish and brought out in Argentina. Several collections followed in English, including *The Itinerary of Beggars* (1973) and *A Disturbance of Gulls* (1983). A four-time Fulbright scholar, he has taught and lectured widely in South America, and he works on translations of Argentinian writers. Founding editor of *Poem* magazine, he is professor of English at the University of Alabama in Huntsville.

ERNEST J. GAINES, a native of Oscar, Louisiana, is the author of five novels, a collection of short stories, and numerous other works. His third novel, *The Autobiography of Miss Jane Pittman,* was made into a highly praised television movie in 1974; his most recent novel is *A Gathering of Old Men* (1983). Gaines has held writing fellowships from the Guggenheim Foundation, the NEA, the Rockefeller Foundation, and Stanford University. He has taught and lectured at Yale, Brown, and dozens of other universities, and he is currently writer-in-residence at the University of Southern Louisiana.

GEORGE GARRETT, who had published two volumes of poems and two of short stories when "The Confidence Man" first appeared in *The Georgia Review*, has since had five novels and five more volumes each of poetry and short fiction. He has written plays, a biography of James Jones, and screenplays for five feature films—including that for "Frankenstein Meets the Space Monster," which received a Golden Turkey Award as one of the 100 worst films of all time. Henry Hoyns Professor of Creative Writing at the University of Virginia, Garrett has edited for *Transatlantic Review*, *The Hollins Critic*, *Contempora*, *The Film Journal*, and *Poultry: A Magazine of Voice*. His most recent publication is *An Evening Performance: New and Selected Short Stories*.

GARY GILDNER, born and educated in Michigan, has lived in Oregon, Mexico, France, and elsewhere. First known as a poet (with eight books now to his credit), he has in recent years published more and more fiction. His first volume of stories, *The Crush*, came out in 1983; in 1987, Algonquin Books will issue simultaneously his first novel, *The Second Bridge*, and his new collection of stories, *A Week in South Dakota*. Winner of the Robert Frost Fellowship and the William Carlos Williams, Theodore Roethke, and Helen Bullis poetry prizes, he currently teaches at Drake University.

PATRICK WORTH GRAY's "Too Soon Solos" was his first published fiction and, as it turned out, one of only two stories he has published during a career devoted mainly to poetry. The other story appeared in *Green River Review* in 1979. Gray reports that " 'Too Soon Solos' is the work of a young man, and 'Love Song' the work of a middle-aged man. I can hardly wait to see what kind of story I write when I become an old man." The owner of an MFA in poetry from the Iowa Writers' Workshop, he took his degree to Vietnam and has since held various jobs. He is living in Bellevue, Nebraska.

DONALD HALL, best known as a poet and essayist, has published stories occasionally in literary quarterlies and in *The New Yorker* and *Esquire*. His first book of poems, *Exiles and Marriages*, came out in 1955; his ninth, *The Happy Man*, comes out this year. Long a teacher at the University of Michigan, he left academe in 1975 to write full time at his family homestead in Vermont. His collections of essays include *String Too Short to Be Saved*, *To Keep Moving*, and *Goatfoot, Milktongue, Twinbird*, and he has written children's books (*The Ox-Cart Man*), literary biography (*Remembering Poets*), and a composition textbook (*Writing Well*). A play, *The Bone Ring*, opened off-off Broadway in early 1986.

BARRY HANNAH earned a National Book Award nomination for his first novel, *Geronimo Rex* (1972). His other books include *Airships* (1978) and *The Tennis Handsome* (1983). He has written screenplays in Hollywood and has taught, among other places, at the University of Montana and the University of Iowa. He is now back in his home state, teaching at the University of Mississippi in Oxford.

T. E. HOLT's handbook for amateur astronomers, *The Universe Next Door*, has recently been published by Scribners. He has completed a novel, *Before the Be-*

ginning of Years, and is working on a study of the Hubble space telescope and another of nineteenth-century English poetry. A recent Ph.D. (1985) from Cornell, he is assistant professor of English at Rutgers University.

MARY HOOD has had five stories in *The Georgia Review*; one of these, "Inexorable Progress," was reprinted in *Best American Short Stories 1984* and in *The Editors' Choice 1984*. Her first book, *How Far She Went*, came out in 1984 from the University of Georgia Press, and a second will be released (by Ticknor and Fields) late in 1986. She lives in Woodstock, Georgia.

JUDITH HOOVER's "Proteus" was her first published story when it appeared in our pages in 1978; she had just graduated from Bennington College, and she went on to work for a time with *The Hudson Review*. She currently lives in Cambridge, New York, and teaches at South Vermont College in Bennington.

JAMES LEWIS MACLEOD, whose ancestry includes the first Presbyterian minister born in Georgia, was himself ordained in the Presbyterian church in 1963. A lifelong student and scholar of education and theology, he has most recently published *The Great Doctor Waddel: A Study of Moses Waddel, 1770–1840*. MacLeod was born in Louisiana but lived as a young man in Milledgeville, Georgia, where he became the friend and informal student of Flannery O'Connor. In 1978 he published *A Season of Grace*, a book of religious meditations dedicated to O'Connor's memory. He lives in Sylvania, Georgia, where he is pastor of a small mission Presbyterian church.

JACK MATTHEWS' many novels include *The Charisma Campaigns* (a National Book Award nominee), *Hanger Stout, Awake,* and (most recently) *Sassafras*. As a prolific short-story writer, he is the author of *Crazy Women* and the forthcoming *Ghostly Populations*. Also, he collects and deals in old and rare books; Johns Hopkins University Press will soon publish his *Booking in the Heartland*, essays on rare books. Distinguished Professor of English at Ohio University, his many honors include a Guggenheim Fellowship and several awards from the Ohio Arts Council.

NAOMI SHIHAB NYE's second collection of poems, *Hugging the Jukebox* (1982), was a National Poetry Series selection. This book was preceded by *Different Ways to Pray* (1980). She has had several stories in journals such as *The Virginia Quarterly Review* and *Prairie Schooner*. She has done reading tours in the Middle East and Asia, and she presently works for PROTA (Project of Translation from the Arabic). Born in St. Louis, Nye lives now in San Antonio.

JOYCE CAROL OATES, one of America's best-known writers, has published numerous works of fiction, poetry, and criticism. (She is one of the very few authors to have appeared in the pages of *The Georgia Review* with fiction, poetry, *and* essays.) Her most recent works are the novels *Solstice* and *Marya: A Life*. Professor of English at Princeton, she co-edits *The Ontario Review* (with her husband Raymond Smith) and helps to run the Ontario Review Press.

A. B. PAULSON grew up in Minnesota, attended the University of Chicago, and received a Ph.D. from the State University of New York at Buffalo in 1974. After teaching stints at Dartmouth and Hamilton Colleges, he is presently at Portland State University in Oregon. Since 1973 his short fiction has been appearing in such periodicals as *TriQuarterly*, *New England Review & Bread Loaf Quarterly*, and *The Ohio Review*. His first book, a novel entitled *Watchman Tell Us of the Night*, will be released in late 1986.

FRED PFEIL's literary concerns dovetail with his interests in politics and history. He is co-editor of two journals, *The Minnesota Review* and *The Year Left: An American Socialist Yearbook*; his essays will appear in *Marxism and the Interpretation of Culture*; and he is at work on an historical novel about Melville, Barnum, and Frederick Taylor. His first novel, *Goodman 2020*, has just been published, while his first collection of stories (*Shine On*) is forthcoming. He teaches writing, literary theory, and film studies at Trinity College in Hartford, Connecticut.

SCOTT R. SANDERS' story here was reprinted in his first book of fiction, *Wilderness Plots* (1983)—a book that began a whirlwind of publication for this Midwestern writer. In 1984 he published *Fetching the Dead*, a collection of stories, and *Wonders Hidden*, a novella based on the life of John James Audubon. Then, 1985 brought *Terrarium*, a novel; *Hear the Wind Blow*, a group of stories based on American folk songs; and *Stone Country*, a narrative about workers and landscape in Indiana. Three more books are forthcoming, including *The Paradise of Bombs*, winner of the 1985 Associated Writing Programs award for creative nonfiction. Sanders teaches at Indiana University.

JESSE STUART (1907–1984) wrote more than forty books: novels, short stories, poems, children's stories, and autobiography. His best-selling novel, *Taps for Private Tussie* (1943), sold more than two million copies. Kentucky, his lifetime home, has honored him by establishing the Jesse Stuart Foundation in Ashland to promote his work and beliefs.

BARRY TARGAN has published two prize-winning collections of stories, *Harry Belten and the Mendelssohn Violin Concerto* (Iowa School of Letters Award) and *Surviving Adverse Seasons* (Saxifrage Award), and a novel, *Kingdoms*, which won an Associated Writing Programs prize. He has also published two poetry chapbooks, as well as numerous essays on art in such magazines as *American Craft*. He currently teaches in the creative writing program at the State University of New York at Binghamton.

ROBERT TAYLOR, JR., has published over sixty stories in journals such as *Shenandoah*, *The Missouri Review*, and *Northwest Review*. His two books are the novel *Fiddle and Bow* and the diptych volume, *Loving Belle Starr/Finding Jesse James* (a novella and a story sequence). Co-editor of *West Branch*, he teaches at Bucknell University and fiddles with the Buffalo Creek Bogtrotters. The Pennsylvania Council on the Arts has twice awarded him literary fellowships.

WALTER S. TERRY, while publishing a number of short stories, has made his living in the aerospace industry. "The Bottomless Well," his most widely noticed work, has appeared in a high-school textbook in England and has been broadcast to China on the "Voice of America" radio network. A Navy veteran of World War II and the Korean War, he lives in Huntsville, Alabama.

DAVID WAGONER, since 1953, has published thirteen volumes of poetry and ten novels. In 1966 he founded *Poetry Northwest*, which he continues to edit, and he has had brief tenures as editor and judge for such distinguished competitions as the Princeton University Press Contemporary Poetry Series, the University of Missouri Breakthrough Series, and the Lamont Prize of the Academy of American Poets. Born in Ohio and reared in Indiana, he has taught at the University of Washington since 1954.

LEIGH ALLISON WILSON was only a year out of college when "From the Bottom Up" was accepted by *The Georgia Review*. She has since won the Flannery O'Connor Prize for a collection of the same name and earned an MFA from the Iowa Writers' Workshop. A native of Tennessee, she now lives and teaches in Oswego, New York.